THE MARMALADE POT

Dedication

For every woman who has suffered in her own home, and in the hope she eventually finds love and happiness.

For Caroline
With best wishes and happy memories

THE MARMALADE POT

STEFAN BUCZACKI

Cato & Clarke

First published in 2020 by Cato & Clarke
Prospect House, Clifford Chambers, Stratford-upon-Avon, Warwickshire, CV37 8HX
www.stefanbuczacki.co.uk
catoandclarkepublishers@btinternet.com
Cover design by Stefan Buczacki

Distributed by Gardners Books, 1 Whittle Drive, Eastbourne, East Sussex, BN23 6QH
Tel: +44(0)1323 521555 | Fax: +44(0)1323 521666

This is a work of fiction and any resemblance of the characters to real people, living or dead, is coincidental and unintentional.

British Library Cataloguing in Publication Data
A catalogue record for this book is available from the British Library.

ISBN 978-0-9934186-1-7

Typeset by Amolibros, Milverton, Somerset
www.amolibros.com
This book production has been managed by Amolibros
Printed and bound by TJ Books Limited, Padstow, Cornwall, UK

Author Biography

Stefan Buczacki has been a writer and broadcaster for more than forty years and is the author of over sixty best-selling works of non-fiction and biography as well as many thousands of newspaper and magazine features. He has received awards and honorary degrees for his writing and is a committee member of the Society of Authors. He has also written, presented or contributed to over two thousand radio and television programmes.

Stefan was born in Derbyshire, educated at the universities of Southampton and Oxford, lives near Stratford-upon-Avon and has travelled widely throughout the world, but many years ago fell in love with the county of Norfolk where this debut novel is set.

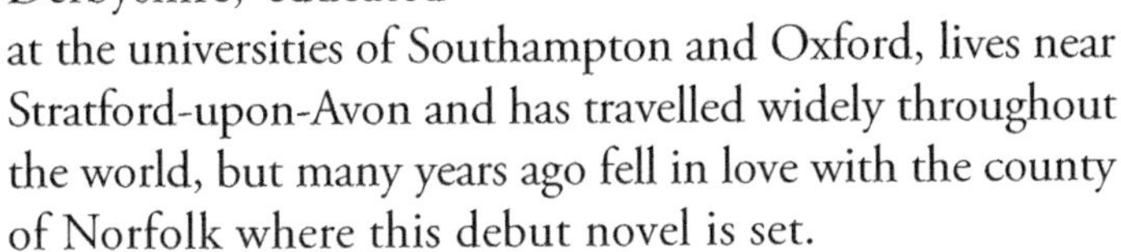

Author photograph: Stefan in Norfolk, Summer 2020.
© Beverley Buczacki

Acknowledgements

Thank you Jo, Nicky, Sarah and Fern for so kindly and generously reading my words and making such perceptive and helpful comments. My gratitude goes also to the experts who have advised me on medical, legal, religious, farming and other matters, while I am, as ever, indebted to the amazing Jane Tatam for so patiently turning my script into a real book.

Prologue

What could have been more perfect, more innocent, more quintessentially English, than a wedding in an ancient village church on a gloriously warm summer Saturday afternoon? Yet the occasion proved to be part of a journey that was touched by tragedy and exposed many of the most basic human frailties. And then, against the background of impending war, it led to a beautiful young woman embarking on a bittersweet exploration of her own sexuality.

Chapter One

The Reverend Humphrey Bellwether exhaled and shifted his substantial weight slightly from one foot to the other. 'Bugger,' he muttered almost noiselessly under his breath. His gout-enforced adjustment was nonetheless hidden from the church's congregation beneath a marginally less than immaculate black cassock, it in turn agreeably and fortunately screened by his pure white surplice. The extensive and unseemly stains that revealed where a bottle of one of East Anglia's finest bitters had been spilled down the cassock front the previous evening, and undone all his housekeeper's laundering labours, would have been plainly visible to the front row pews; and might not have been viewed particularly kindly by the wedding guests seated there.

The occasion that Saturday afternoon in June 1938 was memorable; although in many other ways wonderfully ordinary. Since the twelfth century, the church in the small Norfolk village of Felsingham St Margaret had seen countless similar nuptials; and the Reverend had personally officiated at a significant proportion of them. He was living evidence for the pointlessness of the principle that a priest should move on from his parish after around seven years. Humphrey Bellwether had been the church's immovable incumbent since King Edward the seventh was on the throne.

Close by the chancel, in the crypt, and locked in an antiquated wooden cupboard, were the Felsingham parish registers. Remarkably, almost all had survived and, in those early twentieth century days, many of the limited range of ancient surnames recorded there were still to be found in the village and its surrounding farms. So it was that Saturday afternoon when the pews were largely peopled with Futters, Atmores, Marsters, Postles, Farrows, Abbs, Ketts and Harmers.

As the hour-hand of the clock on the old square tower approached closer to two, the Reverend Humphrey drew a wheezy breath and prepared for his task to join in holy matrimony two young members of the parish's best known, if not universally or uniformly best loved families.

Charlotte Farrow was twenty-four and unarguably the most attractive young woman in the village. She was of medium height, elegantly slim while appropriately and alluringly curved in all the most important of feminine ways. And then there was her hair. Such hair! It was auburn and perfectly Pre-Raphaelite in its long tumbling waves that fell about the soft-paste porcelain skin of her pale and shapely shoulders. Wedding day or not, there was to be nothing tied up and coiffured for Charlotte. She was a woman who already in her tender years could, did and rather frequently had, caused strong men, young and not so young, to tremble at the knees; almost always metaphorically but a highly select one or two quite literally. Charlotte appeared fragile, almost frail, as if she would dissipate into a hundred pieces when anyone picked her up, gave her a hug and squeezed tightly. But as the chosen and fortunate group who had done just that could testify, nothing was further from the truth. That pristine skin and outwardly delicate frame belied a steely strength within. Brought up where she still lived on her parents' ancient Six Oaks Farm at the edge of the parish, where Felsingham touches the larger neighbouring settlement of Middle Turney, she could fork hay, sort turnips, stack straw, clamp potatoes and swedes and be midwife to sheep, pigs and cows alike with a skill, energy and fortitude that put many men of her age to shame. She was unarguably a young woman apart, a lifetime's treasure for the man who won her heart but a lifelong challenge for the one who tried to tame that free and adventurous spirit.

That very individual was sitting close to the gout-ridden Reverend and waiting alongside his best man at the front of the church for Charlotte's arrival. Frank Atmore was four years his bride's senior, tall and handsome in a rugged Norfolk open-air kind of way. He certainly had a fresh, healthy complexion that betrayed a coastal upbringing. Before his parents retired to Felsingham, the family had owned a small fleet sailing herring boats out of the charming little nearby port of Yaxton-next-the-Sea and his youthful summers had largely been spent on deck. The fleet had been sold some years ago but the Atmores still retained ownership of its associated smoke-house. Generally displaying around two day's stubble, Frank was today clean-shaven and the place of his usual informal yellow neck-tie was taken by a neat grey knot, the appropriate accompaniment to a morning suit of almost perfect fit, collected in Norwich the day before from Jessup & Sons, Tailors to the Landed Gentry (Dress Hire a Speciality).

'Well, my old bor, you've almost done it,' said Harry, the best man, in an accent that revealed a Norfolk upbringing through and through. 'You must be the luckiest man in Felsingham.' 'I certainly am,' replied Frank, smiling nervously, although knowing perfectly well that luck had played no part in bringing him to where he was today. And best man is overstating the standing of Harry Kett. He was simply the best available. Harry was the village factotum, a role at which he apparently earned most of his income; but only apparently. The rest was the subject of much speculation and had attracted more than a passing interest from the local constabulary. Nonetheless, there was certainly nothing – and not many of the village girls – to which or to whom he could not turn a hand (or two), given half a chance. It was fairly certain, however, that an attempted seduction of Charlotte on her way home from school had given him no chance whatsoever and until about three days before the wedding they had not spoken since 1928.

While the congregation waited, glorious music was emanating from the church's three-manual organ. Seated at it was Daphne de Jong, the sometime school music teacher and now in retirement, parish organist, dutifully keeping one eye on her rear view mirror. Intensely proud of a Dutch ancestry and descent from a family that had settled in King's Lynn two centuries ago, she was almost as permanent a fixture in the parish as the vicar. She was also deeply, avowedly and implacably committed in equal measure to music and to chastity, although there was a widely held view in the community that the chastity was self-enforced as a consequence of some unadmitted adventure several years earlier, following which she deemed her virginity to have been reinstated.

Then, as the tower clock dutifully twice chimed the hour, so Daphne changed her tune. She had caught sight of a vision in cream entering from the church porch and the beautiful organ transcription of Bach's Cello Suite No 1 gave way to a necessarily slow rendering of Grieg's Wedding Day at Troldhaugen; a piece chosen deliberately by Charlotte in the full and mischievous knowledge that probably no-one in the church – apart from Daphne the virgin organist – could possibly know where Troldhaugen lay or alternatively, what it might be.

The cream vision that walked so majestically down the aisle to the accompaniment of Grieg that warm autumn afternoon was a revelation indeed. Charlotte had chosen her dress with infinite care, no little expense – and a profound wish to cause comment – on a specially arranged visit to London with her mother the very day after Frank had made his proposal, all of six weeks ago.

Felsingham and probably much of south-east Norfolk had never before seen such a dress. It epitomised perfectly the liberated female of the 1930s, still a fairly rare animal in rural East Anglia. After all, it was only ten years earlier that women of Charlotte's age first acquired the right to vote. Moreover, her mother had been a profoundly committed suffragist and still wore the suffragette colours whenever the occasion allowed; of which her daughter's wedding day was naturally one. Not for nothing had Charlotte been christened Charlotte Emmeline, although she had her own highly individual interpretation of Emmeline Pankhurst's suffragette values, among which a feminine appearance was certainly applauded, although modesty in dress – especially on her wedding day – was not.

The dress showed off Charlotte's always elegant figure to its most spectacular advantage. The neckline departed from her graceful shoulders to plunge downwards into a cleavage of eye-watering depth. Old ladies sighed; young men sighed, not necessarily for the same reasons. A single *sotto voce* comment came from among the onlookers standing outside the church but was heard only by the closest individuals: 'Bloody hell!' But how many wedding guests noticed what one or two of them suspected – that the dress appeared to bow outwards ever so slightly around the waistline?

Taking his daughter's arm was an immaculately suited and distinguished appearing forty-nine year old man of medium height bearing a full head of prematurely silver-grey hair and sporting a distinctive neat grey beard. There was still enough in John Farrow's well-worn face to betray that it had once been handsome but it now revealed a paternal pleasure into which the strain of a deep-seated physical hurt intruded. He stooped slightly and walked with just a hint of a limp that pride would not now permit him to reveal in its full painful manifestation. A walking stick stood discarded in the porch.

'Are you nervous, my dearest?' he had asked as the pair approached the west door of St Margaret's.

'Papa,' she replied, 'only a bit, and that's for you. I am happy.' John noted she had not exactly answered the question and he was conscious of the merest glistening beads of perspiration on his daughter's forehead although he hoped it was simply due to the especially hot afternoon.

All bodies then turned to the nave as Charlotte and her father processed towards the waiting trio of vicar, best man and groom. Positioned prominently to the left on the front row pew was a blue hat of epic diameter. It was adorned with silk flowers of suffragette white, purple and green. Beneath it was Phyllida Farrow, the bride's mother, and one could see clearly the origin of Charlotte's hair in her still graceful tresses, now more than slightly tinged with the grey of the East Anglian North Sea that lapped at the shore just a few miles from the village. Her formerly flawless face was now slightly lined but it was evident she rivalled her daughter in once being possessed of quite startling good looks. On her arrival at the church some ten minutes earlier, she had stared implacably ahead, taken her seat and continued to stare implacably ahead. But now she turned to indulge herself in a proud and satisfied glance at her husband and daughter as they appeared in her peripheral view, while most studiously avoiding any eye contact with the party sitting opposite her to the right of the nave.

Arrayed behind Phyllida on the bride's side of the church were around thirty more figures, mostly stalwarts of the village or local farming communities with a few family representatives. Charlotte's older cousins, Archie and Caroline Farrow, had made the journey from Ely and were seated next to their long-widowed mother, Charlotte's Aunt Peggy. Her husband, Arnold, John Farrow's brother, had died on the Somme where John himself had suffered a life-changing experience and acquired his unavoidable limp. John's only sister Angela, also from Ely, had been too frail to make the journey.

Nearby was a scattering of more distant Farrow relatives and behind them four or five members of the local farming community with their spouses. Behind them, in turn, was the benign and reassuring ginger-haired and kilted figure of Dr Callum Fraser, an ex-patriot Scot who had settled in Felsingham some ten years earlier to become the village's much respected general practitioner. Alongside him was his wife Margaret, the practice nurse, an equally valued member of the community who had brought with her a profound trove of nursing and midwifery skills and an almost impenetrable Aberdonian accent.

Next to Margaret in the same pew sat another pillar of the community who had seen countless young Felsingham residents through their most formative years. Connie Harbutt was headmistress of the village primary school, a post she had held for twenty years. The school was modest in size and had never taught many more than forty children at a time, including those who made the daily journey by bus from even smaller outlying communities. But the quality of education provided by Miss Harbutt and her two colleagues was admirable and consistently gained high praise in its periodic inspections. In addition to presiding over the school, imbuing her pupils with their times tables, guiding them through selected works of John Bunyan and Daniel Defoe and the dates of kings and queens, Miss Harbutt also taught biology and as she sat in the church that afternoon, she found herself unavoidably wondering whether Charlotte was walking down the aisle because or in spite of the way she had inculcated her with the facts of life and love.

Then, a row behind and keeping a discreet presence but never appearing less than dignified, was the imposing moustachioed and slightly balding figure of Sir Arthur van Vliet, fourteenth baronet, with his toweringly tall wife Matilda and their daughter Hannah. The van Vliets were generous benefactors to the community and major employers of local labour who owned Felsingham Manor and its Home Farm Estate, the largest holding for miles around, together with the freeholds of many village properties. Their family was among the oldest in Norfolk and one of Sir Arthur's ancestors had built The Manor close to the heart of the village with its magnificent great hall, tall chimneys and distinctive red brick crow-stepped gables in the sixteenth century. Hannah van Vliet looked after The Manor stables and she and Charlotte had always been extremely close, Charlotte deeming Hannah as almost a surrogate elder sister and confidante whose counsel was destined to become so precious in the times ahead. She had naturally offered her services as maid of honour but Charlotte had been insistent she would walk the aisle alone with her father.

Hannah was by most people's judgement a fine young woman, elegant, handsome although not exactly pretty. She was, like Charlotte, an only child, in her case because her twin brother had died some years ago in circumstances about which no-one now spoke, but which had deprived the family of an heir. Hannah had moreover never been seen with a close male companion, a matter that was the cause of much gossip, speculation and elevated local eyebrows.

Seated close by were the Farrow farmhands Ted Grantley and Tommy Marster with their wives. The men between them had fifty-five years of devoted service at Six Oaks and collectively had forgotten more than most men ever knew about working the local soil. Alongside was Jenny Peasgood, committed spinster, Phyllida's housekeeper, cleaner, cook and launderer and a woman of completely indispensable value and impeccable virtue. In years past, she had been nursery nurse and nanny too and viewed Charlotte as almost her own daughter.

Finally, at the back of the church, were seated three villagers who collectively knew everything about everyone. Nothing, but nothing could happen in Felsingham St Margaret outside the knowledge of this group of individuals whose occupations gave them an especially keen insight into village happenings. They were referred to with some feeling as the three witches: Fanny Handley, village post-woman and occasional part-time cleaner, Gladys Fellgood, operator at the local telephone exchange, having a rare day off work, and Betty Crabtree who was once gainfully employed at the village shop but now spent her waking hours keeping herself impeccably up to date with everyone else's business by any method available. Sitting with them was a man who had himself been the subject of significant gossip in connection with a village girl young enough to be his daughter: Billy Harmer, landlord of the Eelcatcher's Arms, who left the service early to check that all was ready for the wedding breakfast in the pub's upper room.

Frank's side of the church was immeasurably more sparsely populated; in truth it was practically empty. Almost no-one liked, admired or had any affinity with the Atmores, for no single definable reason although they were commitedly anti-social, never appeared at village functions, never sent (and in consequence never received) Christmas or birthday cards, never supported village charities and were considered mean. They were also a family riven with political divisions. Frank's parents Clarice and Vic were, like the Atmores and as befitted small business owners, true blue Tories who kept an extremely low, almost invisible profile. However, old man Jack Atmore was a quite different political animal. He was Frank's paternal grandfather and although now the retired skipper of a herring drifter, Jack Atmore never forgot the abject misery of his early years as a deck-hand on a trawler and he had always been a card-carrying member of the Communist Party. Like many other disenchanted individuals in the 1930s, he was full of admiration for Stalin's Soviet empire and advertised his support of its British fellow travellers, and appalled the village every 22 November, when he flew a provocative red flag outside his cottage to celebrate the birthday of the Communist Party's General Secretary Harry Pollitt. Although Frank was not as far left in his politics, he was nonetheless devoted to his grandfather, a devotion that was manifest in an enduringly powerful commitment to the Labour Party of Clement Atlee.

Together with grandfather Jack, the front row pew was occupied by Frank's parents and whether or not entirely in the imagination of those seated nearby, possibly by a faint aroma of bloaters. The handful of other guests arrayed behind the family included around half the village cricket team, three of them still in their whites having come straight from a net, and a small group of somewhat odd looking young men whom no-one could name but had apparently been Frank's boyhood companions in Yaxton-next-the-Sea.

At the back, pointedly separated from the rest and only seated there because they arrived late and wanted to make the church appear more balanced, was an interesting couple. Trainee dental nurse Lily Abbs was a most likeable albeit constantly giggling girl of tender years. She was usually referred to as Laughing Lily and had been Frank's companion for a short time until a few weeks ago when he suddenly and wholly unexpectedly began to be seen in Charlotte's company to form what in the eyes and opinion of most of the village was a complete and scarcely believable mismatch. With Lily and occupying much of the rest of the pew was her latest consort, a huge and utterly charming young man called Nigel Futter, member of an old village family of equally huge people. Nigel was the delivery van driver for Allcocks, the grocery store in Middle Turney. He was possessed of a rich bass-baritone voice and was considered a gentle giant with a heart of gold that belied his fearsome size. 'Every village needs a Nigel,' someone once said, 'but only Felsingham is lucky enough to have one.'

And so the proceedings began, Humphrey Bellwether

reciting the words he had recited countless times before and that the fabric of St Margaret's had been hearing word for word totally unaltered since 1662. 'There will be no revised service nonsense here,' he declared to the Parochial Church Council at regular intervals, usually with an accompanying reference to the 'abhorrence' of the unauthorised prayer book of 1928.

He paced himself carefully with just an occasional surreptitious glance at his wrist-watch to ensure he was well placed in the wedding sweepstake that was always run in the Eelcatcher's Arms before such occasions. A half-crown was wagered on who could most accurately predict to the minute the length of the service, timed from '*Dearly* beloved, we are gathered together…' to 'I pronounce that they be Man and Wife together, in the name of the Father, and of the Son and of the Holy Ghost. *Amen.*' The fact that the vicar could influence the result was customarily overlooked.

Then, at exactly nine minutes to three, it was all over and despite his best efforts to manipulate the timing, the vicar had lost his half-crown by four minutes to Jack Postle, the village milkman. By then, he had repeated one of his stock wedding orations, three hymns had been sung, a ring had been placed on Charlotte's finger – but none on Frank's – and she had agreed to love, cherish and to obey. There had also been the traditional 1662 reference in measured and marginally elevated tones to the satisfaction of men's carnal lusts and appetites and the avoidance of fornication – at which point Charlotte dropped her eyes – while an unfortunate clearing of someone's throat had occurred at the back of the church just as Holy Humphrey, as he was widely known – although not usually in his hearing – asked if anyone present knew any impediment why Charlotte and Frank may not be coupled together. There were in truth stifled noises from many of those present who knew they had been very firmly coupled together at least once already.

After signing the register, the newly wedded couple led the convoy from the church and paused while the obligatory group photograph was taken outside the porch for posterity while PC Bertie Edwards watched from across the road. Nothing much missed his eagle eye and he had cycled over from the police house in Middle Turney to ensure the thrice-daily bus to Norwich or the even more unlikely possibility of a passing car did nothing to disturb the occasion.

The wedding party then continued the two hundred yards along Church Street, the village's main and only significant thoroughfare, past the drive leading to The Manor, past the Post Office where Fanny Handley plied her trade and spread gossip, then on past old Fred Wellbeloved's newsagent's and shop where one could buy almost anything, then Dickie Barnfather's butchery, closed for the afternoon in order for him to replenish his stock of pork sausages ('from the finest local Norfolk pigs'), to end at the ancient edifice of the Eelcatcher's Arms where the wedding breakfast prepared by Billy Harmer's wife Doris and her assistants was devoured by some, rearranged on the plate by several and carefully avoided by the rest. The magnificent peal of six seventeenth century St Margaret's bells however was silent, John Farrow having vetoed it on the grounds that bells should only ring on joyous occasions.

The speeches, mercifully brief, were concluded, Frank reminding everyone *ad nauseam* how fortunate he was, while Charlotte looked awkward and her mother gazed upwards to carry out a detailed appraisal of the rafters. John Farrow said the barest minimum in praise of his God-given daughter while wholly avoiding any reference to his new son-in-law. Then Frank, having drummed in to his best man – under threat of castration – that he must not under any circumstance whatsoever disgrace himself or embarrass anyone, Harry delivered an excruciating five minutes of platitudes and concluded with a joke littered with some of the more obscure bits of Norfolk dialect that no-one – fortunately – understood.

Finally, the new Mr and Mrs Frank Atmore, by then changed into more appropriate clothes, departed in the van Vliet's horse and carriage, freshly spruced up for the occasion and expertly driven by Six Oaks farmhand Ted Grantley, to the railway station at the nearby market town of Fenton Bishop en route to a short honeymoon in Caister-on-Sea.

Chapter Two

For all their brave faces and public sang-froid, the wedding had been an excruciating experience for John and Phyllida Farrow and it was solely their deep and committed love for their only child Charlotte that had prompted them to organise and pay for it and then to attend. Powerful opinions and forceful words had been exchanged many times between them in the Six Oaks farmhouse during the weeks between Charlotte informing them of her pregnancy and the ceremony itself. John had threatened a boycott on several occasions. To say he disliked Frank Atmore was an understatement of some magnitude. Charlotte's parents both viewed Frank as lazy and unreliable although John preferred an Old English expletive that he enunciated with a particularly memorable resonance to which his rich baritone voice gave full savour. He was in no doubt that Frank Atmore was a shit who had forced himself – metaphorically and in his perception probably literally – on their daughter.

On being told of her pregnancy, their first notion had been that like many another young woman in the 1930s, pregnant out of wedlock, Charlotte must be spirited away quickly, perhaps to live with her cousins in Ely for a holiday of appropriately decent length. There had then followed protracted conversations about the feasibility – and desirability – of endorsing a wedding but keeping it quiet and simple: a Register Office marriage perhaps out of the public gaze in Norwich. But Charlotte herself had been insistent that she remain in the public view throughout her wedding and pregnancy.

'I am not cowering away,' she maintained. 'I just don't care that the village knows the circumstances. I will not be seen to appear ashamed. This is a situation of my own making. I may have been extremely foolish and let you down but I do want a proper white wedding – after all I shall only ever have one. I am so sorry, Papa, about the cost but please try to understand.' Charlotte then threw her arms around John's neck and began unavoidably to sob.

He said he did understand, and of course cost was not an issue but nonetheless he and Phyllida had to perform a most delicate act of emotional balancing because while Charlotte was fully aware that her future husband could not possibly have been her parents' choice as son-in-law, she never knew the extraordinary lengths to which they went to keep from her the abyssal depth of their true feelings.

The family conversations followed a regular pattern. 'You know he is not my favourite person,' was a typical Phyllida comment. 'But he is at least doing the honourable thing and I have no doubt you will come to love him in time.'

'I do love him, Mama, I love him now, despite everything,' was Charlotte's usual response although the comment always sounded unconvincing, hollow and elusive, something her mother never failed to notice. 'I know this was all hardly planned but I am sure there is a decent man beneath it. He works hard, he has a proper job and I believe he will be a good father to our baby.'

There was nonetheless no doubt in the minds of everyone else in the village, not only that the marriage had been a shotgun affair, but that Charlotte had clearly married far beneath herself. She had committed a disastrous error of judgement and was now suffering from serious delusion. 'That was just so brave of the Farrows,' was a typical comment in the community after the wedding. 'It must have been awful for John and Phyllida. Frank Atmore of all people! Can you imagine?'

The village liked the Farrows as much as it disliked the Atmores and knew they had not had the easiest of lives – lives scarred by John's appalling war experience with the loss of his only brother and the fact they could have no more children – and hence never the son John craved to follow him on the farm.

How had it happened, how and why had Charlotte fallen into the ambit of Frank Atmore? How could it be that he was now apparently living the dream of which so many others had, well, just dreamed while his new parents-in-law were experiencing a nightmare?

Frank and Charlotte had attended Connie Harbutt's village school together and, being four years older, he was already well established there when she enrolled at the age of five in the lowest class. At first they barely noticed each other. In truth she never did notice him – she had no reason to – and he only became aware of her as young womanhood began to manifest itself and sculpt her shape shortly before the time came for them both to change schools at the age of fourteen. Frank, for all his rough appearance and generally gauche manners, was no fool. He had, as his mother Clarice was wont to say whenever prompted and to whomsoever would listen, 'A good brain on those shoulders.' It was no fault of hers that he had turned out to be quite so wayward. She blamed first, the boys with whom he associated in the village, and second, the fact that his father was away at sea catching herrings for much of the time Frank had been growing up and metamorphosing from boyhood to adolescence.

But while Frank used his undoubted, if too often disguised intelligence, to pass the selective examination to the nearest secondary school in Fenton Bishop, Charlotte's parents dug deeply into their pockets and her mother's family inheritance to send her to St Jude's Hall in Cambridgeshire, a boarding school of modest renown for the daughters of gentlefolk.

Unfortunately, it was a little too gentle for the free spirit that was Charlotte and instead of achieving her parents' objective of producing a well-mannered, demure and chaste young woman, the school turned out a well-mannered, highly educated girl with a constantly simmering potential to break free from the conventions of the 1930s' middle classes. Her parents had hoped that in the absence of a male heir, Charlotte might run the family farm but they had aspirations for her to progress to university first and study an appropriate subject. However she harboured other ideas, had had enough of academic learning and examinations and at the age of eighteen, launched straight in to becoming her father's lieutenant with an unbridled passion for the land and a keenness to learn on the job. As the years passed, John Farrow's war wounds sapped his energy ever further so for purely practical reasons, Charlotte taking over sooner rather than later did make much sense.

Frank Atmore also avoided further education – in his case out of idleness – but he was as implacably opposed to entering the family fishing business as Charlotte was committed to farming and it was this unswerving stance that encouraged his parents to sell the boats and retire. Instead, and at their prompting, he joined a small accountancy firm in Great Yarmouth. An excellent aptitude for figures was the motivation and although he never had the application required to study and take the examinations to acquire chartered accountant status, he managed to develop a modestly successful career and had recently left the firm to set up his own business specialising in farm accounts, based in his small rented cottage on the Norwich Road. He had on one occasion visited Six Oaks to tout for business but John Farrow had given him the shortest of shrifts – 'Bugger off' was the more courteous of his valedictions – and Charlotte had, almost, although not quite literally, to pull them apart.

But farming was not the only pursuit to have a claim on Charlotte's time and intellect. Like her parents, she took a close and informed interest in matters of national and international concern. She differed from many young women of her time and age in reading the newspapers daily – once John Farrow had finished with his copy of *The Times* each morning, he passed it to his daughter.

And although not then old enough to vote herself, she had campaigned vigorously for the local Conservative MP in the General Election three years earlier.

And it was as a committed Conservative supporter that she attended the fateful meeting in March 1938, the meeting that was to change her life for ever. The prospective Labour Party candidate for the Norfolk Southern constituency was holding a widely advertised hustings in the town of Diss, close to the border with Suffolk and about thirty miles from Felsingham. Frank Atmore, as one of his most passionate supporters, was to be alongside him as part of the platform group. Always keen to fight the Conservative's corner and urged on by her father, Charlotte decided to attend and her devoted friend Hannah van Vliet, who was comparably enthusiastic in her politics, offered a lift in her elderly Austin 10. It proved to be a packed and extremely lively meeting where Charlotte and Hannah found themselves embroiled in vigorous debate with the platform over the gamut of world political events. They ranged from the Sino-Japanese conflict through the relative merits of Eden and Halifax as Foreign Secretary, the German invasion of Ethiopia and annexation of Austria, the British response to the Nazi persecution of the Jews, the Czechoslovak problem, the possibility of an Anglo-Irish Trade Agreement and inevitably to the relative merits of Chamberlain and Atlee as party leaders.

Thanks to his grandfather's admittedly biased tutelage, Frank was no political slouch. He, like Charlotte, was extremely well informed and well read in political matters and unquestionably took a special delight in crossing swords with her although all present agreed she gave an exceptional account of herself and revealed a deep and perceptive knowledge and understanding of local, national and world politics; although having an especially challenging problem in justifying Neville Chamberlain and his principles.

But it was when the subject moved suddenly to the likely impending end to the Spanish Civil War that things took a turn for the more unpleasant. Addressing Hannah van Vliet directly, Frank called her a fascist. 'It was your people,' he said, 'who supported Franco. Your upper class lot. We all saw the pictures of the British aristocracy raising their arms in the fascist salute and leading innocent workers to the firing squads.'

'Heh, steady on,' shouted an anonymous voice from the floor of the hall. 'It's all right,' responded Hannah, and then looking directly at Frank continued. 'I am not a fascist. No-one in my family is a fascist, in fact no-one I know supported General Franco and just because we have been honoured with an ancestral title does not mean we endorse everything that other titled people may do or believe. And anyway, if you are so committed to the Republican cause, where were you when the International Brigades wanted support?'

A quiet but firm voice from the meeting chairman, Councillor Fred Pinfold, then intervened. 'I am sure we all have extremely committed and strong views on such matters but the war in Spain seems to be drawing to a close, whether or not we like the outcome, and all of us who watch international affairs closely will be more than aware that something far more ominous and far more relevant to this country is happening elsewhere on the European continent. As far as this meeting is concerned, the matter of the Spanish war is now closed so may we return to the core business of considering the Labour Party's exciting policies for the next General Election.'

At the time, neither Councillor Pinfold nor anyone else could have predicted that the ominous events to which he referred would render impossible a General Election in the foreseeable future, but night was fast approaching and after another fifteen minutes of Labour and Conservative banter, the formal meeting drew to a close.

As it ended however, the personal sparring between the Felsingham residents continued outside the hall and did so for more than half an hour until peace broke out when Hannah declared it was really becoming so late that she must return home. She had never enjoyed night driving and the headlights on the Austin were almost apologetically dim, even for a summer evening.

'That's all right, Hannah,' responded Frank, now restored to using a more civilised form of address. 'I can run Charlotte back on the bike. I'm afraid we all got a bit heated in there.'

'The bike' to which Frank referred certainly knew its way in the dark. It was a black, highly polished, large and adoringly tended machine that could not fail to impress any road user on two or four wheels. The Series A Vincent Rapide for which Frank had paid all of £140 – most of his savings – just a year ago was at that moment, the love of his life. And Charlotte, never one to reject an adventure, accepted with alacrity.

Chapter Three

It was a month later, and in company with Hannah, that Charlotte – despite her friend's almost daily prompts – finally confided in detail what then took place. 'Please, please tell me, C, exactly how it happened,' Hannah asked. 'There's so much dreadful rumour in the village. I overheard the three witches gossiping yet again the other day in the Post Office. Everyone is saying you are expecting. Is it true?'

And tell her, Charlotte did. The half hour after they left the door of the Diss meeting room found her on the bike's pillion seat, her arms enveloping Frank with the tightest of clutches while the Rapide swallowed up the thirty miles to Felsingham. Charlotte never denied she was already feeling an all-embracing sense of elation, her emotions heightened by the evening's intense political debate, and she now clung to Frank's waist while her thighs absorbed the pounding of a thousand ccs of Vincent V-twin engine. Knowing her life quite literally depended on Frank's riding ability along the twisting dark Norfolk lanes, with hedges crowding in on either side and the occasional soft leafy tree branch brushing through her hair, she found the journey took on an indescribably erotic edge. It had been all of two years since she had last slept with a man and she was now being rendered more vulnerable by the minute.

'As you know, darling,' Charlotte told Hannah, 'his cottage is on the way to Six Oaks and he pulled over and suggested we might continue our discussion over a night cap – and you remember how partial I am to Scotch. Papa always said it would be my downfall – especially because it's blends I like not his single malts – but I can't imagine he could have foreseen this.'

'I should have said no, but I didn't. And yes,' she continued, 'I drank far, far too much of the whisky while Frank, I think, deliberately kept within limits so he was still capable of running me home. We argued about the evening, especially Chamberlain and Atlee, but to be honest I soon forgot everything I ever knew about the Spanish Civil War and the conversation drifted and, yes, I do not deny it, I found him more and more attractive and, well you know the old saying, one thing led to another...'

'Oh, God, Charlotte, did you have no idea what you were doing; and more importantly, did he?'

'No, darling, I didn't, not by that time; I really didn't,' answered Charlotte, pointedly ignoring the second part of the question.

'And he didn't use – you know – to try and stop anything happening?'

'No – well obviously not.'

'I suppose it was at least, what's the word they now use, consensual?'

'I know it sounds absolutely awful, Hannah, but I am

just not sure if it was consensual – yes, that is the word. You can imagine – or perhaps you can't – what Papa said. At one point, he actually told me I must have been raped but I was not having that. I went to Frank's house of my own free will and he made a point of seeing me several times afterwards and asked how I was. When I broke the news to him that I was late, he seemed genuinely concerned – for me, not just for him. Then the day before yesterday, Dr Fraser told me he had heard from the laboratory that yes, I am definitely pregnant, Frank said immediately that he would marry me if that was what I wanted.'

'Oh, dear God, C, my dearest girl. So it's true. You really are, are you? Expecting? And was it, is it, what you wanted – not getting pregnant I mean, but marrying him?'

'Yes, I am, my darling. I really am expecting a baby. I am pregnant. I am with child. If you had asked me that question two months ago – if I wanted to marry Frank Atmore – I'd have laughed uncontrollably. But now, yes, I think I am doing the right thing. A child needs a father and to be honest I am not at all sure I could bring one up on my own. Goodness knows what the village will say. I'm sure I shall be cast out as a fallen woman, a disgrace to my family and everyone else. You remember what happened to that girl from Middle Turney last year. No-one would speak to her and she had to go and live with some obscure aunt and uncle miles away. I'm not even sure she ever came back.'

'I can't believe it will come to that, C. The village knows and loves you – and I shall be here for you at least,' said Hannah and embraced Charlotte. Without saying anything more for all of ten seconds, she held her tightly and began to stroke her hair. Then, as she gently pulled away, she said softly, 'You weren't a virgin were you, C?'

'No, no, there have been two others – and only two I might add!' was Charlotte's response. 'You remember Jeremy, that rather beautiful boy from the Young Farmers' Club? He was my first. Then there was your lovely cousin Torquil I met at your parents' Christmas party.'

'Yes, yes, of course I remember Jeremy. But Torquil! Wow! My gosh! I never knew you and he…but anyway, do go on.'

'Yes, I've always been very fond of Tor. But that's it really, except that now I'm rather terrified,' Charlotte said. 'Tell me, darling, you think it will work out. It's just the way it all began. I have been so completely stupid and I've told myself over and over again – if it hadn't been for that wretched evening, this would never have happened. Would I be marrying Frank? I know I certainly wouldn't in a million years. I had never really thought much about him before.'

'I know it's hardly relevant, C, but what about Laughing Lily?' asked Hannah. 'I thought she and Frank were pretty seriously committed.'

'Oh, they were certainly together, although I am unsure about seriously committed. I did hear talk of a possible engagement but she's very young. I asked him the same question of course and I don't know what he said to her immediately afterwards but once I knew I was pregnant, he said of course he would break it to her the next day and end everything.'

They were taking tea in Hannah's bedroom at The Manor where she was as understanding as she could possibly be in the circumstances; the circumstances being that she had never had – and almost certainly never would have – an intimate relationship with a man and would never experience sexual intercourse in the generally accepted sense. 'Have your parents come to terms with it?' she asked. 'I realise it's all very sudden and they haven't had long. When are you due?'

'Probably the ninth of January. Have my parents come to terms with it? Only just about; at least, I think Mama has, but I am sure Papa never will. He was absolutely appalled, devastated, horrified, all those things. In fact he just went quiet for most of the day and has hardly said anything this morning. He really loathes Frank who seems to be everything he isn't – in life and in politics. He just cannot relate to him and never has done, and now he will be the father of his grandchild. How he will behave towards the baby when it's born I dread to think. You truly are the one person I can talk to properly and honestly, Hannah, but I can't make up my mind if I am – if I have been – just unbelievably stupid or I am really, really wicked.'

'C, don't be ridiculous! You are certainly not wicked. You are one of the most sincere, kind and well-meaning people I know. Now this might seem a completely odd thing to say, but you know you will have to talk about it to the vicar if you want to be married in church, which I assume you do. I'm pretty sure it will up to him to decide – you being as you are.'

'Holy Humphrey!' Charlotte's voice rose, heavily

imbued with incredulity. 'Heavens! Surely not! He's the last person I would want to tell about it.'

'I think you misjudge him,' said Hannah. 'And he *will* have to sanction it. You've always been a church-goer and a Christian believer. There will need to be banns and everything. No, the reason I say this is that when my own situation – for want of a better word – dawned on me and I certainly couldn't tell Mummy and Daddy, the vicar was absolutely wonderful and was really understanding.'

'Well, now you've started, what exactly is your situation as you call it. What is it he understood?'

'I am in love, really, seriously in love, and I am having a relationship – a proper sexual relationship – with another woman.'

Charlotte smiled for the first time that day. 'I think I might just have guessed that, darling. I just knew there was something you were dying to tell me. I am *so* pleased for you, Hannah – at least I am pleased you have found someone special. Am I allowed to know who she is? Do I know her? Do *your* parents know now?'

'Yes, and they have been just marvellous – at least they seem to be now though it took quite a while, for Daddy especially. I think these things must be that much harder for fathers. Do you know her? No, you don't. Her name is Emily, Emily West-Walton and she's a really wonderful girl I met a few weeks ago at a mutual friend's party over in Leicestershire. I'm really sorry, C, I haven't told you before – you must think me awful – but I just didn't know how you would react. You must meet her. Does it shock you, horrify you?'

'No, no, not at all. I do enjoy female company –

well you know that! – but I've never been sure about the physical bit. I've read about these things in books although of course I've never done it, but, when I was at school, a younger girl did have some sort of fairly serious crush and in fact once made a pretty explicit overture. But I do really like other women and I can certainly see the appeal – and I think it might make life less complicated than mine has now become. Women can do whatever they like with each other – it's not like two men, and there's nothing illegal about it – and you will certainly never get pregnant. But West-Walton you say her name is; isn't there an M.P…?'

'Yes, Geoffrey West-Walton, her father. He's actually a junior Foreign Office minister and also a very strong supporter of Churchill. He and Emily's mother Fiona have been immensely understanding, though it's a bit tricky because it's just the sort of thing the papers would love – you can imagine the headlines: 'Government Minister's daughter has female lover…'

'Hmm. Yes, I can see. But will you bring her to the wedding?'

'That's very sweet of you, C, but good heavens no; we are nowhere near ready to go public yet – if ever! So far we have been meeting privately – secretly if you like – at The Manor and at Emily's home in Leicestershire and I'm afraid it might have to continue like that. I'm not at all sure which would be harder for Felsingham to cope with – your out of wedlock pregnancy or having two lesbians in its midst!'

'Of course; I'm sure you may be right – but back to the vicar for a minute because I'm interested in what you say – he approved did he, of you having a girl friend, a lover, you and Emily?'

'No,' Hannah hesitated. 'No, he didn't; not exactly; in fact not really at all because he said the Bible's teaching would not allow that and he quoted something from, I think, the Book of Romans, about unnatural acts – sounds awful doesn't it for something we find so beautiful? But he also talked about human love and the important thing was he made me feel better about it, and certainly not guilty.'

Charlotte gave it all a few moment's consideration. 'I can see it's difficult for you both – and will of course continue to be. But you'll have to make it known publicly some time – and Emily's father I suppose will have to cope with it. I wonder what Churchill will think! Personally, I can't see anything to be ashamed of. After all some of the most famous women in history have had female lovers – like, well, Sappho for a start! Though I can't actually think of another off-hand. But you may be right about Humphrey and yes, I suppose I do need to have a conversation.'

'Queen Christina of Sweden is another one – famous lesbian that is – if you're really interested; and the writer Virginia Woolf according to what I've read!' Hannah replied. 'Though we were talking about Holy Humphrey, who certainly isn't! But when you see him, I'm sure it will go well for you, C. I really am; but never forget, whatever Humphrey or anyone else says, I shall always be here for you, my sweet.' And Hannah gave her a prolonged embrace before they parted.

So, two days later, and having thought further about

her friend's advice and telephoned for an appointment, Charlotte found herself walking along the gravel path leading to the front door of the vicarage, doing her best to avoid trampling the seriously neglected herbaceous borders that were creeping inwards from the edges and narrowing the carriageway such that visitors could no longer walk two abreast. The exquisitely picturesque timber-framed edifice was even more venerable than its resident and was on the diocesan list for possible replacement with something smaller and more modern; much as the diocese had the same long term aspirations for the incumbent.

The vicar admitted her to his study, a sanctuary of learning and knowledge in which almost every horizontal surface was stacked precipitately with books, religious tracts – and railway magazines. Like many a clergyman before and since, he found railways fascinating and the history of the Great Eastern Railway company was one of his enduring enthusiasms. The study walls were hung with bookshelves in the precarious way it is with timber-framed buildings where the structure, created at a time when books were rare treasures and the ability to read an asset accorded to a choice few, was not designed to support the weight. There was a faint aroma of beeswax and bleach, evidence of the cleaning and polishing labours of Mrs Hascombe, the vicar's housekeeper, who consistently did her dutiful best to keep him, his laundry and his home, in a reasonably civilised and disinfected state. She was a kindly, ever tolerant and well meaning Christian soul, the sister of Doris Harmer from the Eelcatcher's Arms and although unmarried she revelled in her honorific title of Mrs, in the way it is with housekeepers and nannies.

The Reverend Humphrey Bellwether had several faults that the whole village recognised with benign resignation. His origin over the border in Lincolnshire and his occasionally lengthy and sometimes unfathomably profound sermons with an elusive railway connection involving steam locomotives, tenders, carriages, guard's vans – and most inexplicably shunting – were the most obvious of them. But no-one could ever hold against him that his thoughts and views were stuck in the nineteenth century from whence he came. For all his antecedents and commitment to the 1662 prayer book, Humphrey Bellwether was a remarkably enlightened, highly intelligent and astonishingly widely read twentieth century priest, a proud product of Balliol. And nor could anyone doubt how well he knew his Bible.

Charlotte sat down in an ancient vicarage armchair, now largely bereft of any padded upholstery, although thanks to its redundant springs, she sank in far further than she had anticipated and found herself well below the vicar's eye level as he sat opposite, something she felt put her at a disadvantage. The words constantly and unavoidably going round in her head were 'Forgive me, Father for I have sinned' and she admitted as much to the vicar. He grinned. 'Wrong church for that of course, my dear. We do not do confession in quite the same way here. But tell me about the problem. I am sure we can understand better than anyone under the aegis of Rome.'

Charlotte told him her experience, repeating what she had said to Hannah and not holding back anything.

The vicar listened attentively. 'Remember, Charlotte, that Mary was pregnant with Our Lord before she was married to Joseph,' he said. 'Technically, yes, you have done what we call fornication and although neither of you is married and so you have not committed adultery, fornication is still strictly a sin in the eyes of God.' The vicar then clasped his hands together and raised his eyes upwards as if reading from an unseen text on the ceiling. 'I need to remind you of 1 Thessalonians 4: "For this is the will of God, even your sanctification, that ye should abstain from fornication".' Charlotte's mouth suddenly felt dry and she wondered what kind of damnation might come next. 'But our God is a loving and most importantly a forgiving God,' continued the vicar, 'and by marrying in his Holy House, before me as his mouthpiece on earth, you will be acknowledging your sin and seeking his forgiveness through your public commitment to each other, and in due course to the child you have created and will deliver into the world and raise together.'

Charlotte analysed the vicar's words quickly in her head and determined he was telling her that everything would probably be all right even though she had no idea what her sanctification might involve. But most importantly, they could marry in church, Holy Humphrey would officiate and she would escape eternal condemnation in the after-life. She thanked the vicar warmly and with a prodigious sense of relief arranged for another meeting the next afternoon when Frank would accompany her and plans be made for the first reading of the banns the following Sunday.

Hannah, meanwhile, had much to ponder because

something Charlotte had said worried her for days and weeks afterwards. If what Charlotte surmised was right, and Frank had stayed relatively sober in order to be able to drive her home, but had still plied her with glass after glass of Famous Grouse until she was apparently unaware what was happening, was John Farrow correct after all? Had her friend been raped?

Chapter Four

It was never destined to be an easy meeting; and how correct destiny proved. Almost immediately after returning from their honeymoon at the beginning of July, Charlotte and Frank arranged to meet Charlotte's parents, John and Phyllida, on an unexpectedly cool Saturday morning in the parlour at Six Oaks. The low-ceilinged room was everything to be expected of a small early Georgian farmhouse, redolent with the history of the Farrow family whose sepia photographs adorned the walls, along with framed certificates for prize barley crops harvested in years past. A stack of recent *Farmers Weekly* and *Farmer and Stockbreeder* magazines was piled neatly on a stout oak table next to a majestic polished mahogany Marconi wireless which before many months were past would be relaying matters of shocking local and national moment. On the central table, the day's copy of *The Times* lay carefully folded open at the Letters page. John's well-worn briar pipe, freshly charged with new tobacco, was propped ready for use in a large ashtray on the mantlepiece above an inglenook where flames from the first logs of the day were flickering silently and filling the room with a reassuring warmth. Holmes and

Watson, John's cocker spaniel gun-dogs lay before the hearth, motionless on a well-worn old rag rug.

It had been agreed before the wedding that John and Phyllida would continue to live in the main farmhouse at Six Oaks while Charlotte and Frank would move into a capacious adjoining cottage that had been built in the early eighteenth century by a family of previous residents to accommodate some of their fourteen children. John had restored the cottage two years earlier with a view to his possible retirement; which in his mind he had now deferred permanently. This arrangement meant he would be conveniently on hand to guide Charlotte in the running of the farm but would not have to face Frank on a daily basis. Frank would give up the lease on his cottage and continue to run his accountancy business from a tiny spare room in the cottage which would serve as his office. The main farm office and study would remain where it had always been in a small room off the parlour. That at least is how matters were eventually decided, Frank's own ideas about taking over the main house having being unanimously and unceremoniously out-voted.

Frank had also made no secret of his wish to take on a much larger role in running Six Oaks Farm and continue with his accountancy work on a greatly reduced part-time basis, meaning his official occupation would change from accountant to farmer. In what was to prove a decision of enormous prescience however, John Farrow put down his foot even more firmly than usual and stopped any such notion in its tracks. Although Charlotte would run the farm, the ownership remained in John's name; Charlotte was effectively his tenant. And under no circumstances would Frank Atmore have a significant say in the way things were done. He could help Charlotte with any especially large or heavy tasks but they would be few because they already had two full-time farmhands in Ted Grantley and Tommy Marster and there was plenty of casual and willing labour available in the village. Big Nigel Futter for one was always enthusiastic.

With a nod towards the day's paper, John reminded them 'There are still one and a half million people unemployed in this country,' and then turning to Frank, added 'and you as a Communist ought to recognise we all have to play a part in trying to bring that figure down. When we need help we shall engage village workers. So instead of filling your time here you can get out on that bike of yours, earn some money and help support the family you have created.'

Frank hesitated for barely a moment before deciding there were arguments here he was destined to lose so he disclosed his assent with 'Have it your own way, John; but just let me be clear. I am not a Communist. I support the Labour Party.'

John dismissed the political nicety with, 'Practically the same thing. And your grandfather certainly is,' and added, 'I *will* have it my own way. Six Oaks is my farm and will be as long as there is breath in my body. My family have farmed this land for five generations and nothing changes without my agreement so never you forget that. You may be living under my roof with my daughter and she, heaven help her, may now have your name but do not for one moment imagine you are here to take over. This house, this farm, this room for God's sake, belong to the Farrow family.'

'I think you've made that perfectly clear, Papa,' contributed Charlotte while her mother added calmly 'Remember we shall all now be living more or less under the same roof. It may not have been our choice – and John we know it was certainly not your choice – but we are where we are and we just have to make it work, not least for our new grandchild.' John Farrow muttered something inaudible under his breath, walked to the inglenook, and carefully stepping over the dogs, removed his pipe from the ashtray, took a wooden spill from the container on the mantlepiece and lit it from the fire. He turned round slowly, looking from his wife to his daughter and then his new son-in-law as he made the first few deep draws to ensure the pipe was well ignited. No-one spoke for at least a minute until John himself broke the silence by turning to Charlotte and saying 'Mama and I will help you remove your remaining bits and pieces to the cottage over the next couple of days.' He then added 'And you and I, Charlotte, need to look carefully at the cropping plans for next year. Please come and see me tomorrow morning after breakfast.'

With that, John gently nudged the dogs into action with his foot and with a brisk 'Come on boys,' walked to the back door, picked up his working coat and walking stick from the small alcove that passed for a cloakroom and left the house.

'He'll be fine,' said Phyllida. 'Just give him time. You know how he is.' With that she clasped her daughter in a warm maternal embrace while glancing at Frank. 'And you simply have to play your part too, Frank.' 'I do know Mrs ... sorry Phyllida,' came the reply. 'And believe me, I do love your daughter very dearly.' Phyllida was not at all sure she did...believe him that is.

The following morning, as requested, Charlotte walked round to the farmhouse, the kitchen still redolent with the appealing aroma of a cooked farmhouse breakfast through which the distinctive individual fragrance of butcher Barnfather's black pudding reigned supreme. John Farrow was nothing if not a creature of habit and despite the constant commitments that running the farm had brought over years, the family would always sit down together for what he called 'a civilised meal'.

'He's gone to do some work has he? I heard the bike,' was John's opening remark as he lifted his eyes from the copy of *The Times* that Fred Wellbeloved's delivery boy had brought on his round before setting off for school.

'Yes, he has a client in Wymondham. You are looking really worried, Papa.'

'I do not like this,' he replied, gesturing to the newspaper and repeating a mantra he had repeated many times before: 'I still think that fool Chamberlain made a monumental error of judgement in trusting Hitler and mark my words, German troops will be marching in to Czechoslovakia before you know it. Another bloody war in my lifetime. It is just so awful and your mother and I do worry about the sort of world your little one will be born in to. But there's nothing you and I can do so let's have a look at the farm where we may be able to make some progress.'

Piled on the corner of the table were numerous brown

and blue, somewhat dog-eared folders, bright red account books and selected recent copies of farming publications as the next two hours saw Charlotte and her father poring over crop returns, looking at the farm accounts and generally tossing agricultural thoughts and ideas to and fro while her mother, Phyllida, plied them with tea and flitted in and out of the parlour as she busied herself with making arrangements for hosting a Conservative Women's committee meeting that afternoon.

Six Oaks Farm's hundred and seventy-five acres were mainly arable and were cropped more or less on a Norfolk four-course rotation of turnips, barley, green fodder and wheat in the historic Turnip Townshend tradition, together with a few acres of potatoes, green vegetables and carrots, although the family always conceded their clay and chalk land was never productive enough to compete commercially with the fenlands and the crops went to the nearest market in Fenton Bishop with a few to the village shop.

John Farrow loathed the eponymous Viscount Townshend who entered farming folklore in the early eighteenth century when he realised the value of turnips as winter stock feed. 'Bloody turncoat,' was his comment whenever his name was mentioned and he refused to acknowledge that on his farm he was following the advocacy of a man who entered the Lords as a Tory but transferred his political sympathies to the Whigs.

'It was all a long time ago, Papa,' Charlotte would say.

'So was Oliver Cromwell but I still do not like the man,' came the predictable riposte.

Together, John and Charlotte decided to make some

slight cropping changes for the coming 1939 season and she always took pride when her father, with all his long experience, took her advice, even if it was on fairly minor matters. Few arable farms, nonetheless, were completely bereft of animals and Six Oaks was no exception. In John's time there were always half a dozen or so Suffolk ewes to be put to a neighbour's ram for spring lambs, three or four Friesian cows for milk, a few Large White pigs to fatten for bacon and ham, and of course this being Norfolk, two or three dozen turkeys for Christmas; John had long championed the striking-looking traditional Norfolk Black and would brook no argument about its matchless flavour. Finally, there was an ever-changing population of chickens and ducks for meat and eggs – ever-changing as some of the eggs hatched and foxes took their toll. New animals were bought from time to time at Fenton Bishop stock sales and because of the close friendship between the Farrows and the Van Vliets, some also came from their Home Farm. The van Vliets' unexpectedly camp estate manager Claude Clinker was a regular visitor to Six Oaks, generally around a mealtime in the hope of catching Phyllida Farrow's legendary beef stew for which he knew she always used the best bottom cuts, plenty of parsley and rosemary and cooked slowly in the old kitchen range for six hours. 'Phyllida, my very own darling, you are such an angel of gastronomy,' he would say.

Charlotte told John that by and large she would continue to keep to his practices with the animals and reiterated how much she adored them, especially the ducks and the cows, of which she had three. They had names, of course: Snowbell because she arrived in Felsingham on a cold white winter afternoon and it seemed a good cow name, Cuckoo because she came the day in April a good many years ago when the first cuckoo was heard calling over towards Turney Wood, and Pretty, because she was. Charlotte always loved Cuckoo the most because she had been on hand during a school holiday to help unload the cart that brought her over from the van Vliet's Home Farm. She was a black and white Friesian and was in time to play an unwitting but critical part in Charlotte's future.

Both John and Charlotte felt the meeting had been productive and no further mention was made of Frank. After lunch with her parents, Charlotte kept to a routine appointment with Margaret Fraser, the midwife, to check the progress of her pregnancy. All being reported well, she returned to make an afternoon crop walk followed by a discussion with Ted on the prospects for the winter barley.

As the days and weeks passed Charlotte detected several things. First, there was a definite thawing of the relations between her husband and father. She thought both of them – almost certainly with third party intervention by her mother – had slowly and inexorably become reconciled to the status quo and an acceptance that they would be part of each other's lives for the foreseeable future. Frank was also taking a close interest in the farm without any longer seriously suggesting he wanted to become more involved. He discussed animal husbandry with Charlotte – and drew more than slightly forced comparisons with herring fishing. He even began to have civilised conversations with John about his cropping plans and demonstrated an above average knowledge of the history of East Anglian farming practices. They had good natured banter about the merits of Turnip Townshend. Conspicuously, domestic politics were seldom mentioned but the two men shared similar ideas about the terrible events still unfolding in Europe.

'I do think there may be some slight merit in the man after all,' John said one evening to Phyllida, although with a barely concealed grudging tone in his voice. 'I always had a sneaking feeling he would come good,' she replied and they agreed that things had progressed beyond Charlotte simply 'making the best of a bad job.'

Twice Charlotte invited Frank's parents, Vic and Clarice, to Six Oaks for dinner and once they reciprocated. On neither of the occasions could the evening have been deemed a success. Vic Atmore was a man of few words and even those few did not make for pleasant listening. He bore an enormous chip on his shoulder for no single reason that Charlotte could pin down but in the time she had known him, she was unaware she had ever heard him agree with anyone about anything. Clarice was immeasurably more voluble but as she had done throughout her life, much of her vocal energy and latent oxygen was expended on telling anyone within range – including her new daughter-in-law – what a wonderful man her son was. She fell short of telling Charlotte she was a fortunate woman but it was clearly implied.

Frank himself was spending more time working at home and less visiting clients in the more distant parts of the county. He began to make increasing use of the telephone. 'Modern inventions are there to help,' he would say 'and encourage home life.' He appeared to be seeing less of his old friends from Yaxton and even his lunchtimes and evenings at the Eelcatcher's Arms declined noticeably – to the extent that landlord Billy Harmer asked Tommy Marster the farmhand one day if Frank had been unwell.

And, above all, Frank was talking daily of their future family, albeit always referring to the unborn child as their son. Charlotte took this lightly however and even began calling him King Henry VIII as he craved a male heir. 'You know what happened to Anne Boleyn when she didn't manage it,' Frank joked; at least it seemed to be a joke. He caressed Charlotte's stomach – rather too frequently for her father's liking – and purred words to the effect that it was he, Frank Atmore, who was responsible for its contents. On one occasion Frank even offered to accompany Charlotte to the doctor for a routine check but that notion was stamped on pretty quickly. He then started to take a questioning interest in the mechanics of childbirth. He had read in a magazine that Prince Albert attended the birth of Queen Victoria's children and suggested he might like to be present too. Even before Charlotte could answer, her mother who was standing nearby said, 'Over my dead body. Don't even think about it, Frank. We may live on a farm but Charlotte is giving birth to a baby, not a calf or a lamb.'

But on a more practical note, Phyllida said to Charlotte one morning as they walked to the village together for some shopping 'I wonder if we may have to think about exchanging homes – certainly when the baby arrives and you need more space. I haven't talked it through it yet with Papa but we really don't need all of the farmhouse for the two of us and it might make more sense for you and Frank to take it on.'

Chapter Five

There is no time of the year when a farm is not a desperately busy place. Crops continue to grow and animals must be fed and milked, so throughout her childhood Charlotte became used to hearing her father say the only time he could genuinely afford to be away from Six Oaks was the first two weeks of November. Rarely, and under pressure from Phyllida, he managed to squeeze in an extra week at other periods of the year. 'Our little daughter so loves the seaside,' she used to say, but John complained constantly that he could not really spare the time and also worried perennially that the farmhands might not be coping; a wholly fallacious concern because Ted and Tommy knew the farm and the routine tasks backwards. 'But what if they have an emergency and I'm not there?' was his constant anxiety. Because of this, Charlotte's main memories of childhood holidays were of those with her mother and cousins and old Aunt Peggy.

A July holiday for anyone was certainly out of the question because harvesting might need to be done at any time when the weather permitted and would require all hands to be at the wheel; almost literally. Charlotte was faced with a quandary therefore when she earmarked a Thursday morning in early July for making space in the big barn so the new season's straw could be stacked in the coming weeks. She knew it was bad practice to stack the new on top of the previous year's bales – of which there were more than usual because of the previous relatively mild winter. However, Ted and Tommy would soon be fully occupied with the harvest as well as all the farm's day to day tasks and she dare not, could not, pull them off, even for a morning, while the fine weather lasted. They had no lights for the machinery – it was not an option on a Fordson tractor of Six Oaks vintage – so they could not work through the night. As it was, she had agreed to help by checking all the animals. And above all, she was becoming frustrated at people – like her father – who used the justification of her pregnancy to try and persuade her to ease off in her personal physical involvement. 'We can cope without you, Charlotte; do take a rest, you owe it to your baby,' was the constant mantra.

But Charlotte was Charlotte and Charlotte knew best. She wanted to shift the old straw that week and would not wait. So, on the Wednesday morning she asked Frank if he could spare a day to help. The answer was a surprisingly firm no. He was due to see a potential new client in Diss; a hugely important client who could catapult their income – his words – into a whole new realm. Charlotte dare not pursue her request further so had to think laterally.

John's health had been particularly poor recently and he was certainly not capable of doing anything useful so it would be unkind to ask. Charlotte was devoted to her father and she simply could not place him in an embarrassing situation and draw attention to the fact that he was no longer the fine strong man he had once been. Nigel from the village, with the strength of an ox, would be perfect so she enquired about his availability, only to discover he was away attending Lily's grandmother's funeral in Nottingham and would not be back for two days. She made soundings of all the other possible sources of village labour, some reliable, some not so, but everyone was committed on other farms and she knew it was unreasonable to ask at The Manor because they were as busy as everyone else and she knew Sir Arthur would feel honour bound to offer one of his own men to help when he could not really be spared. It would not be fair to him, or Claude, his estate manager, and she considered it would abuse their friendship.

Later in the day, Charlotte needed to visit the Post Office. It was, as always, like walking into the opening scene of the Scottish play, although on this occasion only one of the witches was present. It was the first witch on duty behind her counter so Charlotte exercised her final option, albeit one she considered with the greatest reluctance. She asked Fanny Handley, the post-mistress, if she knew anything about Harry Kett's whereabouts. If was a pretty naïve question because of course Fanny knew everything about everyone and would be bound to have an answer. Although Harry had been Frank's best man, Charlotte had seen or heard nothing of him since the wedding and although he did not have a reputation for reliability, probity, sobriety, hard work or any other virtue, and she could not stand him; and had never forgiven him for his attempted seduction of her on her way home from school all those years ago, he might just be capable of shifting straw.

'Oh, don't say you haven't heard, Charlotte,' said Fanny, absolutely salivating over the finest piece of gossip to have come her way since Charlotte's pregnancy. 'It'll be in the paper this week. Harry's being detained at His Majesty's pleasure.'

'Good lord! What's he done?' asked Charlotte.

'PC Edwards caught him blind drunk outside the Eelcatcher's two nights ago, throwing bricks at passing vehicles. In fact, it's even worse, because Harry took a swing at him and PC Edwards had to use his truncheon. He's up before the magistrates tomorrow with a big bruise, charged with public nuisance, being drunk and disorderly in a public place and assaulting a police officer.'

'Well, well! Thank you, Fanny, for telling me. Frank has said nothing so I assume he doesn't know if it's only just happened. Honestly though I can't say I'm surprised. I always knew Harry could end up in serious trouble. Presumably this won't mean prison.'

'Unlikely – probably a fine and bound over,' said Fanny, loving very minute.

Back at home in the evening, Charlotte could not wait to mention to Frank how far his best man had fallen from grace; how he had gone from best to worst. Frank said he did not know about it although Charlotte was unsure how much conviction his denial had and she wondered if the Felsingham-Yaxton grapevine had been at work. Nonetheless, she took him at his word and asked him once more over dinner. 'Are you sure, Frank, you can't possibly help tomorrow? Do please try,' she said, and explained how she had drawn blanks everywhere else. 'Sorry, Lottie, old girl,' he said. Frank had taken to calling her Lottie although he knew how much she hated it. He had become obsessed with an obscure silent screen film star called Lottie Pickford who had died two years earlier and claimed he just loved the name. He said it was just a tease; Charlotte thought it unkind. 'Sorry,' he repeated, 'I'm afraid you'll just have to manage or put it off until the weekend. This client is simply too important to lose.' Waiting until the weekend was not an option because Charlotte had promised, and she was not a woman to break a promise, even to herself.

The next morning, Thursday, dawned gloriously. The sun shone so brightly through the east-facing kitchen window of the cottage that Charlotte had to draw the curtains while she ate her breakfast. Frank had left early in order to be on time for his meeting in Diss. She had heard Ted start up the tractor just after six and head out to Long Mead, the furthest field from the farmhouse, where he and Tommy would be working all day. She cleared away quickly, walked across the yard to cast an eye over the livestock, fed the chickens and pigs and collected the eggs, which she returned to put in the pantry.

She then walked back across the yard and entered the magnificent old Six Oaks barn. It pre-dated the Georgian farmhouse and had once served a much earlier farm on the site. Experts had dated it to the late sixteenth century and it stood now, as proudly against the weather as it had done down the years. The roof had been re-thatched in Charlotte's childhood and she clearly remembered watching the skilled local thatchers weaving magic with their sheaves of Norfolk reed. Inside, the glorious hammer-beam roof stood a silent testament to the countless crops of grain and straw it had protected over the centuries and, in even earlier times, the cattle that had been over-wintered there. One end was now kept screened off and functioned as a garage where John Farrow kept his beloved dark green Riley Kestrel saloon.

Charlotte looked up at the stacked remains of last season's straw and realised she would need to climb to the top and then throw down the old bales one at a time onto the trailer she had asked Ted and Tommy to park there the previous evening. There was a wooden ladder at the side of the barn, big, old and heavy, but Charlotte was no weakling and she manoeuvred it to the side of the straw stack and climbed confidently to the top. It was about ten feet high and once there she began to drag the heavy bales one at a time and tip them down on to the trailer. It was after she had done four or five that it all happened, although afterwards she could not recollect the sequence of events. It seemed, however, that she must have missed her footing on the closely compacted straw which was shiny and slippery. One moment she was at the top and the next she was ten feet down on the barn floor, apparently having collided with the ladder on the way which toppled over, and by serendipity, narrowly missed her before coming to rest against the trailer.

Initially, Charlotte just felt shocked and after a few moments eased herself into a siting position and moved her arms and legs. 'Thank God! No broken bones,' she thought to herself. It was then that the pain struck. When they asked her later, she could only liken it to the most intense period she had ever experienced. The pain was then followed by something else that caused her to panic. She became aware of a warmth and wetness between her thighs. She screamed as she had never screamed before, and by the greatest good fortune she did so at just the moment her mother was driving into the yard with the Riley.

Chapter Six

'Oh, my dearest sweet C,' said Hannah as she entered Charlotte's bedroom at Six Oaks Cottage to find her friend resting prone on the bed, and immediately ran across to throw both arms around her neck. It was four days since Charlotte's fall and Hannah was desperate to give her support and learn more about the tragedy. 'Your mother showed us up,' she added, the plural 'us' immediately explained because following Hannah as she crossed the room was a short, dark-haired young woman of around Charlotte's own age – a bit younger than Hannah herself. Charlotte looked up from where she was lying to see the newcomer was wearing an elegantly tailored fairly close-fitting summer dress with bare shoulders. It ended around knee level and revealed she had shapely legs, a tiny waist and barely discernable breasts. Charlotte looked more attentively to see a petite, kindly face and piercingly brown, almost black eyes. 'Hello, Charlotte,' she said in a voice that was possibly even more refined than Hannah's own. 'I'm Emily. I'm sure Hannah has told you about me but I'm really sorry about this. What an occasion for us to meet! I know how close you both are but I could never have imagined our first meeting would be in such circumstances. I am so, so sorry for you, Charlotte.'

'That's really kind, Emily,' Charlotte replied, 'and thank you for coming. I'm sure we shall soon get to know each other very well.'

The visitors then responded to Charlotte's gesture to sit down, Hannah at the foot of the bed and Emily on a small armchair. 'I just cannot imagine, C, how absolutely terrifying it must it have been,' said Hannah. 'We've come as soon as we could. We've been away in Leicestershire collecting more of Emily's things to bring to The Manor.'

'Can you bear to tell us what happened?' asked Emily. 'Your mother – isn't she lovely by the way? – has told us the basic outline – about the fall in the barn.'

'Yes, I need to talk about it and in fact I want to try and remember everything,' was the reply. 'More importantly, I hope you can bear to listen. Well, there I was on the barn floor screaming my head off. It's ridiculous really but I can remember seeing a mouse run between the wheels of the cart and watching it stop and nibble some grain. It was greyish and it sat up on its back legs and its whiskers twitched. I thought that's a field mouse not a harvest mouse; it must be, because you don't find harvest mice in barns. Can you imagine it – nature watching at time like that? I was in some sort of other worldly state. I can clearly remember the mouse and I can tell you exactly what the weather was like but not how I fell.

Mama obviously realised what was happening and somehow got me into the car. By this time, I felt the blood running down my legs and it was only because I was wearing my jodhpurs and the thick cloth held it all in that my insides didn't end up on Papa's car seat. We went straight to Dr Fraser's and he and Margaret said they would have to get me onto the couch thing. By then the pain was almost unbearable and they undressed me and then as they took off my trousers, it all happened. There was this great rush of blood with all sorts of red lumps in it. It was like a huge bright red dam bursting between my legs.'

Emily intervened. 'Oh, God, I'm so sorry, Charlotte. I'm not great with blood. I shall have to go out.'

'That's fine, Emily,' Charlotte replied 'Are you all right, Hannah?'

'Yes, C. I need to hear this. I love you, and although thank the Good Lord I will never experience anything like it, I have to share it with you so please go on. I've seen some pretty awful things with the horses and I am sure you have on the farm. And I shall never forget how wonderful you were to me that time when we were out hacking and I was thrown and broke my arm and the bone was sticking out all red and bloody.'

'Well, there were great clots of blood and one bigger lump which just sort of fell out. I didn't need to push or anything. That big lump was my baby. It was just a few inches long and all covered in blood and Margaret said I am so sorry, Charlotte, but there was just nothing we could have done to save your baby. Dr Fraser said he was so terribly sorry for me and Frank. They then cut through the cord – it was just like cutting a piece of rope and I felt nothing – and they asked me if I wanted to see it, so Margaret washed the baby and told me it was girl and I said I wanted to see her properly, so Margaret held her in her two hands and showed her to me. She looked like a tiny doll. I hadn't expected that – that she looked like a proper person. And I could see her little face and her nose and her arms and her legs, they were all sort of held tightly together as if she was hugging herself because she was frightened. Margaret asked me if I wanted to hold her but I didn't. It was silly really but she seemed so fragile I was afraid of hurting her. Hurting her – how crazy was that, Hannah? She was dead. She was dead before she had ever been properly alive. I still don't know if I should have done it – held her – but anyway I didn't. Then they took her away and I don't want to think about what they did.'

Charlotte then lost her hitherto stoic composure and broke down, sobbing uncontrollably. 'I expect they just threw her in a bin,' she said. Hannah embraced her friend and held her tightly for a minute or more while neither said anything, the silence only punctuated by the soft sounds of both women now crying unashamedly. Their faces were pressed tightly together, both now drenched, and as the tears flowed downwards, their lips could taste each other's saltiness.

'At least I saw her,' said Charlotte at last, the words unavoidably distorted because her mouth was still pressed against Hannah's cheek. 'I now know I can make lovely little babies. I would have called her Ophelia because it's your middle name and I love it. Then there was the worst part really because there were extra bits still inside me and they had to get them out. Are you still all right?'

Hannah then eased herself away from Charlotte and

nodded and shook free some of the tears. 'Yes, I'm fine, C. Are you? Gosh – Ophelia! Oh, my dearest sweet friend…do go on.'

'Well, I'll spare you the details but basically I had to have – you know – what they call a D and C. You know what that is? Not very pleasant! I was only vaguely aware before but I certainly do now. They said the bleeding wouldn't stop until then. I had been lucky because it was all fairly straightforward and I didn't need go to hospital, provided I took precautions afterwards to keep the bleeding under control and I have these things – you know, to soak it up. They said I could come home in the afternoon, which was what I wanted, and Mama brought me. I have to rest in the mornings and do light things in the afternoon. They kept stressing that I must let everything take its time to settle. Our bodies are wonderful at healing but they mustn't be rushed they said. I'm still in pain but they say this will gradually go. Papa has been lovely but he just hasn't really known what to say. I know he thinks I was stupid to have gone into the barn but I keep saying I did try to get help. It's so ridiculous but he even blames himself because he says I should have asked him.'

'Where was your mother while this was all going on?' asked Hannah. 'She was sitting at the back of the room. She kept out of the way. She wanted to let Margaret and Dr Fraser do what they had to do, and of course she had been a VAD nurse in the war while Grandmama and Grandpapa were looking after me, so she knew quite a lot. She had certainly seen lots of blood, but what I didn't know until she told me afterwards was that she had had two miscarriages – early ones – before she had me. People keep saying it's not unusual although it usually happens early on because something is wrong with the baby. Not after four months when the baby is normal and healthy and the mother is stupid and climbs high ladders. I do blame myself, Hannah. I shouldn't have done it. The job could have waited until someone was available to help. It was just me wanting to get ahead of things on the farm.'

'That is going to be seriously hard for you, C, but you will have to be really strong – Farrow strong! But I haven't even asked you about Frank. What did he say?'

'Well, Mama told him of course as soon as he got home from work and he came straight upstairs to see me. He looked white and didn't really know what to say. He still kept calling the baby him and he was really very odd when I said I should not have gone into the barn until he or someone else was there to help me. He obviously didn't want to talk about it. And that's about it really. I've told him to carry on going to work as usual. Mama is here to help me and it's so wonderful that you and Emily have come over. Do come as often as you can. Oh, do call Emily back now – tell her it's safe to come in! She's really lovely, isn't she? I can certainly see the appeal!'

Over the next few weeks Charlotte, to a degree against her instincts, did as she had been told. She went for check-ups and was told all was progressing well. She went to see Holy Humphrey every week at the vicarage and they prayed together for Ophelia. She could not bring herself to go to church services however because she felt she was not yet ready to be on show or to be questioned by anyone outside the family and close friends. She went to see two friends of her mother who had experienced late miscarriages and one week she went with her mother to a meeting in Norwich with other mothers who had been through the same sort of loss, but she came away frustrated. Every woman had had a different experience, every one seemed to have reacted differently – and above all, every one of them had experienced early miscarriages, miscarriages induced by nature, not late ones caused by the baby's mother. But nonetheless she was slowly, ever so slowly, educating herself back to normal life. Frank however remained odd and was clearly uncomfortable talking about it – and Charlotte, Hannah, Emily and Phyllida all felt there was more to it than the usual male attitude to what are essentially 'women's things'. Phyllida said he always shut up like a clam whenever the subject was raised.

But for all her obedience to the medical strictures, for all her being careful and not rushing back to a normal life, Charlotte still went through phases of feeling appallingly guilty – not at having let Frank down – that never occurred to her for one moment – but at having let down her tiny unborn daughter. She had betrayed this barely formed four-inch long being because she had been stubborn and would not listen to reason. The only solace she could find was in telling herself over and over again that if she was ever blessed with another pregnancy – if she could bring herself to face another pregnancy – she would think of her unborn Ophelia every day and never, ever do anything that might endanger her future brother or sister.

Chapter Seven

The van Vliets' boundless generosity was no better expressed than in two summer garden party gatherings at The Manor. They were major highlights of the village's year and occasions everyone looked forward to with huge anticipation. The domestic and estate staff and their families were entertained at a small party first, generally with a Punch and Judy man or other performer to entertain the children. Then came the time-honoured event when family, close and treasured friends and a handful of village notables were invited to what was in truth, less a garden party and more a buffet dinner of truly memorable sumptuosity on The Manor lawn, held to the tasteful accompaniment of the South Norfolk Chamber Ensemble. What the van Vliets' cook Mrs Fiddler and her assistant were able to produce from The Manor's kitchen and the amateur ensemble were able to produce from their quartet of strings were constantly remarked upon miracles. 'It's my proudest day of the year,' was the culinary lady's regular mantra.

This year, there were two reasons for the guests to be especially appreciative. The ever darkening political situation on the European continent led unavoidably to everyone wondering, although scarcely daring to suggest, if this could be the last such gathering for some while. But almost surmounting this in everyone's perception was the knowledge of Charlotte's all too recent miscarriage which led to some stifling of conversation. This was the almost unmentionable subject.

It was Charlotte herself who decided the party would be her first proper public outing six weeks after the miscarriage and she attempted valiantly to put her fellow guests at their ease by introducing the matter delicately and subtly into her own conversations, and reassuring everyone that she was feeling 'all right'. A swift switch to Hitler then eased the conversational progress still further, although the guests were divided among those who saw recent political developments in Germany as an encouraging sign and those, like Arthur van Vliet and John Farrow, who considered them all further evidence of the deviousness of the Fuehrer and the horrors yet to come.

The van Vliets had invited around sixty guests, including ten or twelve of their own family, who could be accommodated comfortably in The Manor's twenty-two bedrooms, and would stay overnight for an exclusively family lunch the following day. The remainder were their closest and dearest local friends, like the Farrows, with a few near neighbours and a sprinkling of the great and good of the local community. It was always considered prudent, even for residents as eminent as the van Vliets, to be on affable terms with Jonathan Walters, the Chairman of the Parish Council.

As the weather had looked slightly threatening and

thunderstorms were forecast, the van Vliets had decided to serve drinks in The Manor garden but to set out the food in the great hall so guests could come and go as they pleased. The hall was looking at its most magnificent and was dominated by the immense portrait of an early female van Vliet ancestor who looked down on the proceedings with an expression that always appeared to be a combination of boredom, misery and serious constipation. Antlered and horned trophies of family stalking and hunting exploits also gazed down from the walls, while close to the long oak table that groaned with the wondrous results of Mrs Fiddler's gastronomic enterprise was one of Sir Arthur's most prized possessions: a cased salmon that those interested enough could discover from its label weighed 44lb 13oz and had been caught by him on a fly in the River Tay on 2 October 1929.

Inevitably, the gathering broke up into small knots of individuals. The more reticent, withdrawn and shy sought out those fellow guests with whom they were most familiar and stayed effectively rooted to the spot indoors for the duration. They angled their eyes downwards, closely examining the old rugs on the polished stone floor, little knowing they were treasured souvenirs brought back from the North-West Frontier by Sir Arthur's father, Major Sir Wilbert van Vliet, 10th Hussars, who had fought with great distinction and valour in the Second Afghan War. It nonetheless came as a revelation to those villagers unaccustomed to such surroundings to realise that wealth, most especially inherited wealth, did not generally equate with disposable loose change and many of the rugs, once gloriously coloured with natural dyes were now faded and in patches almost threadbare.

The more outward going and gregarious among the gathering circulated from knot to knot of guests, both indoors and out, and the van Vliets themselves were impeccable hosts and attempted to speak at least once to everyone and put the entire assemblage at its ease. The fly in the evening's ointment was always however destined to be Frank. His parents-in-law had had quite sufficient of the diplomacy of dealing with their son-in-law on a daily basis so studiously stayed out of his way, preferring to catch up with fellow villagers, farming friends, van Vliet relatives and others whom they saw much less frequently; and in most cases, not since the wedding. Frank and Charlotte had, as it turned out somewhat unwisely, gone their separate ways on arrival and the first nobly to engage Frank in conversation was the formidably tall and imposing Matilda van Vliet. 'We were so, so desperately sad to hear of Charlotte's recent misfortune – so, so dreadful,' she said, her always resonant contralto voice embellished with just the hint of superciliousness as she looked down on Frank from her greater height. At almost six feet himself, Frank was not used to looking up to women, either metaphorically or, in Lady van Vliet's case, literally. 'A terrible matter and one of great sadness of course for you both,' she added. 'Yes,' Frank responded. 'We were all really sad for Lottie and I'm properly sick that I shan't have a son after all.' Seldom one to be lost for words, Lady van Vliet nonetheless took a full three or four seconds to reply. 'I understood it was a daughter, Frank,' was all she could offer.

'No chance,' he said, 'they got it wrong but we'll have another go and make sure it hatches properly.' And with that the couple parted, Matilda to seek out a more kindred spirit and Frank to the tray of champagne, held somewhat precariously by a pretty young blonde girl, Betty Warburton, Lady van Vliet's chamber-maid who had been pressed into waitress service for the occasion. Frank lingered uncommonly long over taking his next glass and gave Betty a look and a wink that suggested quite unambiguously that he would have welcomed pressing her in to service of a quite different kind. She blinked furiously and uttered a giggle worthy of Laughing Lily.

After Charlotte, and of course, Adolf Hitler, the third pivotal point for conversation that summer evening was Emily, now on public view with Hannah for the first time. And a striking figure she struck with her fine and delicate facial features, closely cut jet black hair, slim figure and impeccable dress sense, although she had deliberately dressed down for the occasion to try, like Charlotte, to avoid becoming a focus of attention. But inevitably one of the first to home in on the pair was Frank.

Looking Emily up and down, he commented 'So you're the other half. I've always wanted to meet a real live pair of lesbians – is that what you call yourselves?'

'We are human beings first, Frank; and women second; there is nothing more to it than that,' said Hannah; and pointedly failed to introduce Emily.

'Oh, come away, Hannah; don't treat me as if I am stupid. Your upper classes are full of it – *homo*sexuality.'

'Frank, you are being utterly offensive. I think you may have accepted rather too much of my parents' hospitality. Charlotte will be totally ashamed of you.' And with that Hannah led Emily away to introduce her to other, equally intrigued but more civilly disposed guests.

Feeling duty bound to maintain a watching brief over her husband, Charlotte soon became all too aware he had exceeded her worse fears. Hannah was correct in both respects. Frank had already drunk too much and she was ashamed of him. She was in truth terrified of her father finding out what he had been saying so she boxed him into a corner and spelled it out in soft, hushed, but unarguably meaningful tones. 'Either you drink no more, apologise to Hannah and Emily and do not step one inch out of line for the rest of the evening or you go home; and I will make your excuses. Oh, yes, the other possibility is that I tell my father and I cannot imagine what he might do. Just possibly kill you.'

Frank looked unaccustomedly abashed and in his own mind opted not to apologise but decided staying in line, moderating his intake of champagne and being as inconspicuous as possible were the best options. 'Fair do's, Lottie. Love you,' he said before camouflaging himself among a group of local farmers.

From the corner of her eye, Charlotte noticed Frank then handing out business cards which she thought may have been tasteless and unacceptable at a social gathering but might just lead to a slight inflation of their income. For reasons he had chosen not to explain, he had recently lost two clients while the new one he said he was visiting so importantly on the day of Charlotte's accident had never materialised. It was then she spotted a sight all too familiar to her at the far end of the lawn admiring a rose bed – a shock of blond hair atop the elegant figure of a man in his mid-twenties wearing a beautifully tailored lightweight tweed jacket and tartan trews. She gently but purposefully eased her way through the crowd to arrive just behind him as he gathered a glass from the tray. 'Hello, Torquil,' she said softly.

Hannah's cousin turned suddenly and broad smiles lit up both their faces. 'Charlotte, my angel; how wonderful to see you. I've only just arrived – horrendous drive south all day.' Extremely close attention to his voice would have suggested to a listener that he had driven south from Perthshire but the accent was essentially English rather than Scottish.

Each instinctively then threw the single arm not holding a glass around the other's neck and exchanged cheek kisses that an uncommitted observer would have noticed were just a few seconds longer than courtesy and propriety might have expected.

'And you of course are married, my dearest sweetest girl – I am so sorry I could not make the wedding – to be honest I was laid low with a broken arm – hunting accident.' Then, using a word everyone else had avoided, 'And your miscarriage, Charlotte. I was so heart-broken for you when I heard and I thought to write, but cowardly as it must seem, I could not bring myself to conjure up the right words.'

'That's all right, Tor; of, course I understand. It was awful when it happened but as they say time is a healer. But it's so good to see you now. How are your parents – and your little brother Alex?'

Torquil was the son of Sir Arthur van Vliet's sister Viola who had married a minor Scottish laird and become a McLeod, but with the van Vliets having no son and Sir Arthur no brothers, it seemed highly likely that Torquil would one day inherit The Manor. 'The family are all well, thank you,' he replied. 'Alex and I have been heavily involved in developing the shooting and fishing side of the estate; but you'll be interested to know that I'm coming south to take up a position working for a major landowner on an estate just north of Thetford. I shall be close to my uncle and aunt which will be good for them – and you too of course,' he added with the most heart-warming of smiles, 'will not be far away. But your husband; is he here? You must introduce us.'

'Oh, he's here somewhere. Perhaps we'll bump into him later,' Charlotte added with what Torquil saw immediately was less than abundant enthusiasm. 'We should go in and get something to eat.'

Frank was still handing out business cards when he heard Charlotte's unmistakable girlish laugh behind him at the other end of the room. He realised it was the first time he had heard its joyous notes since the event of a few weeks ago and turned to find out what had finally lifted the awful pall of gloom from his wife. He saw her in animated conversation with a young man he did not recognise but after his dressing down, thought he would save his enquiries until later.

Meanwhile, as Charlotte and Torquil both performed the juggling act of simultaneously balancing plates and glasses, their conversation continued, each seemingly oblivious to all others around them while they caught up on two years of events, personal, national and global. Charlotte learned that Torquil was still not married and he was intrigued to know her plans for Six Oaks Farm. Then as the evening drew on, Torquil realised he had all but ignored his hosts and after making profuse apologies to Charlotte, said he really, really hoped they would see each other again soon; if not before he returned to Scotland, at least in the early spring when he moved south.'

'I shall certainly look forward to that,' she said. 'I certainly shall.'

As the evening drew to a close and the guests were giving their thanks, John and Phyllida collected Charlotte and Frank for a promised drive home. The Manor was only about half an hour's walk from Six Oaks but it was now pitch black outside and everyone was tired so the lift was welcome. More or less oblivious to what had transpired, Phyllida made small talk in the car though Charlotte conspicuously was extremely quiet.

It was not until she and Frank had said goodnight to John and Phyllida and hung up their coats in the cottage that the issues of the evening inevitably arose. 'So let me guess,' started Frank. 'The blond tartan chieftain who had your undivided attention. I suppose that was Torpid?'

'Torquil; yes, Hannah's cousin.'

'He's the one you fucked before me.'

Charlotte's astonishment was palpable and visible. 'Frank, please don't say that. It's absolutely coarse and disgusting.'

'But true. You told me. You admitted it when you said you weren't a virgin. I never know what's correct though. Who actually does the fucking, who fucks who? Was it you or him?'

'Frank, please stop it. You're still drunk. I've told you before how I feel about that word. It should only be used in the most intimate way when a couple are making love, not as a way of expressing something vulgar.'

'I'll tell you what's vulgar, Lottie. It's you making me look stupid and humiliating me in front of the entire village by fluttering your eyes at your long-lost Bonnie Prince Charlie. Don't you dare do anything like that ever again. As your husband, I forbid you to speak to him. And I may as well tell you now, I have never liked that Hannah woman. I don't like you seeing her either.'

'What do mean "That Hannah woman"? She's my best friend and always has been.'

'She's queer. Having sex with other women. Those two are freaks. Do you know how they manage to do *their* fucking? It's not normal though it's all quite interesting if you're a bloke. It's all very contrived and mechanical – all those bits of equipment they use. Must be fascinating to watch. Have you ever seen them do it?'

Charlotte was used to being shocked but Frank was now being vulgar beyond anything she had ever heard, from anyone.

'Frank, stop, stop it, stop it! Stop using that language and being so vile and coarse. I know you've had far too much to drink but you know I hate it. And let me tell you, you cannot and will not ever forbid me to do anything.'

'Love, cherish and *obey*. Isn't that what you agreed?'

'Love and cherish, Frank? You don't know the meaning

of the words. And as for embarrassment, you were a complete disgrace. You were extremely rude to Hannah and Emily, you abused the van Vliet's hospitality and I just wanted to disown you. And now you are saying things that are more disgusting than I have ever heard in my life. I'm tired and I'm going to bed. And I shall sleep in the back bedroom tonight.'

With that, she was gone, although she resisted the temptation to slam the door behind her which even in her seriously disturbed state she thought would be unseemly and undignified. She more than half-expected Frank to follow but was relieved to find he said, and did, nothing as she made her way up the stairs.

Once undressed, Charlotte buried her face in the sweet smelling fresh cotton of the sheets and pillow, laundered and neatly prepared by housekeeper Jenny for some unknown guest who would now, in all probability, never be invited; and she sobbed her heart out. This was not in her wildest nightmare how she ever imagined spending the night after the first Manor garden party of her wedded life. She had married a man who embarrassed and disgusted her beyond imagining and was coarse beyond belief. She was almost hourly realising, not so much that she did not love him, but that she did not know how to love him. She had lost a baby she knew had not been conceived in anything approaching affection and Frank had changed, almost overnight, since her miscarriage.

And she had been reminded in the past few hours that decent, honest, loving men really did people the world beyond the gate of Six Oaks Farm. Surely, she thought, things could get no worse. She then dropped to her knees at the bedside, clasped her hands together and said a silent prayer for her lost Ophelia, and for herself, then fell into bed and cried herself to sleep with the name Torquil on her lips.

Chapter Eight

The start of the day after the party was saved from being unbearable at Six Oaks Cottage by the fact that Frank had risen early, before Charlotte awoke, and left for work somewhere in the far-flung reaches of the county. So she was her own woman again, with her own time and her own space to do what she wanted. She would attend to farm matters and have a lengthy talk later with Ted and Tommy, who had been left too much she felt to their own devices of late. She could spent a small amount of time with her parents reviewing the previous night – or at least the censored parts of it – all in the hope that by the evening Frank would have returned to something approaching civility.

But this is not how marriage was ever intended, she thought; and she could not remove her dear friend Torquil from her mind, without really deciding if that was good or bad. She realised she and Frank never did anything together. They did not go out as a couple, they did not socialise, they did not invite guests. And strange as it seemed to her, she was only now realising that, in truth, they had no friends and no interests in common.

After breakfast, and on an impulse, she telephoned

Hannah. Without any planning or forethought of what she was to say, the conversation matured into the first of what were to be many occasions when Charlotte opened her heart to the woman who had always been her beloved surrogate sister. She told her – in sanitised language – about the aftermath of the party. 'You know, my darling, how I feel about one or two old words in the English language that have become corrupted. You know the ones I mean. It's probably silly really but that's me and it hurt me so much to hear him misusing them.' Hannah then confided what Frank had said to her and to Emily at the party and Charlotte uttered a sound that was wordless but unarguably expressed disgust. 'He hasn't apologised for his behaviour even though he was drunk at the time,' Charlotte added. 'We can't go on like this, Hannah. He's getting worse; in fact now I think about it, he's a totally changed man since my miscarriage. He's becoming seriously embarrassing in public – and I haven't told you everything about what he does in private. Perhaps one day…If my parents knew half of it, they would, my father would, well…think about it, Hannah. It was an unwanted pregnancy with a man I didn't and still may not love – and I've had a miscarriage. Until I am ready, physically and psychologically, I need to refrain from love-making but Frank can see none of this. He seems to think of me as some sort of plaything, always on hand to satisfy his any and every bedroom need – some of them really very strange.'

'Let's meet up, C, you, me and Emily as soon as we can and have a good girls' talk about it all. You know I – in fact *we* now – will always be here for you.'

Later in the morning, Jenny the housekeeper came into the Six Oaks Cottage kitchen with a look that was hard to define. Was it shock, horror, disgust, fascination, surprise, perplexity? Perhaps it was all of them. 'I found these under the desk, Charlotte,' she said, 'while I was tidying the office. What shall I do with them?'

She held out a bundle containing a dozen or so magazines. On the top one, Charlotte could see immediately the cover photograph, which was of a naked girl in a most peculiar pose, and the magazine's title, something in German she did not understand. She took them gingerly and flipped through the pages. It was her turn to be shocked and disgusted and she closed them quickly. 'That's awful, Jenny. I am so sorry you've had to see this. Leave it with me.'

Charlotte took the magazines with her to the parlour and pondered what to do. Should she say nothing, put them back under the desk and pretend they did not exist, wait until Frank asked where they had gone; or confront him with them immediately and ask for an explanation? After a few minutes, during which she again looked at two or three pages and confirmed it was as all as disgusting as it had seemed, she decided on yet another option. She would leave them conspicuously on the table so Frank would see them at dinner time, but on a sort of impulse, she first pulled out two at random, put them in a large old envelope and secreted them at the bottom of her wardrobe.

What Charlotte had not anticipated was that her mother would pay her a visit half an hour later to borrow some tea, having inadvertently omitted it from her shopping list at Wellbeloved's. She immediately spotted the literature on the dining table. 'What on earth are these, Charlotte?'

'Oh, don't look at them, Mama. They are awful. They are Frank's. Jenny found them and I am going to see what he has to say about it all.'

Despite her daughter's request, Phyllida was intrigued, picked up the top magazine and began carefully to turn the pages. It was not every day such things turned up in Felsingham St Margaret.

'Extraordinary,' she said. 'Fascinating. Oh, my goodness, how do they...well, well, well, I would never have imagined people could...where did they come from? Why does Frank have such stuff?'

Charlotte snatched back the magazine and slammed it on the pile. 'I don't know but I intend to find out. They are just disgusting.'

'Yes, yes, of course but...' said Phyllida who felt her education had suddenly, at the ripe age of forty-eight, suddenly acquired a whole new dimension. She returned to the farmhouse with the packet of tea, a slightly wiser woman than when she had left five minutes earlier and called out, 'Do let me know what you discover. But I don't think it would be a good idea to let Papa know about them.'

As intended, Charlotte spent most of the afternoon on the farm, caught up with some of her writing and farm records, and was reading the local newspaper when Frank arrived home at around six. He walked straight into the parlour where the magazines were staring back at him from the table. Was he embarrassed? Was he defensive? To Charlotte's disbelief, he was neither and appeared completely unabashed. 'Oh, I see you've found my reading matter,' he said. 'I don't need to look at them now so they can go back in the study.'

'Frank, how can you be so casual and matter of fact? They are disgusting. I could hardly bear to look. I've never seen anything like it. Jenny found them and I'm sure she'll now have nightmares.'

'Stop fussing. They are just entertainment for active young men. You don't have to look at them – although you might learn a thing or two and get some fresh ideas.'

'You are horrible. Where did you get them for heaven's sake?'

'One of the lads is on the boats and he buys them in Hamburg.'

'Well, I would like you to put them totally out of sight and ask that you do not bring anything like it into my parents' house again.' Charlotte hesitated but decided not to tell Frank that her mother had seen them and certainly not that she had spirited two of them away. Both matters could be kept in reserve for another occasion and in one sense, disgusted with him as she was, she was relieved that Frank had brushed it aside as a storm in a teacup and the episode had not led to another major dreadful confrontation.

But a few days later, another publication made its presence felt in Charlotte's life. The telephone seldom rang at Six Oaks Cottage on a Sunday morning; certainly not before nine o'clock. But it did the weekend after The Manor garden party. Frank was still in bed and Charlotte picked up the phone. There was an agitated Hannah on the other end. Agitated is an under-statement. It was a wholly furious Hannah. There was not even the usual 'Hello, C.' She launched straight in with 'Have you seen the *Sunday Voice*?' 'No, we never get it,' said Charlotte, 'Papa won't have it in the house. We only take *The Sunday Times*.' 'Well you need to see it today,' was the response. 'Just let me read this headline to you: "Top Tory's daughter frolics with younger woman at private party".'

Charlotte's response was slow and measured as she stressed every word. 'Oh, my God.' Then after a pause. 'Wherever has that come from? What more does it say?' Hannah elaborated. 'It mentions Emily, as the daughter of Tory Minister Geoffrey Wells-Weston. It doesn't mention me or give any other names and it doesn't say where it took place other than "A private house in Norfolk". They obviously tried to contact Emily's father but it says he was not available. It also says they contacted Churchill's office because he and Geoffrey are very close but they would not say anything and also the Cabinet Office because Geoffrey is a Junior Minister. They played it straight as you might expect and said they do not comment on salacious and unfounded rumours about Ministers' families. As you can imagine, Geoffrey himself is incandescent and my father is beside himself. I have never seen him so angry. He rang back to apologise to Geoffrey personally as soon as we heard.'

'And frolicking?' asked Charlotte. 'How could they possibly claim anything like that?'

'We've thought about that and you know how the papers will read something into nothing. We remembered that at one point we did briefly forget ourselves and hold hands. I expect someone noticed and that would be quite enough for them.'

'This is just so awful, darling,' said Charlotte. 'How has Emily taken it?'

'She is distraught and hasn't stopped crying. My mother is comforting her. I didn't say but she's still here. She decided to stay on for a few days – in fact I'm hoping she will move in properly soon and help me with the horses. As I think I told you, we've been so careful to keep our relationship private because this is what we always dreaded might happen. What we couldn't understand at first was how anyone discovered her full name. We know that Wells-Weston is very unusual so she was really careful to introduce herself to people just as Emily – we had agreed that beforehand – but she does now think she may once have allowed herself to say it in full when she met the Chairman of the Parish Council. As you know, he's always a bit formal and pompous and would have given his own full name; he probably called himself Councillor too.'

'Jonathan Walters? Yes, he is pompous and formal but he is also the soul of discretion so it just could not have come from him.'

'That was our conclusion. So someone must have overheard. We need to work out who was standing nearby and might have wanted, for whatever reason, to contact the papers. Was there someone there who had a grudge against Geoffrey? There are plenty of people in politics who are jealous of his rapid advancement but there were certainly none of them at our party so that seems pretty improbable.' Hannah hesitated. 'Or even a grudge against me perhaps, though I'd surprised if anyone cared that much.'

Charlotte hardly dare think her next thought but Frank's shocking comments about Hannah and Emily were still raw in her recollection of the events of a few days ago and she thought quickly. 'I do not like that Hannah woman,' he had said and described her and Emily as freaks. And of course Frank's politics were as far removed as they could be from Geoffrey Wells-Weston's. Frank despised the Tories, at least he despised what he thought they represented – power, influence and all that goes with it. Charlotte had to make up her mind quickly. If she told Hannah her suspicions now, it would immediately reach not only Emily's father but her father too with consequences that did not bear thinking about. She decided to keep her counsel for the time being and told Hannah she would think very carefully about who it might have been; adding, 'Of course we may never know.' She put down the phone after again expressing her dismay but felt deeply uncomfortable about being evasive and holding back from her dearest friend what she was sure must be the explanation. Frank would have to be confronted with it. Another frightful episode loomed.

About twenty minutes later Frank came downstairs and into the kitchen hoping to find some breakfast.

'Did I hear the telephone?' he asked.

'Yes, it was Hannah. Do you know anything about the *Sunday Voice*?' Frank was looking away at the time so Charlotte could not see any facial response but he simply said, 'A bit of a rag but a good read sometimes. Why?'

'Not a good read today apparently. There's a story in

there about Hannah and Emily at the party. At least it doesn't name Hannah but it mentions Emily as an MP's daughter and it says "A house party in Norfolk".'

'Is she? An MP's daughter I mean? I'm not sure I knew that. What about them anyway?'

'It's the usual *Sunday Voice* stuff about them being…' she hesitated, '…intimate friends. Now the van Vliets have worked out that Emily only mentioned her surname once at the party and that was to Jonathan Walters. He wouldn't say anything so someone must have overheard and told the paper. Frank, it couldn't have been you could it? I know at one time you were standing close to Jonathan handing out your business cards – a pretty crass thing to do I thought in fact. You don't like Hannah or Emily and considering what you said about them two nights ago – freaks was your word – I need to ask you straight. Did you contact the *Sunday Voice*?'

'No, I did not.'

'Again, Frank, you really didn't?'

'No. I've told you. May we now have breakfast?'

'All right, I'll say no more, although I'm sure my parents will find out about the story and they'll be pretty curious too.'

It was not until much later that Charlotte realised that when she asked if Frank had telephoned and he denied it, she had not asked the obvious follow-up question – "But do you know who did?"

The rest of the day passed fairly normally. There had been a modest thawing of her relationship with Frank since the aftermath of the party and he had uttered no more comments, vulgar or otherwise about Hannah; or anything else, burying himself for most of the time in the office. Ted and Tommy normally took turns to work on Sundays but as she had given both men the day off, it was down to her to see to the animals. She milked the three cows, checked their food, fed the pigs, cast an eye over the sheep in Alder Carr Meadow, fed the chickens, ducks and turkeys, and collected the eggs. And all the while she thought through the newspaper story. Although the van Vleits and Wells-Westons knew immediately what was being referred to, not everyone in Felsingham necessarily would. Most had never heard of Emily, let alone met her, and almost none knew she was an MP's daughter, including Frank if he was to be believed. Most people in the village were not at the party although almost everyone knew there had been one.

A possible awkward moment did come when Charlotte and Frank went round to the farmhouse for lunch. There was an informal arrangement whereby Phyllida and Charlotte would take turns at cooking Sunday lunch, the most significant meal of the week. Charlotte and Frank agreed a truce and used their amateur theatrical skills so nothing would appear amiss. And by and large, it worked. Phyllida and John had at that stage heard nothing about the news story. There was naturally nothing in their *Sunday Times* and it was too insignificant to be reported on the BBC news in a week when world events were crowding out such trivia. It would be later in the week after *Sunday Voice* readers in the village had added two and two together that it became common knowledge.

Charlotte decided however to pursue some discreet enquiries of her own when she was in the village two days later. While in the shop, she asked Fred Wellbeloved about his newspaper deliveries. How many people in the village took the *Sunday Voice*? He checked. 'Usually seventy-one or seventy-two,' was the answer. He did not ask why she was interested but gave her a knowing look.

On reflection, she realised that information told her nothing so she then went to the Post Office. This time there were two of the witches present. The first witch was behind her counter as usual but the second witch, Gladys Fellgood, the telephone exchange operator, was there too. Charlotte threw her a tempting poser.

'Gladys, tell me. Has anyone telephoned the *Sunday Voice* newspaper recently?'

'I wondered if anyone might ask that,' she said. 'Yes, on Friday afternoon. I had to look up the number because I've never had a call to there before.'

'Do you know where it came from?'

'I do. It was the phone box on the back road.'

'The one to Yaxton?'

'That's it.'

'Do you know who made the call?'

'No.'

'Can you say what was said?'

'No, and even if I had listened in, I would be breaking the rules to talk about it.'

It's never stopped you before, thought Charlotte. But there the matter had to rest for the time being. Clearly the story had originated locally but in fact Frank had been working at home on Friday afternoon so he had told the truth – he did not make the call. And Charlotte could think of no way in which she might discover anything further.

Chapter Nine

Charlotte and her husband had settled to a fairly fixed morning routine. Frank as a creature of rigid habit – borne of his days at sea – dictated it. He rose first, washed and went to his desk in the little ante-room adjacent to the parlour that served as his study and prepared for his day's work – a farm visit, paperwork at home or occasionally assisting at Six Oaks if no-one else was available; which Charlotte tried to ensure was as seldom as possible. Charlotte had now taken to sleeping separately in the back bedroom and, despite occasional mutterings, Frank had accepted her explanation that 'for the time being' she was not sleeping well and did not want to disturb him when, as happened, she often had to get up during the night.

Once Frank had risen however, and in the one indulgence she generally felt able to afford, Charlotte soaked in the bath, the gas heater supplying enough water for one bath at a time. But one morning in September, just a matter of weeks after her miscarriage, events took an unexpected turn. The day was already promising high levels of autumn warmth so the water in Charlotte's bath cooled slowly and she could afford the luxury of a slightly longer soak than usual. But when she emerged from the bathroom wrapped in her robe she found Frank had returned to the main bedroom and was searching through her underwear drawer.

'These really are old women's things,' he said, completely unabashed by her sudden arrival and holding up a pair of pink knickers. 'A man expects his young wife to look more provocative than that,' he added. 'I'll tell you what, Lottie. I want you to get some new underwear. I want to feel the way a man should do when he sees his woman undressed. Silk knickers, brief black silk knickers like you see in the magazines, that's the sort of thing you need. You've got a really beautiful body and it should be properly displayed. A man needs to be aroused.'

'And what sort of a thing is this?' he added, gingerly holding aloft a white brassiere as if it was contaminated with some unspoken virus. 'You've got great tits so let's see them properly displayed and not buried away in these shopping bags. Your wedding dress had the whole village talking but since then you've not been making the most of yourself.'

'I was four months pregnant if you remember, and then I had a really bad miscarriage.'

'Sure, but you don't need to be a frump.' Charlotte winced. 'And you've also got great legs but no-one ever sees them. Don't tell me you get pregnant in your legs. I love it when other men look at you. It's a real turn on.'

'I wasn't aware that married women were supposed to dress to appeal to other men. Do you now really find me so unappealing, so unattractive that I have to be dressed up like a doll? Anyway it's not always practical, Frank, to work on the farm in a skirt,' she added looking at the well-worn jodhpurs hanging on a chair and that were her usual working attire.

'I know, but you must be able to do better than this,' and he glanced back at the drawer where he had now returned the offending articles.

Charlotte was so surprised by this turn of events she did not realise her bath robe had fallen open. Frank moved closer and placed his hands on her breasts. 'They really are terrific,' he said, squeezing firmly, 'and such gorgeous nipples.' He then lowered one hand and placed it between her legs. 'And what about our beautiful pussy?' he asked. 'If I stroke her fur nicely would she like to play a little game before I go to work?'

Charlotte pushed his hand away, gently but positively. 'You know I've told you I'm not ready yet, Frank,' she said. 'I'm really sorry but Dr Fraser said I must take my time. He said a sixteen-week miscarriage is serious and I must wait until my mind and my body tell me it's right again.'

'Fine,' said Frank, 'but don't you keep me waiting long. That reminds me – look at this, I kept it specially for you.'

He then returned to the bedroom and to his jacket hanging on the door. He took a small folded piece of paper from the pocket and handed it to Charlotte. It was a newspaper cutting, apparently from something downmarket like the *Sunday Voice* and she read the headline:

"I Couldn't Wait To Have Sex Two Days After My Miscarriage Says Randy Dolores"

Charlotte glanced at the article. 'Don't be ridiculous,'

she said. '*Please* try to understand. Look at it. That woman had a miscarriage after five weeks, not much more than a heavy period. Frank, I miscarried after sixteen weeks. My world and my body were turned upside down and inside out. For the first month I hardly thought about living, letting alone anything else.'

'Fine, if you say so,' said Frank. 'Anyway I'm getting late now so I'll skip breakfast. And don't forget that shopping.'

After he had gone, Charlotte dropped her bath robe and looked in the mirror. She did have a fine figure and despite her instincts, perhaps Frank was in some ways right. She had not been making the most of herself. She would try to please him and give him his treat although feeling slightly anxious that if he became too aroused, as he put it, it would become even harder to reject his advances for which she really was not yet prepared, in her mind as much as her body. She had lost a child, a life had ended before it had begun and although she told herself it may seem odd to a husband – at least to *her* husband – she actually needed to mourn.

Having dressed and had her own breakfast, Charlotte wondered where she might be able to satisfy Frank's wish. She certainly wouldn't find provocative black knickers in the village shop and smiled inwardly at the thought of asking for them when any of the witches were present. She then remembered having seen an exclusive women's dress shop in Fenton Bishop that might just fill the bill. It was a gloriously warm morning and she decided some time away from Felsingham would in any event be good for her, so an hour later she was on the bus.

Charlotte was right in her recollection. The shop had a wide range of items for women of all ages and tastes and she explained what she wanted – although without saying why. She clearly did not need to explain because the assistant took evident delight in pulling out a drawer from behind the counter. 'This is our really special range madam. They are not cheap and you can't get them in many places but the manager imports them for our more discerning Norfolk ladies – some of them titled, I may say. I am sure these will give you much pleasure,' she suggested. 'And no doubt your husband will be very pleased too.' Charlotte smiled, tried on various items in various colours, some so brief she had to be reassured they really were intended for women of her size, although they did make her feel rather special. Then, finally, she made her choice and was pleased. Surely no husband could possibly complain now. 'Shall I gift wrap them for you, madam?' the shop girl asked. 'No, thank you – in fact I'll wear them,' said Charlotte, realising that while the intention was to make her look provocative, they actually caused her to feel good and feminine too.

Frank arrived home at six as usual, the meal was uneventful and the evening passed fairly normally and amicably – which meant conversation was minimal but most of the common courtesies were observed. They both said please and thank you, no-one shouted, no-one hit out or threw anything and underwear was not mentioned by either of them.

Having cleared away, they both then settled down to read, Charlotte picking up *Under the Greenwood Tree*, her favourite Thomas Hardy and Frank the *Farmers Weekly.*

They then listened to the BBC news on the wireless.

Still Charlotte said nothing about underclothing and finally made her way to what had become her bedroom at the rear of the cottage, and Frank to what was still, notionally at least, the marital bed. She then, as she was to say later, took her life in her hands, prayed he would like what he saw and prayed even more it would serve its purpose of making him kinder to her. She took off her dress and walked into Frank's room wearing only her gloriously provocative and extremely brief new black silk bra and knickers and without speaking stood just inside the door. Frank was in the process of getting into bed but stopped as suddenly as if he had seen a phantom. He muttered something but Charlotte could neither hear nor later remember what it was. He then simply said, 'Don't move,' and walked across to look at his wife in the most analytical and intimate detail. 'Turn around,' he said. 'Now walk up and down...again, turn around, walk up and down and keep walking up and down.' This was not at all what Charlotte had expected and she now felt like an exhibit or an object being assessed prior to purchase. Frank was not just looking; he was inspecting her.

'Do you like them, Frank?' she said, with frightening naïvety.

'I like them,' said Frank, now sitting at the end of the bed. 'I like them very much. That is more like the woman I married. Just stand there a minute while I look at you properly.' Charlotte stood and waited for what was far longer than a minute and felt more like five while Frank continue to ogle. 'Have you just changed into them?' he asked. A curious question Charlotte thought, but one she answered honestly. 'No, Frank, I've been wearing them all day.' 'Excellent, really excellent,' said her husband with an expression on his face that Charlotte could not recall having seen before, 'and in this warm weather too. Now,' he said, 'now take off the bra...now take off the knickers.'

She did as he asked, dropped them on the floor and stood naked in front of him. This was becoming more and more like a burlesque show Charlotte thought; although worse was to follow.

'You are absolutely gorgeous Lottie. You have the most wonderful body. I do so wish other men could see you like this, I really do. I would just *love* that.' The remark terrified her and she wondered for a moment if he truly meant it and was planning to put her on display somewhere.

'Now, will you come to bed and make me even happier?'

'I wish I could, Frank, but I told you this morning,' she said, 'I am really not ready for it yet. I promise I shall tell you when I am although it might be quite a while,' and held her breath for fear of what his reaction might be. Would he go mad, would he force himself on her as he did all those months ago?

His response was not at all what she expected but left her feeling riven with disgust. 'All right,' he said without a hint of an objection, 'but you mustn't keep me waiting long.' He then slapped her on the bottom to send her on her way to the other bedroom. 'But I mean it – don't keep me waiting.' He then picked up the bra and knickers, pressed them to his face, smiled a libidinous smile and said, 'Wonderful. Warm and damp! I'll manage by myself tonight,' and climbed into bed, taking the underwear with him.

Once in her own room, Charlotte shuddered almost uncontrollably out of fear and the realisation of what she had done. She was now convinced he wanted her used underwear in bed with him at least as much as he had wanted to see her wearing it. She had played right into his disgusting little scheme and for several minutes she was too shocked and too ashamed even to cry. But as the minutes passed, she more than made up for it and sobbed until her pillow was wet.

Chapter Ten

It was a week after the underwear episode, about which neither Charlotte nor Frank had spoken again, although she had now come to dread each minute she was alone in his company for fear he would formulate some fresh and even more bizarre desire.

It had also been a terrible evening. This time Frank had turned his attention to her cooking. He had been complaining for several days that their meals were boring, that he could eat far better at the Eelcatcher's Arms, and that it might make sense if he only came home to sleep and had dinner on the way from his office. Here, Charlotte thought, is a possible way back without the risks attached to anything that involved clothes or the bedroom. She knew dinner had been less exciting recently while her mind was on other things. But she never doubted her own skills in the kitchen – skills she had inherited from her mother and grandmother before her.

She said she was sorry he didn't enjoy the meals and that she would try her best to do better for him, so the next morning saw her in Dickie Barnfather's butchery. It was replete with tempting cuts and joints that Dickie obtained from local farmers together with the sausages and other processed products he made in the shop. "All our meat come's from good Norfolk farm's not more than twenty mile's away" was his slogan, Dickie being of the school of grammatical thought that considered an apostrophe the essential precursor to any and every use of a terminal letter 's'. At the village school, teaching English to Dickie had always been the low point of headmistress Connie Harbutt's week and it had been clear throughout his education that carving carcasses rather than parsing sentences would be a far more appropriate outlet for his talents.

Charlotte asked Dickie if he had any particularly choice cuts available that would be appropriate for a special meal and he directed her to some new buck roe deer venison he had just obtained from a large estate the other side of Fenton Bishop. Charlotte's eye lit on a haunch joint, already boned and rolled. It looked splendid. It was probably the most expensive item in the shop but what the hell, she concluded. Trying to repair her marriage was worth more than a haunch of venison. She was determined to make a real effort and was sure she could do it justice. That must surely please Frank she thought. Most men enjoy their food and he was no exception. How could any husband be unkind after a meal like that?

Although Phyllida had cooked venison many times, Charlotte wanted this to be entirely her own creation so she said nothing to her mother but back at Six Oaks, took down her grandmother's hand-written cookery notebook dating back to the nineteenth century and found her personal recipe. The book agreed with Dickie

Barnfather's suggestion that the haunch would benefit from two days of marinating. So she pushed out the boat and did exactly as Grandmama suggested with a marinade of oil and a generous helping of port (discreetly 'borrowed' from her father's wine cellar), laced with salt, pepper, cloves, thyme and rosemary. She immersed the joint in the mixture and kept it covered and hidden in the larder for the whole two days, glancing at it and turning it whenever she had the opportunity as her excitement and anticipation built.

It was a Friday, two days later, when the meal was to see the light of day. Charlotte took it from the larder around lunchtime and slow-roasted it for four hours in the range, basting regularly with the marinade so it would be cooked to perfection by the time of Frank's early evening arrival. She garnished it with a bunch of freshly picked parsley and prepared root vegetables from the farmhouse kitchen garden as accompaniment. She then spent the best part of an hour to tidy the parlour and dress the bare wood of the table with a fresh clean table cloth, polish the wine and water glasses and carefully arrange the place settings. She then carefully ironed her best linen napkins and placed them neatly in position.

The Vincent growled its way into the yard at just before six and Frank came in to the cottage and as usual hung his leathers on the hook by the door. Charlotte had changed into clothes rather better than her normal day-time attire and went over to give him an unaccustomed hug to which he responded with a less than enthusiastic brief kiss on her neck. Over her shoulder he could see the table as he had never seen it before. 'What's all this about, Lottie?' he asked.

'I've taken on board what you said, Frank,' she answered. 'I'm really sorry. I know I've not been giving our meals all the attention I should so I thought I would start the weekend with something a little better. Go and clean up and come and sit by the fire.' She then uncorked a bottle of two year-old Bordeaux that Fred Wellbeloved had suggested. She had not dared revisit her father's cellar for a loan on this occasion.

Frank returned five minutes later and did as she had asked, taking his seat in one of the two armchairs. Charlotte brought over two glasses and raised hers in a toast to 'Better understanding.' Frank said nothing but emptied his in one unceremonious go. They then chatted a touch awkwardly for about ten minutes and Charlotte asked Frank how his day had gone. He was pointedly non-committal so she then asked him to sit at the table to which she transferred the wine glasses and re-filled them.

Almost glowing with pride at her achievement, she brought the haunch to the table along with two bowls of root vegetables each of which she had augmented with a knob of the farm's butter and finally, a boat of a rich gravy which like the marinade had also benefited from a dash of her father's port. She then asked Frank if he would like to carve and handed him the implements; at which point everything went disastrously wrong.

'Beef?' he asked, peering intently at the sumptuous joint from which a wisp of steam and an exquisite aroma now arose.

'Venison,' said Charlotte with an inner satisfaction.

'Oh, no,' said her husband, putting down the carving knife. 'You know I don't eat meat from wild animals. It disagrees with me. You have it. I'll go to the Eelcatcher's and get some proper food.'

Charlotte stood open mouthed and was quite literally rendered speechless for about ten seconds during which time tears welled up and poured down her face. She then shouted as she had never shouted in her life. 'You've never said that before, Frank. In fact I'm absolutely sure – I know – I've served you game. You are a brute,' she said. 'You are an unkind, cruel, horrible brute. I tried my very best. I went out specially to find something I hoped you would like. I have spent two days working at this meal. I desperately wanted to please you. I just want you to be kind to me. But you can't, can you? You can't be kind and loving like normal men. I hate you, I hate you, I hate you.' And as the last three words left her lips in a crescendo of outrage and disgust, Frank, who had until them simply stood his ground, swung his right hand at the side of Charlotte's face. It was not an open right hand delivering a slap. It was a firmly clenched fist and it struck her with such force that she fell backwards into one of the armchairs.

'Don't you dare talk to me like that again, Lottie,' Frank said, 'or you'll feel something that'll really show you who's in charge here.'

And with that he stormed to the door, grabbed his leathers and went out. A few seconds later, the big V-twin engine burst into life and propelled the Vincent and its rider up the lane and on to the Eelcatcher's Arms.

Charlotte sat almost stock still for what could only

have been fifteen minutes but seemed much longer. At the end of it she was exhausted, partly from the emotional trauma, partly from the pain in the side of her face and partly from the fact that she had been sobbing almost uncontrollably. She then heard her parents' car draw up in the yard. Thank the Lord, she said to herself that they had been out for the evening and so would have heard nothing through the house wall. She was also thankful they did not come round to the cottage and ask why the motor-bike was not outside because they had become used to the fact that Frank often absented himself in the evenings.

If she had not realised it before, Charlotte was now in no doubt her brief marriage was disintegrating before her eyes. She knew that once Frank had resorted to physical violence, a line had been crossed. It was not a matter of if, but when it would finally end. At some stage she would have to share all of this with her parents but she knew that if she did so now, her father was quite capable of doing something everyone would later regret. She just had to keep this evening's events from them. And getting to her feet, Charlotte then went to the bathroom and the mirror to see what damage Frank had done to her face which was now throbbing mercilessly.

She drew back her hair and saw there was a small trickle of blood arising from just in front of her ear and a large fist-sized red patch which would surely soon metamorphose into a bruise. Fortunately, Frank had struck her so far back that if she was careful over the next week or so and ensured her hair hung as freely as it usually did, it would in effect create a concealing curtain.

Having satisfied herself that the damage could be kept more or less secret, Charlotte then turned her attention to the meal still languishing untouched on the table. The vegetables would be consigned to the bin of pig swill outside and she could salvage the venison by keeping it in the pantry and inviting Hannah and Emily for lunch when she could serve it cold or made into pâté with salad. Waste not, want not, had always been her mother's maxim, although it surely had never before been quite so severely tested.

Charlotte slept inadequately that night and heard Frank return around midnight. She eventually fell asleep at about three o'clock then woke again at six and decided to come downstairs and prepare some breakfast. While knowing the marriage was living on borrowed time, she decided she had to keep acting normally – not of course as if nothing had happened – but to try and maintain her own sanity over the coming days and weeks.

Charlotte continued preparing breakfast and then waited until Frank came down. She had no idea what his demeanour would be and had not rehearsed what she herself might say. As things turned out, he spoke first. 'I should not have done what I did last night, Lottie,' he said, looking her in the face but then glancing away as soon as he caught her eye. It was wrong of me to hit you even though I was provoked.'

'It wasn't just wrong. It was wicked and cowardly. There can never be a justification for a man to hit a woman and it will take me a long time to get over it. It still hurts like hell. Look,' she said, drawing back her hair and pointing to a glowing bruise at the side of her temple and still a slight smear of blood beneath. 'Now let me spell this out, Frank. I don't forgive you for hitting me and I don't forgive you for how cruel and horrible you were about the meal – though for what's it's worth, I had no idea you didn't eat wild meat as you call it. I don't forgive you and I can't forgive you, but if you change your ways – and believe me, I do mean change your ways – I shall say nothing to Papa. Because I meant what I said at the van Vliets' party. If he knows what you have done – especially now – I really do think he could kill you. Remember he was a soldier and he has killed people before. So I mean it. This is your very, very last chance.'

'How will you explain the bruise?'

'I shall have to lie and say it was some sort of accident.' And as things evolved over the coming days, Charlotte did lie, and Phyllida once caught a glimpse of redness when the wind blew Charlotte's hair aside slightly but seemed satisfied by the explanation that it was the result of her daughter having walked carelessly into the handles of a farm cart.

Chapter Eleven

As the relationship between Charlotte and her husband was clearly approaching an all-time low in late October, an innocent shopping trip by her mother to the village led to the filling in of one more piece of what was becoming a jigsaw puzzle.

'Mrs Farrow! How are you? I haven't see you for weeks.'

Phyllida was making her first visit for some while to the Post Office to buy stamps for her Christmas cards and found witches numbers one and three in occupation. Number three, Betty Crabtree, was hovering by the door just listening but it was number one, Fanny Handley, behind the counter who had spoken.

'Oh, you know how it is,' said Phyllida. 'I've been so busy with one thing and another so Jenny has been doing all the shopping.'

'I'm glad I've seen you though,' said Fanny, 'because Charlotte was in here a few weeks ago asking about the *Sunday Voice*.'

'Yes.' Phyllida sounded interested.

'Well, I don't know much but I made a few enquiries and my friend Mrs Kerrigan who runs the Yaxton

Post Office spoke to me a few days ago to ask if I was interested to know about a letter in an official *Sunday Voice* envelope she had just delivered to a local address. It seemed a bit of a coincidence,' said Fanny with a mischievous glint in her eye, 'and I thought I would pass it on as soon as I saw any of your family.'

'Well, well, well!' responded Phyllida. 'And do you still have that address?'

Fanny took a slip of paper from her drawer and handed it over. 'But you won't say where you got this information…'

'Of course not.'

Having rushed through the rest of her shopping, Phyllida hurried back from the village bearing the revelatory nugget which she could not wait to impart to her husband. He, however, was as usual engrossed in the day's copy of *The Times* and she was barely through the door when he called out 'I thought the wretched *Sunday Voice* business had died a death but I see that fool Sir Peter Wallis has been stirring things.'

'Sir Peter Wallis?'

'You know. He was a right-wing Tory MP but he lost the whip after making improper suggestions about Winston's parentage and he now sits as an Independent. Apparently he referred to the *Sunday Voice* article in the House yesterday and asked Chamberlain a question. Listen,' and John read from *The Times* Parliament page: ' "Does the Government have plans to look again at the Criminal Law Amendment Act and bring the law for women into line with that for men and make homosexual physical acts between females illegal and punishable by imprisonment?" '

'Good heavens! What did Chamberlain say?'

'He said no!' John referred again to his newspaper. 'He stated the position that although the Commons agreed to a change in 1921 to make what were called sexual acts of gross indecency between women illegal, the Lords threw it out. And they have no intention of bringing it back. I can remember it at the time, all we young men were amazed at what women can get up to.'

'How fascinating!' said Phyllida who had hitherto found little time or necessity in her day to day routine to ponder such things as sexual acts between females, indecent, gross or otherwise. However it had all now become much closer to home given Charlotte's friendship with Hannah and Emily and, without of course letting her husband know, she had understandably become intrigued and eager to learn more. And she had to admit to herself that the German magazines had further fuelled her curiosity.

'Well, I have some very interesting first hand information,' she said.

John looked up, riveted and shocked in equal measure by this significant change in the scope of his wife's experience. 'About gross indecency between women?'

'No, my dear, about the *Sunday Voice*.'

More than a touch relieved, John said, 'Go on then, tell all.'

Phyllida recounted her experience in the Post Office and handed John the slip of paper. He read: "Mr Lewis Cottrell, 27 Harbour Road, Yaxton-next-the-Sea, Norfolk."

'Right,' he said. 'I shall pay Mr Cottrell a visit and finally I hope get to the bottom of this wretched business.

And let's see if we can properly pin it on that dreadful son-in-law of ours.'

'I think, dear, it would be best if you and Arthur followed it up together,' said Phyllida. 'After all, it was all about things that took place at his house and with his daughter. Charlotte was not directly involved. And Arthur being a magistrate, he will know how best to handle it. I'm afraid you might go in all guns blazing.'

John agreed, and telephoned Sir Arthur the same morning who said he would take a few soundings from his contacts in the police. When he reported back to John later in the day, it transpired that the address was a low grade lodging house used by sailors; and almost certainly a brothel. The police were aware of some petty crime possibly being associated with it and were sure it was the source of some pornographic German magazines that had been circulating locally. But with many bigger commitments and a war in the offing, they had not followed up anything though gave Sir Arthur a few useful pointers. He suggested he and John pay it a visit. 'But let me do the talking, John…'

The following morning, the two men drove the few miles from Felsingham to Yaxton, approaching from the west past the Atmore family's smoke house and then turned into Harbour Road, a long depressing street of tired-looking early Victorian houses leading down to the less salubrious end of the little fishing port. Smoke curled laboriously upwards from most of the street's chimneys, adding even on a fine late autumn day to a distinctly sombre pallor. As they drove slowly past the serried ranks of identical terraced brick houses looking for the address, several children quite inadequately dressed for such a chill morning stopped playing ball in the street, two exhausted women took the opportunity to pause with their heavy shopping bags and a weary looking man wearing a sailor's cap who was leaning against a house wall took the cigarette from his mouth and lifted tired and bloodshot eyes to look. It was not every day that a two-tone fawn and black 4-litre Daimler Straight 8 saloon appeared in Harbour Road and such a thing had most certainly never before been seen in the vicinity of number twenty-seven. Arthur parked outside and he and John got out and looked around. 'I said we should have brought Hannah's Austin; or even my Riley,' said John. 'This thing sticks out like a cavalryman in the infantry. Don't let it out of your sight.'

A half-pint milk bottle was on the door-step where the milkman had left it several hours earlier when the world was still dark, evidence that the occupants were either out, still in bed or not in need of anything as nutritional and wholesome.

Sir Arthur knocked soundly on the almost bare wood of a door that appeared once to have been painted red. After several minutes, the sound of locks being unbolted and chains withdrawn was followed by the door opening a few inches. A face, apparently female, appeared in the gap, although it was mostly obscured by a mass of lank hair imbued with a curious colour akin to vomit and that in its creation obviously owed more to some amateur chemistry experiment than to nature or its owner's parentage.

'Good morning, Miss,' said Arthur.

'It's Mrs, though God help me for marrying the bastard.'

'I'm so sorry. I do understand and I must apologise for intruding. But does Mr Lewis Cottrell live here?'

'Who wants to know? You the rozzers?'

'No, but do tell us please if Mr Cottrell lives here. We really would like to speak to him on a most important matter. Could you possibly open the door?'

'Not likely you bleeding pervert, I've got nothing on. Lew, there's some blokes want you.'

The female face disappeared and the door closed again firmly to give time for Sir Arthur Lancelot van Vliet, Baronet of the United Kingdom and Justice of the Peace, to try and recall when, if indeed ever, he had last been called a pervert.

After an intensive but inconclusive search of his memory, Sir Arthur knocked again just as the door reopened, now to its full width and a fully clothed figure, this time male, appeared. He was aged about thirty with short, reddish hair, a face bearing around seven days stubble and wearing clothes that could have been either day or night attire but which had clearly never been in intimate contact with anything resembling an iron. He was accompanied by an aroma of something that had originated in the sea but since died.

'Mr Cottrell?'

'You the police?'

'Not exactly, but we do have connections with the local constabulary. I understand you are a seafaring man.'

'I'm on the ships if that's what you mean, yes.'

'And you visit Germany, from time to time.'

'Yes, but I'm nothing to do with them Nazis.'

'That may well be so, and I am pleased to hear it, but do you purchase items in Germany to bring back to the United Kingdom for possible sale?'

'What do mean items?'

'Items on which perhaps you may have forgotten to pay import duty or which may be prohibited in this country.'

'I don't know anything about that. What sort of items?'

'Well, let us start with obscene literature.'

'Obscene? Oh, you mean the dirty mags. You can't get 'em here you know and the lads really enjoy 'em. But I don't have 'em now. They've all been sold so you are out of luck gents. You could try me again in a few weeks. But anyway, how do you know?'

'Are you familiar with the Obscene Publications Act of 1857?'

'No. What's that mean?'

'Well under its provisions, it is illegal in this country to offer for sale items of an obscene nature,' – and Sir Arthur clearly revelled in quoting the next part and put on his most sonorous Chairman of the Bench voice – 'whose tendency is to deprave and corrupt those whose minds are open to such immoral influence and into whose hands the publication might fall.'

'Blimey! That sounds bad doesn't it? I never knew. What are you going to do? Report me?'

'In fact, that does not concern us particularly, nor any other items you may have imported although I am sure the customs authorities would be extremely interested. However, we have a more specific question to ask and if you answer truthfully, the other matters can perhaps be overlooked for now. Does the *Sunday Voice* mean anything to you?'

'Well, it's a newspaper isn't it? In what way do you mean what does it mean?'

'We think you know in what way Mr Cottrell. Did you telephone the *Sunday Voice* newspaper with a story about two young women at a house in Norfolk, a story they subsequently published?'

'Well...'

'The customs authorities, Mr Cottrell.'

'All right, yes, but it was just a bit of fun, a joke like.'

'Not for the women concerned, or their families. It upset a great many people. But may we ask how you came by that information, that story?'

'A friend gave me a tip-off and he said if they published the story, they'd pay for it and we could split the money.'

'And the paper did pay you. They sent you a cheque recently.'

'Yes. Last week. Five quid. How do you know that?'

'And who was the friend?'

'Oh, well, it wouldn't be fair to let on.'

'The customs authorities Mr Cottrell...'

'All right. It was a bloke called Frank Atmore. In fact Frank told me to ring the paper again because he said he might be able to get some more info and even some photos but the paper said they'd got several bigger stories and they lost interest.'

'Thank you.'

'And you won't report me?'

'Just keep the right side of the law in future, Mr Cottrell, and choose your associates with more care. Good morning.'

Arthur and Frank returned to the Daimler. It was John who spoke first. 'I always said my son-in-law was a shit. Now he's turned out to be a mercenary shit.'

As the two men drove back to Felsingham, they debated what to do with their new-found information. John Farrow was, as his wife had predicted, rather in favour of' going in 'all guns blazing' and confronting his wayward son-in-law. Sir Arthur counselled much less haste and much more caution. Despite the question in the House of Commons, the story had more or less run its course, no lasting harm had been done to Emily's father and all the women, Emily, Hannah and especially Charlotte had already suffered enough at the hands of Frank. In view of the way things were going and from what he had learned from his daughter, he confessed to John that sadly he could not see the marriage enduring, but anything that caused further antagonism at this juncture was perhaps better avoided. John was unsure and wanted a line drawn under it all so after further discussion it was decided John would tell Charlotte and she in turn would tell Hannah and Emily. 'After all,' said John, 'it was my family – or at least one pathetic part of it – heaven help us – that was the cause of all this. I'm so sorry for you, Arthur – although it pains me to have to apologise on behalf of such a useless waste of space as Frank Atmore – and I shall write to Geoffrey Wells-Weston.'

Chapter Twelve

After yet another tearful and almost sleepless night in the back bedroom – which she had now taken to calling *her* bedroom – Charlotte cycled into the village one morning in early November and was in Fred Wellbeloved's shop buying bread when she spotted Lady van Vliet's young chamber maid, Betty Warburton.

'Hello, Betty. How are you? I'm so pleased I've met you because I haven't seen Hannah for some time and I really do want to talk to her. Is she away?'

Betty looked long and carefully at Charlotte. Although Betty did not know her well, she was familiar with her many visits to The Manor and she had always struck her as elegant, confident and happy, usually smiling. It was a different Charlotte she saw today. Although it would have been improper and impertinent to stare, not least because she was a servant, Betty could see she wore no make-up and even at a brief glance, it was apparent there was redness in her eyes. Her clothes were far from the neat appearance Charlotte normally presented. Even when working about the farm, Charlotte was always properly, even smartly dressed. But not today.

'Yes, she and Emily have gone to visit some of Emily's

relatives in Somerset,' said Betty. 'They will probably be back next week.'

'Oh, dear! That really is a great pity. I do need to talk to her.'

'I don't have a telephone number but I do know the address,' said Betty. 'I can it give to you so you could write to her.' Both women then took notebooks from their handbags and Charlotte jotted down the details and as soon as she was home, she sat down to compose a letter. Nearly two hours later, she had completed it.

Six Oaks Farm House
Felsingham St Margaret

Fourth of November 1938

Darling Hannah

I just have to talk to you but I was devastated to discover that you are away with Emily's relatives for two weeks so please forgive this letter. Betty gave me your address. I am almost at my wits end. In fact darling I am totally distraught and there is no-one I can turn to. Mama might understand and I think, in fact I am sure, she suspects something serious, but I just dare not risk Papa finding out how bad things are. I know he always seems a quiet calm man and he is lovely but he can be aggressive – not violent of course – about things he feels passionately about. I am sure the war affected him more than we really know. He often reminds me I am his only daughter and he would do anything for me because he loves me so much. That's what makes me afraid and why I just have to keep it all to myself.

First, I am truly sorry about the Sunday Voice story and especially the way it upset you and in a way seems to have come between us. You have been rather distant since then and I am convinced that must be why. I'm sure it's not Emily's fault that things have gone a bit cool because she seems to like me and I like her very much and am <u>so</u> happy for you both. I wish I could have a tiny bit of the sort of happiness you have found together so please forgive me if I had any part in the story though I don't think I did. But I do understand how difficult it must all have been for her because of her father's position. And of course it was really terrible and embarrassing for him too. I am so truly sorry. I do still suspect Frank had a part to play but you know he denies that he telephoned them. Perhaps we may never find out but please Hannah do not let it come between us and our friendship which I value more than anything – and even more so now.

I know I have talked to you about things

not being right here but it's far worse than I have said. In fact Frank gets more awful almost every day. He has been more and more hateful to me ever since my miscarriage. He's a completely changed man. I don't know why. I don't know if he was always hateful and was just putting on an act when I was expecting because he seemed really kind and caring for some time and even Papa was beginning to get on better with him. Perhaps he really did want a child – although he still always called it our son. But perhaps he just can't adjust to the fact that we lost it – or rather I lost because he seems to think it was my fault. And in a way he is right. I was the idiot who went up a ladder when I was four months pregnant.

I was once proud, strong, ambitious, all those things. You have known me long enough to realise that. You remember the wedding, when I said no to your kind offer to be my bridesmaid. I wanted to stand up, alone with Papa, to hold my head high despite the situation I had got myself in. But now I feel crushed. He has broken my heart and now he is trying to break my soul. Frank criticises what I wear, how I look, he controls – or tries to control – the money I have and how much I am allowed to spend. Fortunately I have never told him about the special savings account I have for the money that

Grandmama left me. If he finds out about it he will go mad. He criticises everything. He even complains about the meals I cook though I always try hard to do the things he likes. Recently I tried so hard to do a really special meal but he took one look and said it was something that would make him ill. I was so upset I just cried in front of him which is something I try not to do because I feel it gives him the sense he has won. And I'm afraid for the first time we actually came to blows. I still have the bruise. He really, really hurt me.

Each time he works away – which is often now – I do him a packed lunch and always try to make it appealing – you know how good my picnics are. I include things like Barnfather's pork pies and my special egg and cress sandwiches but he never even says thank you.

He criticises my friends. He is horrible and just vulgar about you and Emily and makes the most disgusting suggestions that I could not repeat. His language is vile and he keeps repeating things he knows distress me. He has even tried to ban me from seeing you. There are even little things that I am sure he does just to annoy me. He always calls me Lottie which he knows I hate.

And he always wants to know where I am when I go out – which isn't very often – and who I might be seeing while he spends almost every evening in the Eelcatcher's.

We can't really have civilised conversations any more. Many of our meal times are awful and night times are unbearable. I am terrified when I go to bed because of the demands I know he'll make. Some of the things he expects me to do are just horrible so I usually sleep in the back bedroom now and even then I am afraid he will follow me although he hasn't actually done it yet. That is not right. It's terrible.

I've mentioned to you that I have not felt up to making love since the miscarriage but it did happen two nights ago although love is not the right word. I didn't want to do it. I didn't want to touch him or even look so for the sake of getting some peace I just knelt down and pressed my face in the pillow and let him get on with it. I am really afraid of getting pregnant again so soon and I was terrified of how painful it all might be – although it fact it wasn't. But Frank understands none of this and expects me to perform what he calls my 'wifely duties.' Recently he even showed me a newspaper cutting about some woman who had sex two days following a miscarriage – but that just was after five weeks. He just does not realise what a miscarriage does to a woman, especially after sixteen weeks. He actually got really aggressive the other night because I didn't have an orgasm – in fact I will be honest and say I never do with him other than fake ones – God, he would kill me if he knew that. And he said I did it on purpose to make him feel bad. Can you imagine that? Honestly Hannah I do not love him any more and I am getting to the stage where I am actually repelled by him physically. What a thing to say about your husband. I never want him inside me again. He just uses my body to masturbate. I'm sorry, darling, but this must all seem horribly strange to you. There are some things you will always be spared.

I found some dreadful magazines the other day – or rather Jenny did and she was so shocked and disgusted I wondered if she might say she would not work for us any more. I suspect Frank gets some of his weird ideas from magazines like that. He wasn't ashamed when I showed them to him and he seemed to think it was normal. It isn't normal is it, darling? We have only been married for a few months.

Apart from anything else, I know things are beginning to suffer on the farm. Ted and Tommy have been wonderful and do more than I have the right to ask. They are lovely, honest hard-working men and they are just so loyal. They know something is seriously wrong, they aren't stupid, but they do need my advice and supervision sometimes. I cannot ask Papa's opinion – any more than I usually do – because he will begin to suspect. And his health is not all that good. I worry about him too.

I woke up this morning thinking things cannot get any worse but I just do not know what to do. I cannot go on Hannah. Please come back soon so I can talk to you. I have no-one else.

I am so sorry to be sharing my problems but I am desperate. What have I done darling to deserve this? I've always tried to be kind to everyone and I just need someone to be kind to me.

My love to Emily

Charlotte

An answer came swiftly.

West Court
Bath
Somerset

6 November 1938

My dearest C

My heart bleeds for you my sweetest dearest friend. Your letter was DEVASTATING. Of course I shared it with Emily and we had NO idea things were so bad. We both actually feel guilty about the happiness and joy we have found together and it is just so terrible that Frank is trying to turn you against ~~me~~ us. WE MUST NEVER LET IT HAPPEN.

Everyone knew that Frank was a bit of a 'bad boy' and it's no secret that we were all anxious for you and wondered if the marriage would work – I am sorry to put it so bluntly. But you ~~were~~ <u>are</u> such a STRONG person that we thought you would overcome it. We could never have guessed that it would be so bad so soon. Emily says she wonders if he is now trying to push you as far as possible for some reason – is he daring you to tell your father or trying to get you to walk out on him? It's just awful to see it not working out how we all prayed it would but you must as you put it still hold your head high. You are a Farrow! You are Emmeline Farrow! Never forget that and be brave for yourself and for your lovely parents.

Of course all is forgiven about the story although I think we would all like to know the full facts. Perhaps as you say we never shall. Who knows.

We shall of course see you as soon as we can. We come back to Felsingham on Wednesday and I have promised Emily for ages that I would take her to see Norwich cathedral on Thursday so could we come over to Six Oaks on Friday morning? I imagine Frank will be out then.

Our fondest love

Hannah and Emily

And Charlotte replied immediately.

Six Oaks Farmhouse
Felsingham St Margaret

Seventh of November 1938

Darling Hannah – and Emily

I hope you will receive this before you leave.

Thank you so much for your lovely kind words. Frank is not often here in the daytime now and he will be in Norwich seeing the bank manager on Friday (so he says) so it would be ideal. Give me time to see to the farm jobs first. Can you come at about 12 and we can have a good talk over lunch – I will just do something simple. I shall expect you then. I will telephone your parents tomorrow to make sure you received my message.

I can't wait to see you my dearest friend.

All my love and kisses

Charlotte

Chapter Thirteen

I told you it was magnificent,' Hannah said to Emily as she took her on the long-promised visit to Norwich Cathedral. 'It's always been one of my favourite English cathedrals – and that's not just because we live in the diocese.' They entered as worshippers had done for over nine hundred years through the west door. The great nave with its magnificent Gothic vaulted ceiling stretched before them and they walked its length to view what for Hannah was the crowning glory – the fifteenth century carved misericords in the choir. Sadly, there was no music to hear because as Hannah explained, 'Strangely, Norwich has no bells and the organ was practically destroyed by fire last year. Daphne, our village organist, was devastated at the time. But I must show you the new St Saviour's Chapel. Both my father and John Farrow were involved in its creation as a memorial to those who died in the Great War,' she said, 'and Nurse Edith Cavell is buried nearby.'

But as they approached the chapel, the familiar towering figure of Nigel Futter, all of six feet three inches tall and comparably broad of shoulder was walking towards them.

'Nigel! How good to see you, but what on earth are you doing here – do you know my friend Emily?'

'No. Hello, Emily. Daphne sent me to see if I might be good enough for the choir and I came for a trial. They say I'm not! Which is no bad thing because I'm sure I could never have found the time for all the rehearsals and that but they did tell me I have a lovely voice which was nice.'

'I think all of Felsingham could have told them that. But you are well it seems. I haven't see you for ages. How is Lily? You are still together I imagine.'

'Oh, yes, definitely. She's well too, thank you but I haven't seen her for a week or so because she's revising for her nursing exams.'

'I hope you don't mind but I have been wanting to ask, how did she take it when Frank – you know – with Charlotte – then found out she was pregnant and had to break the news to her? I'd heard there might even have been the possibility of an engagement.'

'Engagement? Never! It was never the remotest possibility. And he didn't need to tell her anything. Didn't you know? It wasn't like that at all. They'd split up several weeks before that political meeting when – you know – Frank took Charlotte home and it happened. In fact Lily broke it off when she found Frank's demands – and I'm sure you know what I mean – were a bit too much. She's only eighteen – seventeen in fact then – after all.'

'No! I don't believe it. That's certainly not what Frank told Charlotte. For heaven's sake, Nigel, don't repeat that.'

'No, no, Hannah, of course not, you know me well enough. I may not have had your education but I am always honest and discreet.'

'I know. You are a good man, Nigel Futter, and we are all very fond of you. Lily is a lucky girl.'

Nigel then hesitated and looked from Hannah to Emily. 'As we are sharing confidences, Hannah, I am going to tell you something else, but promise, promise me, you won't breathe a word of it to Charlotte. I know how close you two are.'

'Of course not, Nigel; but what is it?'

Nigel looked around and dropped his voice. 'Well, a few days after Lily broke it off with Frank and shortly before the political meeting, he was in the Red Lion in Middle Turney with some of his mates; not village lads but a pretty rough bunch – sailors I think mostly – that he knows from Yaxton. I'd just finished work with the delivery van and was in there with an old school pal. We were sitting in the corner by the dart board and couldn't avoid hearing what was being said although Frank had his back to me and never knew I was there. The lads were sharing experiences they'd had with their female conquests – you can imagine the sort of thing – bragging what they'd done with this girl and that girl. How far each one had gone. They were even talking about girls they'd shared – at the same time! It was all extremely coarse. I'm a fairly broad-minded bloke but I always respect women so even I found it disgusting. It was just the way they obviously treat women as trophies – with no respect for them at all. Sickening really. Anyway, I can't remember everything and the pub was noisy but Frank was boasting that he was on the look out for some new challenge – I do remember him calling it 'the ultimate challenge' – and he said, quite clearly, I often have fantasies about f… – about having sexual intercourse with a girl in the village called Charlotte Farrow; only begging your pardon – and being in a church – he didn't actually say "having sexual intercourse". He said she was the most ravishing girl he'd ever seen.'

'My God, Nigel. That's awful; just awful. Poor C.'

'Yes, I agree, but remember, it's just between us. It's really worried me though since the wedding, in fact I've had sleepless nights about it. Should I have said something before? Should I even have spoken out in church when the vicar asked if anyone knew – you know, why they should not be married? But I'll tell you why I didn't. I didn't because Charlotte was expecting. I thought she's got enough to handle without being warned off the man who was the father of the baby. And after all, he did propose to her straight away so I'm told. He did say he wanted to marry her and as far as I know, he's actually not been a bad husband, at least in the early days. So I thought – what's the expression – a leopard can change its spots. Although I hear on the village grapevine that things have not been so good between them since Charlotte lost the baby.'

'However do you know that, Nigel? Not that I'm commenting one way or the other. And the expression is a leopard *never* changes its spots!'

'Oh, yes, I see. But how do I know? Come on Hannah! This is Felsingham. You've lived here all your life. You can't keep secrets in our village for five minutes! Remember when Billy Harmer from the Eelcatcher's had that affair with Gladys Postle who was young enough to be his daughter, if not his grand-daughter? He thought no-one knew but Doris his wife used to go the Post Office every morning to get the latest news about it from the three witches. He only survived by the skin of his teeth because he was the official landlord and Doris couldn't risk being made homeless. That's the Felsingham gossip machine for you!'

'Yes,' said Hannah, 'I do remember. Look what kind of a community you've become involved with Emily! It all seems quite funny until this sort of thing happens with someone you know and love.'

'But look,' said Nigel, 'I'm sorry but I must be getting back and daren't miss my bus. I'm sure I shall see you again soon. Goodbye, Emily, it was lovely to meet you.'

'Bye, Nigel.' The words struggled to tumble from Hannah's lips as Nigel turned and made his way back to the west door.

'Well, what was all that about?' said Emily. 'Let's sit down and you can tell me.'

The two women moved to a quiet pew close to the now dormant organ. Hannah knelt down and said a silent prayer. Emily sat next to her, laid an arm around her shoulders and sat with her eyes closed. After several minutes Hannah sat up, took a deep breath and spoke very quietly.

'I can hardly believe what we have just been told, although I don't doubt Nigel's honesty – nor his memory – for one moment. But you heard what he said. What you don't know is that when Frank discovered Charlotte was pregnant he said quite clearly to her that he would have to break the news to Lily, who Charlotte thought – assumed in fact – was still his girl friend. That is what Frank said, quite unambiguously. He said he realised it was the end of things with Lily and he would tell her everything the next day and that would be that. Charlotte told me she's never been certain that Frank didn't deliberately ply her with whisky to lure her into bed although of course she's always tried to convince herself she was wrong – and to be honest I have always tried to reassure her she was wrong too. But from what Nigel says, it must have been even more contrived and it was Frank's intention all along. He was just looking for the opportunity so he could brag about it to his friends, but it all went wrong because he was with Charlotte at a bad time of the month, he didn't take any precautions and she got pregnant. Frank has obviously never had respect for any women and he obviously doesn't now, even though they are married. It's sickening, as Nigel said.' Hannah suddenly realised a group of visitors accompanied by a robed cathedral official were within earshot so immediately dropped into even more hushed tones and all but whispered, 'Clearly the bastard planned everything.'

'That is just appalling. What can we do?' asked Emily.

'That, my sweet one, is the almighty question. You heard me promise Nigel faithfully that I wouldn't tell Charlotte and I can't go back on it. He'd never forgive me and I'd never forgive myself. But she really, really needs to know and to know now. She's entitled to it. How can I see her tomorrow without saying something? Oh, God, what a mess.'

After a moment, Emily spoke quietly. 'You promised him, Hannah, but I didn't. I said nothing to Nigel. I didn't even know Nigel. And I am coming with you tomorrow.'

Chapter Fourteen

Once the sun finally broke through the dark and mist of the early morning, Friday 10 November promised one of those unexpectedly cheerful days one does not feel entitled to at that time of year. The crackle of frost on fallen leaves marked every footstep Charlotte made as she walked from the cottage, first to Old Sawpit Field to cast her eye over the cows, then Alder Carr Meadow, historically wet but now free draining and perfect for the sheep, then to the pens where the pigs snorted and snuffled and the chickens, ducks and turkeys chuckled and cackled. She thought the turkeys were filling out well and she was sure her customers would be pleased with their usual succulent Six Oaks birds for Christmas. The order book was always full because the regulars re-booked in January, as soon as the old carcasses had been turned into warming winter broth.

Charlotte Atmore was a young, healthy woman with her life ahead of her. She lived and worked on the farm she loved, in the county she adored, and with her devoted parents close at hand. But there was also no mistaking that Charlotte Atmore was unhappy, and anyone who looked carefully into her beautiful twenty-five year old face would soon see there was almost always the slightest reddening of her gorgeous big brown eyes, betraying that something had been amiss within the previous twenty-four hours. There were now the faintest lines on her forehead, lines that by right should not have appeared for another twenty or thirty years. And when her glorious auburn hair blew to one side in the wind or as she bent down to attend to her tasks, an observant viewer might catch a glimpse of a small scar and a large and fading but still evident bruise on her left temple.

Frank's days were now seldom spent at home and when he was not visiting clients, he was in a tiny office he rented in Middle Turney and he often departed again after dinner – on the occasions he even came home for dinner – to commune with his mates in the Eelcatcher's Arms. It grieved Charlotte deeply that the marriage had become a state of co-existence and little more. It was a marriage in name alone. Time after time, Charlotte told herself she wanted to love her husband, but she was coming increasingly to the conclusion that he was a man who could not be loved. He was not receptive to any affection she could offer. He had done some dreadful things and she had forgiven them almost all – his rudeness to and about her friends and his apparent betrayal of everyone over the *Sunday Voice* story, his demands over what she should and should not wear, the weird episode of the underwear and his hateful dismissal of her cooking when he struck her so hard that her temple exuded a small pool of blood. The one event she could not forgive or forget, at least not yet, was an attempt he made to cut off her beautiful flowing hair. But was she repeatedly giving him one more chance after one more chance simply to save her own face, so the proud, strong Charlotte Farrow would not appear weak in the eyes of her family, friends and the wider village? How much more forgiveness did she have within her?

There were just a few glimmers of brightness. The pain from her miscarriage was now a fading memory although the psychological wound from the loss of her child and the belief she could have avoided it would be with her for all time. Not the least of her pain now stemmed from the need to keep almost everything from her parents for fear of what her father might do. She had become a past-mistress at conjuring excuses for Frank's absences but it was the abject loneliness of her life that above almost anything else was slowly wreaking its toll. Which is why she wrote to Hannah and why today she could look forward to seeing her dearest, closest friend once more and would within a few hours be able to open her heart as she not done for many weeks, and discuss freely at last how it might some time be resolved, how it might all end, what, where and with whom her future really lay.

How little could Charlotte have guessed that the resolution would actually come that very day, in truth much of it within the next half-hour.

She was walking back towards the cottage with her basket of eggs when she heard the sound of a bicycle bell and a diminutive figure on an extremely elderly 'sit up and beg' bicycle rode into the yard. She recognised Doreen Hascombe, the vicar's housekeeper, not least by her battered trilby hat. 'Good Morning, Mrs Hascombe,' said Charlotte. She was pleased to see a friendly face, albeit not of someone she knew especially well, although they always exchanged pleasantries when they met and they had chatted on her visits to the vicarage. 'What brings you here to enhance this bright frosty morning?'

Mrs Hascombe dismounted and leaned her bicycle against the cottage wall. It was then that Charlotte noticed her usual calm and gentle face had a seriously worried look. 'Is something wrong? Do come inside,' she said.

Once in the kitchen, Charlotte offered Mrs Hascombe the usual symbolic pleasantries. 'Please sit down. Would you like some tea or coffee?' 'No thank you,' the housekeeper replied. 'And I'll stand if I may.' 'What is it then?' asked Charlotte. That was the required catalyst and Mrs Hascombe barely took breath over the next ten minutes or so.

'Well, Mrs Atmore.'

'Please call me Charlotte.'

'Right you are, Mrs Atmore. I wasn't at all sure I should come. I've been worrying about it for quite a time because I am a good Christian you know, Mrs Atmore, I am truly a devout and believing Christian that's the way I was brought up and I always follow the Bible's teaching as far as I possibly can. My father was a lay preacher you know and he introduced me to the Good Lord. So I talked it over with the Reverend, with Mr Bellwether. In fact, that took me a long time too before I approached him and I asked if I could tell him something in confidence and of course he said yes, his being a man of the cloth and all that, so he took me into his study and asked me to sit down but I preferred to stand. I do prefer to stand you see at times like this, not that I've ever had a time like this. But he was very kind and very understanding and said he realised the predicate I was in and I told him all my concerns and all my worries and what I had seen and what should I do about it and he told me there was nothing exactly in the Good Book that answered my questions but that I should – what was the words he used – Oh, yes, I should follow my conscious. I've then prayed in the church every morning for the Good Lord's help and I felt he was guiding me and it was his hand on my handlebars when I turned off the road and he took me down the lane to your beautiful cottage and here I am.'

'Goodness,' said Charlotte, by now nearly as breathless as Mrs Hascombe. She was almost tempted to ask if it was Mrs Hascombe or the Good Lord who had rung the bicycle bell but then thought better of it, suspecting the reason for her call was probably too serious to trivialise. 'But what's it all about?' she said.

That was the second catalyst of the morning and Mrs Hascombe was off again.

'Well, you know I do for Mr Bellwether and although I says it as shouldn't but I am quite good as a housekeeper and a cook. In fact sometimes I help out my sister Doris at the Eelcatcher's in the kitchen there when they have busy times or parties or someone is off sick. Well it was like this. My sister Doris knows Joan Willis, who is the cook at the Boatman Hotel, you know off the Cromer Road, and she had a problem two weeks ago when her assistant Annie Pettigrew who is a bit sickly at the best of times, anyway she was even more sickly than usual and you can't have people being sick in the kitchen can you at meal times or really at any times – pardon my saying this when you've just had your breakfast – which meant she was short-handed as it were. So my sister Doris knew how helpful I have been to her in the Eelcatcher's when she is busy that she asked me if I would be able to help out at the Boatman Hotel at lunchtime on a few occasions. I said I could do it if I caught the bus because it's long way to cycle in winter and there's a stop outside the hotel but I hoped they would pay my bus fare. And I said of course I would have to ask Mr Bellwether and he said of course you must do it to help so I did. Well, it was about three weeks ago that I saw it first and like I shall tell you I saw it again several times.'

Charlotte was by then becoming just a trifle exasperated and asked 'Mrs Hascombe. What exactly was it you saw?' little knowing Mrs Hascombe's answer was to stretch her powers of forgiveness almost to breaking point.

'Well, there was this woman, quite a pretty woman she was, about forty I would guess with curly blonde hair and I don't exactly know who she is but I think she is something to do with the hotel because I have seen her there most days when I have been working.' Mrs Hascombe then took a deep breath. 'Well she, this woman that is who I don't really know who she is, she was in the bar talking to a gentleman, only they weren't talking. They were touching each other and although I say it as shouldn't, being a Christian woman like I said, they were touching each other in places where people shouldn't touch each other, not at least in a public locality like that. Then they went away from the bar together and I didn't see them again until about an hour later when they came back to the bar. And they kissed each other and the gentleman left. And this happened about four times on days when I was there helping. The last time was the Tuesday just past, Tuesday this week.'

'Yes,' said Charlotte.

An even deeper breath emerged from Mrs Hascombe.

'God forgive me for saying this, but the gentleman was Mr Atmore, your husband.'

Charlotte said nothing for about a minute. She then swallowed hard, looked at the wall, then at the door, then at the ceiling, then at Mrs Hascombe. 'You are quite sure it was Frank?'

'Oh, yes, I'm certain. I recognised him because I have seen him in the village and that time he came with you to the vicarage about the banns and he always has a yellow scarf thing round his neck. And when he left I heard a motor-bike and I know Mr Atmore has a big motor-bike.'

'Mrs Hascombe, you say the man, Mr Atmore, and the woman, went away from the bar for about an hour each time. Do you know where they went?'

'I can't of course rightly say and I mustn't assume, being a Christian as I am, but I will only say they went through a door that is just for residents. It leads to the bedrooms.'

Charlotte's response appeared unemotional, almost matter of fact. 'Mrs Hascombe. Thank you for telling me this. You must not feel guilty. You have done exactly the right thing, as a Christian, and whatever I decide to do now, I shall not of course say where I discovered this information.'

'Thank you, Mrs Atmore. I'll be on my way now if you please because Mr Bellwether is expecting me back. God bless you and protect and guide you in all you do, Mrs Atmore.'

And with that Doreen Hascombe was gone, leaving behind her a life in even greater turmoil than when she had arrived.

Charlotte sat down feeling utterly numb. When she thought about the events later, as she did many times in retrospect, she repeatedly came to the conclusion that in her heart of hearts she was not surprised, in truth almost expecting it. Frank after all had become a demanding, uncaring bully, cruel to her and in a sense, even worse, he had been unkind to her. He had hit her and hurt her, he had displayed an interest in pornography that seemed to guide his physical actions, he had caused a rift between her and her most treasured friend purely for reasons of personal self-interest, and she was increasingly sure it was he who had created problems for innocent third parties far beyond the little village of Felsingham St Margaret, and that had even caused ripples in Westminster. His best man was now in trouble with the police and Frank himself – and she thought about this more and more as time went on – may have forced himself upon her while she was his defenceless victim. What else could there be? Now they were married, he might as well throw infidelity into the mix. But even then, Charlotte could not know there was yet more to be told.

It would be another two hours before Hannah and

Emily were due to arrive and Charlotte needed to clear her head. She was still wearing her outdoor clothes so she went back outside and did something she had not done for many weeks, and hardly since her miscarriage. She spent the next hour walking the fields and paths of her beloved farm, redolent with memories of the magical time when she was growing up at Six Oaks. But first, she had to walk close to the great old barn with its terrible reminders of her fall before she passed the two ancient oaks, the only survivors of the original six that gave the farm its name three centuries ago, and past her much loved animals where she gave a reassuring pat to Cuckoo, her favourite cow, who thrust an inquisitive nose over the fence as Charlotte paused to pass the time of day with her. Then she walked on and over the stile to Brick Kiln Lea where the winter barley was now showing green and strong and Ted's drilling skills were revealed in the crop's geometric lines. The path then took her into Broad Meadow, a meadow no more but a field filled with Townshend's turnips alongside the willow-lined banks of Bunting Stream just where it turns north, eventually to add its waters to the wide reaches of the River Yare which carries them on to Great Yarmouth and the sea. Charlotte recalled this was just the spot where her cousin Archie once caught a 2lb brown trout on a worm and where, less ambitiously, she and Hannah used to sink old baited bottles to trap minnows. Hannah being two years older and wiser, always caught more, and was the first to realise the bottles had to be sunk with the necks facing up, not down stream.

She lingered for a couple of minutes by the gnarled old

hawthorn where Jimmy Wellbeloved, the shop-keeper's son, had given her that first kiss and she remembered clearly how much she enjoyed the novelty and how she had boldly returned the gesture. Jimmy was now Mr James H. Wellbeloved, architect, happily married with a handsome house on the road to Diss and the father of two beautiful twin daughters; and a little boy crippled with polio. How paths diverge, she thought, and how cruelly nature rolls its dice.

By the time Charlotte had crossed Ten Acres and skirted Jackson's Plantation, the best hide-and-seek locality in the parish, she realised that at her ambling pace, she would barely be back by noon so she took the old short-cut across the freshly ploughed mud of Little Slade where the spring barley would go and where her father once picked up a Roman coin that the museum had said was very rare and dated to the Emperor Augustus. Where is it now, she wondered. As she approached the great barn once more, a rabbit scuttled out from under a log pile and Charlotte rued not having brought her gun. But then she looked up at the barn and remembered all life is precious and was pleased she had left it locked safely in its cabinet.

It had taken her just over an hour and although she did not feel she had returned a new woman, it all brought back memories of a storybook childhood and of – what had seemed to her – gloriously carefree times when the sun always shone and the summers were endless, and the world had done with war. Her beloved father had returned to his family from the horrors of the trenches – about which he never spoke – for her mother to nurse him through his wounds while everyone looked forward to an enduring peace. It convinced her even more that no man, no-one, and certainly not Frank Atmore, would ever take this away. She returned to the cottage fortified for who knew what was to come.

Chapter Fifteen

The clock of St Margaret's had just completed its twelve noon strikes when the purr of Sir Arthur's van Vliet's Daimler announced the arrival at the cottage of Hannah and Emily; the loan of the car a paternal treat for the two women on a chill morning and a luxurious change from Hannah's own Austin 10 with its apology of a heater.

Charlotte could hardly wait to open the door and welcome them in to the cottage which was warm from the radiated heat of the kitchen range and the fire in the parlour grate. 'I am *so* pleased to see you,' she said, and hugged them both in turn.

'I've prepared a simple lunch but we must talk first. Do sit down. There is so much I have to tell you,' said Charlotte. 'But before anything, I must pass on something Papa told me two days ago. He and your father, Hannah, felt it was right I should say it. That awful story in the *Sunday Voice*. I am sorry to say we now know it did come from Frank and I want to apologise on behalf of all our family. Papa is writing to your father, Emily. I don't know how they found out but it seems Frank told some dreadful friend from Yaxton and he actually made the phone call to the paper. But this is the sickening bit. They did it for money. They were paid for it.'

'Well, it was no more than we suspected,' said Emily, 'though it must have taken some detective work to get to the bottom of it. Doesn't it confirm what we all really suspected about Frank? Is there anything to which he won't lower himself? I am really sorry for you, Charlotte. It was none of your fault.' And with that Emily gave her a prolonged and firm hug.

'I am just so pleased you are both here,' said Charlotte, because I feel the whole world is against me and I've fallen into some sort of marital waste bin; a scrap heap of people's affections. I've come to realise I could cope with him not loving me. But I can't cope with him being unkind. He has to be in control. I don't know if it's some medical condition or there's a special name for it but it's become unbearable.'

And she then recounted, almost day by day, the diary of her marriage. She described the details about Frank's cruel rejection of her beautifully and lovingly prepared meal and the pain of the bruise, the story of the lacy underwear, and of her special shopping visit to Fenton Bishop because she had thought it would please him, and perhaps make him kinder towards her. She told Hannah and Emily how he made her parade around the bedroom in them and then undress while he ogled her naked. 'He slapped me on my bottom as if he was herding a cow and then took the bra and knickers to bed with him. I could only guess why.'

Hannah and Emily both made noises that simultaneously signified repugnance and revulsion.

'Then one night he did – or tried to do – something even more hurtful. He said he did not like my hair – that it was too long for a woman of my age, and he wanted me to cut it short. I said no. I said my hair *was* me. It was my identity. But he wouldn't have it and even went to look for some scissors. I actually screamed at him before I ran to my bedroom and locked the door and although he made unpleasant comments about it afterwards, thank God he never tried again. Fortunately my parents were out or they would have heard my screams.'

Hannah rose from her chair, walked round to Charlotte's side of the table and gently eased her to her feet. She then hugged her extremely firmly. 'That is terrible, terrible, my dear, dear C. That's the worst thing of all. You are right – your hair *is* you. It is so much of what is wonderful and gentle and feminine about you. Frank wanted to castrate you. I am so, so, so sorry.'

And with that Hannah released her embrace, placed her hands gently on either side of Charlotte's face, pushed back her hair, looked straight into her eyes and kissed her on her lips, firmly and with totally unambiguous intent. Charlotte was so taken aback she stood riveted to the spot with her arms hanging limply at her sides. Her mouth stayed closed for all of the ten seconds or so the kiss took, more out of numbness than lack of want she said much later, and what she remembered most was the novel taste of someone else's lipstick.

After what seemed an age, Hannah finally pulled away. 'I think perhaps I shouldn't have done that. I am sorry, C. I must have shocked you terribly. I am really sorry but I was so appalled by what had Frank had threatened,

I wanted to hold you and comfort you and reassure you that people do love you. I hadn't really expected to do that though.'

'No, darling,' said Charlotte, now looking dazed. 'Not shocked. Very, very surprised, yes. Not shocked. But much more than that – I am flattered that it should seem such a natural thing for you to do. Perhaps it should have appalled me but the extraordinary thing is it didn't. It gave me a wonderful feeling of warmth and security having you hold me and do that. I think I need to sit down.'

Hannah looked down and placed her hands on Charlotte's shoulders. 'All right, C,' she said. 'I suppose now is as good a time to tell you as any other. My dear, lovely friend, you need to know I've been attracted to you since you were about fifteen but I have never let on, and I have never done anything because I was sure you weren't inclined the same way and I was terrified – and I do mean terrified – of losing your precious friendship which means more to me than almost anything. Please tell me I haven't done that now. Tell me I haven't lost you. You never gained a hint of my feelings did you?'

'No, no, I never did. Never. God, no, I had no idea. No, of course you haven't lost me. But Oh, Hannah what a surprise. I think I mean what a lovely surprise.'

'I am so, so pleased I never let it slip, that you never suspected,' Hannah intervened. 'But then, C, you always were one of life's lovely innocents.'

Charlotte glanced across at Emily expecting to see a look of abject horror. But Emily was smiling and sitting calmly and almost serenely on the other side of the table.

'It's fine, Charlotte,' she said. 'Hannah told me about her feelings for you almost from day one of our relationship. You and I are no threat to each other, please believe that, although in another life and another time you could have been in my place. You are Hannah's closest friend and I am her lover and hope to be her life partner. I pray that will always be. But I am so glad you now know.'

Hannah continued. 'When we were girls I came to realise, when I was about twelve or thirteen, that I was a bit different. Mainly I suppose because I never found boys all that much fun. Most of the other girls had boy friends – but not you of course, my lovely C, because you were always a bit naïve and shy.' She gave Charlotte another hug. And I always found the company of girls more appealing and then I became attracted to them in physical ways – although I never found the right one until I met Emily. But I knew there could be never be anything of that kind between us because I could tell you weren't like that. I just wanted you to be what I hope you are, and will always be, my life-long best friend and confidante.'

'I am, Hannah darling, I am. But no, I am sure – I mean almost sure – I am not that way inclined as you put it,' Charlotte replied. 'Do you remember when you first told me about Emily and I said a younger girl at school had once made – I think I called it an overture or advance – towards me? Well I have never ever told anyone this, but it was in my last summer just before I left school and it was after a late tennis practice. We were in the sports pavilion alone putting away the equipment. Suddenly she took off her top and bra. I thought at first it must be the warm evening…'

'One of life's innocents,' Hannah repeated.

'…then she asked me to – you know – with her. I was absolutely stunned and I said nothing and simply stared. I had seen girls undressed in the changing room of course all the time, and not thought much about it, but then I was just mesmerised at how beautiful her body was, its shape, her skin, everything. In those few moments, who knows what a different turn my life might have taken. But something deep inside held me back. I was within seconds of doing what she asked, and what she certainly wanted, but something, I do not know what, stopped me. I have never seen or heard from her again and I had not really thought about it much since until I saw the happiness you and Emily have together, and the abject misery of my situation. I can't believe a woman would do to me what Frank has done. It will be a long time before I feel I can love and trust a man again.'

'There are some kind and lovely men out there,' Emily intervened, 'and it really isn't your fault you have landed yourself with this one. But this has certainly been a day of discoveries and confessions hasn't it, so let me add one more big one and then we can all talk about what's best for you.'

'No, wait a minute and please let me have my say,' said Charlotte. 'I have more things to tell you; really, really important things.

Emily started to speak, desperate to convey Nigel's terrible disclosure. 'No wait, wait, Emily.' Charlotte cut her off again. 'There's more, but first I'm going to show you something that will really shock you but I want you to see it so you know what I have to put up with, and perhaps make what I have to say a bit clearer. I think I mentioned some magazines in my letter.' Charlotte then went to the back bedroom and took the brown envelope from the bottom of her wardrobe.

'Look at these. Jenny our housekeeper found them. This is what it's come down to. Do you wonder I don't know how to deal with it all?' Charlotte pushed the envelope containing the two salvaged magazines across the table. 'Don't dwell on them though. It's awful stuff.' Hannah pulled the two magazines from the envelope and she and Emily gasped simultaneously. 'I'm embarrassed to say this even to you, such dear, loving friends,' Charlotte said, 'but I imagine this is where Frank gets his ideas for some of the things he expects in our bedroom.'

'Oh, God, C, you can't put up with that,' said Hannah. 'It's disgusting beyond belief,' and just as Charlotte and Phyllida had done, she merely flipped through the pages to reinforce the impression the covers had given. 'They're German,' said Charlotte. Hannah intervened. 'I can see that,' she said, turning to Emily. 'You speak German, don't you?' 'Yes,' Emily replied, never having imagined her extremely costly Swiss finishing school education would come in useful for translating German pornography. 'That title,' she said. 'Aufregung. It means excitement. But my God, the hypocrite, after all he has said about us.' 'What?' asked Charlotte. 'This one here,' said Emily, 'just look at the cover – you hardly need to speak German to work out what that means – Spezielle Lesbische Ausgabe – Special Lesbian Edition. It's awful, just awful.'

'Let's sit down, C, because there are things you need to

be told,' said Hannah and looked at Emily, both women ever more anxious to reveal their shocking discovery.

But Charlotte wasn't listening. 'No, let me finish first,' she said, 'because I have discovered something this morning even more important that I have spent the last hour trying to rationalise, and I am trying to tell myself I can still forgive.' She paused, swallowed hard and looked from Hannah to Emily. 'Frank has been seeing another woman, sleeping with her in fact.'

The chorus from Hannah and Emily was loud, instinctive and simultaneous. '*No*!'

'I can't tell you how I know but the source as they say, is impeccable. This woman's a tart basically; some sort of worker at a hotel and he goes there regularly and they have sex.'

'C, my dearest girl,' said Hannah, 'that is the absolute end. Surely there can't be a way back now. Now it's your turn to sit quietly and listen. Let's try and plan a way ahead for you. Let's think if he has done anything against the law. I imagine those magazines might be illegal. And he hit you, C, and hurt you. That must be assault at least.'

'Yes,' said Charlotte, 'but it'll always be his word against mine. As a woman I am powerless. The law does not protect us.'

'Surely the police would believe you,' said Emily. 'The word of a well-educated woman from a very good family and with the respect of the community – and loads of character witnesses – us for start! – against a known left-wing bad boy who hardly anyone will have a good word for.'

'Yes,' added Hannah, 'but you could say he also comes

from a good family, who like us vote Tory! You can't condemn a man because he belongs to the Labour Party and his grandfather's a communist. And remember, he maintains we are all fascists and that doesn't exactly look good in 1938. No, Frank is no fool. He's also had a good education and as far as I know he's never been in trouble with the law. His best friend may get into difficulty with the police but he can't be condemned by association. It's very difficult and speaking personally – I don't know what you will say Emily – but I just don't think trying to involve the police will get you anywhere except all over the papers. And let's face it, you've already told us you can't reveal the origin of the information. It could be Almighty God himself but if you can't say so openly, it's again your word against Frank's.'

Charlotte smiled for the first time that morning, thinking that although not quite Almighty God, her bicycling source was not all that far removed.

'And I doubt if this hotel woman is going to spill the beans either,' continued Hannah.

Emily intervened. 'I agree entirely with Hannah,' she said. 'I think – if this is what it's come to – you have to tell him to go and then see what happens. Don't threaten him with the police but with your father.' She hesitated. 'And I'm now finally going to tell you something I think will convince you once and for all that you simply have to end it. Hannah has known you since you were little girls and she believes you have to do it; and for what it's worth, so do I.'

Emily began. 'We haven't known each other long, Charlotte, and you still don't know me all that well. But

I like you a lot, I really like you a lot, you love Hannah and I love Hannah and I know how much you mean to each other. So now, *please*, sit tight, don't interrupt and let me tell you. It's something Hannah can't say without breaching a solemn confidence, but I can because I haven't given any undertakings or made any promises, although let me add that this is also from a wholly trustworthy person, but again one I can't name. I won't even say if it was a man or a woman. I really can't bear doing this after all you've told us, as if you haven't suffered enough, but you just have to know this. Prepare yourself, Charlotte.'

Charlotte looked anxious and Hannah moved her chair closer and held her hands.

Emily continued. 'The night it all happened with you and Frank after that Labour Party meeting wasn't chance. We've been told by someone who overheard a conversation in a pub – not the Eelcatcher's by the way – that Frank was just looking for an opportunity. It seems he had what almost amounted to a bet with his awful chums, a bet that he couldn't get you into bed – couldn't seduce you. Having sexual intercourse – that's putting it much more politely than he did – having sexual intercourse with Charlotte Farrow was what he called the ultimate challenge. That's why he got you drunk. And he wasn't still going out with Lily. She had broken off with him several weeks earlier because he was expecting too much from her – you know how I mean? Hannah says she's not much more than a child. Well that's it. I am so, so sorry. As if you haven't had enough shocking news today. Charlotte, are you all right?'

Charlotte's face had turned an unusual colour. She

said, 'I think I might be going to be sick.' Two minutes later she was, only reaching the bathroom with seconds to spare.

Chapter Sixteen

Once Hannah and Emily had managed to restore Charlotte to something approaching normality, the three of them – Charlotte only just – sat down to eat the modest lunch she had prepared. She was full of sincerity and gratitude for having her friends with her again and apologised profusely for the end result. Was she strong enough to cope with what was bound to happen she asked. To which her answer was to quote from Hannah's letter.

'You are right. I am a Farrow,' she said. 'No-one is going to pull me down. And certainly not Frank Atmore. I will be strong and proud and raise my head again.'

But after Hannah and Emily left, she did not want to talk to her parents and avoided the main farmhouse. The decision that had to be made that day would be hers and hers alone.

Then, all afternoon she busied herself, trying to prepare for what she knew would come, but also attempting to act as if was a normal day. She did nonetheless spend an uncommonly long time in front of her mirror.

Four o'clock came and with it the darkness of a

November evening; then five, but Charlotte waited until she heard the Vincent pull into the yard and tried her best to appear nonchalant as she busied herself at the range preparing a meal; but not one of her special meals. In the circumstances, cooking anything had been a challenge and it was about as basic a dinner as she could contrive.

Frank called out, 'Hello Lottie,' as he came into the kitchen. Charlotte did not reply as he took off his boots and hung up his riding leathers. He then walked over to the range and looked into the pan of almost colourless soup bubbling away. Charlotte still said nothing.

'What's that? Doesn't look like much of a meal for a man after a busy working day. I suppose it'll have to be the Eelcatcher's again.'

Charlotte then turned to face him, and did as she had rehearsed several times that afternoon in front of the mirror. Although she was trembling inside, she hoped nothing showed outwardly as she looked him straight in the eye. 'Where were you last Tuesday, Frank?' she asked.

Frank looked shaken, and then after a brief pause, and feigning puzzlement as he dug deeply into his perfectly sound memory, said, 'Last Tuesday? Let me see. Oh, yes, I told you. I had a new client in Wymondham, potentially a good client with a big account and we need the money.'

'Big account my foot. Big something else more like. You are a compulsive liar, Frank. You weren't in Wymondham. You were in the bar at the Boatman Hotel off the Cromer Road talking to a woman. Well, not just talking. You were groping each other and you then both crept away to a bedroom for God knows what. You were seen, Frank, so do not for one idle moment try to deny it. Who is she?'

Frank saw with dismay that argument was futile.

'Her name is…'

'I don't care a damn about her name. What is she? Where did you find her?'

'She works at the hotel.'

'Oh, I see, a barmaid. Just about your standard.'

'In fact, she's the manager.'

'Well, she's certainly managed you all right hasn't she?'

'I don't think being abusive is much help.'

'So you expect me to be polite and courteous about my husband's mistress. What sort of a fool do you take me for?'

'She is not my mistress. She's...'

'Don't play semantics with me, Frank. She is a woman, who is not your wife, who you are sleeping with on a regular basis – in fact whenever you get the opportunity, as often as possible, apparently. I know you have been there with her several times. There are witnesses. I'm sure there's always a vacant bedroom at the hotel. How very convenient. Trust you to choose someone with facilities on tap.'

'That is really unfair. I didn't choose her as you put it. We just sort of fell in together. She's not my mistress…'

'Oh, tripped up, tumbled headlong. An accident was it? Oh, dear! Did you call Dr Fraser? But no, of course, you are right, Frank. My mistake. Big, big mistake. She isn't your mistress. That is much too dignified a title. Some of the greatest men in history have had mistresses, and some have been amazing women. And sometimes their wives have known, and sometimes they have even approved. This woman is not your mistress, no, she's a whore, a tart, a – what's that good old word – a slattern – no, I know what she is, a slut. Yes, that's it, she's a slut and you have been sleeping with her and then coming back to sleep in our bed. I shall have to ask Jenny to disinfect everything before I ever go back in there.'

'Look, Lottie, just calm down and let's try to talk this through. How long have you known me? For God's sake, you must realise by now that I have…Oh, let's be honest – fairly red-blooded male needs. I told you pretty bluntly when I asked you to buy that underwear and I didn't apologise for those magazines. It's sex, Lottie. It's what men do.'

Charlotte rolled her eyes.

Frank continued his monologue. 'And you can't deny that over the past weeks, especially since the miscarriage, you have been, well, less than accommodating. In fact, if I'm honest, our relationship, at least the sexual aspect, has been downhill all the way since we were married. So one evening when I was on my way home and feeling pretty worked up, I stopped for a drink, and this very attractive woman came over. There's really nothing in it. I don't love her or anything. It's just a bit of fun.'

'Is it?' Charlotte paused, looked straight at Frank again, albeit fleetingly this time, then unavoidably found herself looking away. She stared at the ceiling as the beginnings of a tear welled up in each eye. Isn't it strange, she thought, how both your eyes always cry at the same time. She blinked several times and swallowed hard but found it impossible to retrieve the salty droplets that now spilled over her lower eyelids and began to roll slowly down her cheeks. 'I must not show weakness, not now,' she told herself. She must take the initiative and gain the upper hand.

'Is it?' she repeated. 'You are pathetic. It's an excuse as old as time isn't it, Frank? Isn't it? Look at me...you clown. It's not love you say. That's right at least, Frank, because you love no-one but yourself. And you know what I have to do now, don't you? Look at me, I said. Of course you would not have married me if I had not been pregnant. I have always known that, my mother, my father, the whole bloody village has always known that. Yes, I was stupid beyond belief to fall into your trap – I now know it was a trap – and I have to live with it for the rest of my life. You planned to get me into your bed that night, you bastard.' Charlotte suddenly found she was hammering her fists into Frank's chest, although to little effect. 'That's why you kept pouring me whisky. You wanted to be able to brag about your latest conquest to your disgusting friends. How was it you referred to me – Charlotte Farrow, the ultimate challenge?'

For the first time since she had known him, Frank looked shocked and was speechless. His face suddenly went grey. His fresh outdoor complexion melted away like the morning frost when the sun rises. He opened his mouth but no sound emerged. He looked as if he wanted to speak, but something in his vocal apparatus would not allow it.

'No, don't even think of denying it, you were overheard. Well, at least I have that to cling on to – I wasn't easy prey and I had to be completely drunk to fall for it. You are a weak and horrible man, Frank. You are evil and I am ashamed to have your family's name. I actually think your parents will be ashamed when they know what their little boy is really like. It's not their fault they created a pervert. Sex and playing with people's emotions are the only things that matter to you. You use people for your own amusement, whether it's your wife or that slut at the hotel. Sex, making money, spending money – preferably my parents' money – and more sex. Do you pay her for it – your hotel slut? Does she give you a regular user discount? Does she dress up for you? Does she pose for you like the women in your disgusting magazines? I should have seen this coming. I should have known from the moment I found you inspecting my underwear. I must have been completely, totally mad, out of my mind, to have indulged you that time. I shall never, ever forgive myself.'

'That's not fair.'

'Don't you dare talk to me about fair, you little worm. You have to be in control don't you? You need to control everything, me, the money, what I do, how I dress, how I look, who I meet, who I talk to, where I go. If you could, you would control what I think and believe. You have brought nothing but shame into my family. You have embarrassed everyone who knows you. You have come between me and my dearest friend. And you just brush aside my miscarriage because all it meant to you was the inconvenience of not being able to have sex whenever you wanted it. It wasn't just a miscarriage, Frank. It was a sixteen-week miscarriage and I lost a perfectly formed little girl ready to have a life of her own. She would have been beautiful. She would have enriched other people's lives and brought happiness to everyone. And now she is gone. Yes, it was my fault, I shouldn't have gone into the barn and done what I did. I have to live with that for ever. But I did try. I asked everyone who might be able to help – including you, but you of course had far, far better things to do. You had a new client to see to. What happened to them by the way? You never told me. God forgive me for saying this but I'm glad I lost my daughter because she wouldn't have deserved you as her father.'

Frank stared vacantly through the window into the unknown; the physical unknown of the darkness outside and what he now realised was about to be for him the darkness of an unknown future.

Charlotte continued, growing stronger and gaining more confidence with each sentence she threw at her husband. 'I now know it was you behind that Sunday newspaper story. Oh, yes, you were clever when I asked if you had telephoned and you said it wasn't you. It wasn't of course but you tipped off one of your low life friends in Yaxton. And you actually did it for money. You betrayed my friends for money. How many pieces of silver was it? Thirty – or just five? How sordid can a man get? I should throw you out, Frank. In fact, I have thought about this all day and I am going to throw you out, out of my parents' house, out of my family's home. But only to give you time to think about what you have done. I want you to go away tonight and I don't want you to come back until you have thought longer and more deeply about what you have done than you have ever thought about anything in your entire miserable life.

I don't want you to go within a mile of that hotel. You can take as many days or weeks or months as you like but when you come back, I want you to crawl. I want you to go down on your knees and beg my forgiveness, to convince me you will never do anything like this, in fact do nothing out of line ever, ever again. I am giving you one very last chance to mend your ways. And I shall make sure my parents and everyone else knows what you have done and what I have done. Now go.'

She then sat down, shaking.

Neither of them spoke again before Frank went upstairs and Charlotte heard him moving from one room to another. She guessed correctly that he was putting some clothes together. He seemed to be taking an age, during which Charlotte had the presence of mind to turn off the range before her gruesome soup boiled away, and then sat down again, still shaking.

It was actually around fifteen minutes later that Frank came down with a bag, walked straight past her, pulled on his boots and took his riding leathers from the hook by the door. He then turned but could not look her straight in the face and he spoke with a voice that did not sound like his own. One of his legs was trembling almost uncontrollably as he delivered his speech.

'I will go, Lottie. I am going but I will not give you the satisfaction of having me back. I will not crawl or beg. I will spend time with anyone I like. I will not be dictated to by a mere woman. You have been so lucky to have me as your husband when you couldn't even give me what I need in bed. It's a wonder I didn't go weeks ago. I did actually try to love you but I couldn't because you and me, we come from completely different places and different backgrounds. We are different people. It would never have worked. I thought at least you could give me physical satisfaction but you couldn't even manage that. Go and play with your girl friends, Lottie – see how much fun you can have in their bed. See if you can satisfy them. That's about the limit of your sexual abilities I reckon – pleasing other women, like that Hannah of yours.'

And with that he opened the door and without turning back said, 'I shall send someone over to collect my things in few days. I don't want to see you again, ever.'

Charlotte sat down, now shaking quite uncontrollably as the reality of what she had done and what had happened slowly began to sink in. She realised she was breathing in the rhythmic, concentrated way she remembered having been taught at her pre-childbirth classes – in through her nose and out through her mouth – the breathing that was never needed, for a childbirth that never happened, and that she thought and still cried about every day of her life.

Only after the sound of the Vincent faded as it went up the drive, did Charlotte begin to calm, if slightly. Her breathing returned to something approaching normality and she became aware that her heart was no longer thumping furiously inside her chest. She then did what English people do in such circumstances. She made herself a pot of tea and sat down and stared into the fire. She watched the flames rise and fall, change colour and chase each other across the grate. She realised she must have been staring into the fire for at least half an hour because the logs were now burning low and she reached to the fireside basket and tossed on two more. She remembered helping Tommy who had cut them from an old dead oak at the edge of Jackson's Plantation back in the summer when the weather was warm and her baby was still a small bump around her middle.

Then, without any forethought or perception, she walked upstairs, went to the back bedroom and wondered how soon she would be able to return to her proper bedroom, how soon Jenny would be able to prepare it for her with clean sheets and pillowcases, smelling of the indefinable freshness of newly laundered cotton. Tomorrow, she hoped. Then, almost as an instinctive action, she went to the old mahogany chest in the corner of the room, opened the drawer that contained her underwear, the drawer she had found Frank sordidly exploring and beneath everything found what she sought. She returned downstairs and sitting in front of the fire once more, watching the flames now licking hungrily around the new oak logs, she supplemented their appetite with two small additions and surprised herself by discovering how silk burns and how soon carefully crafted garments, beautiful in their way and the results of some unknown seamstress's skill, shrank and curled and shrivelled, flickered briefly with the smallest of flames and then fell apart leaving a pile of gritty ash. There was a smell just like the time many years ago when she singed her hair on a candle. Charlotte felt an inner satisfaction; the way she imagined people feel when a funeral pyre burns, a life has ended and a new leaf is turned. And for a brief moment as she looked at the disintegrating, shrinking pieces of blackened silk she saw in them an image of her marriage.

It took Charlotte over another hour before she felt strong enough to go next door to see her parents. Phyllida was preparing her own dinner in the kitchen while John was in the parlour, absorbing the latest sobering information from his beloved newspaper while listening to the BBC news on the wireless. He did not hear Charlotte enter but Phyllida did, although she continued with her cooking without turning to look. 'Hello, Charlotte,' she said, 'has Frank gone out somewhere? I heard the bike earlier.' There was no answer but she instinctively knew something was wrong; parents have that sort of sixth sense. As she turned, Charlotte threw herself into her mother's arms. She became her daughter again, her baby, and she desperately needed the security of a maternal embrace.

'What's wrong, my dearest?' she asked.

Charlotte's answer was punctuated with deep, serious sobs and her words struggled to come out. 'He's…he's been seeing another woman and I have told him to go. It's all over.'

'Oh, dear God,' said Phyllida. 'But I honestly can't say I'm surprised. How did you find out? Who is she? Come on in and tell your father.'

Still oblivious to the drama that had been unfolding in the kitchen, John Farrow looked up from his newspaper and was shocked at what he saw in his daughter's eyes. 'Oh, my dearest, whatever is wrong?'

Phyllida was the one to speak. 'Frank has gone. Charlotte discovered he has been unfaithful.'

John stood up, turned off the wireless and repeated the word that was being used increasingly frequently about his son-in-law: 'The bastard,' then he added his personal customary embellishment: 'The shit.'

Over the next hour, Charlotte told her parents practically everything she knew, about the increasing unpleasantness and cruelty, the vulgar language, the criticisms of her clothes and her cooking, the underwear she had bought – although she could not bring herself to say Frank used it to masturbate – the threat to cut off her hair, the obscene magazines – which Phyllida now admitted to her husband she had seen – and the remarks about Hannah and Emily. She said she had told him that everyone now knew the facts behind the *Sunday Voice* story and she told of how inevitably, bit, by bit, Frank had alienated himself from her in every aspect of their lives. She said her marriage was a joke, a folly, a ruin and told them about Frank's valedictory speech with as much of its bile and anger and hate as she could recall. 'I did offer him another chance,' she said, 'but in my heart I knew there was no way back.'

Even then, Charlotte could not bring herself to disclose the terrible row about her meal when Frank had hit her, the weird demands he had made of her in their bedroom and above all the fact that as Emily told her, Frank had contrived to get her into his bed in order to satisfy his fantasy, and then be able to report the success to his friends; and had plied her with drink in order to do so. If her father knew that, she was in no doubt it would sign Frank Atmore's death warrant.

Her parents in turn, finally felt bold enough to reveal their long held feelings and anxieties, John repeatedly saying he always knew it would come to this and Phyllida saying with marginally less certainty that it did not surprise her.

'You must move back into the main house with us Charlotte,' said Phyllida, 'and now do have some dinner, it's almost ready.'

'No, Mama, I want to prove I can be independent. Please understand. I want to continue in the cottage. We can talk again in the morning but I need to go to bed now. And I'm sorry, Mama, I couldn't eat anything.'

And with that Charlotte hugged both her parents and went back to the cottage, back to the rear bedroom where she undressed and prayed, prayed as she always did for her unborn Ophelia, prayed forgiveness for having told Frank she was glad she had lost her and prayed for herself. Then, at the end of a day such as she could never have foreseen twenty-four hours earlier, she fell asleep and for the first time for many days, did so without any tears. She was now just too tired to cry.

After she left, John and Phyllida talked long into the night and took turns to blame each other for not having supported their daughter better or had the insight to see what was taking place just next door.

'I've never said this to you before, my dearest,' John said, 'but what I always suspected now makes sense. Once Frank got Charlotte pregnant, he didn't offer to marry her to legitimise the child and make amends for what he done. The bugger saw it as a way to get his hands on Six Oaks but he was thwarted because he found me firmly in his way.'

'And I can now see,' replied Phyllida, 'that not getting Six Oaks would just have left him the baby and becoming a father – and I would like to guess even that only appealed to him because it proved his virility. Then, when Charlotte lost the baby, there was nothing to keep him in the marriage. He never loved her, and he just took it out on the poor girl. Oh, our poor, poor angel, what has she been through? She is going to need us so much John over the coming months and we must keep the closest watch over her.'

Chapter Seventeen

Two weeks after Frank left in early November, a strange looking and scruffy, unshaven young man wearing a thick, dark blue, knitted fisherman's wool sweater parked a van in the farmyard, knocked on the door and produced a list of Frank's possessions to be collected. Charlotte and her parents supervised their departure, watching his every move like hawks. Without comment Charlotte watched a cardboard box being loaded; a box she knew contained a pile of German reading material.

Then, over the coming weeks, she worked desperately hard in an attempt to pick up her life. She realised she could not act as if nothing had happened but as Christmas approached, activities on the farm kept her busy. Barnfather, the butcher, took away the pigs and turkeys for slaughter and all made a decent financial return. When she and John reviewed the year's activities they were as pleased as any farmer is ever pleased. The barley had made a good price, the other crops had done as well as could be expected and the next cropping pattern more or less took care of itself – thanks to that man Townshend and his rotations again. They considered the improvements the farm needed: replacement fencing was certainly a priority for which Ted had been recommended a new contractor. It was decided they could afford a slight increase in Ted's and Tommy's wages and a new plough might be necessary because so much on the old one had been welded and re-welded that little of the original structure remained. But a new tractor was out of the question for the moment and the old faded orange Fordson would have to keep soldiering on.

The income from Frank's accountancy activities had gone – not that Charlotte had ever seen much of it – and long conversations with her father confirmed it would be pointless to try and claim any maintenance support from him, at least for the present. That might come later when any separation was on a legal basis. For the time being, John was able to reassure her he could fill the financial gap and there would in effect be a return to the state before Frank appeared. He told her not even to think of touching her Grandmother's legacy to cover any costs; that was for her and her future, not to keep the farm functioning.

But Charlotte now needed the opportunity to do something quite out of the ordinary, to convince herself – let alone anyone else – she had taken control of her life again. She wanted once more to regain the free spirit Charlotte Farrow had always had, a spirit Frank had all but squeezed out of her. But she certainly could not have predicted what it was or from where it was to come.

The Ely cousins drove up for Christmas Day and for a few hours, the misery of her marriage was forgotten and a traditional Six Oaks celebration temporarily lit up all their lives. The next day, John and Phyllida went back to Ely with the cousins to stay for a week with John's ailing sister Angela and his sister-in-law Peggy, leaving Charlotte with the Riley. Ted and Tommy would be taking care of the farm for a few days so she could go where she liked and do what she wanted. No-one would know. She was beholden to no-one. She was liberated. She was Charlotte Farrow again, her own woman, not Charlotte Atmore, under Frank's controlling fist. She even began to debate returning to her proud maiden name but demurred before gaining some advice in case it threw up legal difficulties.

Hannah had suggested Charlotte might join her, her parents and Emily for the Boxing Day meet of the South Norfolk hunt at The Manor. John Farrow was no longer able to ride because of his wounds and Charlotte had always been equivocal about hunting. As a country woman, she recognised it as one of the pivotal traditions of rural England. She was a passably good horse woman – although not in Hannah's league – and the spectacle, the fascination of hunting etiquette, the high standard of horsemanship and the social company and camaraderie were undeniable attractions. But she always felt something of an outsider at the climax, the moment the fox was cornered; and she had shrunk away when at the age of six she had been daubed with blood in the traditional way at her first kill. And since the miscarriage, she was aware that her attitudes to life and death, in whatever form, had changed and softened. All living things she now considered precious. She reminded Hannah she had not ridden for over a year and was more than slightly anxious, the more so since the miscarriage.

However Hannah assured her she would find a quiet, well behaved and experienced gelding, so she succumbed and said she would join in; for what was to end in a quite extraordinary outcome.

Charlotte dusted down her long neglected and beautifully tailored black riding jacket, a present from her father when her figure was just an inch or two slimmer although when she glanced in the mirror before leaving the cottage she thought how much its slightly tighter fit enhanced her widely admired curves. Her brown breeches, much to her relief, still fitted snugly post-miscarriage and she spent an hour polishing her black boots. For safety reasons her hair could not be left wild and free for once but was carefully confined in a net under her riding hat. She thought to herself that despite all she had endured, she was indeed still a good looking young woman and unconsciously held her head a fraction higher as she told herself she had much to offer to the world, and to people who cared for her. 'To be honest,' she said in her head with a complete lack of modesty, 'you are looking rather gorgeous, Charlotte Farrow. Appearing like this, you could even see yourself on the front page of *Country Life*!' Yes, there was no doubt that a move towards a return of pride and confidence in herself was already under way.

As the dark of night-time was driven away by the new morning, Boxing Day emerged bright and clear with just a hint of frost in the air, enough to layer the thinnest of ice on the puddles of The Manor's stable-yard. The low December sun struck the forty or fifty riders marshalling there at the lowest of angles, so causing crisp, elongated shadows to be thrown across the doors of the now vacated loose boxes. The snorts, neighs and snuffles of the horses combined with the animated chatter of the assembled riders produced an atmosphere of thrill and expectation. Small, white, misty clouds of exhaled breath emerged from men, women and horses alike and drifted upwards to the accompaniment of that unique, wet, equine smell familiar to country-living folk everywhere.

Charlotte collected Jason, Hannah's warmly recommended lightweight sixteen-hands black and tan gelding, already saddled by a stable lad. The horse looked directly at her, his ears pricked and his eyes wide open. He seemed to be imbued with the innate insight of a good and experienced hunter. Encouraged by his calm, quiet demeanour, Charlotte placed her left foot in the stirrup and lifted herself in a smooth and graceful movement across his back. As a young girl, she had been taught the fast disappearing skill of riding side-saddle but now preferred to be astride when she felt much more in control. Once she was comfortably settled on Jason, she immediately became aware of the dual feelings known to every rider – of superiority at being so far above ground level and mere pedestrians, and of the vulnerability that comes with knowing it is a long way to fall. She was placing her safety and well being jointly in her own skill and the behaviour of the animal beneath her who was already shaking his head from side to side in anticipation. Spotting the Master nearby she offered him a customary greeting and then nudged her heels gently into Jason's flanks and joined her fellow riders. The South Norfolk was a traditional shire hunt, its gentleman members all clad in striking pink while most of the accompanying riders, like Charlotte, were impeccably turned out in black. It had always intrigued Charlotte as one of those perfectly ridiculous, yet wonderful English traditions, for folk to dress up in their most immaculate clothes only to spend the next couple of hours doing their utmost to cover them, themselves and their mounts with a generous helping of countryside mud.

Charlotte nodded and smiled at those fellow riders she recognised, chatted briefly with those she knew better, and prepared with them for the thrill of the chase. Then, the ritual of the stirrup cup completed, and to the accompanying applause of a hundred or more Felsingham residents gathered to admire the spectacle, the huntsman sounded his horn and the clattering of hundreds of hooves on old cobbles accompanied the cavalcade of horses and riders as they moved from the yard into Manor Lane and thence into the wider countryside. Given her long absence from the saddle, Charlotte determined to let the experienced riders, including Hannah and Emily, hunt with the main pack while she held herself back with the field and kept Jason towards the rear, avoiding the most challenging fences.

At the end of the chase over some ten miles of compellingly beautiful Norfolk winter countryside, Charlotte was hot, tired, perspiring heavily and had an ache in her inner thighs, not yet readjusted to the saddle after a long absence. They will hurt more tomorrow, she thought. But she felt invigorated – and excited. She dismounted, removed her hat and shook her hair free, before handing back Jason, thanking him and the stable lad for their efforts and prepared herself for the evening.

There was always a memorably fine party after the hunt and Mrs Fiddler, The Manor cook, threw herself body and soul into preparing a spread of game and other matchless winter fare much as she did with summer dishes at the garden party. She was a slightly unworldly soul whose horizons more or less ended at her kitchen range, but she was not so detached from reality as to realise that world events just might dictate this to be the last Boxing Day hunt party for some while.

Charlotte returned to Six Oaks to bath and change, then repeated her journey to The Manor in the evening and arrived about fifteen minutes after the event had reached its fullest exuberance and the great hall was packed. Her ever-striking figure was unarguably now shown to its best advantage since her wedding day with a high neckline, tomato-red shoulder-padded dress, around knee-length to reveal her long, shapely legs and the result of a special shopping visit to Norwich just before Christmas. Heads were unavoidably turned in admiration and intrigue as she entered. That was exactly what she intended. Long gone was the Charlotte of the summer garden party when she had dressed down to avoid attention after her miscarriage. This was the Charlotte Farrow of old, who wanted to be seen and noticed.

She felt good, purposeful and emboldened by her choice of wardrobe and she soon engaged – and in turn was engaged – in lively conversation by all whom she met. She saw Hannah and Emily across the room but they were occupied with family guests and Charlotte did not intrude. After an hour or so however she found herself locked in a less than welcome discourse about modern farming practices with the Master of the hunt, widely considered an outstanding horseman but also a crashing bore, when at a most convenient moment, she heard a rich and elegant female voice just behind her.

'Hello, Charlotte. Still playing tennis? I saw you out in the field and was sure I recognised the hair tucked under that riding hat.'

Charlotte turned round. 'Oh, my goodness, no it can't be. Is it? Julia? Yes. It is. Dear God! How absolutely amazing. I'm so sorry, I forget, what was your surname?'

'Fitzgerald, it still is.'

'Yes, of course, Julia Fitzgerald.'

'So, am I still playing tennis? Yes, occasionally, but not perhaps quite as you must remember! Of course you were two years behind me at school weren't you? But what on earth brings you here?'

'In a sense you do, my sweet! A friend of my father's told me about the hunt because I ride fairly often – though usually just a hack – and when he mentioned Felsingham I had an idea you lived locally and thought the opportunity was too good to miss – so here I am.'

Charlotte looked Julia up and down, just as she had done that summer evening in the sports pavilion eight years earlier, although Julia's exquisitely slim, firm figure and pearl-like skin was now demurely concealed by a perfectly tailored silk gown. Her hair, almost jet black, was cut with a side parting and a neat fringe that complemented beautifully sculpted waves, beneath which a pair of sparkling diamond drop earrings were just visible.

Charlotte drew in breath. 'You look absolutely

wonderful, gorgeous in fact. It really is *so* good to see you, Julia. I know we weren't all that close at school – socialising with lower forms was a bit frowned on – but I always thought you were great fun. I'd love to know what you have done since. There's so much we could talk about.'

'Then why not come and stay with me tonight, my sweet? I'm renting a little cottage about three miles away for a couple of days. Could you manage to get away or – Oh, dear – I spy a wedding ring. Is there an adoring husband waiting somewhere?'

Charlotte realised afterwards that it took barely a moment's thought before she answered.

'I'd love that, Julia,' and glancing at her left hand which she instinctively covered with her right, almost spilling her wine as she did so, added, 'No, there's most certainly no adoring husband – I'll tell you later. Let's meet up after the party.'

'Marvellous. That's really marvellous. We can share a bottle of wine or two and catch up on news and reminisce about school. Do you remember Miss Phillips, the deputy head, who was copulating with Colin the groundsman? Her name was Gertrude and we all called her Dirty Gertie! And Janice Peters, the sadistic gym teacher, who was always so free with her cane? I can feel it now. Lovely! What great days they were! There's only one bedroom but we are old friends after all. You might even find out what you missed all those years ago! Good for you, Charlotte Farrow, live a bit…'

Two hours later, Charlotte was driving her father's Riley, and following Julia's little Morris Minor, along the local lanes to the rented cottage in the nearby village of Wester Dyke and as she entered it, her pulse rose with a feeling of excitement such as she had not experienced for many months. Once they arrived, and Julia had unlocked and let them both in, she looked carefully around the little four-room cottage. She wanted to absorb the feel of the place, a place where she had an extremely good idea of what might be going to happen.

'Do look around, my sweet,' said Julia, as she rearranged a small mound of waiting logs and pieces of coal in the fireplace, pushed some old newspaper beneath and put a match to it. 'It belongs to an old friend of my mother and it's really rather sweet,' she added. The flames soon devoured the newspaper and embraced the logs and coal to ornament the dimly lit room with flickering shades of yellow, red and blue.

The cottage was replete with what estate agents call character: timber framing and centuries old wattle and daub, the living room dominated by the newly illuminated inglenook fireplace which had been painted black with the soot of fires past; not so different, although smaller, Charlotte thought from the fireplace in her own home at Six Oaks. And like Six Oaks, it had undoubtedly seen human dramas and emotions of all persuasions played out down the years. Tonight might just see one more. Off the living room was a small but sensibly organised kitchen and a tiny bathroom. At the other end of the room, Charlotte opened a latched door to reveal a short straight staircase that led directly into a bedroom occupying the entire first floor and into which the warmth from the fire would soon be filtering upwards. She explored further, and saw the room had a large double bed, covered with a Paisley-patterned counterpane. There were the same matching blue and red floral curtains as in the living room – rather to my own taste she thought – and she lingered for several minutes, noting as much detail about the bedroom as she could take in. The wardrobe door was half open, revealing several high quality country clothes, the possessions Charlotte decided, of a woman of style and discernment.

By the time she returned downstairs, the little living room was already filling with warmth and becoming imbued, she thought, with an atmosphere conducive to relaxation and perhaps the loss of inhibition. And further to fuel a loss of inhibition, Julia had produced two glasses and was uncorking a bottle of 1935 Valpolicella. 'My favourite tipple,' she said. 'I always pop two bottles in the car when I am going away – you never know…'

Despite both women having an extremely good idea of what might be coming, Charlotte found Julia in no hurry as she gestured her towards a small settee on one side of the fire. 'Do sit down, my sweetest,' she said, adding, 'I'm sorry the wine isn't quite the right temperature yet.' She then stood the bottle in the hearth to rectify the fault and sat opposite in a leather bound armchair.

Julia raised her glass: 'To friendship.'

Charlotte reciprocated: 'To lost friends found again.'

The ensuing half-hour or so of conversation was animated and gloriously happy for both women, regularly punctuated with gasps and laughs as memory after memory of their mutual school days flooded back. Having been two years apart, their experiences were not always identical and they revelled in exchanging stories about their fellow pupils and the members of staff. Julia topped up the glasses a couple of times and opened a second bottle as Charlotte became increasingly overwhelmed with a feeling of ease, relaxation and no little tiredness after her day on horseback. The tiny room was now becoming decidedly warm and at one point she found the need to push the little settee a foot further from the fire. 'I'm afraid I'm becoming rather hot and sweaty,' she explained, conscious of her high and now rather constricting neckline.

'What a glorious thought!' said Julia. 'Now tell me about yourself, my sweet. Your family farm nearby don't they?'

'Yes, Papa is the owner but he suffered badly in the war and finds things hard now so basically I run it – though I'm still learning. I have no brothers or sisters, you see. They couldn't have any more after me. And I just love the farm. It's what I always wanted. Perhaps you will come one day. I'd really like that. Mama is still alive and well and as busy as ever – she's big in the local Conservatives and in fact I take a pretty close interest in politics myself.'

'Good, that's all good – though I'm a committed Liberal,' responded Julia with a broad smile. 'One of my cousins is distantly related to Archie Sinclair – you know, the Liberal leader. But never mind that. Now tell me, though only if you want to, about your marriage – about being married. What's lies behind that wedding ring?'

And tell her Charlotte did, about the marriage and the miscarriage, sparing little. She dwelt – perhaps unfairly she thought to an unmarried listener – on her unborn

Ophelia but Julia seemed genuinely moved and listened attentively with an occasional interruption for the odd clarification over almost half an hour.

'That's a truly awful story, Charlotte. I am so sorry for you. You deserve far better.'

'Yes, and I shall have far better, Julia. I'm in the early stages of turning a new leaf, though there's an awful lot to put behind me. But now it's your turn. Where do you live?'

'I have a sweet little place – a cottage a bit like this – in a village just south of Holt. It's a pretty town. You'd be most welcome any time you're in the area.'

'And what do you do?'

'I'm a teacher. I teach at a girls' school, history and geography mostly. No, it's all right. I can imagine what you might be thinking. They are quite safe. I wouldn't lay a finger on them. I have absolutely no interest in young girls.' She smiled. 'It's their mothers who need to look out!' Julia then suddenly appeared more serious. 'Have you ever thought back to that time after tennis? I was only sixteen but I knew what I wanted and it was you, my sweet. I can remember it now so clearly. I really, really fancied you, Charlotte. With the benefit of hindsight and maturity, I now know it wasn't just a schoolgirl crush. You were the first girl I had real feelings for and when I took my top off I was desperate for you to hold my breasts. I was so upset when you didn't. I cried floods back in the dorm.'

Julia then took one more large drink from her wine glass before putting it down. She left her chair, sat next to Charlotte on the little settee, put one arm around her shoulders and whispered 'Why not make up for it now, sweetheart?' She then ran the fingers of the other hand through her hair. 'You always had the most glorious hair. I was so envious. You still do. You were a beautiful girl at school and you really have become a most beautiful woman. Honestly, my sweet, I have never forgotten you and always prayed we might one day meet again.' Charlotte's pulse was now racing in anticipation and she wondered if Julia could actually hear her heart pounding because she was all too well aware that by showing not a hint of resistance to such explicit advances, she was giving her the licence she needed.

Charlotte placed her arm around Julia's neck and in the same moment, Julia turned Charlotte's head towards her and kissed her on the lips. This time, Charlotte knew precisely what was coming and knew exactly how she wanted to respond. Unlike Hannah, who had given her the fright of her life, Julia had prepared the ground and made quite clear what she had in mind. So, far from keeping her lips sealed, Charlotte now opened her mouth invitingly and the taste of a rather good 1935 Valpolicella passed back and forth from one woman's lips and tongue to the other.

⋆

Julia was in the tiny cottage kitchen preparing coffee and toast by the time Charlotte emerged the next morning, more than a touch bleary-eyed and draped loosely in a dressing gown she had found hanging behind the bedroom door. Despite what had transpired in the previous eight hours, a deeply inborn modesty still required her to cover up, if only as a token gesture. Julia had already re-lit the fire.

'Well, good morning, my lovely farmer.' Julia stopped her breakfast preparation, put her arms around Charlotte's neck, looked her straight in the eye and kissed her. 'Did you have a good night? I rather got the impression you enjoyed all that. And if, as you told me, it really was your first time, well done you! I've been around a bit, Charlotte, my sweet and not many women manage to give me three orgasms in one night – unfortunately I've never been one of those multi-orgasm girls!'

'Goodness! Does it sound ridiculous, Julia, for me to say thank you? Yes, I did enjoy it enormously. You can't imagine how terrified I was when we drove back here and then, when you kissed me on that settee, my blood pressure must have been somewhere on the thatched roof. Although it's all very new to me, you probably know that Hannah is inclined the same way as you…'

'Don't be afraid or shy to say it, Charlotte – we are lesbians.'

'…yes, I know, of course. But what I was going to say was that, despite being so close to Hannah for all my life, she only confirmed it to me recently after she met her lovely girl friend Emily, but I really only had a vague idea of what women do with each other – much of it was guesswork. Hannah has called me one of life's naïve innocents which I don't think is quite fair! But you were so understanding. I'm not surprised you are a teacher!'

'My sweet girl, there was nothing naïve about you last night. And if it really was guesswork, believe me, sweetheart, you certainly guessed right! I'll be honest

Charlotte, you were wonderful for me too – and though I'm being totally immodest in saying it, I'm a fairly experienced woman for all my twenty-three years! Given a chance I think – I'm almost sure – I could rather easily fall in love with you. But let me add something, because I know what happened here was actually a step – an enjoyable step – towards Charlotte Farrow trying to escape or trying to find something – although I'm not entirely sure what it is she's looking for. Perhaps she doesn't either and just needs to prove something to herself. But please don't be afraid of me, Charlotte, because of what we shared last night. I think, I suspect, your long-term future may be with a man – a decent man I mean, not another Frank – look at me, Charlotte – and believe me when I say I will not pursue you or pester you. I promise you that with all my heart, but I shall always be there for you if you want me. I loved last night so much because it wasn't just what we did with each other – it was what we talked about in between. That would sound ridiculous to many people but I imagine it's the same when a woman is sleeping with a man – though I wouldn't know of course. I never have.'

And Charlotte thought back to all those awful married nights with Frank when here had been no talking, no conversation, no love making, just raw physical sex and she had hated it.

Julia continued with her breakfast preparation and poured the coffee – tastefully Charlotte noted into neat cups with saucers, not mugs. The toast, fresh from the grill, was piping hot and came from a rich and tasty home-made loaf with just a hint of sourdough. Julia had

had obviously brought it from home. It had certainly not originated in a Fred Wellbeloved production. Charlotte then spotted a printed label on the marmalade pot. It read "Julia's Jams" and underneath in neat handwriting "Marmalade 1938".

'What's all this?' she asked.

'Oh, just a little diversion. I make batches of all sorts of things like this, a lot of them from hedgerow fruits like blackberries and damsons, and sell them to local shops and restaurants when I have enough, or give them to friends. I always have a pot with me when I go away. You must take this one with you – souvenir!'

Charlotte thought that what she would be taking away had rather more to remind her of the previous twelve hours than just a pot of marmalade but nonetheless accepted with gratitude, not realising how her future was about to be haunted by that small glass container.

One of the most extraordinary passages of her life had however now come to an end, the farm awaited her and a return to what passed as normality. She went to the bathroom for a swift wash, then back to the bedroom to change and gather her possessions. When Julia came to the door to say goodbye, both women had tears in their eyes. And when Charlotte fired up the Riley which hesitated just a few seconds as a gesture to the cold morning, Julia turned while closing the cottage door and called out, 'If ever you want to see me again, sweetheart, you know where to find me…'

Having swallowed hard several times to nullify the tears, Charlotte found she was talking to herself on the drive back to Six Oaks and realised she was rehearsing a speech to say to Hannah – although she was not at all sure she could or should ever actually deliver it. 'That really was the best, the most wonderful thing I have done for ages. It wasn't the sex – although it was surprisingly enjoyable, really very enjoyable in fact – Julia is so experienced in these things and knows exactly what she is doing – you will know all about that of course. No, it was the fact that it liberated me. It was on the face of it such an outrageous thing for me to do; me, Charlotte Farrow from Six Oaks Farm in Felsingham St Margaret. But I thought, what the hell! Can you believe that of one night in bed with another woman, something I have never done and in reality couldn't ever imagine me doing? Though I can't deny that time you kissed me did kind of prepare the way. But it's given me back a lot of my self-confidence. It's what I needed to put the past months behind me and move on. I can't imagine I shall repeat it – although Julia made it quite clear she would like to. But she promised she isn't going to pursue me and I believe her – I suspect there are plenty of other pebbles on her beach. But she did make it clear she will be there if ever I want her. Who knows?'

On her return home to Six Oaks, Charlotte felt elated. Her head was in a spin. She had done something so reactionary, so bold, so outrageously unexpected; but for the moment at least, she could share it with no-one, tell no-one. Despite the speech written in her head, she would not repeat it to Hannah, in time perhaps when the moment was right, but not yet. And her parents would undoubtedly go berserk if they knew. She found herself thinking back to what Hannah had said when she confided her lesbianism to the vicar. Something about the Book of Romans, understanding but not forgiveness wasn't it? For the moment however she must put such concerns aside. Surely Holy Humphrey and the greater being he represented would look kindly on an honest soul trying to reclaim and rebuild a fractured life.

Chapter Eighteen

In the days and weeks of early spring 1939, Charlotte could not avoid her mind being occupied with the Boxing Day experience. Try as she might, it was impossible to concentrate on matters of routine domesticity and farming. She told herself she was permanently 'on a high.' She felt this is what it must be like after taking a narcotic. And she found she was increasingly talking to herself, usually in her head, but on a few occasions she realised it was out loud, and she prayed that neither her parents nor anyone else was within hearing range.

Although she adored her farm and all that went with managing it, she knew she needed to keep up the momentum that had reinforced her self-confidence and self-belief, the momentum that in truth had catapulted them into an entirely new realm. She must not let that lapse again; she must not let Frank Atmore re-emerge in any shape or form, to dictate the rest of her life. And a sudden thought – an impulse in truth – struck her. She had learned to drive a tractor on the farm when she was only twelve or thirteen and once she reached the age of seventeen, her father was happy to allow her to undertake short drives in his car on the public roads. More recently, he had always been generous in permitting her the use of the beautiful Riley when there were no convenient buses. But now, she thought, what better way for her to strike a further blow for independence than to have her own car. Provided it was not too costly, it would be an ideal way to indulge a little of the inheritance from her dear Grandmama. The old lady, like Charlotte's mother, a suffragette, would surely have approved, just as she would have been disgusted at the way her beloved granddaughter had been treated at male hands.

The nearest possible source of a car was the garage in Fenton Bishop where the Riley was serviced and she thought it only a courtesy to take paternal advice, which John was delighted to provide. He telephoned a man named Bill, the owner, whom he had known for many years, and who also dealt with any farm machinery problems that were beyond the scope of Ted and Tommy. His friend confirmed he had half a dozen possible small cars in stock so the following morning, Charlotte drove herself and her father there in the Riley.

Guiding them into his little showroom, Bill was about to give his potential customers a conducted tour of the available vehicles when Charlotte stopped. She had seen what she wanted. Nothing else in that showroom mattered. She had found her car. It was an exquisitely alluring looking little machine: a five-year old, two-seater MG Midget sports car in sparkling red with gleaming wire wheels and a low mileage, having had the proverbial one careful local owner. Charlotte was in love. The next quarter of an hour saw her father examining it most carefully. He even managed to kneel down – something he did not achieve very often and never without significant pain – to look underneath. Satisfied with what he saw, a conversation with the proprietor resulted in confirmation that the car was ready for the road, had a full tank of petrol and all the paperwork was in order, while John's long-time loyal custom facilitated a slight reduction in the asking price. The deal was done for £125 and was followed by ten minutes of instruction for Charlotte, not least in the crash gearbox. The fairly smoothly synchromeshed Riley Kestrel was the only car she had previously driven but she had coped with the 'crash and hope for the best' gearbox on the Fordson tractor and soon took to double de-clutching the MG with the minimum of effort – and only a few grating sounds ensued before it became second nature. Then, after thanking the proprietor and giving her father a prolonged hug, Charlotte drove away from Fenton garage an independent motorist and, even more importantly, with the knowledge she had taken one further stride towards becoming a fully independent woman again.

Charlotte could not wait to show her new acquisition to Hannah, so without bothering to telephone, and once her mother had drooled over the car at Six Oaks and muttered 'If only I was 25 again!' she took it the short distance to The Manor and parked it with a most satisfying crunch on the gravel outside the front porch. The massive oak door was ajar and Charlotte had just manoeuvred her way out of the Midget and was about to mount the three entrance steps to go inside when the doorway darkened and the familiar towering figure of

Matilda, Lady van Vliet, appeared at the top. She was just like the illustration Charlotte remembered of Queen Nefertiti in the Children's Encyclopaedia. Her ladyship was clothed from head to foot in what may have been either a bath robe or a ball gown but had the effect of making her seem even taller than her natural six feet and one inch. Moreover, given the additional height of the steps, her height had now been elevated to around six feet nine and Charlotte had to crane her neck significantly upwards to return the habitual and predictably fulsome greeting, one she had rather hoped to avoid.

'My very dearest Charlotte,' Matilda boomed downwards. 'What a splendid and unexpected surprise – it is so, so wonderful to see you again – it has been so, so long – surely it was Boxing Day when last you were here – how are you – are you now much recovered after that frightful, frightful experience – what a terrible thing it was – that man – that marriage – Frank was he called – such a common name don't you think – that you happened to find – Oh, and your loss of the child – such a terrible thing for you – it happened to your dear Mama too of course – twice as I recall – but much sooner so much, much easier to overcome – you are looking very well though – your hair is so lovely, I always say that to Hannah – if only you had hair like Charlotte – and your scarf too – how jolly and gay it is – I always think Italian silk is the best – Hannah does sometimes buy such cheap things – and your ever-delightful parents – are they well – is your dear, dear Papa still suffering – such a brave, brave man – we all feel so much for him – we simply *must* have you all over for tea – it's been so, so long – or even better for supper – before the week is out – I shall arrange it forthwith, *forthwith* – I shall speak to Mrs Fiddler this very day.' Lady van Vliet then spotted the MG. 'And *what* is that adorable little object? Is that yours, my dearest? Oh, Charlotte, what a wondrous thing it is. Did Papa buy it for you? It isn't your birthday is it? Oh, God in his mercy, I haven't forgotten it again have I?'

By this time, Matilda had – literally and metaphorically – descended to earth and was leaning over the MG and stroking its seats of beautifully matured leather, still redolent with the fragrance of a restorative wax treatment.

'Hello, Lady van Vliet,' responded Charlotte. Despite a lifetime's close acquaintance, she was all too well aware that Hannah's mother thrived on formality and the notion of ever addressing her as Matilda would definitely be a step too far. Charlotte contemplated trying to answer her fully but decided there would be such a cacophony of yeses and nos in response to Lady van Vliet's questions and comments – the earlier of which they had both already forgotten – that there seemed little point. So she opted to concentrate on the most recent.

'Yes, it has been a long time I am afraid. But no, it's not my birthday – my own little indulgence. And thank you for kindly asking after my parents. They are fairly well I think, but I am sure would love to see you and Sir Arthur again.'

'You have come to see Hannah, I expect, and to show her your prize,' said Matilda. 'You know she has Emily now – have you met Emily – yes, of course you have, how foolish of me – a good influence – she has moved in here you know – and we do like her father too – just the right sort of politician don't you think – Winston's man – exactly what we need in these terrible times – yes, Emily, such a nice, refined girl – not what Arthur and I had planned for Hannah of course – a young man with land we had thought – and a title naturally – a small barony would have so, so perfect – but we are where we are as they say in the newspapers – Hannah is so, so happy and that is what matters isn't it, dearest – Oh, and here they come.'

Hannah and Emily had walked round from the stables after hearing the unfamiliar rasping sound of the MG's engine and both women embraced Charlotte warmly. 'Is that yours?' asked Emily. 'Goodness, what a beauty! I am so envious.' And then, turning to Hannah, added 'Rather puts your old Austin in the shade doesn't it?'

Hannah laughed. 'It's gorgeous, C. Is it a present?'

'No, your mother asked me that too. It's my special treat to me. I decided I needed a little something to cheer me up – you know after everything. I must give you a spin – but one at a time I'm afraid – only two seats!'

'It's been too long since I last saw you both,' she continued. 'We must catch up on news. I have felt so different after what happened on Boxing Day…' Charlotte stopped abruptly.

'Boxing Day? Oh, you mean the hunt?' responded Hannah. 'We hardly saw you at the party but there were just so many people we hadn't seen for ages. I did catch sight of you chatting to a pretty dark-haired girl. Who was she?'

'Oh, I can't remember. I talked to so many people that night – and you know I'm dreadful with names.

But look, your mother has kindly invited me to come over with Mama and Papa for dinner.' Charlotte turned to Lady van Vliet who was still standing next to the car, smiling imperiously at all around her. 'Yes, yes, indeed,' she said. 'You girls can all talk then.'

'That's wonderful,' said Hannah. 'Now, we must get back to the horses and we'll wait to hear. Drive carefully, C! Don't bend it!'

Lady van Vliet was true to her word and a few days later, Charlotte and her parents were entertained at The Manor. Everyone was in sparkling form although several remarked later that Charlotte seemed a little reserved; preoccupied was the word one of them used. And preoccupied was right because despite the joy of her new sports car, her mind remained a blend of elation and turmoil about the decisions she knew had to be made.

Chapter Nineteen

Back at Six Oaks, Charlotte kept turning over in her mind the momentous event that had followed her previous visit to The Manor, that unforgettable Boxing Day night. She had become all too aware that something had happened deep inside her psyche. She was intelligent and perceptive and she always knew – how could she possibly avoid knowing – that she was a highly attractive young woman. And it took the merest glance in her mirror to reveal that the slightly furrowed brow, those faintly emerging premature facial lines, the sad eyes that marriage to Frank had induced, were now fading by the day. Anyone else could see that. But what they could not see was something she did not think she had ever felt before – and apart from that first fateful whisky-fuelled encounter, certainly not with Frank. Charlotte now felt sexy, sometimes extremely sexy to the extent it even distracted her from concentrating on her daily work. That was wholly novel – in truth she had always been led to believe such a thing was purely a male phenomenon. It was not something women experienced. She now knew how false was that widely held perception but it nonetheless created two conundrums. First, was the inescapable truth that the feeling was due, not to the influence of a man, but to another woman. It was Julia who had stirred her emotions and set her hormones aflame. And second, and most importantly and practically, she needed an outlet, a relief, for her new found physical feelings. At night, she increasingly felt she had to comfort herself in ways she had seldom previously found necessary – some of which Julia had actually taught her. 'That's all right,' she kept saying in her head, 'and satisfactory and perfectly harmless as a short-term expedient,' but she knew it was certainly no substitute for the company of another human body, not least in her bed.

She regularly lay awake, not soaking her pillow with tears as she had done so often during the marriage years, but simply because her head was in a whirl. The question 'How can I possibly follow that experience with Julia?' was constantly in her mind and begging for an answer. And although it seemed, even to her, a naïve position to be in, she found herself asking on some nights what she really was or possibly what she had become. What was the real Charlotte Farrow? Was she like Hannah and Emily, a lesbian, or was she just passing through a long-delayed period of what should have been, ten years earlier, an adolescent experiment on which she had somehow missed out? The problem for her was that she did enjoy both the company and sexuality of men – even though not one called Frank. Somewhere, in a magazine a little while ago, she had read an article about an Austrian neurologist called Sigmund Freud who wrote about something he called psychoanalysis and introduced her to the word bisexual. He apparently thought all men and women have some inbuilt attraction to both sexes. So is that what she was? Bisexual? She couldn't help thinking it sounded more like a kind of flower that self-pollinated.

Charlotte could, of course, have put Julia's marmalade pot in the pantry, bought another from Wellbeloved's and so removed the daily reminder of that remarkable night. But she did not in her heart of hearts want to forget Julia, and seeing that little label every morning on her breakfast table was in a most bizarre way offering her a comfort. Even after a fortnight, when the home-made marmalade itself had gone, she had washed out the little pot, being careful not to remove the label, and now kept it constantly on her windowsill to display a few tiny seasonal flowers.

On five or six occasions over the early weeks of the year, Charlotte took out her address book, opened the page headed 'F', and stared at the entry she had written on that extraordinary morning: 'Fitzpatrick, Julia, Lavender Cottage, Westington, Nr Holt, Norfolk – Phone Holt 176.' Three times her hand hovered over the telephone receiver with a finger ready to dial, but three times her hand retreated. Julia had so far been true to her promise. She had not pursued Charlotte, she had not pestered her and Charlotte believed her undertakings. Surely, she told herself, whatever your past experiences and even if you are more than slightly promiscuous, you do not do as Julia had done and look straight in the eye of someone with whom you have just spent a most gloriously intimate, frank and open-hearted night – and lie to them.

But – and it was an ever-present but – Julia said she believed she could fall in love with her and Charlotte repeatedly came back to the thought that if she did telephone her – or even drive to Holt in her glorious newly acquired red transport – she would be crossing a Rubicon and indicating she might be willing to take on some sort of commitment. It was a risk – and hitherto Charlotte had never thought of herself as a gambler.

She was now in her mid-twenties and despite that one awful marital experience, she was not someone destined be alone. She needed company and she adored the company of what – she now had to admit – was her somewhat limited circle of close friends. Aside from her time at boarding school – and look what that had led to! – practically all her life had been spent in rural Norfolk. Although she could drive, it was only now she had bought herself the real freedom and the four wheels to take advantage of it. And she adored her home, her farm, her village, her county. She did not want to travel far, and certainly not to live anywhere else to expand her horizons. She so desperately wanted companionship but she wanted it here, just where she was now. She wanted someone to come to her and bring happiness with them, arrogant and selfish – and extremely improbable – though it might seem.

One night, she sat bolt upright up in bed, startling herself at the sudden recollection of what Frank had said in that last hate-fuelled tirade. It was something along the lines of her only being able to satisfy other women. 'Oh, my God!' she said to herself. 'Could he have been right?' It was a conundrum that somewhere, with someone, she needed to resolve. Perhaps, after all, she should talk to Hannah about her feelings – although of course she could not do so without revealing the truth about Julia, something she was equally sure she was not yet ready to do. The absence of Hannah as an intimate confidante was actually beginning to fray her nerves. But there was just no-one else to whom she could turn and who would understand, and also be discreet. Or was there?

Charlotte began to think back over her life's experiences. There were no other women friends close enough, physically or emotionally. She loved her cousins in Ely and they had spent many gloriously happy childhood hours together but both Archie and Caroline were unmarried and had very different lives of their own. She thought of Jeremy, the beautiful boy from the Young Farmers' Club as she had described him to Hannah. Charlotte was nineteen at the time and they were in his parents' house while they were away. There had been a late night dance and a significant consumption of beer and it was then she had given him her virginity. At least, she always believed she had given him her virginity, but so inept had it been she was never quite sure. He *was* beautiful in his way, but he too was a virgin and they had fumbled their way through a token coupling – as much as anything because it had been thought such a grown-up thing to do. It seemed, as they both said afterwards, a good idea at the time. The blessing was that it had been painless and harmless, although hardly an ideal introduction to the world of adult intimacy. The most important consequence was that they had been able to laugh about it afterwards. 'You put your left leg in

...' sang Jeremy to uncontrolled, inebriated giggling as Charlotte hysterically added '...and shake it all about.' She had no idea where Jeremy had ended up, but heard a suggestion recently that he was married and already had three sons – so presumably must have discovered a little more accurately about what to put where and when not to shake it.

No, it was not Jeremy but Hannah's cousin Torquil, who in her mind was the one to whom she had really surrendered her maidenhead. He was so loving, so kind, so gentle, so caring, even if technically he hadn't been the first to cross the hymenial line. He had, in fact, been so understanding that he had provided her with her first conjugal orgasm, not something any woman easily forgets. 'He was a real gentleman, Mama – and no, before you ask, he didn't hurt me one bit,' she had told her mother after confiding that her beautiful baby daughter was quite definitely no longer chaste, pure and inviolate. So what about Torquil? He had told her at the garden party that he was moving from Scotland in the spring to manage a sporting and forestry estate north of Thetford and so would only be a few miles away. What better way for the MG to stretch its legs than to pay him a visit? She recalled that Hannah had been asked to pass on his new address a few months earlier and sure enough several minutes rummaging in the study produced it: Pines Lodge, The Sandyheath Estate, near Thetford, Norfolk. Sadly, there was no telephone number and a quick check indicated nothing in the directory. She would have to take a chance; and a spin on the road in her exciting new sports car on a bright sunny day could certainly do not harm.

The word 'bowling' kept coming into her mind as she drove south from Felsingham along the pretty southern road to Thetford. Why was it that motor cars were always said to bowl along country lanes, she wondered. She had no answer but no matter. Charlotte was thrilled to be free, to be away on her own and the purr of the MG's hard-working four cylinders drowned the sound of the birds in the hedgerows as she pushed it to just over 70 mph and swept through Bungay and the little towns and border villages: Homersfield, Wortwell, Harleston, Needham and Thorpe Abbots – and on through Diss, South Lopham and Rushford. So to make up for the loss of the birds, Charlotte sang herself. She had always been a reasonably good soprano – not church choir standard but pleasant enough – and in any event it didn't matter here where no-one else was listening. The musical play of the moment was Cole Porter's *Leave It to Me* and its songs were ever-present on the gramophone at home. So taking a cue from having heard it during the previous week, and thinking it an appropriate way to express love for her adored father, Charlotte gave South Norfolk her own personal rendering at the top of her voice of '*My Heart Belongs to Daddy*'.

Charlotte was undeniably happy and as the tiny windscreen on the MG offered little real protection, her hair was blowing wildly where it was not confined by her head scarf. It all added to an overwhelming feeling of freedom, liberation and being utterly carefree. She saw hardly another vehicle for all the forty or so miles and then as she approached the town of Thetford, a discreet painted sign loomed up on her left. "Sandyheath Estate" it read, "Private Road". She followed it down a firm, but unmetalled track lined with tall, reddish-barked pine trees. After about half a mile, a group of smart buildings – stables, workshops and what appeared to be a small saw mill – loomed ahead. There were stacks of cut timber here and there, and two fairly new bright red tractors that put her old Fordson decidedly in the shade. It all smacks of someone not too short of funds, she thought.

She brought the MG to a halt close to one of the log stacks where a man in overalls with a pot of paint was marking the cut ends with letters and numbers. 'Excuse me,' she said. 'I'm looking for Torquil MacLeod, the manager. Is he here?' 'Worken in Estate Office, Ma'm, at end of rud. Least he say he do,' came the reply in one of the richest Suffolk accents she had ever heard and with an intonation that sounded as if Charlotte was being asked a question rather than given information. The man gestured towards a small brick building about fifty yards away, so Charlotte eased herself stiffly from her seat and walked towards the building, noting as she passed, the intense heat radiating from the MG's bonnet as the engine regained its composure after the drive.

The office door was ajar and as she approached she could see the object of her journey seated at a large wooden desk surrounded by papers and books. Torquil raised his eyes on hearing the approaching footsteps, then leapt to his feet, dropping a pen and a large box file, scattering its contents on the floor.

The words 'Bloody hell,' came first, followed immediately by 'My dearest sweetest angel. What a surprise! What joy! How are you? What are you doing here? Come in, do have some tea.' Then glancing over her shoulder 'My goodness! Magnificent motor car, Charlotte!'

Torquil then took a large stride in Charlotte's direction and enveloped her in an all-embracing hug that suddenly conveyed to her an image of something she had once seen at a Highland games. He kissed her on both cheeks and she noted the rather strong smell of the resin from recently felled pine trees.

Having released her from his grip, Torquil took Charlotte by the hand and led her in to his office, stepping none too carefully over the scattered papers muttering 'I do hate the admin.' 'Sit down,' he said, gesturing towards a small swivel chair in the corner, picked up an elderly kettle with several dents, shook it to ensure it contained water and placed it on a small gas ring which he then lit.

They talked and laughed together, drinking cup after cup of tea, for around half an hour, catching up on each other's news, good and bad. And Charlotte slowly and using her utmost tact, steered the conversation towards Torquil's relationship status and probed to discover what, if any, serious feelings he had towards her. As the message seemed to have reached its target, she introduced the question 'Am I grasping at straws?'

Torquil suddenly became rather more serious. 'May I give a bit of advice, from an old bosom friend to someone who will always be so utterly special to me? Whatever happens, Charlotte, be assured that one day you will meet the right person, and I am sure when that happens you will know who it is. He will come charging along on a great white horse. I just know he will. But whatever you do, Charlotte, don't clutch at straws. Not that I am saying I am straw – I think I have bit more fibre than that.' He laughed at the imagery. Charlotte laughed, but less convincingly. 'I shall always have a really soft spot for you, Charlotte, and don't imagine I haven't thought about you a great deal and I will be absolutely truthful and would tell you if I thought there was any possibility we might make a go of things. You are an incredibly beautiful and personable woman with a golden heart and I was totally gutted that your marriage did not work out. And to lose your baby was just terrible. Terrible. I literally cried oceans for you, my sweetest. You deserve so much better and I know one day you will find the right person. But I can't be that person – at least not in the foreseeable future – and it would be frightfully unfair and arrogant of me to give you hope and keep you waiting. Though I would never say never! I know I can be totally honest with you Charlotte and tell you that daft as it seems, I am not really sure where I belong. In Bonnie Scotland? Here? I don't know. I do love my work here. And on a personal level, I can't deny I've had some wonderful times – and I mean in and out of bed – with several women, some utterly fantastic, some certainly peculiar. When I saw you last summer, I was in an on-off relationship with a woman fifteen years older than me who taught Scottish dancing. Can you believe that, my angel? Anyway, our Highland fling, as my brother Alex called it, came to an end when she went back to her last husband but two. I'm now with someone else although I have absolutely no idea how or if it will all work out.'

'Oh, I am *so* pleased for you,' said Charlotte, realising with wholly undisguised sadness she could almost certainly now cross off one possible direction in which her life might have veered.

'Go on then, Tor, tell me. I expect she is totally gorgeous and probably rich as well.'

'No,' said Torquil, 'he is!'

'Oh, my God! Tor! No, you haven't! You aren't! You don't!'

'Sorry, Charlotte. I've completely shocked you haven't I? I don't think I'm queer – in fact I'm sure I am not, not properly queer – but he is terrific company, very intelligent, artistic and perceptive – he's called Larry and he's a professional musician. It's all very new for me – a sort of life-enriching experiment – and although it's great while it lasts, I do think that eventually I shall settle down with someone shaped like you!'

Charlotte burst into uncontrolled laughter. 'I'm sorry, Tor, I'm not laughing at you. I'm really not. I'm laughing at myself and our situations. Now, don't you laugh, but on the subject of life-enriching experiments – I do love that expression and shall use it again – I have to tell you I recently slept with another woman and enjoyed it enormously.'

'Charlotte!' said Torquil. 'That's just wonderful! Good for you!' And he gave her the most all-embracing hug and the aroma of pine trees returned. 'Who is she? What is she? You simply *must* tell me.'

Charlotte continued. 'It's not going anywhere – at least I don't think so – and she may be predatory. She's a school teacher and she sort of told me she has a predilection for married women who are lesbian virgins – and I don't think she was joking! Anyway, I obviously filled the bill. In fact, believe it or not, I knew her at school and she tried it on with me then but I hadn't seen her since and met her quite by chance at The Manor hunt party. I don't *think* it's anything I shall do again. It taught me lots about myself although it may have asked more questions than it answered. I started to wonder if I might be something called bisexual – have you heard that word? It's rather good, I think, but I'm still not sure – that night didn't exactly clarify things! Though I do now have a bit better understanding of Hannah and Emily's relationship. She's a really wonderful girl, you know, your cousin Hannah, and I just do not know how I could have got through the last year without her. I would simply have gone under. Anyway, as I was saying, I think that if I am to have a long-term companion, it will be with a man, but when or where I shall find him, I have absolutely no idea. Wonderful men don't exactly grow on trees in the wilds of Norfolk and as far as I can see none are beating a path to my door. And you have obviously ruled yourself out of contention, at least for the time being. Curse you, Torquil McLeod! But I'm glad I did what I did, Tor, because after the marriage and an odd experience with Hannah herself, it's gone part of the way towards answering a question I have been asking about myself. No-one knows any of this so *please* keep the confidence. I may in time tell Hannah but I'm not sure.'

'Of course, and you likewise. I think my aunt and uncle – let alone my parents – might go mad if they knew what I am doing. Not least, of course, because Uncle Arthur is a magistrate and what Larry and I do is illegal. Apart from anything else, they'd probably cut me out of the will!'

Charlotte was still mentally reeling. 'You really do it, do you? The illegal thing? What men do together? I've never met anyone who actually… No, don't tell me, Tor. Spare me the details! Heavens! I may have to get some fresh air. This will take a little while to sink in.'

Charlotte then composed herself. 'Actually, Tor, sharing these really private and intimate confidences with each other is enormously heart-warming and reassuring. I have always felt a huge affection for you and I feel it even more now. You are a wonderfully kind and honest man and we shall be friends for ever. And although neither of us has mentioned it today, you do know you were only the second man I ever slept with. You were so gentle and understanding and so concerned not to hurt me that I have never – and will never – forget it. When I compare it with what my awful husband did – but no, I mustn't. I've moved on from that. Anyone who knew me as a child would think that what I did with Julia – with that woman – was completely out of character. Shy, naïve Charlotte Farrow who has lived a sheltered life – even Hannah has called me that, along with saying I am one of life's innocents. But boarding school changed me and gave me the potential to be rebellious and not to want to conform. I think it has taken this horrendously awful marriage to a man who almost literally crushed the life out of me for it all to come out. Honestly, I have been through such a mill of emotions this past year that I now just feel liberated. I feel I could do anything and not care a damn.'

Torquil made another fresh pot of tea and the pair chatted on in his office for another half hour about her farm and his estate before Charlotte said she must return to Felsingham. Torquil told her she was welcome to stay. 'They provide me with a rather nice little house on the estate. There's masses of room. In fact I tend to rattle around in it rather.'

'That's very sweet, Tor, but perhaps another time,' she replied as she was now beginning to feel rather deflated. In her mind, she had unwisely built up hopes that Torquil might be her saviour but it was now dawning on her that much as she was fond of him, she really was clutching at straws. She conceded it was all too much of a reaction on the rebound.

Charlotte drove back rather more slowly than she had done earlier and thought long and carefully about her conversation with Torquil. She had never knowingly encountered a male homosexual before, although most people in Felsingham did have strong suspicions about the Van Vliet's estate manager, Claude Clinker. But that the first confirmed one should turn out to be her beloved Torquil was not easy to take – even if what he had said was correct and he was only queer temporarily or on a part-time basis. 'What Larry and I do is illegal,' he had said. Charlotte was aware of that and was not as naïve as Hannah might claim. She knew perfectly well what homosexual men did together. She once picked up an illustrated volume of classical Greek vase paintings in a second-hand bookshop during a school outing and became so engrossed that she only just managed to replace it on the shelf before her teacher appeared. But the thought of it, of the physical act, made her feel uncomfortable. It was no longer something abstract, something to be seen in books. It was real, it was Torquil. He had been inside her and she now tried, not particularly effectively, to put out of her mind the image of him inside another man, naked and unashamed. Doesn't that expression come from the Bible somewhere, she then wondered. Oh, yes, the Bible! Holy Humphrey would have a field day. This is not just fornication and adultery and the Book of Corinthians. This is Sodom and Gomorrah! Yes, she confirmed to herself, what Torquil does is sodomy – or is it buggery? Then, becoming far too distracted as she wondered about the difference, Charlotte had to make a sudden swerve to avoid introducing the MG to the back of a farm cart laden with manure.

With the road again clear ahead of her, Charlotte mused further. But who was she to judge Torquil when she herself had committed what the vicar had told Hannah were unnatural acts? But it is different, she then told herself, now with far better knowledge than most people, of having sex with both men and women. Sex with a woman is very different. That must be why it isn't illegal she decided. But the technical, physical details aside, she knew she had done something she could not imagine confessing to Holy Humphrey. She had done more than stray. In his eyes – and those of many other people too – she had become a sinner, although she could not bring herself to believe she was wicked; not in the way Frank had been wicked. She had hurt no-one. She had been unkind to no-one. She had broken her wedding vows but they had become the vows of a meaningless marriage, a marriage in name alone.

Her visit to Torquil had been revelatory and as it turned out highly necessary. It cleared the decks because she could not now see him as a partner, ever. She did not want him as a partner but she would still love him as her closest male friend. Knowing what he did changed the way she viewed him sexually, but not the way she viewed him as a person. He was still the same Torquil but in effect, while she could be bisexual, she could not accept the same for him.

Chapter Twenty

Although fencing and ditching were traditional winter jobs on the farm, Charlotte decided to bring forward the fencing repairs that she and her father had agreed were essential. There were gaps appearing in too many places and she could never be certain the animals were always where she had intended. She had even had to call Ted late one night when a motorist drew up at the farm to report there were sheep on the Norwich Road. She remembered he had been recommended a new fencing contractor so she asked him to put the work in hand at the end of May. They could not however afford to replace the wooden fences in the ideal way, so opted for barbed wire as a medium-term measure. That decision was to prove momentous.

It was early one morning, a few days later, that Charlotte heard a vehicle draw up in the yard, followed by men's voices. She was not yet dressed, but peering through the curtains she could see a small lorry with something about fencing written on the side. Ted was giving instructions to the driver. She thought no more about it. Ted was completely reliable and she could relax with getting dressed and preparing for her own day's tasks.

About fifteen minutes later, Charlotte heard her father outside shouting. He did not often raise his voice, so that alone caused her concern, and at first she could not make out what he was saying, but as she opened the cottage door she heard more clearly. He was saying 'No, no, no, not here,' with an anxiety, a fear almost, that she had never heard before. Her mother then appeared and said, 'Take your father inside, Charlotte, quickly. I'll deal with this.'

She did as she was asked and shepherded John into the farmhouse, took him through the kitchen and sat him down in the parlour. 'Whatever is it, Papa?' she asked.

He was trembling slightly, and his response was all but incoherent with only a few words strung together in meaningless phrases. 'No, not here. I can't. Not again. We never have. Who did it? Phyllida knows. I'm sorry, my dearest, but I just can't.' When it was apparent Charlotte was unlikely to make any more sense of what he was saying, and there was nothing obviously wrong physically, she went to the kitchen, made some tea and brought it for him along with a large Scotch.

By the time Charlotte had brought the drinks and John was sitting quietly, her mother had returned and Charlotte then heard the lorry drive away. Phyllida confirmed her husband was now calming down and beckoned Charlotte into the kitchen. 'Don't worry. He'll be all right, but it may take a while. It hasn't happened for a very long time, several years in fact,' Phyllida said, 'and I'm really sorry you have seen him like that, but of course we've never talked about it – and I have never told you.'

'Told me what? Well, please tell me now, Mama. I was terrified seeing him like that.'

'I'm sure you've heard of shell shock.'

'Yes, of course. After the war the men would still hear the sounds of the guns and so on – and it all came back to them and almost drove them mad. But that never happened to Papa did it?'

'No, thank God. But what affected him this morning is not so different. And you weren't to know and nor in fact did Ted – but it was seeing the barbed wire that caused it. You know, of course, that your Uncle Arnold died in the war. Well, we've always spared you the details, but he was in the same trench as Papa one morning when they advanced – you know, went over the top. What the men dreaded almost more than anything were the great tangled rolls of barbed wire which could trap them. And I'm afraid that's what happened to your uncle. He got caught on the wire and was shot and wounded. The medical people couldn't get there to pull him back because of the machine gun fire and he just hung there, screaming for about half an hour, before a huge shell landed and everything was wiped out. They never found any trace of him afterwards. That's why he has no grave, just his name on a memorial in France. But I am afraid Papa saw it all happen; saw his brother killed like that and could do nothing. It's the sight of rolls of barbed wire that brings it back. I should have told you. He can cope with it on the fences – you know, single strands. That doesn't affect him, but seeing them unloading all those rolls this morning was too much. If I'd known you were going ahead with the fencing, I would have asked you to arrange the delivery at a time when Papa was out of the way. I am so sorry, Charlotte. I should have said.

I'll take Papa out later and we can discuss having the fencing done on some other day when he's not here. I told the men and they understood.'

It was ten days after the barbed wire episode and one of those glorious early summer evenings. The Norfolk sky was at its most blue and expansive. There is always so much more sky in East Anglia than anywhere else in England and although she grew up with it and accepted its beauty as a fact, Charlotte never ceased to appreciate the wonder, the splendour, of the county in which she lived; the county she considered her own. Frank had moved out just seven months ago and in many ways life was returning to what she had known as a girl. But while it was good, there could be no pretence it was easy. Despite the cushion of her parents' bank balance – ever-present although certainly not bottomless – and the knowledge that her father was there to help in whatever way he could – generally with advice but almost never now with physical labour – she had to work desperately hard to ensure there was a small surplus at the end of the week or the month. And she had to keep a close eye on the outgoings, the wages for Ted and Tommy. With Frank gone, she had to learn how to manage the accounts, although her mother was a godsend in that regard and it gave her an excuse, if excuse was needed, to go in to the cottage and spend evenings with her adored daughter. But Charlotte was managing, and if nothing else, being busy was helping to push Julia to the back of her mind – on most days.

One evening, a while later, Phyllida had taken John to the cinema in Fenton Bishop to see the new film

Wuthering Heights which had been glowingly reviewed recently. It was part of her attempt to diminish the effects of the recent barbed wire episode. Charlotte was alone, catching up on book work, when farmhand Tommy, who had been working late, knocked on the cottage door before entering.

'Sorry to disturb you, Charlotte,' he said, 'but I think you should come and see your Cuckoo. She's damaged her leg – and I'm feared it may have been my fault. Can you come? I'll show you.' Like any farmer, Charlotte was concerned for all her animals but Cuckoo, the cow, always held a special place in her affections, so she quickly followed Tommy to Old Sawpit field where Cuckoo was standing forlornly in one corner. 'You can see where she's torn it,' said Tommy, pointing to a badly lacerated left front leg.

'Poor old thing. It looks jolly painful,' said Charlotte, 'but what makes you think it was your fault?'

'I took down some of the old barbed wire a couple of weekends ago ready for the new stuff and I reckon I must have left a little coil somewhere although I can't rightly find it. I'm real sorry, Charlotte. But it's beyond what I can do to put it right.'

'These things happen, Tommy,' said Charlotte, having seen far worse in her years at Six Oaks. 'But you're right. I think it needs the vet.'

'There's a new man now you know with old Dick Harris being retired. Chap called Cartwright over in Middle Turney. Claude at the Home Farm says he's very good,' added Tommy.

'I'll track him down,' said Charlotte. 'You get off

home now – your Elsie will be waiting. I'll see you in the morning.'

And with that Charlotte returned to the cottage and telephoned the vet's practice number her father kept pinned to the kitchen notice board.

'Hello, is that Mr Cartwright? This is Charlotte Atmore at Six Oaks Farm in Felsingham. We haven't met, but your predecessor Mr Harris looked after our animals for many years while my parents were running the farm. They have partly retired now and I am more or less in charge. My husband is …' There was then the briefest, the most fleeting, pause of which only she was aware before the word 'away' presented itself; 'and I know it's getting late but I'm afraid I need your help with one of our cows.'

'I see, what's the problem?' The voice at the other end was measured, soft, gentle, reassuring, what Charlotte might have expected from a medical or a veterinary man. She guessed its owner must be in his early forties and had a hint of an accent she could not place. It was certainly not Norfolk.

'She's obviously torn her front leg rather badly. We think it's from barbed wire although I couldn't find any. She didn't like me touching it.'

'I think I'd better have a look.'

'Do you know where we are?'

'Oh, yes, I have been to The Manor which isn't far past your lane. I'll be there as soon as I have finished here.'

It was about an hour later that the sound of a car drawing up in the yard was followed by a knock on the back door and Charlotte opened it to be faced with a tall, rather handsomely weather-beaten man in well-worn but still stylish tweeds and rubber boots. Her immediate impression was to think he had a kindly face.

'William Cartwright,' he said, smiled and held out an impressive hand.

'Charlotte Atmore,' she responded, taking his hand firmly in hers. 'Shake hands as if you mean it,' her father always told her, 'can't stand grabbing a piece of dead cod.'

'Thank you so much for coming over. You are highly recommended by our friends at The Manor. As I explained on the telephone, it's one of our cows. She's called Cuckoo. Daft name really but she came to us five years ago in mid-April on the day when the first…'

'Of course.' William smiled and immediately understood the connection. 'Yes, The Manor, charming people. I've been two or three times to see to a sheep and then the horses. They have some rather fine livery stables there.'

'Yes, you'll have met Hannah van Vliet, the daughter. She's my dearest and oldest friend,' said Charlotte. 'Now, I'll show you the way. Goodness, that's an impressive looking motor.'

'Oh, yes, it's a Humber Pullman. It was my father's and it's a bit of a tank but it does carry a lot.'

It took them just a few minutes to cross the stock yard and enter the field to find Cuckoo still standing close to the water trough, more or less as Tommy had left her. William put down his bag and knelt close to the cow's leg.

'Oh, yes, I can see; it's that left fore-leg. It looks a bit nasty.'

His hands may have been large and strong but they

were also evidently tender as they caressed the animal's injury. And he had a smile that she thought betrayed especial warmth. Without thinking further, she told him so.

He raised his eyes briefly from the cow's hoof. 'Thank you, Mrs Atmore, that is a most generous sentiment,' he said with hint of a smile.

'No, I mean it,' she replied. 'You must have a special warmth in your heart to turn out for an animal – someone else's animal – so late in the evening like this.'

'Oh, it's not for the animals; it's for the fee,' came back the swift response.

'I do not believe that for one moment. And please, it's not Mrs Atmore. It's Charlotte,' she countered and they both smiled, he a little more broadly and she with one of those deeply revealing smiles that seem to originate from somewhere unseen and far, far down.

'Will you bring a bucket of warm water please?' said the vet and Charlotte obliged, returning a new minutes later. William poured in some antiseptic and washed the affected leg carefully, but thoroughly, before delving in his bag for a cloth, wiping it dry and then binding a bandage in place.

'I'll come back in a few days to check and change the dressing,' said William, 'but I'll give you a ring first. Do make sure I have your number.'

'Yes, of course. And thank you, William, if I may call you that. I am so grateful,' replied Charlotte. 'The least I can do is offer you some refreshment, unless you are in a tearing hurry.'

He assured her he was not, and added there was

nothing he would like better. It was now rapidly getting dark as they retraced their steps to the kitchen door, pulled off boots and went inside to a welcome warmth from the constantly radiating kitchen range. Although it was now on the threshold of early summer, the nights were still chill and the unseasonably warm days of early April seemed a long time ago. Around two years in five Felsingham had a May frost and it felt as if tonight could be one of them.

Charlotte was correct in her appreciation that William Cartwright's accent was not East Anglian. What she had failed to identify was its origin in north Derbyshire. He had an eclectic background and was born near Buxton to a family with wide-ranging talents. His mother was a school teacher and his father, like his father before him, an artisan metal worker, blacksmith and farrier from whom William acquired a lifelong affinity for the land and for animals. He treasured the times he had accompanied him on his visits to farms and stables. But his mother came from a long line of medical men and it was a combination of both families' callings, an extremely sharp brain and a commitment to hard work and study that led him to Liverpool University and, five years later, a veterinary degree.

He revealed all this to her – apart from the possession of a sharp brain which she quickly realised – while they sat in the kitchen sipping mugs of freshly made tea and devouring her home-made scones which she had slipped into the oven as they arrived. They were still reassuringly warm and the freshly churned farm butter soaked through the pastry.

'That is so fascinating,' Charlotte said. 'It was also through my father that I realised my future was going to be with the land. My parents – mainly Mama in fact – wanted me to go to university but I never thought I had the brains or the necessary application. And of course because I'm an only child, they were actually thrilled that the farm would stay in the family because there was no-one else who could take it on.'

She offered William another scone which he did not hesitate to accept.

'One of my earliest memories is of learning to milk,' she said. 'My father was so patient – and come to that so was the cow. The first time I tried, I pulled a bit too hard and fell backwards off the milking stool. I often think back to it when I do the milking even now. Do you have any one special memory like that?'

'Not perhaps a single occasion, but a repeated one,' he replied and then told her how over all the years since, he remembered with fondness, affection and privilege the hours he had spent in his father's forge, watching as bare lengths of iron were plunged into the furnace flames to become red, then white hot, before being withdrawn and wrought by a hammer held in a strong and skilful hand into objects of enduring craftsmanship. And he especially recalled working the bellows to force the furnace heat, and how the beech wood handle, which was just within his reach at its highest point, had been worn to half its diameter over untold years of sweated energy.

Charlotte, now relaxed, assured that Cuckoo was in safe care and feeling remarkably at ease in the company of this stranger, then asked a question and long afterwards wondered what could have prompted such boldness. 'Do you have a wife, a family?'

'I'm a widower.'

'I am so sorry, I shouldn't have asked. Impertinent of me.'

'No, that's quite all right; but perhaps I'll tell you more another time because you'll have to excuse me. There's some paperwork I must finish tonight. Thank you, Mrs Atmore – Charlotte, sorry – for your really kind hospitality. Wonderful scones! I have so enjoyed our little talk. And do let me know if Cuckoo does not show signs of improvement before I ring you in a few days time. I'll see myself out.'

Charlotte half rose from her chair as he left and then sat down again and remained quite still for a few minutes, staring at the family photographs on the dresser as the Humber burst into life outside and William drove up the lane. She felt an indefinable inner happiness that she realised had been extraordinarily rare of late; and it was not just because her cow was being expertly treated. 'I did enjoy that. What a lovely man,' was the thought that lingered momentarily in her mind before she caught sight of a small marmalade pot on the windowsill, now full of spring flowers.

Chapter Twenty-one

True to his word, William rang five days later and arranged to call at Six Oaks to check on Cuckoo, although Charlotte did tell him she seemed immeasurably better and was now walking freely. 'I'd still like to come to check,' he said and arrived just over an hour later in the early evening.

For reasons of which she was not seriously conscious at the time, Charlotte changed from her working farm clothes into something a little more appropriate to a summer evening before he arrived. She walked out to meet the big Humber as it parked in the yard. 'Good evening, Charlotte,' said William, the formality of Mrs Atmore having clearly already been consigned to history. 'And if I may be so bold as to say, how delightfully summery you look.'

Charlotte smiled a broad smile that obviated the necessity of a verbal response and they walked together to see Cuckoo.

'Has it been a busy week?' Charlotte asked, wishing to make casual conversation while not appearing too intrusive. 'Oh, you know. Pretty much as usual. Varied,' said William. 'That's why I like a mixed practice, small and large animals. I do have a young colleague though, fresh from university, Amanda, and she will taking on most of the small animal work in future.'

Once Cuckoo had been checked and her dressing changed, William said, 'That should work itself off in time but if not, just pull it away, or get your man to do it. I shan't need to see her again.'

Pleased as she was for her cow, the last remark put something of a damper on Charlotte's demeanour so she decided to grasp the nettle and give voice to a notion that had been running around in her head for the past few days. 'Oh,' she said, 'then I wonder if you might like to come over for a meal, one evening – I mean a proper meal, not just scones! I'm a fair cook and it's lovely to be able to do it for someone else.' William glanced up from the repacking of his bag and, unless it was her imagination, looked Charlotte more directly in the eye than he had done before. 'That is most kind,' he replied. 'I would like it enormously. Being alone all the time, I do weary a little of my own culinary efforts, although they are not all that bad! But I don't think I put enough variety into my cooking. Perhaps it will be a chance to meet your husband. Thank you so much, Charlotte.'

'I'm so sorry,' said Charlotte. 'I should have explained. My husband and I are no longer together. I'm on my own now.'

'Oh, I see. I had no idea,' said William with an intonation in his voice that a perceptive listener might have thought blended surprise, intrigue and pleasure.

Back in the cottage, Charlotte and William compared diaries and the dinner was arranged for the following week. Charlotte purposely selected a day when her parents would be attending an event at the local Conservative Club. She certainly had nothing to hide but did not want to fuel her mother's inquiring mind too soon. It was to prove a week in which Charlotte kept telling herself she was behaving like a lovelorn school girl. It was impossible to keep everything bottled up and although her parents suspected nothing, they commented to each other that she seemed happy, although permanently distracted and with her thoughts many miles distant. 'That girl's got something on her mind,' said John to his wife, 'but whatever it is, it's certainly giving her pleasure, thank the Lord.' And then looking Phyllida straight in the eye, added, 'But don't you dare ask.'

It took only a hour or so after William had left before Charlotte decided exactly what she would serve for the dinner. She would take the opportunity to exorcise that terrible evening with Frank and prepare the same meal of roast venison having first said a small prayer to herself that Barnfather the butcher would have some available. She telephoned his shop the next morning and was reassured that a new delivery would be arriving from the local estate in two days time. 'Please reserve me your best haunch joint,' she said.

The next few days passed for Charlotte all too slowly until William arrived on the appointed evening, and almost to the minute at the time agreed, clutching a bunch of assorted flowers. 'From my garden,' he said, 'not perhaps the best colour blend. I'm afraid I don't have my wife Jane's touch with flowers.' Charlotte thought it slightly odd that he had brought his late wife into the conversation quite so soon but she let it pass unremarked him and thanked him for his kind gesture. William had, as Charlotte's mother would say, scrubbed up well. He appeared every inch the country vet with an almost perfectly fitting suit of lightweight tweed, a touch heavy for a warm evening Charlotte thought, but he does look a real gentleman. And a real gentleman he proved to be, thanking Charlotte effusively at every stage of the evening.

Any slight anxieties either of them had about this first social encounter were soon dissipated and the venison was received with the greatest appreciation 'My word, you certainly can cook,' said William. 'That was absolutely wonderful. I adore wild meats, game and so on.' Charlotte smiled a cathartic smile. 'In fact I haven't eaten venison like that since...' and his voice trailed away before any earlier event or other person could be mentioned by way of comparison. The conversation was relaxed and Charlotte carefully but deliberately brought up the subject of her marriage without going into any sort of detail. 'It just wasn't to be,' she said but felt it necessary to mention her miscarriage because it was common knowledge in the village and William would be bound to hear about it from elsewhere, and certainly if he ever encountered the three witches.

The evening passed only too quickly and both agreed it had been immensely enjoyable. They also agreed they should do it again but William insisted he would be the host, although warning Charlotte that the cuisine could not possibly approach her standard. 'But it will be more than just a sandwich,' he said as they parted. Charlotte did wonder if he would be bold enough to give her the merest hint of a kiss on the cheek but discretion prevailed and William shook her hand positively, but did then add his left hand by way of further emphasis.

Charlotte was truly excited, and desperately wanted to share the pleasure of her experience. She realised she had not seen Hannah for some while so having cleared away after the meal she made a late-night telephone call to The Manor, knowing Hannah had always been something of a night-owl and would be bound to be awake. After the two women had exchanged warm pleasantries and snippets of family news, Hannah asked pointedly, 'What is it you want to tell me, C? You are obviously very happy about something and I can't remember the last time you telephoned me this late. So who is he?'

'Oh, darling, you know me too well! All right, yes, I am happy. Do you remember meeting the new vet, William Cartwright? Well I am now seeing him.'

'You're not! You mean seeing him – *seeing* him?' was the immediate response. 'You and him? Are you? How far has it gone? You haven't, have you? Good for you, C. I only met him twice but he struck me as charming – rather good looking too. Bit older than you. Not married I hope!'

'Not married; widower. He's been here for dinner and I am going to his next week. Probably won't lead anywhere but it's so wonderful to be with a really lovely man. I'll keep you posted…'

The seven days before the return invitation passed all too slowly, during which time Charlotte thought most carefully about what she should wear and what she should take as a gift. She opted for a demure, but beautifully tailored lightweight country jacket and skirt but with a fairly tight fitting plain white blouse beneath that left little scope for speculation about the nature and quality of her curves. As a thank you, she took a copy of a small book – of which she had been left several copies – written by her grandfather containing his hints for successful trout fishing.

Charlotte proudly drove over to Middle Turney in her beloved MG and found William's cottage relatively easily. It was just off the main road, a short way down a quiet lane and externally she thought a trifle forbidding: a brick built semi-detached Edwardian building standing in a small, carefully tended garden. The adjoining cottage had been converted to accommodate the veterinary practice. Having parked the MG alongside, she was about to knock on the green-painted front door when it opened and her host appeared, smiling broadly. 'Do come in, Charlotte,' he said, I've been looking forward so much to this. I do hope it won't disappoint. Oh, my goodness, is that your car? Where was that hiding when I came over?'

'Oh, it lives in the barn. It was part of an indulgent pick-me-up after my marriage broke up,' she said, realising as she did so that she had begun speaking of it in the past tense, almost forgetting she was in fact still married and still had a husband. And unavoidably she recalled the even greater pick-me-up that was Julia Fitzpatrick. But that really was the past, tonight was the present, and just possibly the future.

William's cottage was what Charlotte would call a bachelor residence: neat, tasteful, the walls lined with books. There was classical English literature, including much Thomas Hardy she was pleased to see, together with topographical, country and sporting books to which the little fishing volume was added with bounteous gratitude. But overall, and as her mother was wont to say 'it lacks a woman's touch'. William poured two glasses of sherry and asked if Charlotte would like to see the practice premises next door which he showed her with evident pride. Back in the cottage, they talked for about half an hour, punctuated by William's periodic journeys to the kitchen to check on the progress of the meal. He was true to his word. The cooking was plain but competent – lamb cutlets with a light gravy, a sauce prepared with his garden mint, potatoes and carrots. 'I'm afraid it's too early for my own vegetables and the crab apple jelly is not mine – no crab apples,' he apologised.

The evening passed too quickly for both of them. At least that is what they said to each other when, at an hour before midnight, Charlotte confided she really must return home. 'It's my turn next,' she said, 'if you really would like to come again.' William said he certainly would, so the next available date was quickly arranged for ten days time before he saw her to the door and then, yes, the hoped for kiss – nonetheless an extremely chaste kiss – on one cheek did materialise.

The following week, as war became ever more likely – probably by the end of the year Mr Churchill had said – John Farrow gave his daughter a piece of advice. 'Make the most of what's in the shops, dearest,' he said, 'because mark my words, the government will be introducing rationing before long.'

'I have been,' said Charlotte, 'and in fact I have a guest for dinner on Thursday.'

Mothers being much bolder in these situations than fathers, Phyllida hesitated not one moment before asking 'It's not that charming new vet who was here the other day is it?' 'How do you know about charming vets?' was the response, made through a barely concealed smile.

Charlotte's choice of meal this time was simpler: a joint of Barnfather's smoked ham, slow-cooked and served with her first digging of new potatoes – 'Arran Pilot', always her favourite – a salad and a Cumberland sauce. It did not take long to prepare, so this allowed her to spend time in the bedroom during the Thursday afternoon, or more precisely, gazing into her wardrobe. Emboldened and assertive as the new Charlotte had become, there was nothing demure this time. She chose a dress she had not worn since before her marriage: a floral print in pale red and blue with bare arms, a slight flair at the hem, just below the knee, and most importantly, a provocatively plunging neckline; not as deep as that of her wedding dress – which had since been consigned to a cupboard in the spare room – but plunging nonetheless.

Again William was on time, again he brought flowers – this time an assortment of local wild blooms that he handed over without reference to his late wife. Again there was much animated conversation and laughter for around an hour over two glasses of dry sherry before Charlotte invited him to the table. Unlike the previous occasion, she then asked if he would carve the joint. 'That really is an honour,' he said. 'I always think that being asked to carve a joint in someone else's house is a mark of real friendship and great trust.'

As the meal progressed, Charlotte became fully aware that William, sitting where she had carefully placed him, directly opposite her, was finding it quite impossible to avoid glancing every few minutes at her breasts. Without herself paying any obvious attention to what he was doing, she knew exactly where his eyes were directed, and that he was experiencing the pleasure of her cleavage. That had, of course, been just her intention, and inevitably there came a point when instead of feigning disinterest, she allowed her eyes to catch his at exactly the moment he was raising them from cleavage level. With a bravura she would never have dared to display in the past – and which if the truth be known she had only acquired since the last Boxing Day – Charlotte said, 'Do you like my dress, William? I chose it specially for you.'

'I do, Charlotte, I do,' he said. 'It looks just perfect on you and I have to say, if you will forgive my unseemly boldness, you are looking especially beautiful tonight. I'm afraid to say I do find you an extraordinarily attractive woman.' Charlotte smiled broadly without saying anything because William's remark coincided with the moment she rose from her seat in order to remove the main course plates and make space for her bowls of summer pudding. As she moved to William's side of the table and leaned unashamedly across him – which her mother had told her often enough was shockingly bad manners – she knowingly and deliberately revealed appreciably more of her breasts at a moment when their faces were but three or four inches apart. In one of those episodes that Charlotte had thought only ever occur between film stars in the pictures, they looked at each other in silence as their lips came ever closer, and then met. Charlotte's eyes closed and she opened her mouth just as she had done for Julia. William's lips were strong, manly, but gentle and as they coincided with hers, his tongue began boldly and ambitiously to explore her mouth.

Their heads were full of mixed and scrambled emotions. Charlotte was the first woman William had kissed with sexual purpose in the five years since Jane died. And William was the first person of any gender Charlotte had kissed with sexual purpose since Julia. Unknown to each other, they were both comparing the sensations with their previous experiences. Julia's mouth had tasted of Valpolicella and her lips of an unidentified exotically fragrant lipstick. William's tasted mostly, albeit not unpleasantly, of Charlotte's Cumberland sauce.

William's own abiding sensation though was not one of taste but of Charlotte's perfect teeth. He had always found running his tongue around a woman's teeth to be among the most erotic of sensations – not that he had done it especially often. But while his late wife Jane had two missing, the result of a childhood accident with a hockey stick, Charlotte's teeth were both complete and perfect. In his younger days, William had enjoyed caving in his native Derbyshire and he now smiled inwardly at a comparison between what his tongue told him about Charlotte's mouth and dentition and a small cave he knew in the Peak District which contained the most perfect newly forming little stalactites he had ever seen.

After that unashamedly erotic first contact, Charlotte decided she had pushed her luck as far as necessary for the time being. She had tested the waters and found them receptive, but then allowed the rest of the evening to pass in a most relaxed and enjoyable atmosphere but without further sexual activity; although the parting kiss, when it came, was almost comparable in its seriousness with the mealtime experience.

After this, William became a dinner guest at Six Oaks about once a week during that 1939 summer and on his third visit, Charlotte took him next door to the farmhouse for a pre-dinner drink and introduced him to her parents. John had briefed his wife in advance not to ask any searching, probing questions about personal relationships of any kind. And for once Phyllida obeyed. It was an hour of civilised conversation and pleasantries with Charlotte taking a back seat while watching and listening attentively, and just a touch anxiously. Phyllida asked a few investigative questions regarding the veterinary profession and also about William's background in Derbyshire. She said she had a distant cousin who lived in Bakewell but assumed William did not know him. She was right. As was his wont, John tended to monopolise William on the subject of the European political crisis. The Government had recently announced an air raid test in London and on the day of Charlotte's dinner, John's copy of *The Times* reported that the Nazi party had closed down the last surviving Jewish businesses. 'Make the most of this summer,' John had said, 'war is just around the corner,' and whereas Phyllida had previously been labelling him a prophet of doom, few people could now deny he was correct.

Chapter Twenty-two

On that third, and then the fourth visit, William and Charlotte kissed as passionately and as long – but no more in either measure – at the beginning and end of each evening as they had kissed the first time. But nothing of much greater adventure transpired beyond a little hand holding and looping of arms around waists. That said, Charlotte was aware that on one occasion, as William embraced her, his right hand and her left breast and his left hand and her right buttock did come into uncommonly close proximity – but stayed their exploration at the last moment. It was on the occasion of the fifth dinner that Charlotte – for she was always the motivating party – chose to advance matters and in doing so further and quite significantly complicate her life.

The air was warm, its movement barely discernable, but it gently caressed anyone fortunate enough to be outdoors in the way it is on a fine English late summer evening. The sun had sunk below the distant oaks of Turney Wood some minutes earlier, leaving them as dark cushions silhouetted against a quickly fading golden sky. The moon was already rising above the horizon and long-eared bats were flitting silently to and fro past the open door at Six Oaks Cottage. The meal had this time been simple but as delicious as ever. It was her braised rabbit, shot on the farm herself, accompanied by potatoes and runner beans from the farmhouse garden. It would have been the envy of many a professional cook – certainly in rural Norfolk. They had both experienced a long and busy day but had now wound down unhurriedly in the pleasure of each other's company.

The suggestion came really from nowhere and Charlotte even surprised herself, although she had been thinking about it in the most general terms in advance, but as they cleared the table and embarked on the washing up, and with the romantic accompaniment of a bowl of hot water and soap, without looking up she said, 'William, would you like to stay the night?'

'Good lord, Charlotte. Are you sure? Well, yes, of course, I would love that. But I haven't brought anything.'

Charlotte then surprised herself even more by responding 'I was rather hoping you wouldn't need much. And I can easily find you a towel and a toothbrush.'

The dishes and cutlery then found their way back to the dresser with just a shade more speed than usual. 'Would you like to lock up?' she said. 'I'll use the bathroom first and leave you the towel. I'll see you upstairs. We'll be in the back room if that's all right.' 'Yes, yes, naturally,' William replied. He knew it would be premature for her even to think of inviting him into her own bedroom and what was still, in theory at least, the marital bed. That would be a Rubicon to be crossed perhaps on some future occasion.

Once upstairs, Charlotte undressed, slipped into her

nightdress, climbed into bed and allowed her head to sink into the welcoming embrace of the soft down pillow. She could not help remembering those many, many nights, beginning with the dreadful time after the garden party, when she had been in the back room alone having left Frank in the marital bed and cried herself to sleep on that very same pillow. Tonight promised something so different. But nor could she erase from her mind the last time she had shared a bed with another person – and wondered what Julia was doing now and with whom she might be sleeping.

William undressed separately in the spare room next door and came in a few minutes later with the towel wrapped around him. He presented a shadowy figure in the moonlight as he approached the side of the bed, slipped off the towel, drew back the covers and climbed in beside Charlotte. The sheets had already been warmed slightly by her presence and without speaking they embraced and kissed, long and passionately for several minutes before, almost it seemed at an unseen signal, their hands simultaneously wandered down from each other's shoulders to explore beneath the sheets. 'You are wearing a nightdress,' said William.

'It was a bit chilly when I first got into bed but I'm sure I don't need it now,' Charlotte replied and with some awkward manoeuvrings managed to pull it over her head and toss it aside without disturbing the bed clothes.

Their kissing and gentle caressing continued for several more minutes to the accompaniment of a multitude of unspoken thoughts in each other's heads and the sound of the softest of summer breezes, now blowing through the cottage window – purposefully left just ajar – and encouraging the curtains to flutter slightly.

Two or three times they each altered position slightly to help hands and fingers that needed more scope for their adventures. Charlotte then gently but positively pulled away from William's lips and with one expansive movement threw aside the sheet and blankets that covered them. The light of the almost full moon now streaming between the gently moving curtains illuminated their bodies in a kind of flickering surreal half-light. It was, of course, the first time they had seen each other naked and it struck Charlotte how beautifully curved the horizontal human form, both male and female, really is. She then slid down the bed until her face was level with William's thighs. She gazed up and into his eyes with a look that spoke simply of love and longing and seemed to go on for ages, but in truth lasted only a few seconds, before she closed her eyes, opened her mouth and did what she thought he wanted and would please him.

William gave a sharp intake of breath and lowered his hands so his fingers could run through the mound of Charlotte's glorious auburn hair, now so wildly strewn across her shoulders that it concealed everything below waist level, including the object of her committed attention. He felt her head move slowly back and forth. After what seemed almost an eternity, but would have been barely a minute, the distant clock on St Margaret's church tower was heard to strike one as if indicating that was enough for now, and Charlotte stopped her action, slid back up the bed, gave William a brief kiss and then buried her face against his chest.

For a few moments neither spoke, then he said, 'Thank you, sweetheart. That was just so beautiful.'

'You know I have never done that before so I hope it was all right and what you wanted,' she responded. Then, with her head still pressed so firmly against his chest that she could clearly sense every pulse as his heartbeat gradually slowed again, she whispered, 'I once read somewhere that no self-respecting girl would ever do that on a first date. But this doesn't feel like a first date, does it?' She then thought back to the number of occasions Frank had asked, practically demanded, she perform the same action on him but she had always refused; sometimes with dreadful consequences. 'It has never seemed right before,' she whispered to William though without mentioning Frank's name. 'Was I very forward? It's just that I do love you, William.'

It was the also first time she had put into words something that had been whirling around her head for some while; the first time she had told William she loved him. She immediately wondered if she had made a mistake. Had she been carried away too much in the passion of the moment?

William stirred from the pillow and kissed Charlotte softly several times on each breast then gently eased himself on top of her, answered her question and repeated the commitment. 'Of course you were not forward. And I love you so much, Charlotte.' She then instinctively parted her legs, unavoidably recalling the time she had done the same for Julia. And she also remembered the awful summer party night, the exchange of anger with Frank and especially *that* word, which he had shouted at her so crudely, so aggressively, so wrongly then and on so many other occasions. Now all was different and although there was no need for either Charlotte or William to say anything, she wanted to, she wanted to use the word as she believed it should be used, an old word she did not think she had ever spoken out loud before, to anyone. But it now seemed the most natural thing in the world as she whispered softly, 'Darling, fuck me.'

By the time Charlotte rose in the morning, William was already downstairs and dressed. 'Hello,' he called up, only a touch awkwardly. 'You don't fancy a lie-in, do you? I could bring you breakfast in bed.'

'That's very sweet,' she answered from the top of the stairs, 'but I have lots to do today walking the crops with Ted; not that I don't have a good appetite!' Once downstairs together, they made small talk, punctuated with coy and rather sheepish looks and smiles each time their eyes met. The first however to mention anything of the night's events was William, who tried his best to appear nonchalant as he poured the breakfast tea and stared fixedly into the cup.

'Anything I say, Charlotte, is going to sound trite, but that was just so beautiful. *You* are so beautiful. You said something about a first date but you were right – it didn't feel at all like that. It all seemed just so natural,' – and then trying to be a touch less serious – 'and long may it continue!'

'It will, darling. If it's what we both want, of course it will.' And Charlotte was almost – yes, almost – sure she did mean it. She felt she might be falling into something over which she had no control; and she thought it was making her happy. Then a few minutes later, as she rose to clear away the breakfast table, the morning's post dropped though the letter box. Charlotte bent down to pick it up and among a magazine and three or four buff-coloured official-looking envelopes was a white hand-written one. She thought she recognised the handwriting. She certainly recognised the post mark – it read Thetford. She placed them all on the dresser to be opened as soon as she was alone.

At around the same time, Phyllida drew back the curtains of their bedroom in the main farmhouse to look out at the summer morning sun now streaming into the farmyard and could not fail to see the big Humber still parked where it had been the night before. She called out, 'John, come here a moment.' Her husband, his face still adorned with shaving soap, joined her at the window and they looked at each other. Phyllida smiled. 'I'm really pleased for her,' she said. 'I think William is just what she needs.'

Her husband did not smile and his face clouded over. 'He may be what she needs but I'm not at all happy at that, not at all happy,' John replied with a gesture towards the cottage. 'They're not married to each other, they're not even engaged. And Charlotte is still married to Frank so she's committing adultery for a start – and under my roof. In fact they barely know each other. Call me old-fashioned – I've no doubt you will – but for a couple to be sleeping together like that, under these circumstances, just doesn't feel at all right. I expect he'll be moving in with her next. And he's a lot older than her – in fact I'm surprised at him doing it. Not what I would have expected of William. I reckoned him a decent, honourable man. Yes, I know you'll tell me she's old enough to know her own mind, the modern emancipated woman and all that – and please don't quote the suffragette heritage to me, I had enough of that from your mother – but I just wonder if we, if I as her father, have gone wrong somewhere. We have tried, Phyllida, to bring her up in a Christian home with Christian virtues, to know right from wrong. She fell in with that awful, awful Frank and we supported her, gave her the fairy-tale village wedding she had always wanted, but look how that's all ended up. Perhaps it was the school, St Jude's. Were we wrong to send her there? Perhaps she picked up too many liberal attitudes when we couldn't keep an eye on things. And you may say it's no-one else's business but I can tell you straight. The village certainly won't like it. Felsingham's a pretty conservative community by and large. And bear in mind that she needs to be very careful if there is to be any future consideration of a divorce. I think she needs a fatherly talking to, that young woman.'

'No, she doesn't,' came back his wife's instant retort. 'You will leave well alone, John. She's been through hell with Frank and you're not going to deny her a new found happiness – whatever Felsingham may think or say. And yes, she is a modern emancipated woman, I'm proud to say. And no, we weren't wrong to send her to St Jude's. It's a fine school – modern in many of its attitudes I grant you – but we live in a modern world. It's the twentieth century, John, not the nineteenth and just because we live in a rather isolated rural village doesn't mean we have to be fossilised in the past. She's a wonderful daughter. We all make mistakes. It's just that Charlotte made rather a big one but I'll say it again, John, she's now happy so don't you spoil it.'

'There are ways of finding happiness without getting into bed,' said her husband and then muttered something barely audible but that could be translated roughly as 'Just you wait and see,' and with that he returned to his shaving bowl.

Back in the cottage, William gave Charlotte an unusually exploratory kiss before he departed for the surgery in Middle Turney and his day's work. He was hardly out of door before Charlotte picked up the letter from Thetford, tore it open, poured herself another cup from the dregs left in the tea-pot and sat down to read. It was written in the same neat, beautiful script as the address on the envelope. It was a kind of hermaphrodite hand she thought – not obviously male or female. She read:

Sandyheath Estate,
Near Thetford

25th of July 1939

Dearest Darlingest Charlotte

Oh! woe is me for not writing long ago to say what a total and absolute and perfect joy it was to see you when you drove here in that magnificent shining red chariot. It bore you like a fairy tale heroine into my humdrum little world. I should have begged a ride in it – and shall do so on the next occasion when I share the ecstasy of your company. You simply must indulge me, my angelic girl.

I am still loving – loving – my work here but remain in an absolute flutter over whether I shall return to my bonnie homeland at some stage. My contract here is for two years and my employer is such a lovely, lovely man with *the* most glamorous wife south Norfolk has ever seen. Excepting you my angel although I still cannot think of you as a wife which I suppose you no longer really are. Which is my point. When you were here I – in far too fraternal a manner it now seems – dissuaded you from clutching at straws but remarkable to relate things have changed and there is now a straw here willing and remarkably anxious to be clutched!!!

My life-enriching experiment has ground to a halt somewhere between the sands of Thetford Chase and the heather-clad hills of Perthshire. Larry the musician is no more. Well, that is to be perfectly accurate, he is no more with me. He left to play his fiddle with another beau!!! He now tells me it was always doomed to failure because he is committed to queerdom on a full time basis. He called me an amateur queer, nasty thing he turned out to be.

So Charlotte my sweetest angel, I am here for you if the offer is still of interest. In fact I could be there for you if it was what you wanted.

Do write, my lovely country girl.

As always

Your ever loving Tor

Charlotte smiled. The letter was just so typically Torquil. He has never known what he wanted and on his own admission, never really known what he is, she thought. Her mind wandered back to that time they slept together when he was so kind and gentle. She would for ever be grateful to him for that. But she, and life in general, had moved on. She had already told herself she could no longer be comfortable in any sort of intimacy with him. She no longer wanted him inside her. And of course, there was now William who had been in that very same place just a few hours ago. While the thoughts were still in her mind and she was still basking in the warm glow of the previous night's events, she decided the breakfast pots could wait, immediately took up her pen and paper, sat down at the table and wrote:

Six Oaks Farm Cottage
Felsingham St Margaret

Wednesday Twenty-seventh of July 1939

My Darling Tor

It was such a delight to receive your letter. I really hadn't expected anything after my visit – which I enjoyed enormously. It was so good to catch up on news and see you in a really fulfilling job – and working in such glorious surroundings. For the family's sake, I do hope you stay here down south although your homeland is also so beautiful that I wouldn't be surprised if it lured you back.

But you mention straws!! Much has happened in my life in the short time since I saw you – when, to be fair Tor, you were hardly enthusiastic about any possibility of us having a future together!! You remember I said that eligible men didn't seem to be beating a path to my door – well one has!! Yes, I have met someone and we have become rather fond of each other…

At that point Charlotte paused in her writing and briefly laid down her pen. For the second time, Torquil's letter had caused her to smile, on this occasion at her own euphemism. 'Become rather fond of each other' was probably a bit of an understatement for having just had sexual intercourse with someone for the first time.

She wrote again:

> ...I don't know if he and I have a future. It's early days – and of course there is the not so small matter of the woman about whom I spoke to you in the greatest confidence. My mind has not yet resolved that conundrum I am afraid. Oh, dear! Such confusion!
>
> And now you, my dearest Tor. I am unsure if I am sorry or pleased for you that your relationship with Larry has come to an end. You know of course that you shocked me but I thought that if it felt right for you then, well, it was right for you. Oh, dear again, I'm not expressing myself very well am I? We are <u>both</u> in a conundrum now aren't we and I do hope that when we see each other again we can talk about these things properly.
>
> This is not a very good letter Tor but I did want to reply straight away so you were not left hanging in any sort of state of uncertainty.
>
> I shall love you always Tor but it can't be in the way I think you think you would like.
>
> As ever, with all my fondest love
>
> Charlotte

Chapter Twenty-three

Over the coming months, the Humber was seen in the Six Oaks farm-yard overnight two or three times a week and John Farrow was right – William was obviously becoming a part of the furniture. John and Phyllida always exchanged lengthy pleasantries with him whenever their paths crossed and from time to time he was invited into the main house for lunch, tea or dinner. Despite all his misgivings about the intimacy of William's relationship with his daughter, John enjoyed their conversations on topics that ranged from farm animals and their maladies to the reasons for the fall in the price of barley and inevitably, and most lengthily, to the terrifying state of European politics. Certainly no-one could fail to observe a change in the demeanour of Charlotte. Phyllida constantly told John she had again become the happy, seemingly carefree daughter they had known for all her previous twenty-five years – and that he should be happy for her.

But also over the coming weeks, and as William spent more nights in her company and in her bed – and on the fourth or fifth time it was back in the marital bedroom – Charlotte could not dispel an ever-present anguish. She believed she was falling in love, and in both thought and reality that did give her immeasurable joy. Nonetheless, the more she believed she was in love, the more she realised she had never been in love before, even though she had slept with three other men and was still married to one of them. And the anguish that was ever-present was the secret named Julia. The more she became close to William, and the more she thought there might be a future with him, the more she became afraid; afraid that when she told him what she had done with another woman, he would find it either unacceptable or unforgivable and she would be alone again.

Charlotte's anguish was the more because it was her secret and almost hers alone. Of course Torquil knew – and for his own very personal reasons, it was not a confidence he was likely to break. Nonetheless, Julia had been true to her promise and made no attempt to contact her and for Charlotte that posed more questions than it answered. She was, however, now convinced she had to disclose it to Hannah, and also thought the time was long overdue for her to do as she had promised and keep her 'posted' on developments with William.

Two days later therefore, Charlotte invited Hannah and Emily to Six Oaks for a simple supper. Not wishing to be too probing and inquisitive, despite Charlotte being her oldest friend, Hannah held back for as long as she could before half-way through her fresh fruit pudding, she could hold off no longer. She blurted out, 'Go on, C. Tell all. The suspense is killing us. Your vet. How is he? What have you been up to?'

'Well,' said Charlotte slowly and feigning coyness,

'it's certainly progressed. We are now sleeping together, have been for a few weeks.'

Hannah's and Emily's faces lit up. 'That's terrific, really terrific,' said Emily to which Hannah added, 'I am so, so pleased for you, C.'

'Yes,' said Charlotte, 'but I do now need to tell you something else that means it isn't all straightforward.'

'You told us he was a widower,' said Emily.

'He is,' said Charlotte. 'He's a free agent so I don't think there's a problem there *except* that I'm sure he's still in love with his dead wife. But I suppose that's understandable. I'm not of course – not a free agent I mean – remember I'm still married to Frank though I confess I often forget it myself. No, it's something quite different, darling, and it's an enormous secret – a *really enormous* secret – I've been keeping to myself for over six months; something I haven't dare tell you. I'm going to confide in you now though. I *beg* you to be understanding.'

'Of course.'

'Right then, here goes. Do you remember all that time ago when you first told me about Emily and that you were in love – and confirmed what I really knew, that you prefer women to men – that you are lesbian?'

'Yes, of course I remember. You said you were pleased and you have always been really sweet to both Emily and me.'

'Well, do you also remember that I told you a girl at school once made explicit overtures to me?'

'Yes, vaguely, I think so.'

'Now, do you remember your parents' hunt party on

Boxing Day and you said later you saw me talking to a dark-haired woman?'

'Yes,' said Hannah; it was a very long drawn out yes.

'Well, they were one and the same. She is called Julia Fitzgerald and – wait for it darling – the night after the party, I slept with her.'

'Wow! Wow! Charlotte,' were all the words Hannah could muster. Emily said, 'Good God!'

'I suppose it's a frightful shock for you both – I can tell you it was a frightful shock for me too! But think about it. I did say the idea of two women making love certainly didn't repel me and that I could see the appeal. Then of course you kissed me – and I was honest and I said I enjoyed it.'

'So I'm to blame?' asked Hannah, but with a broad smile that implied she was not being entirely serious.

'I do think you may have played a part, but,' continued Charlotte, 'the really important thing is not just that I had an amazing night with Julia, it's that I've not been able to get her out of my mind since. I'm not sure you will be able to appreciate this but I can't even get Julia out of my mind when I'm in bed with William. I keep comparing the way he and I make love with the way Julia and I made love and – this will sound completely crazy – although I have only spent one night with a woman and rather a lot of nights with men – some of which I grant you were horrible although William is wonderful – I don't know which feels right, which I prefer, which is the more natural for me.'

'Yes, and you know you really aren't comparing like with like. One night with a woman, loads of nights with men – sorry, don't take that the wrong way! But come on, C! Two big questions then,' said Hannah. 'First, we assume you haven't told William.'

'Correct, and it really gnaws at me because I know I shall have to do it sometime, and I'm absolutely terrified it will turn him away and I would lose him.'

'That in itself means you don't want to lose him, C. But it might also mean you want to have your cake and eat it. There are rather a lot of people who genuinely can't choose and don't want to choose. But they need jolly understanding partners.'

'And the longer it goes on without you saying, the harder it will become,' said Emily.

'I know, Emily, I know.'

Hannah intervened. 'But the second big question, C, is what happened to – what was her name – Julia? Where is she? Have you been in touch with her again?'

'No, that's just it. When we parted, she said she thought that given the chance she could fall in love in me, but she would never pursue me, and she hasn't. She said she would be there if I wanted her. But I really don't know if I do.'

'Oh, God, C! What a pickle you've landed yourself in.'

'I know and it bears out you telling me I am one of life's innocents. The irony is that after I slept with Julia, it make me feel terrific, not just sexually, but because I felt I was reclaiming my independence after Frank – being my own woman again. Then along came William and sort of pulled the independence rug from under me. But I must continue to be honest with you both. I had actually been hoping to find a new man. I even went to see Torquil but realised that wouldn't go anywhere. So, yet again, you may well say, Charlotte Farrow, it's your own fault. I have deliberately encouraged William. And now of course he will be horribly hurt if I call a halt.'

'You really don't help yourself do you, C?' said Hannah. 'Think about it. There's too much he doesn't know. He doesn't know about Julia. I assume he doesn't know about the way Frank trapped you and let's be honest may have raped you. He doesn't know about the way Frank treated you – in every way. There is far too much for it to be the basis for a continuing relationship. As my dearest, oldest friend, I'm telling you, you have some really, really serious decisions to make if you aren't to end up hurting yourself as well as anyone else. You've been through too much, C, to do it all again. We shall always be here for you but ultimately, you have to decide which way and with whom you want your life to go.'

Chapter Twenty-four

John's comment at the bedroom window about divorce when they were looking at the Humber, and first realised William was staying overnight, kept preying on Phyllida's mind over the next few weeks. Seeing his car at the farm more and more often prompted a number of thoughts. She personally felt increasingly at ease with the situation and was sure it was all beneficial to Charlotte's long-term well-being. She also realised that, by contrast, her husband was increasingly ill at ease with the matter and she had periodically to rein in his more reactionary suggestions. But she also felt that if things went on as they seemed to be doing, she was sure Charlotte would want, would be bound, at some stage to think of a divorce so she would be free to plan her own life again and make a fresh start; and this was true even if it was not to be with William. She believed her daughter had to be rid of Frank formally, properly, legally. So she came to a decision, and early in August emboldened herself tactfully to raise the subject with Charlotte the next time they had tea together. Charlotte thought her mother was being far too premature. 'For heaven's sake, Mama,' she said, 'William and I have barely begun sharing a bed, let alone our lives.' The last thing she needed was to have her mother take over the steering wheel of her future. She had enough conundrums still to resolve before she felt anywhere near to committing to a life with William and argued that she would much rather wait a while. But the more Phyllida insisted that being forewarned is being forearmed, the harder she found it to resist without revealing all the quandaries in her mind. Eventually, therefore, she capitulated but on the clear understanding that this was simply a fact-finding exercise and that William's name *must* be kept out of any conversation, and her father *must* not under any circumstances be told.

'Agreed,' said Phyllida, having for the first time in some while won an argument with her daughter. 'I'll arrange to see the family solicitor. He certainly knows his law although he is a bit odd. I've only met him a few times but he's your father's lawyer and I think his father and even his grandfather used the same firm. But I agree, Papa must know nothing of this or he may jump to unwarranted conclusions and then goodness knows what he might do.'

So a week later, and on the pretext of a shopping excursion, Charlotte took her mother in the MG to Norwich and they made their way to Fenman's Walk, a tiny alley not far from the cathedral. The heavy old door of number twelve had once been a cheerful blue but the paint was faded and peeling and it was now more the colour of large and painful bruise. Phyllida rang the bell and they were admitted by a slender, middle-aged gaunt-looking woman wearing precariously balanced and ridiculously outsized spectacles. As they shook hands, Charlotte noticed immediately that her long bony fingers had neglected and broken nails and showed no trace of ever having borne any kind of ring. 'Mrs Farrow and Mrs Atmore? Mr Palfreyman is expecting you,' the woman said and showed them into an inner office, dark, almost windowless and smelling of old paper and something else they could not exactly define. It might have been cat urine.

The office's occupant stood up to greet them as they entered. Her mother had been right about him being odd, and Charlotte thought Simeon Palfreyman of Palfreyman, Wheedle and Crockett, could have walked straight from the pages of her literary hero, Thomas Hardy. She could imagine him setting up business in Casterbridge. Phyllida had said that Wheedle and Crockett had long since departed, and Charlotte felt Palfreyman could not be far behind them. He wore a dark suit that had obviously been inherited from someone appreciably smaller. He was balding, clean shaven, of above average height and well below average width with a complexion like that of a well worn window leather, and a slightly elongated neck that bore a large Adam's apple but little flesh. Charlotte looked at it and remembered she had seen a lizard in the garden recently. Phyllida, ever creating her wondrous dishes in the farmhouse kitchen, said the expression that came to mind when first she met him was scrag end.

The women sat down in two highly polished Windsor chairs facing Mr Palfreyman's desk. They were not close, but near enough to detect the merest hint of halitosis. It was Phyllida who began. 'I mentioned to you on the telephone, Mr Palfreyman, that Charlotte is now living separately from her husband Frank, and in time, certainly not yet, but in time, she *may* need to consider the matter of divorce.' Charlotte nodded. Phyllida continued 'I feel – and please understand Mr Palfreyman that for the moment we have not discussed this with my husband, with Charlotte's father – I feel we need to know the legal position. I think I have read that the law has changed recently; and that it may now be more helpful to Charlotte.'

'Divorce, yes, always a most difficult and sensitive matter.' Mr Palfreyman's voice was thin and decidedly irritating, with an unusual accent neither woman could place, but so quiet it was not always easy to discern what he was saying; an unfortunate trait in a lawyer. 'You are quite right,' he said, 'in that two years ago, Mr Alan Herbert MP introduced what passed into law as the Matrimonial Causes Act. It does make several changes to the existing law, most notably that adultery is not now the only ground for a divorce. Other factors the Court may take into account are desertion for two years, incurable insanity and cruelty.' Mr Palfreyman then looked up with a peculiar expression on his face. 'Also a proclivity to incest or sodomy.' Phyllida visibly winced. Charlotte thought of Torquil. Mr Palfreyman continued. 'There was additionally a suggestion that the period to elapse before a divorce can be granted should be increased to five years.' Charlotte's face fell. 'But it has in fact been settled on three.'

'Now, I need some details.' Mr Palfreyman opened a large and impressive leather-bound book, turned the pages until he was about half-way through and reached the next blank sheet, slowly unscrewed the cap from his fountain pen and began to write. 'First the date,' he said. Even viewed upside down from about a yard away, Charlotte could see his script was tiny, meticulous, almost copper-plate, and formed with an extremely slow movement of his bony fingers. It seemed to take an eternity for him to complete each entry because although he generally made his notes with just a few words, he prolonged matters by using a blotting pad after almost every pen stroke.

'Now the names,' he said. 'You are Charlotte Atmore née Farrow. Is that right?'

'Yes,' replied Charlotte. 'I am Charlotte Emmeline.'

Mr Palfreyman raised his eyebrows and wrote it in his book. 'I see. And your husband is Frank?'

'Yes. That's what he's known as. He's actually Francis Drake Atmore.'

Mr Palfreyman again raised his eyebrows.

'Unfulfilled parental ambition,' said Phyllida.

Mr Palfreyman wrote again.

'You were married on?'

'The twenty-fifth of June last year, 1938.'

'And Mr Atmore left the marital home on?'

'In early November. I threw him out.'

'Very soon. I see. We now need to know more about this.'

'Well to be honest, I did give him another chance but he decided to go.'

'Ah, that might be significant. It could be argued that he deserted you. But in any event, we need to know why you threw him out, as you put it.'

'It was simple,' continued Charlotte. 'He admitted he had been sleeping with someone else.'

'I see. Do we know the identify of this lady. I assume it was a lady?'

'She's no lady. She's a slut. But yes. At least I know where she works and what she does. I don't actually know her name.'

'So Mr Atmore admits adultery?'

'Yes, at least he does to me. I don't know about publicly.'

Mr Palfreyman wrote "Admits adultery", then added, "Privately".

'And since then you have been living alone at the marital home?'

'Yes, but…'

Phyllida intervened. 'Charlotte has a gentleman friend.'

'I see. And are you cohabiting with this gentleman?'

Mr Palfreyman's extremely quiet and peculiar voice did not help and Charlotte thought he said "copulating". She looked quizzically at her mother, mouthing the word silently.

Phyllida clarified. 'Cohabiting, dearest.'

'Oh, you mean does he live with me? No.'

'Does he stay with you?'

'Sometimes.'

'Have you been partaking of sexual intercourse with this gentleman?'

This time, Charlotte certainly knew what he meant, though she had never thought of what she and William did as 'partaking'; but she answered, 'Yes, from time to time.'

'So not constantly?'

Charlotte wondered how anyone could partake of sexual intercourse constantly. Even for her, a young woman running a busy farm and doing it once a night about three times a week was quite enough. She was certain Mr Palfreyman himself couldn't manage anything like that, and she gave a shudder at the thought of him trying.

'No, sometimes.'

'May we know the name of the gentleman?'

Phyllida opened her mouth to speak but Charlotte said it first.

'Not at the moment, I am afraid.'

'Is he married?'

'He's a widower.'

'I see. But you therefore also admit adultery?'

Charlotte thought back to that meeting with Holy Humphrey when he told her she had fornicated but not committed adultery. Now she had obviously done both, and in her mind she was also aware that she had since committed unnatural acts; not that she intended revealing that to Mr Palfreyman.

'Yes, I suppose I do.'

Mr Palfreyman carried on writing, "Also admits adultery."

'Now we must move on to other considerations. Is there anything apart from him sleeping with another person that prompted you to throw him out, and that might under the new Act be considered grounds for a divorce? Mr Atmore, I deduce, is not incurably insane?'

'Not I am sure in the medical sense.'

'He may however quite possibly be deemed to have deserted you. What then about cruelty?'

Charlotte looked seriously at her mother.

'Yes, he has certainly been cruel,' said Phyllida, 'but what exactly constitutes cruelty in a legal sense? He has behaved extremely badly and rudely and horribly to Charlotte many, many times and often brought her to tears. In fact I know she cried almost every night in the later stages.'

'I see,' said Mr Palfreyman once more. 'That might well do and I am saddened to hear it. But has there perhaps been any physical violence?'

'No,' said Phyllida.

'Yes,' said Charlotte.

'What!' said Phyllida.

'I have never told you, Mama. It was only once and I screamed at him first.'

Phyllida looked horrified. 'What on earth prompted it? Did he hurt you badly?'

'It was a few months ago. Remember when I had that swelling on the side of my face that I covered with my hair? I said I had walked into the farm cart but in fact Frank had been horrible about a special meal of venison I cooked for him and I really shouted at him.'

Mr Palfreyman looked fascinated.

'Yes, Mama, I shouted at him and he hit me – with his fist.'

'Good God,' said Phyllida, 'this goes from bad to worse.'

Mr Palfreyman made a few more notes. "Fist. Special venison."

'I have made a note,' he said.

'Charlotte, you and I need to have a serious conversation later,' said Phyllida.

Mr Palfreyman interrupted the domestic exchange. 'Is there anything else?' he enquired. 'We do not I trust need to think about incest or sodomy.'

'Good lord, no,' said Charlotte, again knowing she had thought of little else but sodomy since the meeting with her dear friend Torquil.

'No, certainly not Mr Palfreyman,' replied Phyllida, with a stare that said "how dare you?"

Did Mr Palfreyman look disappointed or was it just Charlotte's imagination?

Phyllida again intervened. 'What about the magazines, Charlotte?'

'Magazines?' Mr Palfreyman suddenly appeared interested again.

'Oh, yes, I found some magazines that were hidden under Frank's desk,' said Charlotte.

'What sort of magazines?'

'Disgusting, sex magazines.'

Mr Palfreyman looked even more interested and he wrote down, slowly and meticulously, "Magazines, sex, disgusting."

'They were German.'

He wrote "German".

'Do you speak German?'

'No.'

'Then how do you know they were disgusting?'

'Because they were full of photographs. They were illustrated magazines.'

'I see. They were what you might call porn-o-graphic?' Mr Palfreyman spelled out the syllables of the word with especial savour.

'Yes, I suppose so.'

He wrote "Pornographic".

'May I ask what they depicted, these photographs?'

'Well, I am sure you can imagine, Mr Palfreyman.'

'I am not sure I can.'

'Well I couldn't bear to look too closely but they were full of pictures of naked men and women doing strange things.'

"Strange things, naked," wrote Mr Palfreyman.

Charlotte thought for one awful moment he was going to ask 'How strange?' but he simply said, 'Do these magazines still exist?'

'Yes, at least two of them do. I told Frank I would throw them all away but he took them back and said he would keep them to himself in future and they went with his other things when he left. I'm sure he will not have got rid of them because he seemed to treasure them, but just in case they might be needed I did keep two and put them in an envelope. They are at the bottom of my wardrobe. Frank didn't notice any were missing.'

'Excellent,' said Mr Palfreyman.

And Charlotte was fairly sure she saw him briefly lick his lips. She was probably right because as Mr Palfreyman looked back at his notes and doubly underlined "Disgusting" and "Strange things", he thought that should this matter come to a full legal action, he would personally need to examine the evidence most closely.

'That's good,' he said. 'I think then Mrs Farrow and

Mrs Atmore, we have covered everything and all options. I do hope I have been helpful.'

'Yes, you have been abundantly clear,' said Charlotte. 'But I suppose that is it. As long as Frank doesn't reappear and go mad, there is no more hitting, he doesn't get the chance to be cruel again, there are no more filthy German magazines and provided we both steer clear of sodomy and incest, I need to wait three years after he admitted his adultery unless we can prove two years worth of desertion and even then we may have a fight on our hands if he chooses to contest it?'

'Yes, I am afraid so. You have summarised rather admirably but do please get in touch with me if you have any further questions or if anything else unexpected and untoward occurs. That is unless of course, Heaven forefend, Mr Atmore should pass on…'

By this time, Mr Palfreyman had become something of a serious irritation and Charlotte who could never resist a tease, interrupted. 'Pass on what – some frightful communicable disease? Not syphilis for goodness sake?'

'No, I mean go to a far, far better place.'

Charlotte now had Mr Palfreyman hooked like a trout and continued to play him. 'Where? He's in Middle Turney as far as I know.'

'No, Mrs Atmore. I mean if he should die.'

'Oh, I see. That's not at all likely unless he falls off his beloved Vincent. He's as fit as a fiddle.'

'Who is Vincent and what might Mr Atmore be doing on top of him?' asked Mr Palfreyman, reopening his book apparently in the hope of identifying an additional co-respondent.

'It's a motor bike,' said Charlotte.

And with that the two smiled at each other, Mr Palfreyman's mouth revealing all too clearly why they had sensed halitosis, and the meeting came to a natural end. The women thanked Mr Palfreyman and were shown to the door by the female assistant. 'That was a bit of a cruel game,' said Phyllida smiling as they walked back to the car.

'Oh, I think he knew exactly what I was doing,' said Charlotte. 'I suspect he's not as stupid as he seems.' But then, much more seriously and on the way home, she and her mother talked through what had happened but what most concerned Phyllida was the physical violence.

'You really shocked me there,' she said. 'Promise me he only ever did it once and that you will not let your father know.' Charlotte promised. 'At least it can't happen again because Frank will never come back. And of course William is there now to look after you,' Phyllida continued. 'We do like William very much, you know, Papa and me, and I know it's early days but I do hope you may find happiness with him.' She then immediately wondered if, despite her husband's views about cohabitation, she might have given Charlotte a misleading – and rather too encouraging – impression.

'Thank you, Mama, thank you,' replied Charlotte and gave her mother's hand a firm squeeze.

Chapter Twenty-five

For a change, the news did not come first from the three witches in the Post Office but through a small item in the *Eastern Daily Press.* John Farrow was relaxing in the pleasure of the Six Oaks garden in the closing hours of a gloriously warm early August day. Although the first flush of the roses had long passed, a few buds of a second peach-orange blooming were swelling on Phyllida's cherished 'Lady Hillingdon' against the house wall. Nearby, the small bed of dahlias she grew to cut for the house was rich in a tapestry of yellows, reds and golds that caught the slowly setting sun. Opposite them the mauves, blues and reds of a planting of asters stood out against the shadowed green of an old yew hedge. It was approaching the end of several hours of Felsingham rural bliss. If this is what semi-retirement meant, John was quickly becoming an enthusiast.

Charlotte was out with William. He had taken her for a meal to a newly refurbished pub in Middle Turney in the hope of helping to wipe from her mind the memory of that awful fall in the barn, a year and a month ago.

The local paper echoed the world news in the day's copy of *The Times* which was headlined "Europe in

Suspense" and reported Mr Churchill saying 'If Herr Hitler does not make war, there will be no war.' 'Come on Winston,' John had muttered, 'we all know the mad monster will do it. You know it's just unavoidable.'

Then, since he had read them all as assiduously as usual in the morning, John was about to fold the papers away and it was only as an afterthought that he browsed the inside pages of the *Eastern Daily Press* where a headline of slightly lesser moment caught his eye: "Felsingham Man on Burglary Charges." He read on with increasing dismay: "Harry Kett, 29, unemployed, of Felsingham St Margaret appeared today at Fenton Bishop Petty Sessions charged with four counts of burglary carried out between 31 July and 6 August. He was also charged with assault on a police officer and resisting arrest. He was remanded in custody to appear at Norfolk Quarter Sessions. As he was led from the dock, Kett shouted at the presiding magistrate, 'It's Frank Atmore who should be here. It was all his idea.' "

After an expression of audible disgust, John showed the paper to his wife who said simply, 'Well, that's ruined another lovely summer evening; best man indeed! I never liked him from day one!' John then telephoned Sir Arthur van Vliet to see if through his own magisterial position, he could throw any more light on it, and above all how his wretched son-in-law's name came to be involved. Sir Arthur rang back just before midnight by which time Phyllida had gone to bed.

'John,' he said, 'I've made some discreet enquiries from a police inspector I know. He was off-duty but he's an old friend and said he would help as far as he was able and we had a long chat. But this is strictly off the record John – for his sake and mine. The background is that Kett is charged with doing four burglaries in local villages a week ago. It was a hot evening and it seems there were plenty of windows left open. He is alleged to have got away with rather a lot of cash, a few items of silverware and some jewellery. The assault charge relates to his arrest. He was seen coming out of the last of the houses by a passing PC and Kett went for him. I can see no alternative to him pleading guilty and being sent down. Now to the worst bit. It seems that Kett's basis for claiming Frank put him up to it is that Frank was getting seriously in debt. Kett says Frank had lost several clients and his income had dropped significantly.'

'That's true, we knew from what Charlotte has told us,' said John. 'Frank kept saying he was going to see a possible new client but they never seem to have materialised. And I know he's lost two or three of his existing ones for some reason.'

'Yes, but – wait for it John,' added Arthur, 'This may explain both things. Kett also said Frank was short of money because he was paying prostitutes.'

'What! Oh, my God,' said John. 'Not that! Can this possibly get any worse? My poor, poor Charlotte.' And then he added, using his favourite son-in-law specific sobriquet, 'The man is an absolute, total shit.'

'I know my dear friend, I know. But there is an interesting slant to this, John, that may give you a lead if you want to find out more – though because of my position as a JP I *must* stay out of it. It seems Kett claims Frank was seeing these women at that house we went to in Yaxton. Kett said Frank was always talking in particular about one woman he met there, a red-head calling herself Flame. My understanding – again unofficially – is that they are not going to charge Frank and may not even call him as a witness. He may have been – probably was – in debt and he may have been – probably was – seeing prostitutes but that's not illegal and doesn't prove he was involved with Kett in the robberies. It may look highly likely – at least to us – but it's circumstantial. There's no evidence to link him. It's just one man's word against another. If it came to court, Kett would claim it and Frank would deny it – even under oath. I've seen this in my own court many times.'

John Farrow lay awake that night and thought long and carefully about this revelation. The first decision was that Charlotte would have to be told about the newspaper item before anyone else showed it to her. And second, neither she nor Phyllida could under any circumstances be allowed to know about the prostitutes. He eventually fell asleep having decided on a course of action.

At breakfast the following morning, he showed Charlotte the newspaper and hardly before she had time to express her shock, shame and disgust, John Farrow told his daughter a lie. He said he had made enquiries and it transpired that Harry Kett was simply being characteristically cowardly and unwilling to face up to his responsibilities. It was typical of the man that he should try to apportion the blame to someone else. Both Charlotte and Phyllida appeared to accept this explanation.

Following his conversation with Sir Arthur, John was

deeply thankful to learn that Frank would probably not appear in court, although his name just might again be reported in the press. But John himself needed to know the truth, for Charlotte's sake as well as his own. He therefore took the decision to return to twenty-seven Harbour Road, Yaxton and see what he might discover. This time he would visit it alone without telling anyone – he would make an excuse for his time away. But he also reminded himself of Phyllida's wise counsel that first time not to go in all guns blazing. If he was to find the women involved and extract the truth from them, it would have to be handled most sensitively.

Three days later, John Farrow arrived back at number twenty-seven to see little had changed since his visit with Sir Arthur seven or eight months earlier. Harbour Road was nonetheless quiet now and the air bore a fresh hint of sea and salt rather than hanging heavy with November's chimney smoke. He knocked on the door, its paint faded further and peeling even more under the influence of another summer's sun. The door was opened, wide this time, but by the same woman with the same vomit-coloured hair, although she was now fully clothed. 'Yes?' she asked. Then after a pause, 'You look a bit familiar. You been here before ain't you? If you want a girl though there's none working till tonight but I can put you on to a pretty little piece at number fifteen who specialises in older gents – *lovely* figure she's got.' 'Puts my sagging pair to shame,' she added, grasping her breasts with both hands as if judging their weight. 'She'll do you very nicely.'

John tried not to look too closely and attempted,

not very successfully, to be indifferent to the anatomical comparison now being demonstrated before him. But at least he thought, unlike Arthur, he was not being called a pervert. 'No, nothing like that. I'm not looking for a girl – at least not how you mean. And let me say I'm not a client and I'm not the police, this is not official but I am making enquiries as a girl's father.'

'Oh, your daughter's on the game, is she? We do get fathers coming looking sometimes. What's her name?'

'No, it's not like that either. It's complicated, but basically I am trying to find a girl who calls herself Flame. I think she has red hair. I wonder if you know her because I need to find out if she had a client called Frank. I can promise that if you help me you will not get into any sort of trouble. You have my word as a gentleman.'

'Frank your son is he? Been a naughty boy? Well, yes, there was a girl called Flame – her real name's Meg – but she's not been here for some while. And we did have a bloke called Frank – came here a lot, one of the real regulars, a big spender I'm told he was though I never saw him personally cos he used to come in the daytime and I work the evenings. And the daytime maid we got now is new so you need to see Flame herself really. Frank doesn't come often now she's gone. Tell you what though, I wouldn't normally do this cos I'm on my own, my bloke being at sea, but you've got a kind face – you remind me of my own Dad, rest his soul – so if you come in I'll see if I've got an address.' And then as John stepped into the house she added, 'But I'm really trusting you, so keep your hands to yourself – what's more I might say than my Uncle Kenny used to do when I was a young girl. Soon as he came in the house he was all over me and trying to get me to open my legs for him, the dirty old sod.'

John winced, then entered, gratified that in addition to not being considered a pervert, nor was he deemed a dirty old sod, and recalled that the last time he had been inside a brothel was in France in 1915 – a low grade *maison tolerée* for officers only – but reassured himself with the thought that 'these things happen in war'.

He found himself in the main ground floor room of the terraced house. The woman called it the reception area. The overall colour of the décor was akin to yellow and not so far removed from that of her hair. Clearly the house must once have had far grander owners because beneath its film of nicotine deposit the wallpaper appeared in the past to have borne a William Morris pattern. The furniture – a table and four chairs – was basic in design, although not Quaker basic, just junk shop basic. The wall bore a small mirror – too high for people of normal dimension John thought – a picture of King George V and Queen Mary torn from a magazine and held up by only three drawing pins and a current year's calendar advertising Castrol motor oil.

'Here, have a look at this while I find the address,' the woman said and took down the well-thumbed calendar and handed it to John. The only writing on it was of entries every two or three days along the lines of Florrie/Jeff, Flame/Harry, Angel/black guy, Angel/Jeff, Clarie/didn't give his name, Florrie/big foreign bloke, Princess/Joe; together with a few Flame/Frank items in the earlier months of the year. It was clearly a record of the brothel keeper's bookings. What John now had to do was confirm the Frank of the calendar was indeed his son-in-law – and awful to contemplate – if he had been visiting Flame during the previous year when he was still together with Charlotte.

'You don't have last year's calendar, I suppose?'

'No, went with the Christmas stuff. Meg might remember though. Ah, here it is in my notebook. Thought I had it somewhere.' And she read out the address of an apartment she said was on the outskirts of Fenton Bishop.

John thanked her profusely and asked how he should explain knowing Meg's address. 'Say Susie sent you cos you had a kind face. Best leave it at that.'

Then John gratefully turned his back on twenty-seven Harbour Road – for the last time he hoped – and drove the few miles to Fenton Bishop, a town he knew well although the apartment was in an area he had never visited and was unaware even existed.

The address was of a large house, probably about thirty years old John thought, and like the Yaxton property, one that had seen far better days. Alongside the green door was a row of bell push buttons. The top one, labelled number six, was his objective and he pressed it once for several seconds. A bell sounded far away and John realised he was hearing it through a third floor window open above him. A female voice called down although no human form was visible when he looked up to ascertain its origin.

'Yes, what do you want?'

John directed his voice upwards. 'Good morning, Miss. Are you by any chance Flame – or is it Meg?'

'I might be but I ain't working.'

'I know that. Susie kindly gave me your address but you need have no concerns. I am not anyone official but I am enquiring about a man called Frank. Susie said you might be able to help.'

'All right, Susie's a good girl and I trust her. I'll come down.'

After around three minutes, the door opened and the woman it revealed was quite clearly Flame. John had seldom seen such strikingly coloured hair. She was about Charlotte's age he thought but of much slighter build, wearing a loose floral dress and looked decidedly under-nourished.

'Like I said, I trust Susie,' she said, 'but I'm not working now.' She patted her stomach. 'I got caught so I gave it up. A few of the girls would though – there are blokes who'll pay a lot extra to have it with a woman who's pregnant. If that's what you want I can't help you.'

John winced for the second time that morning. 'Good Lord! No, nothing like that, nothing at all. I know you aren't working, Meg. That's not why I'm here. It's about Frank.'

'Oh, yes? I've known two or three different Franks. Which one is it?'

John took a photograph of Frank from his pocket, a piece cut from the picture of the official wedding group in front of St Margaret's church porch – the picture Phyllida had removed from the mantlepiece and hidden in a cupboard as soon as Frank departed. John had sliced off everyone else although it had been difficult to exclude all parts of Charlotte's dress.

'Blimey! Yes, I thought it'd be that Frank but I didn't know he was married. Most of the older men are but he'd only be what – less than thirty? That's a bit unusual. Something wrong with his wife I suppose. What's he to you – you his dad?'

'No, I'm pleased to say, and forgive me but I'd rather not explain what my connection is though it's really important for me to know as much as you can remember – if anything that is.'

'Oh, yes, of course I remember Frank – never knew his other name naturally – he was one of my regulars, always wanted me, not the other girls. It was the red hair he liked. Said it turned him on something special. He paid me lot – I mean a lot – because he didn't just want a quickie. He'd stay for hours some days, even bring his lunch would you believe. I had to keep my wits about me though because he'd often ask for extras, odd things.'

John was utterly aghast, not at the idea of odd things, but at Frank having brought the packed lunch which would have been the one his beloved Charlotte prepared for him every day; brought it to a brothel to share with his favourite prostitute! He then hesitated – not after all being either a pervert or a dirty old sod – before asking 'And did you oblige – with the extras?'

'Sometimes, sometimes not. I have my limits, my pride if you like, what I call my red lines. He'd bring magazines, German I think they were, and ask me to do what was in the pictures. Some of it was really weird stuff, things I definitely wasn't about. One time he even wanted to bring his mates to watch but I wasn't having that.'

'I know this may be difficult but do you have any idea how many times you saw Frank?'

'Oh, yes, more than that, I can tell you the actual dates. I'm very careful about these things. Comes of being a bookie's daughter I suppose. I keep a diary with dates and clients in it. I saw him for about six months I reckon all told last year and a bit this before I gave it up. Wait a minute and I'll find it.'

And with that she closed the door.

After a short while, Meg returned with a small pocket diary for 1938.

'Would you mind if I noted the dates when you saw him?'

'Be my guest. Doesn't matter much now I've given up. Here, I like you and it's nice to have someone to talk to. Come in and I'll make you a cuppa. What did you say your name was?'

'Thank you. I didn't, but it's John.'

'Funny, most of them say that…'

Meg led John into a dark, tiled inner hallway, then into a room off to the right which appeared to be a communal kitchen. She filled a kettle and boiled it to make tea for both of them on an extremely basic gas stove that might have fetched a shilling or two from a collector of curios. She then handed John a steaming 1936 Coronation souvenir mug with coloured drips down the sides that revealed it had recently been used for something quite different. He put it to one side as he went carefully through the diary, copying down all the 'Frank' dates into his own notebook. It took him about five minutes, which meant he only had time to take three sips of Meg's pale sepia-tinted brew through which, with little difficulty, he could see clearly the bottom of the mug from which a smiling image of King Edward VIII looked back at him. The diary dates confirmed that Frank's regular visits had indeed been during the months of his marriage. An appalling thought then occurred to John. He glanced down at Meg's bump.

'That wasn't by any chance…?'

'No, not Frank, couldn't be. Not *your* Frank at any rate. The dates were wrong. I've tied it down to five or six possibles but that's all I can do about it really.'

As John departed, leaving the remains of the pale sepia tea, he thanked Meg – who called out, 'Come again some time, John' – and wished her well, then sat in his car and before leaving Fenton Bishop, contemplated his newly found information. So Frank had not just been unfaithful with the woman at the hotel. He had never been remotely faithful at any time and had been spending his earnings – the family's earnings – on prostitutes throughout his marriage. What should he, could he, do with this information? Simply telling Phyllida and Charlotte was never an option. They had been hurt enough by Frank already and Charlotte would just go to pieces. Could the knowledge be useful in the event – the inevitable event – of divorce proceedings? Almost certainly not, because he had given his word to the women that what they said would be treated in confidence and, no matter how they earned their living, he was not a man to break it.

John then drove away even more disgusted with his son-in-law, and disgusted and informed in equal measure, at a side of Norfolk life of which he had been wholly unaware. And as he drove back to Six Oaks, he unavoidably had women on his mind, although his daughter Charlotte was but one of them. Above all, he could not help brooding on the personable red-headed Meg, pregnant by an unknown client – one of five or six possibles for heaven's sake – carrying a child conceived in lust, living alone in a miserable apartment with who knew what future ahead of her. Who was paying the rent he wondered – and in return for what? It did not bear thinking about. In his mind he could only draw one parallel between Meg and his beloved Charlotte. She too – in his perception at least – had been made pregnant in loveless lust but there the resemblance ended. She had a loving family and an assured future – perhaps it seemed with a man called William. But who and where are Meg's parents? Does her bookie father know what she does? Where *is* her father? Dead? Alive? Try as he might, John simply could not translate himself into that father's position. He tried to picture his Charlotte working as a prostitute. It did not endure imagining. He suddenly wanted to turn around, go back to that house and talk again to Meg, he wanted to become *her* father, talk to her as *his* daughter, to learn more and above all – to do something.

Then, there was Susie. Where was the father with the kindly face when she was being abused by her uncle? She said he was now dead. Under what appalling circumstances did she come to be where she was: a part-time brothel keeper entering sordid bookings on a calendar and satisfying strangers' lusts to make ends meet? What could he do about her?

Then he told himself common sense had to prevail. 'You simply cannot correct the wrongs, injustices and unfairness of the world,' he said silently in his head. And he knew there were far, far greater injustices being played out on the European political stage that in time, a time very soon, others would have to try and correct.

Then, as Six Oaks drew nearer, another woman came into his thoughts. Where is *she* now? Did she survive? Is she alive? Did she ever find love? Is she married? Does she have children? For the first time in countless years, he remembered her name. She was called Eloise, a lovely, musical, poetical name – at least Eloise was what she said – that tiny, dark-haired girl, all of eighteen, who had satisfied his own lust one hot afternoon in a shabby apartment in Amiens twenty-four years ago to the constant accompaniment of distant artillery, an apartment with broken shutters and tattered lace curtains that did not meet in the middle and gave no privacy from the queue of his fellow subalterns waiting their turn outside. He still remembered the massive, ancient iron bedstead with its peeling black paint that creaked loudly under every bodily thrust and the dirty threadbare rug with a sleeping dog – a brown and white mongrel creature it was – lying there quite oblivious to all the carnal moans that emanated from just a few feet away. He thought on, and down the years came the memory of the briefest of conversations and the faintest smell of something like sulphur drifting on the wind through the open window. Could she really have been as old as eighteen? That was his idea not hers. She did seem much younger. 'Quel âge as tu?' he had asked her in his finest Rugby School

French – he had after all won the Third Form language prize. 'Quel âge voulez-vous que j'aie?' she had replied, and dix-huit was the first French number that came into his head – simply because it was his dark-haired sister Angela's age. So had he, Lt John Farrow, been an abuser too, was he no better in his own way than Susie's Uncle Kenny?

John thought on again. When the new war comes, how many more squalid make-shift brothels will there be in France for officers like him – and separately – and even more squalid – for other ranks? How many more little girls called Eloise will rent their young bodies to foreign soldiers for a handful of centimes? How many more young men from decent English families will abuse and fornicate with girls who look just like their own sisters?

'No, John, gather yourself together,' he told himself. 'You must not feel guilty. You cannot change things. You cannot, must not, think that way. The world is too big. England, Norfolk, Yaxton-next-the Sea and Fenton Bishop are all too big. Look to your own family, John. Look to Charlotte. Charity simply has to begin at home.'

By then he had arrived back at the yard and he parked the Riley in its accustomed place next to Charlotte's MG in the shelter of one end of the great barn. Lunch was already on the table – a simple but delicious Phyllida farmhouse lunch with bowls of garden-grown salads, a freshly baked Fred Wellbeloved loaf and thick slices of ham from a Six Oaks pig, killed and cured by Barnfather the butcher. This pig, for anyone who remembered, had been called Jennifer.

'Was is it a good morning, dear?' asked Phyllida of

John's visit to a farmer friend in Middle Turney to talk about the supplier of a new variety of turnip seed.

'Yes, very good,' replied her husband. 'Very good indeed. I learned far more than I could ever have imagined.'

'I would never have guessed two men could talk for so long about turnips,' said Phyllida.

After the meal had been cleared away, John sat down for a quiet contemplation of his morning's experience. Charlotte was sitting opposite, a notebook on her lap jotting down some ideas for a talk she was to give to the local women farmers group. John looked across at his daughter. She was suddenly not quite as tall, much slimmer, paler of complexion, slightly and faintly freckled – and with startling red hair. 'What are you staring at, Papa?' she asked. 'Are you all right? You look as if you are miles away.'

'Yes,' he said, 'I'm sorry. I was, my dearest, just miles away.'

Chapter Twenty-six

By the end of August, and in common with the rest of the nation, the residents of Six Oaks had been following events with increasingly alarm and foreboding as the world news unfolded, terribly. For day after day, John Farrow had been reading the reports in his copy of *The Times* that spoke of war with a resigned inevitability. Then on 1 September came word that Germany had invaded Poland and the outlook appeared even more certain and even more bleak. On 3 September, the wireless at Six Oaks was kept switched on to the BBC Home Service from early morning. Ted and Tommy came in from the farm periodically to see if anything new had transpired. However, they were out in the fields when at ten o'clock the announcer Alvar Lidell reported that the Government had given Germany until eleven that morning to withdraw its troops from Poland. The family was still listening at eleven-fifteen when a further announcement was made: 'You will now hear a statement by the Prime Minister.' It was to be the fateful broadcast reporting that Hitler had failed to withdraw his troops from Poland by the required deadline and as Chamberlain's thin voice continued '… consequently this country is at war with Germany.'

The room fell silent as the family listened to the entire five minutes of the Prime Minister's broadcast without anyone speaking. John Farrow was sitting at the dining table, gazing with an impassioned stare at a family photograph on the wall. Phyllida sitting opposite him stared at the floor. William placed his arm around Charlotte as they both sat motionless side by side on the settee. As Chamberlain finished with the words 'I am certain that the right will prevail', the room remained silent for about five more seconds then John spoke first. 'What was it he said, something about being unable to have done anything more or anything different? I don't think so, Prime Minister. If Winston had been running the show, Hitler would have backed down already.'

Foreseeing a long and pointless monologue, William intervened. 'I think that's highly arguable, John, but anyway, we are where we are. We have been fairly sure for some while it was going to happen, and at least we now have confirmation. But Chamberlain was right in that those of us in jobs that are – what was his phrase – essential to the maintenance of the life of the people, are certainly going to have to pull our weight. Are we fortunate in being engaged in what they are calling reserved occupations? To be honest, I would rather be in uniform and doing my bit that way.'

'Don't think being in uniform is anything like a soft option,' said John.

It was on the day Britain declared war, 3 September, that the government strengthened their existing limited powers and formally introduced conscription. 'Very sensible – very sensible indeed,' said John, recalling that in *his* war, it had not been done until spring 1916 'By which time unfortunate buggers like me had been shot to pieces and sent home. Lloyd George was forced into it, you know,' he said. It appeared no-one else in the room did know. 'But it lost him four cabinet ministers.' The family nodded in resigned agreement.

About a week later, there was knock on the cottage door. Charlotte was on her own clearing away the breakfast and opened it to find her view darkened by the imposing figure of Nigel Futter. 'It's been ages, Nigel. How are you? Do come in and tell me all your news,' she said.

Once seated by the range and having had a cup of coffee thrust into his large and appreciative hand, Nigel said, 'I've actually come, Charlotte, to say good-bye – well to be honest I sincerely hope it's just au revoir! I've answered the nation's call as they say and signed up.'

'Nigel, the village will be so proud of you and we shall all pray for your safety, wherever you end up. What exactly will you be doing?'

'Well *exactly* Charlotte, I don't know, but you've heard all young men are required to register for military service. They have to, legally. So I rolled up at the recruiting office in Norwich with a whole load of other blokes. It's a joint office for army, navy and air force and I really fancied the air force – becoming a pilot you know. They gave me a medical – pretty personal I might say! – and they said I was in great shape but too big to fit in a cockpit, which was really disappointing. I could be ground crew but I thought I wanted to see some action so I opted for the army and will be having six weeks training and then joining an infantry regiment. After that, who knows? But you will be really interested to hear this – I think!'

'Go on,' said Charlotte, intrigued but with a slight suspicion of what might be coming next.

'One of my mates was there two days later when – guess what – Frank was ahead of him in the queue. Frank didn't know him, but Jim, my mate, recognised his name from what I've said about him. Now this sounds really pathetic, and I'm sorry to say it but I know you two aren't together now. It appears Frank turned up in glasses and said he had bad eye-sight! Well, the medical orderly soon scotched that, even though Frank then tried to claim he couldn't read the eye test! Can you believe it?

'In fact, yes, I can – but do go on.'

'Well, this is the even more interesting bit. Frank then said he was in a reserved occupation so wouldn't have to enlist. At first, he said he was a farmer and when they quizzed him, he claimed to be part owner of Six Oaks – by virtue of his marriage.'

'No! Cheeky beggar! Funnily enough, when we were first married, he tried to persuade Papa to let him be a part-owner which would actually have made him a farmer but – well you know my father! – that was pretty smartly stamped on. But go on.'

'Yes, well they put an end to that by saying they would telephone the registered owner of the farm – your father I assume – and check the legal paperwork.'

'Frank then said that technically, legally, perhaps he wasn't actually a farmer after all. He said perhaps, strictly, he was more of a fisherman, and mentioned the family smoke-house. So they then asked him when he last caught a fish and he realised that was going nowhere either. The recruiting guy then asked him what he really was, and Frank said he was a farm accountant, but he said he knew that like farmers and fisherman, accountants were exempt too so he wouldn't have to enlist. The man then checked Frank's age – you know he's twenty-nine – and completely floored him by saying accountancy only becomes a reserved occupation when you reach thirty!'

'No! Is that right? So my devious husband tried to get out of serving his country but they finally got him. Well, well, well. I have absolutely no sympathy. So what's he going to do?'

'It seems that once he realised he'd lost the argument, he opted for the navy – given his family background. But I gather the recruiting people took a pretty dim view of it all and were none too gentle with parts of his anatomy when he had the medical!'

'Serves him right. You know me well enough, Nigel, to realise Frank and I have no future and I am already moving on in my life. Of course, I hope and pray he doesn't come to any harm, but I am really grateful for you telling me. But more importantly, I hope you will keep in touch with the village whenever you can. I'm sure there will be several other young Felsingham men serving too and we shall be praying for all of you.'

Through the late autumn of 1939 and on into early 1940, life at Six Oaks and more widely in Felsingham seemed not too different from any other year. At the end of

September, all householders had been required to register the names of everyone living in their home and from this information, identity cards and ration books were issued with their invaluable coupons that had to be exchanged to obtain essential goods. That said, rural residents like those at Six Oaks with a ready supply of butter, eggs, milk and other products fared significantly better than city dwellers and there was much dissent at the perceived unfairness of the system. 'Town folk should realise what hardships we farming families have to go through to keep them fed,' said John Farrow. 'A few perks are no more than we deserve.' Phyllida and Charlotte made jams and jellies from damsons and Charlotte's rose hip syrup soon became the admiration of the village. Then, from the garden and farm itself came peaches for jam, tomatoes for juice, potatoes, onions and of course precious eggs from the Six Oaks chickens which they increased to create a small flock. They also took in five more pigs, two more cows and six more sheep while much of the ornamental garden was turned over to productive output, leaving only a small area for cut flowers.

The first Christmas of the war was a little more low key than usual but the Ely cousins managed to come by virtue of several changes of bus on the way. William was on veterinary call through the holiday period but became a greatly appreciative family guest on Christmas Day itself. The Boxing Day hunt was no more but one member of the household – had anyone been paying close attention – was noticeably quiet and reflective in the evening. The relatively modest military activity led in the New Year to the newspapers calling it the phoney war.

The three witches were naturally the conduit by which news about Felsingham men serving in the armed forces was disseminated locally. In the late autumn, not long after his enlistment, word had arrived that big Nigel was with his regiment in the British Expeditionary Force that had been sent to help defend France from what seemed the inevitable German invasion. By mid-May however, it became evident that the force was not faring well and was being driven back towards the French coast. Then, for eight days, the nation collectively held its breath as the British Forces were evacuated from Dunkirk. Never normally one to advocate retreat, John Farrow – extremely vocally on this occasion – led the tributes at Six Oaks to Vice-Admiral Ramsay who planned the whole extraordinary undertaking. And John nodded with approval when in early June, after more than three hundred thousand men had had been evacuated, Winston Churchill said this must not be considered a victory. 'Wars are not won by evacuations,' the Prime Minister had cautioned.

As the days and weeks passed, however, no word was heard of Nigel, and his family and friends were left in a state of limbo. He had not returned to England with the evacuation, but whether he was dead or had been captured, no-one could discover. Charlotte said Lily would be heartbroken and she made a point of seeing her several times to offer such support as she could to the young girl. The only consolation, if consolation it was, being that none of Nigel's fellow soldiers had seen him fall. But the war was no longer in the slightest bit phoney and was coming ever closer to home.

Chapter Twenty-seven

Since Frank's departure, his name had hardly been mentioned at Six Oaks although Charlotte occasionally saw or read or heard something to remind her she was still married, and had a husband serving his country somewhere. But by dint of now living in Middle Turney, he fell outside the scope of the three witches' information sources. From time to time, Phyllida and John privately discussed the possibility of a separation and the likelihood of divorce, but never mentioned anything to Charlotte – nor indeed to William – and John's advice was, 'Let's see. We are at war and no-one has any idea what's going to happen. Think of poor Nigel.' Phyllida moreover was at great pains to ensure her husband did not know that she and Charlotte had already sounded out Palfreyman, the lawyer.

Following the Dunkirk evacuation and through the early weeks of that 1940 summer, a German invasion appeared all but inevitable although the daily appearance of RAF planes in the sky above South Norfolk gave Felsingham's residents some grounds for hope. Once again, as the newspapers carried daily reports of the ebbing and flowing of the air war, the nation was in a state of collective dread. On Six Oaks Farm nonetheless, life had to go on, and the importance of producing the heaviest crops possible to help the country's food supply was more important than ever. An official came one day to discuss the need for volunteer land girls to assist on the farm but the conclusion was that they would be better employed elsewhere. Tommy and Ted, with Charlotte's support, could cope, although if as seemed likely, the outlying meadow fields had to go under the plough, some help might well be needed then.

Then one day in March, when Charlotte was in Wellbeloved's shop, in walked a couple she had not seen, apart from those few dinner occasions, since her wedding day. Her parents-in-law Vic and Clarice Atmore had always kept themselves to themselves and had made no contact with her – or she with them – for almost two years.

They exchanged pleasantries and common courtesies, but it was Clarice Atmore who made the conversation. 'I'm sure you have heard nothing of Frank, Charlotte – and nor I expect do you wish to. For our part, we are sorry how things turned out and the loss of your baby – *our* grandchild – must have been terrible. Frank was not the husband you were entitled to and we should have made contact and written sooner. But there we are. We have seen you now and I know Vic shares my views.' The silent Vic nodded.

Charlotte was more than slightly taken aback. 'I must confess, Clarice, that is most unexpected but nonetheless welcome. Thank you. You and I have never fallen out and I appreciate what you have said.'

'You probably won't be interested,' added Clarice 'but you may wish to know that Frank is now serving on a corvette, HMS *Sunrise*, but of course we don't know where he is. He writes from to time but I must be honest and say he never mentions or asks after you.'

'No, well…I suppose he wouldn't, but I pray he is safe,' was all Charlotte could say, aware that her prayers would carry little weight with the Atmores who were committed atheists. She then paid for her few purchases from Fred Wellbeloved, bemoaned the absence of bananas and oranges – no chance of any more home-made marmalade, she thought – handed over the requisite number of ration coupons, asked after Fred's son and grandchildren, learned that the little boy with polio was holding his own and being really brave, gave a polite valediction to her parents-in-law and returned home.

William was in the cottage having just completed a farm visit and decided he would have a snack with Charlotte before going back to his surgery in the afternoon. Charlotte was pleased to see he was starting to lay the table for lunch when she arrived. She knew she would not, should not, mention her morning encounter but was then to receive her second shock of the day; one even more significant. She had her back to him and was putting her purchases in the pantry when he said, 'By the way, Charlotte. There's something I've been meaning to ask you for quite a while. Do tell me about Julia.'

Charlotte experienced one of those moments when people learn what it means to feel something strange in the pit of their stomach. A multitude of thoughts went through her head in as many seconds, of which the most important were: Why is he asking? What does he know? Who on earth has told him? How can he have found out? She knew she needed longer to work out her response and concoct a suitable explanation so again without turning her head, she stalled. 'Give me a moment. I must use the bathroom,' she said and went upstairs at speed, giving every impression of someone experiencing a major urinary emergency.

Once behind the safety of a locked door, she quickly decided this would have to be the moment she had dreaded for so long. She would come clean, tell William that Julia was an old school friend she met again by chance and that she had been seduced by a younger women while under the influence of strong Italian wine. She was unsure what she may have done with her, but it all meant nothing and she has never seen her again. She hoped none of that was wholly untrue. She was prepared to be evasive for the sake of any relationship with William she might have, or hope to have. But she must not tell him a bare-faced lie. She thought again through her account and told herself it would have to do, although she knew all too well it could end their beautifully blossoming relationship. And she realised it all sounded horribly like a re-run of her first encounter with Frank – the details of which she reminded herself, William was still unaware. Nonetheless, it could make her appear stupid and gullible. But there was no way out, so she finally flushed the lavatory, took an extremely deep breath and walked slowly downstairs to the parlour where William was just finishing the table.

'Now William – Julia. You were asking about her,' she

said, but then before she could launch into her poorly rehearsed speech, William interrupted.

'Yes,' he said, 'it's that marmalade pot with the name Julia on it. I just wondered if you knew who she was and thought if that's the only flower vase you have, I might bring you a prettier one from home.'

Charlotte mentally erased her speech and breathed a heavy and almost audible sigh of relief. 'Thank you, that's kind, but it's fine,' she said. 'I like the shape and size - it's just right for little flowers. Mama asked me the same thing recently.' And then she told a white lie. 'It came from a produce sale and Julia must have been the person who made it.'

That evening, all the residents of Six Oaks were together for dinner and the conversation inevitably turned to events on the European stage. Everyone now opened their newspapers and listened to the wireless daily with constant anxiety and dread. It was just under a month since Prime Minister Neville Chamberlain had endured a particularly rough passage in the House of Commons and failed to form a coalition. German forces had then turned their attention to France, Belgium and the Netherlands, Chamberlain had resigned, King George VI sent for Winston Churchill and he had addressed the House for his first historic speech as Prime Minister at the head of a National Coalition government.

John Farrow was so elated at the development that observers suggested he was actually taking personal credit for the appointment. 'The right man at last,' he said. 'I've been saying so for months but no-one would bloody well listen.' William had endured a particularly spirited exchange with him on the subject the previous day. 'Churchill doesn't have a magic wand you know, John,' he said. 'You know what he said. Blood, toil and all the rest of it. And don't underestimate how difficult it's going to be for the farming community. Mark my words, imports will shrink because the U-boats will be hitting the convoys and we are going to have to feed ourselves as a country like never before. Every acre of land will need to be more productive. There will have to be more intensive cropping, recreational land and grass will need to be ploughed up…'

Serious as it all was, Charlotte and William had to smile at her father's implacable, dogged enthusiasm for the new Prime Minister and his apparently blind faith in his ability to see the nation through it all. The conversation could have gone on all day but William had a clinic to attend although they all knew the debate would undoubtedly continue at regular intervals.

'I was right though with what I said yesterday about the farming,' he told Charlotte. 'It is going to be very difficult for us. And I do wonder about young – and not so young couples – planning their future. Is this a time to be bringing new life into the world when every day so much is being taken from it?'

William was touching on a most sensitive subject – for her and many others among her contemporaries. She had in fact discussed this very matter with Hannah who had expressed relief that the dilemma over bringing children into the world was something she would be spared. But Charlotte was interested to note that William had spoken of farming as 'us'. He really did now seem to identify himself with her and Six Oaks. Did that make things easer or harder for her?

After a few minutes of silence, William spoke again. 'You've never said, Charlotte, and probably I should not be asking. But do you ever think about Frank, wonder what he is doing? You are still married to him, awful man though he may have been to you.'

Charlotte answered, truthfully, 'From time to time, William.'

Chapter Twenty-eight

In July of the previous year, The Manor had been visited by officials to assess its suitability for housing evacuee children from London, should it become necessary, but in the event, nothing more transpired and it seemed it was not required. Many of the children who had been evacuated were returned to their homes, but things were now different. Invasion had become a real possibility and a new evacuation was planned. In the middle of June, Sir Arthur van Vliet received a formal letter from the government requiring him, to his astonishment, to provide accommodation not just for a few children but for an entire primary school.

He read the letter aloud to his wife: 'As a result of the survey made by officers of your property The Manor, Felsingham St Margaret, Norfolk in September 1939,' it said, and continued, 'you are required under the Government's wartime provisions and the new Government Evacuation Scheme for the safety of the residents of London to provide accommodation without limit of time for thirty pupils, male and female, aged between six and nine years of age, together with three female members of the teaching staff. You must provide two classrooms and the children must be accommodated in at least two dormitories with the sexes separated, together with washing and lavatory facilities, also separated. The female teachers should ideally have individual bedrooms although it is recognised this may not be feasible. There must be provision for the preparation of meals – which may be taken to the classrooms for consumption – and also an isolation room to accommodate any children who develop contagious diseases including but not limited to chicken pox. You will be recompensed at the Government's agreed rate which will be recovered from the children's families viz. 10/6 per week for one child and 8/6 for more than one.'

Sir Arthur drew breath before reading on: 'Additionally, you are required to provide classroom accommodation for approximately a further thirty children who will be billeted in other properties nearby and transported to The Manor from Monday to Friday by bus, for which you will not have to pay. It will be helpful if you can indicate at the earliest opportunity by letter or telephone call to the above address the names and addresses of any local owners who have appropriate facilities. Any shortfall will result in a further visit by our assessment officers whose decisions will be binding on property owners.

'You will be notified of the date of the children's arrival which will probably be at Norwich Railway Station where buses will be provided. Members of the Women's Voluntary Service (WVS) staff will be present to assist in the process.

'May I thank you on behalf of His Majesty's

Government for your assistance at this difficult time in the nation's history and remind you that the above requirement is compulsory and that any person(s) refusing to accommodate evacuee children without good reason may be fined.'

'Well, that's pretty clear,' said Matilda. 'We simply must do our duty, Arthur. I'll talk to Mrs Fiddler today about how we can allocate the rooms. I shall think about menus straight away. I expect the government will supply extra food and of course the desks and chairs and I'll talk to Phyllida for ideas of other people who will be able to provide. I'm sure they'll take some at Six Oaks. I find it all so very exciting, Arthur, and it will be so, so good to have little children about the place – after all, Hannah is never going to provide us with any! We can pretend they are grandchildren.'

'I'm not sure I ever intended having thirty or sixty grandchildren,' said Arthur, 'though of course we must play our part. But this is not a game, Matilda. We are helping the nation of course but we shall be taking on a huge responsibility for these little ones, who will be parted from their families. I have no doubt it will all be very traumatic for them, although they may at first think it's just a holiday – which I suspect most of them have never actually had.'

Matilda was on the telephone to Phyllida almost before her husband had put down the letter on his desk. 'Oh, Phyllida, dearest, such, such an exciting thing has happened – we are going to have our own school with lots and lots of lovely little children who will have such, such fun with us. Can you believe that? They can play in the grounds and make model boats to sail on the lake and Hannah can teach them to ride. And you must have some too my dear…'

'Just slow down a bit, Matilda, dear. What on earth are you talking about?'

Lady van Vliet began to try and explain more clearly but it was evident there was burgeoning confusion at both ends of the telephone line so reluctantly she handed over to her husband. Arthur explained in precise detail what he had received and outlined the need for the village to accommodate thirty more children to which Phyllida immediately responded. 'Oh, I am sure we could take two. We have two small bedrooms in the main house. It's the least we can offer. I'll talk to John.'

Further details soon arrived, but any expectation Matilda van Vliet had that they would be hosting a rather exclusive private educational establishment for the sons and daughters of gentlefolk, was soon dispelled. They were told they were to accommodate two classes of the Wharf Lane Church of England Primary School from Limehouse, in the East End of London.

And so it was that on the afternoon of Friday 7 June 1940, a large reception party gathered in front of the imposing Victorian façade of Norwich railway station, awaiting the arrival of a train from King's Cross. There were dozens of Eastern Counties buses parked outside with a crowd of several hundred local residents, because the Felsingham school evacuation was replicated several times across the small towns and villages of Norfolk. Awaiting The Manor group were the van Vliets and their staff with Hannah and Emily, the Farrows with Tommy and Ted from the farm, Charlotte and William, a motley assemblage of other householders from Felsingham and nearby hamlets who had also agreed to take children, Holy Humphrey to give the whole exercise his blessing, a large number of WVS volunteers, PC Edwards, a local newspaper reporter and a photographer together with assorted civic dignitaries, some bearing large chains of office, who hung around looking important but with no clear idea what they were expected to do – which was actually nothing.

The train eventually drew in just before four o'clock and the extremely elderly black LNER engine came laboriously to a halt, its brakes complaining loudly, while its chimney and far more than the regulation number of boiler exhausts filled the station with steam and clouds of faintly sulphurous dirty grey smoke containing tiny black particles that stung the eyes. The railway company, required at extremely short notice to provide hundreds of extra trains, had been obliged to delve into the limits of its ancient motive power and rolling stock resources. The once varnished and uniformly smart teak brown but now uniformly sooty carriages, disappeared temporarily in the haze and then, as the smoke dispersed, a vast multitude of doors opened almost in unison to disgorge a mass of infant humanity. Like a miniature football crowd streaming towards the turnstiles after a match, hundreds of children were marshalled by their teachers in the direction of the station exit.

As they slowly emerged from the smoke and walked towards the reception party, there appeared to be approximately equal numbers of boys and girls. They were all wearing outdoor coats despite the warm afternoon, and each carried a little suitcase. Every child also had a small bag containing a gas mask, while a label bearing his or her name hung around their necks or was attached to some convenient part of their clothing. Some of the children were smiling; most were not and looked worried, dazed or frankly terrified.

It was Phyllida who spotted it first. There was an extremely large number of doors because each compartment opened individually. These elderly carriages, intended just for short urban journeys, had no corridors and no lavatories. And the nervous, anxious and frightened children, away from home for the first time had been travelling for nearly five hours.

It took around two hours more for the groups to be separated and their respective reception parties and coaches identified. The Felsingham contingent from Wharf Lane Primary did, as expected, number approximately sixty and it was first come, first embarked on the coaches. Once the thirty destined for The Manor had been loaded, a queue was formed of the remaining children and three of the WVS women ticked them off against a list of the other host residents. When the alphabetical list reached Six Oaks Farm, the next two children were a brother and sister. Their labels identified them as Annie Partington aged six and Gordon Partington, aged eight. They were obviously siblings and had a joint angelic look; a look that was to prove more than slightly misleading in the weeks to come.

In addition to John's Riley, William had brought the Humber Pullman because it had the most room, and he and Charlotte helped the two children on board with their luggage. They were accompanied by an undisguised and clearly identifiable smell of urine and faeces. Charlotte turned to William and mouthed the word 'bath' as they both opened the windows. John, Phyllida, Ted and Tommy followed in the much more fragrant Riley.

Little was said on the journey back to Felsingham except that Charlotte turned round periodically to give the expressionless siblings a reassuring smile. She said they were going to live on a farm and she would explain all about it when they arrived. 'Isn't it exciting?' she said. The extremely tired Annie and Gordon appeared wholly unconvinced.

On arrival at Six Oaks, the still more or less silent children were taken into the main farmhouse and properly introduced to the small army of strangers. 'It will be a bit confusing for you at first, Annie and Gordon, because there are four of us here at the farm,' said Charlotte. 'This lady and gentleman are my parents – I call them Papa and Mama. They are Mr Farrow and Mrs Farrow. So that's what you call them and you will live here in the big house with them. I am Mrs Atmore, so that's what you call me and I live in this part of the house which we call the cottage. But we shall do most things together and have most of our meals in the big house. My husband, Mr Atmore, isn't here because he is away on a ship fighting the Germans. This nice gentleman is Mr Cartwright and he stays here some of the time. You call him Mr Cartwright. He is a vet – do you know what a vet is?' Annie and Gordon looked utterly blank.

'Well, he's a doctor for animals. So when the cows and sheep and pigs get poorly, he looks after them.' Charlotte said afterwards that she might as well have told them he had two heads and five feet for all the credibility they appeared to attach to what she had said.

'And sometimes,' Charlotte continued, 'you will see a lovely lady called Miss Peasgood. She helps us in the house. Is that all right? Do you understand?' The children nodded in unison. 'Now let's see what's in your suitcases,' and together they then unpacked from each case an assortment including some underclothes, slippers, socks, a toothbrush, a comb, a towel, a tiny piece of soap, a face cloth and some handkerchiefs. 'I'm sure we can find any extras you need,' Charlotte added after looking at her mother. 'Now, Mrs Farrow will show you your bedrooms where you will sleep – they are right next to each other – and then I think you both need a nice warm bath after your journey. Then we shall have some tea and I think it will be bedtime. Tomorrow, we shall show you the farm and the animals. Then, on Monday, you will go to school on a bus with all your friends and your teachers at a big house near here. Now, is there anything you want to ask?'

It was Gordon who spoke. 'Will Mam and Dad come here too?'

Phyllida answered in her most reassuring maternal voice. 'No, Gordon, they will stay in London because they have to go to work, but they want you to be safe here with us until all the fighting is over. Then you will go back. But they want you to write little letters to them and they will write back with all their news.'

Somewhat unexpectedly, Gordon then looked at his

sister and said, 'We like that, don't we, Annie? We like it here on our own.'

The following morning after breakfast – at which juncture Phyllida declared, 'Heavens, we shall have to make a start on table manners!' – Charlotte and William took the children on a tour of the farm. It was then the reality struck home. Not only had they never had a holiday, never seen the sea and never seen a farm, they had never seen a cow, a sheep or a pig and their first close encounter with all three caused them serious alarm.

But with the Six Oaks adults as their guardians and guides, anxiety soon turned to wonder as over the coming days and weeks, Annie and Gordon were introduced to an entirely new world they had no idea, no conception, had a reality of existence beyond the pages of their school books. During that summer of 1940, the adults – Charlotte and William especially – showed the children the life and ways of the countryside they themselves knew so well, and imparted their own love of everything around them; although with the air battle daily intensifying in the skies overhead, inwardly wondering how long such bliss could continue. Charlotte, without at first realising it, had discovered a new purpose to her daily existence. They fished in Bunting Stream and Charlotte re-lived her own childhood days with Hannah catching minnows in an old wine bottle. And Annie was delighted beyond measure when it was she, rather than her elder brother, who caught the first 'proper' fish on her line – a roach weighing fully half a pound.

The children watched with wonder-filled eyes every time they were exposed to some new and revelatory manifestation of country life. One day it was a hare loping across Ten Acres; on another a fox in broad daylight skulking along the hedgerow that divided Broad Meadow from Brick Kiln Lea; then the rabbits that daily darted everywhere from field to field; the songs of skylarks and the thrill of trying to find the insignificant little brown birds from which such glorious melodies came; the sparrowhawk chasing – and catching – an unidentified finch along the track that skirted Lammas Field; and the wheeling noisy rooks that were forever overhead. It was as if page after page of an encyclopaedia was being turned daily for Annie and Gordon's all too evident delight.

Annie chased butterflies along the rides and soon learned to tell a Red Admiral from a Peacock or a Small Tortoiseshell. The pair collected wild flowers and were fascinated to be told that every kind of flower had a name. And Charlotte, and of course Charlotte alone, saw the irony when they asked – to which request she willingly agreed – if they could take on the task every few days of renewing the little flowers in the marmalade pot.

William taught Gordon how to find and collect birds' eggs – for in the less enlightened days of 1940 bird-nesting was *de rigueur* for every country boy. But even then, William was sensitive enough to country matters – the words environment and ecology were not then in anyone's vocabulary – to ensure just one was collected and only from the nests of the most common birds. Watching admiringly as Gordon held the eggs gently in his fingers and used a needle to make holes in each end of the shell preparatory to blowing the contents, William thought it probable the little boy might one day earn his living from the application of some artisan skill.

On the sidelines, watching William wholly absorbed in his role as rural guide and teacher, and seeing Annie and Gordon relaxed as they revelled and laughed in his company, Charlotte thought – although felt she could not at that stage possibly say – the four of them collectively looked almost like a family.

But one day, a crude reality struck home and threatened briefly to undo all the collective good. Searching unsuccessfully for a lipstick in her bedroom, Charlotte realised some bars of soap and a pot of face cream had also vanished. On an instinct she went to Annie's bedroom to discover a small treasure trove of powder, soap, scent, lipstick, face cream, sweets, biscuits, sugar and a brooch. Speaking to the school teachers and to other evacuee hosts later, she learned that, for many of the children, petty theft was a way of life. A firm but understanding talking to did the trick.

That first evening, when the children were given their baths and the residue of all those hours in a train with no lavatories had been removed, the Six Oaks family had discovered what many another evacuee host was to discover: many of the children arrived lousy. As more infestations were unearthed almost daily, Phyllida decided to telephone The Manor where much the same problem had been identified and the children from all the outlying billets were gathered together to set about the problem in earnest. She insisted that every child – clean and dirty alike – should have their heads washed in paraffin and oil, allowed to soak for two hours then shampooed, washed out and a pungent oil applied. It did the trick and lice were never heard of again.

Gradually, the young Partingtons were adapting to a world and people so different from anything to which their short life experiences had previously exposed them. It spoke volumes, John Farrow said, for the quality of a hard East End upbringing that these young children who had never been away from home, seemed to have adapted astonishingly well to their new surroundings.

'It'll be a slow process, dearest,' Phyllida had said to her husband after the first two days, 'and we need to do it one step at a time. It's a lot for them to take in, but we must make a start on their manners and general hygiene. And have you seen the state of the lavatory?' To her and everyone else's surprise, Annie and Gordon proved quick learners and did not resist the many changes in life habits that were being demanded of them. They learned to open the door for ladies, to say please and thank you, consistently to hold both a knife and a fork simultaneously, discover the difference between holding a knife and holding a pencil, and basic bathroom etiquette – the plea of 'Gordon, you must put the seat down after you've finished,' soon became unnecessary.

Chapter Twenty-nine

As the eventful and historic summer of 1940 wore on, the news on the BBC and in John Farrow's daily copy of his beloved *Times* became ever more confusing – alternately encouraging and dispiriting – for the residents of Six Oaks and for the rest of the nation. If local people were still in any doubt that the war was not to remain phoney, that doubt ended late one afternoon in early July when enemy aircraft were heard to the north of the village as Norwich suffered its first raid although Felsingham only knew it had happened because of what the residents had seen themselves in the sky, and heard by word of mouth. John Farrow did not read it in his newspaper because the names of cities attacked could not at that stage be divulged in the press or on the wireless. Further isolated raids then took place locally through the coming weeks, but the fact that the raids were isolated, did still lead many people in Felsingham to believe the war would soon be over.

One day in early August, when the evenings were still warm and balmy, the leaves on the Turney Wood oaks had begun to show the merest hint of turning brown and their acorns were becoming daily ever more ripe and full, William and Charlotte were relaxing by the fireplace, its logs still unlit and dry awaiting the late summer chill that would be the signal for the start of the first fire of the season. The children were safely in bed and the couple were enjoying tea after dinner while the bliss that was the Hallé Orchestra playing Elgar's Cello Concerto drifted across from the gramophone. 'Did you know,' said Charlotte, 'that has been Papa's favourite piece of music ever since he discovered that in the cottage in Sussex where Elgar lived and wrote it, he had been able to hear the sound of artillery from across the Channel during the war? Papa felt it somehow bound the horror of the war with the land they were all fighting for, and it reminded people at home how close and awful it all was. I adore it too. It seems to encapsulate everything that is so moving and beautiful about England. I think about it often and it comforts me when I realise the terrible danger we are all in now.'

'I do love you, Charlotte,' responded William, 'for just that sort of thing. You and your family are so sensitive and – well – human.'

Sitting on the rug opposite him on the other side of the fireplace, Charlotte took that as a cue and gave voice to her thoughts and first introduced the subject. 'Do you ever think about what it means to have Gordon and Annie living here, next door in the house? To us, I mean. Don't misunderstand what I am saying, and don't think I am being premature or anything, but they have been here for two months now and it seems as if in a strange way, we are a family. But one day, God willing and now we are in Winston's hands, this awful war will end and

I do worry about the effect it will have on us when they go back. It will be a terrible wrench and personally I shall feel bereft, but I keep saying it's an awfully selfish attitude to have. After all, it's their happiness and their future that matters.'

'I agree with everything you say, Charlotte. I too shall miss them terribly when they do go back to London, and to their real family, but the fear I have is a bit different – though perhaps not. My fear is what we shall find to replace them in our lives.' William had come as close as he had ever dared about raising the possibility of his inability to become a father.

'I know, I know, and it occurred to me looking at you now across the room, because it has struck me recently, and especially tonight, how much you are looking at home here, William,' she said. 'I suspect Gordon and Annie have contributed to that, but I can't tell you how much it means to me to see you, us, like this – is this what they mean by domestic bliss?'

'It certainly feels very blissful and very domestic to me,' he replied. 'Despite the war, I have not been as comfortable and relaxed as this since...' There then followed a long pause and William looked deeply into the fire '... since Jane died.' Over all the months they had known each other, Charlotte had made a point of never mentioning William's wife, although she was aware that on that first meeting when he came to tend the injured animal and disclosed to her he was widowed, he had said, 'I'll tell you another time.' But apart from the occasion he brought the bunch of flowers, her name never passed his lips and he had never mentioned her on any occasion, in or out of bed. If their relationship was to continue, as she had begun to expect it would – or did she mean hope? – she had to know. What had happened; what were the circumstances of Jane's death? Charlotte needed to ask, and ask she did. In an hour's time she was to wish perhaps she should not have done so.

'It's been five years now, but it all happened so terribly quickly,' said William. 'One minute we were a happily married couple with a future and, we hoped and prayed, the joy of a family stretching out for a lifetime before us. A month later, I had lost everything and my private hopes and ambitions were in ruins.' William paused, put down the cup he was holding, visibly gathered himself together, shuffled across the carpet to be next to Charlotte on the opposite side of the fire, put his hand on her knee and stared distantly into the awaiting logs.

'Jane was a bit older than me. She was also a vet in a nearby practice and we met at a professional conference in London. It wasn't love at first sight but we had shared interests – not just veterinary medicine – but country living, hunting, shooting, fishing and all that goes with it, gardening – Jane was a terrific gardener which I wasn't at the time, but she dragged me to flower shows and taught me lots. I'm much better now and I really enjoy my kitchen garden. It reminds me of all the lovely vegetables and fruit we grew together.' William caught his breath. 'I'm sorry, Charlotte, but it does hurts me still to talk about it. I loved Jane so much.'

'I am so, so sorry, darling,' she said. 'I should not have asked.'

'No, it's right that you should,' William replied. 'You

need to know, and it is good for me not to keep it bottled up. There were no dark clouds on our horizon until one day Jane woke up and said she had a rash on her body. Neither of us thought much of it but as it lasted several days, she went to see our doctor and he sent her for some tests. To spare you the details, she then developed other symptoms and it transpired that Jane had cancer of the pancreas.' Charlotte drew in breath. 'I don't know how much you know about it – I knew almost nothing and I don't think the experts know that much. But it's apparently one of the fastest spreading kinds of cancer and once it's diagnosed, it's really too late to do anything. They exposed her to masses of radiation but that made her feel far worse and the pain was terrible. They kept giving her morphine but, and this was the hardest thing of all, she soon reached the stage where she knew she was going to die, and everyone else knew she was going to die; and, this was so awful…' William paused, sobbing, now almost uncontrollably and took several minutes to collect himself again. 'I had reached the point where I actually wanted her to die, wanted my beautiful wife to die, to be released from it all.' Charlotte gripped his hand tightly.

'But she was just so stoic, so strong. She was the most wonderful example to everyone of how to die with dignity. I was with her when it finally happened. I was holding her hand. It was four weeks to the day since that rash. I was just devastated, as you can imagine.' The words were now coming much more slowly; and more tears were coming too. By the time William reached an account of Jane's funeral, the funeral Jane herself had planned in meticulous detail, it had become almost unbearable to watch and see. But he pulled himself together once more and continued. 'Don't let this frighten you, but I had even begun to think of taking something from the practice medicine store. If it would anaesthetise a horse, I thought it would be fairly painless.' Charlotte caught her breath. 'I had no close relatives who would be hurt. There was no-one who would miss me – apart from the cows and sheep! I just felt I could not go on because I thought I would never be happy again. I could not see a way through it. But after I met you, and especially recently,' he turned to look her straight in eye, 'I have come to believe – to know – that happiness can – has – come my way again but I haven't dared mention Jane for fear that I would begin comparing her with you – or that it would frighten you off. Oh, Charlotte, my sweet, that must sound so awful, you must think I am saying you are second best which could not be further from the truth. You have been – and I hope will always be – my salvation. I can't ask you never to mention Jane again because she was part of my life, so she must now be part of yours too. She is in my soul, and always will be. But I am a realist, I am not stupid, I am an intelligent educated man, a scientist even, and I know that physically she has gone but like you I am also a Christian and I know that what remains is something different. It's the way she has enriched me as a person. Some people with perhaps greater faith than I have would call it her soul. I prefer to say it's her legacy on earth. The William you see now is a far, far better William for having known and loved Jane. I can't honestly say you wouldn't love me if Jane hadn't existed. I don't know. You would certainly have been faced with a very different man. This must sound absolutely ridiculous, but I want you to love Jane as much as I did. Loving Jane is a part of loving me.'

Charlotte had never heard William, had never heard anyone, express their innermost feelings, expose their soul, so openly before. She had never heard the sentiments he was describing and it took a while for her to absorb, not least because it confirmed for her what she felt she had always known. William was still deeply in love with his dead wife and she had to wonder if that meant there was any room left in his heart for her. He had called her his salvation. That was an enormous burden, an unbearable responsibility for anyone to have to carry. It all made her own personal conundrum no easier.

She had to choose her words especially carefully in order not to hurt him or to raise false hopes for either of them. She said, 'William if I am to love you, then it will be to love all of you, past, present and future and if Jane is part of that, then of course I will love her memory too. I know that in many ways she will always be with you and that neither I nor anyone else could ever replace her. First loves are like that. I don't think people for whom their first love is also their last love, their only love, can ever understand. But may I ask two things? Sometime, when you feel up to it, please show me a photograph of Jane; and perhaps one day, we might visit her grave together and say a prayer.'

William swallowed hard. He too had never heard anyone express such difficult sentiments so bravely and honestly. He knew then, if he had not known before, precisely how much he loved Charlotte and that, God willing, they were looking ahead to a shared life together. There were only two small pebbles to ripple the tranquillity of William's domestic pond. First, he was aware Charlotte had said *if* I am to love you. And despite the frankness of their conversation, Charlotte had not asked the one thing he really hoped she would; but that he himself had dared not raise for fear of losing her. She had never asked exactly why there had been no children, so she had never given him the opportunity to say that it might, but only might, have been because of an inability on his part to father them. He was not to know then that she had not dared to ask for the fear of hearing just that answer.

Chapter Thirty

By late summer, many of the airfields that were to become such a feature of the East Anglian wartime landscape were already operational and planes with stirringly patriotic names like Blenheim, Anson, Hudson, Defiant and most impressively, the big bombers called Wellingtons, were seen regularly flying over Felsingham on coastal reconnaissance and other duties, much to the delight of Annie and Gordon. Occasionally a pilot – generally one with some local connection and with less regard for his rules of conduct – would beat up the village with a low flying pass and everyone would rush outside to wave.

However, the feeling of national relief at the conclusion of what Churchill called the Battle of Britain and the apparent abandonment of a German invasion plan turned to dismay when the Luftwaffe began to intensify their nightly bombing of London and other cities in what was to become known as The Blitz. At Six Oaks, the terrible events were followed at a distance as the newspapers and the BBC – which were now allowed to report details – conveyed daily reminders that the war was never far away. There were still occasional raids on

Norwich, and one stray German bomb did fall about two miles west of Felsingham, but caused nothing more than a big hole in some waste ground. Then, one Saturday afternoon, around three weeks after William had opened his heart to Charlotte about Jane, a British plane, a Blenheim light bomber returning to its base after a training flight, crashed in a field adjoining Six Oaks Farm. There was no official comment and PC Edwards and the local ARP wardens were tight-lipped about what had happened although it was rumoured there must have been casualties among its crew of three.

The following day, Sunday, the church was almost full for Matins and the vicar Holy Humphrey alluded to the crash in his sermon – which was otherwise mostly about the scriptural significance of railway guards' vans in wartime. Then, after praying for the King and for wisdom among the nation's political leaders, he offered special prayers for those 'closer to our Felsingham home' who have been touched directly by the war.

Prayers were also said, as they were every Sunday, for Nigel, for his parents and his girl friend Lily and all the members of the Felsingham village family as Humphrey put it, who have 'those loved and dear to us, serving on land, in the air and at sea,' looking directly at Charlotte as he intoned the final words. Daphne the organist then played a few bars of "I vow to thee my country" and tears ran down many cheeks.

After Sunday lunch, and at William's suggestion, it was decided to take Annie and Gordon with Holmes and Watson, John Farrow's cocker spaniels, to walk the mile or so across the farm fields to see the crash site. As they approached, they could see tiny wisps of smoke still rising from the wreckage and it was evident that the plane had collided with a large pine tree which now leaned crazily to one side. The front part of the Blenheim had largely disintegrated and was blackened from fire while the tail section seemed mostly intact although it was protruding upwards at an unnatural angle, like a giant camouflaged fox heading down in to its earth. Charlotte said to William, 'I can't see how any of the crew could have survived that.' As they approached closer, one of the three men raking through the wreckage gestured wildly to them and was heard to shout, 'Keep those children and dogs away.' William told Charlotte to stay put and walked across to the plane as the same man shouted again, 'Don't let them come, there's a part of an arm and a couple of legs over there.' They all heard it and none of the group said much as they walked back. The children were noticeably quiet. The war was coming closer. They could not know how soon it would be closer still.

It was four days later, and the autumn sun was streaming through the windows of the parlour at Six Oaks Cottage to illuminate the interior and, as Phyllida was always keen to point out, highlight where and how recently Charlotte had attended to her dusting. She had inherited about three-quarters of her mother's passion for house-work and it had become something of a family joke for Phyllida to pass a comment – albeit gently – whenever she visited her daughter in the cottage at a time when Jenny the housekeeper was away seeing her family in Ipswich.

'I must get on with some housework,' Charlotte

commented to William in anticipation of her parents joining them for lunch in a couple of hours. William, who had no clients until the afternoon, was in turn making a detailed study of *The Times* leader page to be ready for John Farrow's customary analysis of the day's war news, his routine condemnation of Hitler and Chamberlain – whom he blamed in almost equal measure for the present state of the world – and his latest expression of faith in Winston Churchill. A sharp knock at the door attracted their attention and Charlotte opened it to be confronted by a familiar police uniform.

'Constable Edwards. To what do we owe this honour on an unusually fine September morning?'

'No honour, madam. I'm afraid I have some very serious news.'

'Oh, dear! Do come in. You know William Cartwright, our vet. Is it about the plane crash?'

PC Edwards removed his helmet and followed Charlotte purposefully past William, through the kitchen and into the parlour. 'Good Morning sir,' he said. Then there was a pause and he looked at Charlotte. 'No, not the plane crash.' Then another pause for a few seconds. 'Mrs Atmore, you have two young children staying here.' He laid his helmet on the table, painstakingly unbuttoned his breast pocket, withdraw his note book, opened it and read agonisingly slowly: 'Annie and Gordon Partington.'

'Yes, evacuees. Brother and sister. They go to the school at The Manor. They are there now. But why, whatever have they done? What's happened to them?'

'Nothing, nothing at all, but you will know of course that the Germans have just started to bomb London most heavily and I am afraid to have to convey to you the extremely sad news that the Partington family was killed in one of the first raids two days ago.'

'Oh, dear God. How…what…'

William immediately put a firm and reassuring arm around Charlotte's shoulders.

PC Edwards returned to his notebook. 'It appears the family was in their home at 6 Bowman Road in Limehouse, London and retreated to the shelter in their garden when the sirens went off. Most regrettably the garden received a direct hit.'

Charlotte now sat down. 'Oh, God,' she repeated. 'That is just awful, awful. The poor little things. Annie and Gordon. You say the family. That's the parents. What about the rest? I think there's an uncle and grandfather too.'

'I am afraid it appears to have been the whole family, madam, plus a neighbour who did not have her own shelter. I have been advised there were five fatalities and no survivors and at this stage the authorities in London believe there are no other close relatives, though you will understand it's most chaotic up there with the raids every night, and I believe that information comes from conversations the local police and ARP people had with neighbours. It was the neighbours who said the children had been evacuated to you here in Felsingham. But that's about all I know.'

William looked ashen-faced. 'I thought the – what are they called – Anderson shelters – were supposed to be blast proof.'

'I believe that it is so, sir, although I understand this

was not a proper Anderson shelter but a sort of home-made structure. And it was a direct hit.'

Charlotte's eyes were already reddening. 'What happens now? We shall have to tell them.'

'When more information is available, the relevant authorities will be in touch with you, but I am advised that for the foreseeable future, they should continue as before attending the school and living with you here in Felsingham. As for telling them, I could do it formally through the school, but if you are willing to break the news, I think that would be kindest. You, of course, know Sir Arthur and Lady van Vliet at The Manor.'

'Yes, yes, we do, very well, we do. We'll talk about it, but obviously we should break it first to their teachers who have known them for a long time. We'll go up there straight away so perhaps Annie and Gordon can be spoken to at lunchtime. Oh, God, this is just so bloody awful.'

At that moment John and Phyllida came in to the room having see the police bike parked outside. 'Constable Edwards – is there a problem?' asked John.

It was William who broke the news. 'Annie and Gordon's family have all been killed in a raid.'

'No, no, no…' was all Phyllida could manage. 'Bloody Hitler; evil, just evil,' was John's addition. 'What can we do? What happens now?'

'PC Edwards says they will continue to stay with us, at least for the time being, and William and I are going up to The Manor now to break the news.'

William drove himself and Charlotte to The Manor and they arrived just as the school's lunchtime was beginning. The side door was open and when they entered, they were confronted by Lady van Vliet talking to Miss Brandish, one of the teachers. William's expression and Charlotte's red eyes spoke volumes. 'Dearest Charlotte – and William,' said Matilda. 'Whatever is amiss?'

'May we go somewhere private?' said William and all four withdrew to the teachers' sitting room.

'I forget if you have met,' said Matilda. 'William, you will perhaps remember Miss Brandish from Norwich station. She's one of our three wonderful teachers.'

William nodded and then with the pleasantries over, Charlotte spoke and conveyed the shocking news, just as PC Edwards had relayed it. 'We now need to break it to the children,' she said, 'and I think it's important we do it here with people they know and trust.'

Miss Brandish agreed and went to collect Annie and Gordon from lunch. She returned with Miss Mulholland, the headmistress, who positioned herself quietly by the door, leaving her colleague to do the talking. 'Sit down here, children,' Miss Brandish said. 'Now, we have something very, very sad to tell you. You must both be really brave when I say this but I am afraid your mam and dad are dead. They have been killed in London. A horrid German bomb landed on your house.'

Annie and Gordon looked at her, then at each of the other adults in turn, then both stared into space and sat motionless and expressionless for about one minute. Gordon briefly moistened his lips and swallowed. None of the adults dared say anything and it was Annie who spoke first. 'Is that what happened – like when we saw that plane? Did it happen to Mam and Dad – did their legs and arms come off?'

Miss Brandish looked numb, shocked and mystified. Matilda van Vliet left the room and stood outside in the corridor. Charlotte turned away with one hand over her mouth. Miss Mulholland gripped the edge of the door.

'We went to the crash site at the weekend,' explained William 'and saw a lot more than we expected.'

'No, it wasn't like that,' said Charlotte turning back to face the children and swiftly intervening. 'Mam and Dad didn't know anything and they weren't hurt. It all happened very quickly.'

'So we shall need a new mam and dad now, shan't we?' said Gordon.

Annie then asked, 'What about Uncle Bert? Is he killed too?'

'Yes, I'm afraid he is,' said Charlotte.

'Oh, well, we don't want another Uncle Bert, do we Gordon?' was his sister's response which prompted all the adults to look at each other.

'And I'm really, really sorry but your granddad died too,' added Charlotte.

'Well, he was nearly dead anyway, so that don't matter,' commented Gordon.

'And I'm afraid a lady neighbour who was with them was killed too,' added Charlotte, relieved she had now run out of awful news to communicate.

'That's Miss Dora,' said Annie. 'She's Dad and Uncle Bert's friend but she only comes round when Mam's away at work. Can we go back now and have our pudding?'

'Yes, yes, of course,' said Miss Mulholland, the

headmistress. 'Miss Brandish will take you, but you must ask us any questions you want. And if you want to come out of class at any time you must say. Is that all right?

'Yes, Miss,' was the chorus from the children as they were led away by Miss Brandish, who laid a reassuring arm around each of them, and passed Matilda van Vliet as she re-entered the room.

'Well, what are we to make of all that?' asked William.

'One can't predict how children will react to such tragedies,' said Miss Mulholland. 'They all behave differently. My feeling is that we should try to carry on as normally as possible. We shall keep a very close eye on them at school, and you should do the same at home, and we must all try to answer honestly any questions they may have. And of course, the way things are going in London, I'm afraid this may not be the last time we have to deal with anything like it.'

'Yes, I'm sure that's right,' said Matilda, now intervening for the first time. 'I may not be sharpest person around and I don't know all that much about children – Hannah after all was largely brought up by Nanny – but I heard from outside the door what they said and am I alone in thinking their comments about the uncle and the grandfather – and the lady neighbour – were so very odd?'

'I agree, extremely odd; disturbingly odd,' said William. Then turning to Miss Mulholland he asked 'How well did you know the Partington family?'

'Not really at all. The children walked to and from school and I only went to the house twice when Annie was ill and I took her home. The first time I went, I met the mother who seemed all right but I didn't warm to her. The second time, I met the father and uncle and they appeared pretty odd – antisocial certainly. In fact, thinking back, the uncle struck me as creepy. I never met the grandfather. I assume the parents wrote to the children.'

'Yes, we have – we had – a letter most weeks,' said Charlotte, 'and the children appeared to enjoy writing back to them. Thinking about it though, they always seemed to talk more about the mother.'

'It's very worrying, and I do hope it's not what we are all thinking,' said Charlotte. 'Of course, now we may never know unless Annie and Gordon choose to say something, but I think we are all agreed we must never probe them about it.'

And with that, the traumatic episode was over, at least temporarily. Annie and Gordon appeared superficially to be behaving as normal, and long and carefully as William, Charlotte, Phyllida and John observed them over the coming days, they never gained a real insight into what was in their young minds.

Charlotte was perceptive enough however, to note a slightly unexpected reaction from John, her father, when she first mentioned their concerns and worries about the children's uncle. 'These terrible things do happen,' he said, with a clear recollection in his mind of a woman called Susie and her Uncle Kenny. 'One hears of close relatives, sometimes even parents, doing unspeakable things to children.'

'You surely don't know of anyone personally, Papa?' asked Charlotte.

'No, no, my dearest,' he replied. 'I just read it somewhere.'

The autumn had started badly. For Annie and Gordon it could not have been worse. But over the coming two weeks, no-one would have known there was much out of the ordinary. They came and went from school as usual, talked about things they had done there, played with each other at Six Oaks, went out into the fields and showed an ever-increasing interest in the ways of the farm and countryside to which Charlotte, William and her parents had spent the past months introducing them. They asked if they could again go fishing, wild flower collecting and bird nesting – and learned that as the summer faded, the birds' nests were empty and the wild flowers now looked so different as they changed day by day into fruits and seeds. The pair continued to display rapt fascination with watching the farm at work – the milking, feeding, the working of the tractor and the way the land was ploughed and the crops were planted. It continued to be as Charlotte first described it – as if a whole living encyclopaedia of a new and exciting world had opened up before their young and enchanted eyes.

They were perhaps noticeably closer physically than before. Annie seldom left her brother's side and seemed reluctant to undertake any activities on her own. Even when Ted gave tractor rides, he had to accommodate both children together. And it suddenly struck Charlotte that, whereas during the summer, both Annie and Gordon had from time to time asked if a school friend could come and stay the night – to which Miss Mulholland was always happy to agree – those invitations were no more. The two little orphan Partingtons had withdrawn into themselves and became largely reliant on their own company, while clearly appreciating and being happy and relaxed in the company of all the Six Oaks Farm adults.

Then something happened after tea one day that with hindsight everyone should have anticipated. But no-one had, and so no-one had prepared a response when Gordon, remembering all he had been taught about table manners and politeness, suddenly said, 'Thank you for our tea. Mr Cartwright and Mrs Atmore, will you be our new mam and dad please?'

Charlotte immediately turned away as the tears welled up quite uncontrollably. John Farrow had hitherto found it difficult to communicate with the children at a level to which they could relate, but this time he came to the rescue. 'It doesn't work quite like that, Gordon,' he said, 'Mr Cartwright and Mrs Atmore do love you a lot and they are looking after you just the same as if you were at home. But it would be rather confusing don't you think if you actually called them Mam and Dad because they aren't Mr and Mrs Partington?'

Gordon nodded. His sister said, 'Thank you, Mr Farrow, but will you please think about it?'

And William was the first to admit he did think about it. 'Just suppose,' he said to Charlotte one evening a few days later, 'just suppose – only for the sake of argument you understand – that one day, and if you parted formally from Frank, we were to become a sort of couple.'

'You mean married?' asked Charlotte, seeking a clarification that was not needed, but she wanted to hear William say the word. 'Not necessarily. I'm not sure if that would be essential. What I was really thinking was if you thought there might be a possibility of adopting Annie and Gordon? You hear all the time about children being adopted by all kinds of different people. And with the war, there will I am afraid be lots more orphans.'

'Good heavens, William,' came the response. 'I haven't given it a moment's thought. It would be a huge decision for any one to make. And it would depend on what other children your so-called couple had responsibility for.'

'Yes, I agree,' said William, once again avoiding any conversation on the possibility that he might become a father. 'It was just an idea, Charlotte. Forget it.'

But forget it was the last thing she would do.

Chapter Thirty-one

Despite John Farrow's war wounds, he forced himself to walk the mile into the village as often as possible to keep himself fit and his leg reasonably mobile. 'Use it or lose it,' was Phyllida's constant mantra. After all, he had only just turned fifty and felt he had much still to offer to Charlotte and to the farm. It was a bright warm morning in early September and it would soon be a year since Charlotte had given Frank his marching orders and taken him out of the Farrow family's life. If her father was able to have a spring in his step, he would have done so. In so far as any man could feel good when his only daughter had endured a miserably failed marriage and his country was at war, John Farrow felt good.

Arriving at Wellbeloved's shop to buy his tobacco, he literally bumped into the GP Dr Callum Fraser as he entered and they spent some minutes exchanging pleasantries, family news and opinions of the war. Then, ensuring no-one was able to hear, the doctor said quietly, 'Actually, I'm glad I've seen you – sorry to talk shop, John – but what with everything else, I've realised it's well over a year since you had a blood test and an X-ray on that chest. I'll ask Margaret to make an appointment and then I'll see you once you've been to the hospital for the tests.'

John could not argue with the sense and logic of this because he always knew the shrapnel fragments embedded in his chest would be there for all time. Some of them were too close to his heart to justify the risk of surgery; but they did need monitoring. A week later, he visited the small hospital in Fenton Bishop for the X-ray and blood test, and thought little more about it. His mind then turned to a local farmers' dinner party in Middle Turney he and Phyllida were to attend. It being wartime with the strictures of rationing governing everyone's lives, guests agreed to share cars to optimise petrol allowances while everyone would take their own food contributions. But there would be a small band and there would be dancing, something certainly not rationed, and it was hoped this would raise spirits all round. Charlotte and William with Jenny the housekeeper would stay with the children.

Phyllida loved dancing and had not had the opportunity to wear elegant clothes on any occasion over many months, so she spent some time during the afternoon selecting one of her favourite dresses. She then needed to choose appropriate jewellery by way of complementation. She had a small but valuable and eclectic range of items, most of them inherited from her mother and grandmother – necklaces, brooches, bracelets and a few rings. Phyllida's box of jewellery was kept in a small cupboard in what she liked to call her dressing room – effectively a small adjunct to her bedroom and adjoining the two children's bedrooms. But when she went to collect it, the cupboard was bare. She asked John if he had seen it. She asked Charlotte. She asked Jenny. She received negative answers all round. She then spent over an hour searching the house and the cottage. Charlotte and Jenny searched too. There was nothing. The box of family jewellery had vanished.

It was Charlotte who said they must think the unthinkable. It was only ten days since Annie had been found guilty of purloining items from her bedroom, and no-one needed to spell out that she must be the primary suspect. 'But why would she take jewellery?' asked Charlotte, to which the only answer was that she had probably never before seen much jewellery and considered it in the same category as lipstick and face cream. And as everyone had said, petty theft was second nature to some of the evacuee children.

'But don't forget – innocent until proved guilty,' cautioned John, and it was agreed that Charlotte would be the one to confront Annie after she arrived home on the school bus. She knew she must tread most carefully, so waited until the children had had their tea before she managed to isolate the little girl from her brother. Tactfully, gently, she made her enquiries. Had Annie ever been in Mrs Farrow's bedroom or any other upstairs room apart from her own and Gordon's bedrooms and the bathroom? Had she ever seen a small brown box that Mrs Farrow had lost? Charlotte drew its size in the air with her hands. Did she know what jewellery is? Had she ever seen any rings or necklaces anywhere in the house – apart from those Mrs Farrow and Mrs Atmore wore?

Annie's answers were consistently and monosyllabically

negative. He face revealed nothing other than that she had no idea what Charlotte was talking about. There was no averting of her gaze, no stifled smile, no parting of the lips, no tears. 'I believe her,' said Charlotte to the family later, 'I really do. I've come to understand a little about Annie and I honestly think she is telling the truth. And if we persist in doubting her, it could undue all the work we've done to make them both feel at home here.'

'In that case and you are convinced,' commented her father, 'we must inform the police although it's all very odd because we've had no break-in – and let's be honest, there can't be many days when there aren't people coming and going in and around the house and farm.'

The dinner party passed off successfully even though Phyllida had to make do without her preferred jewellery choices. The following morning, her husband telephoned PC Edwards while Phyllida drew up a list of the missing items, in so far as she could remember them, and posted it to him at the police house in Middle Turney. He telephoned two days later to acknowledge receipt and said he had forwarded the list to his inspector at police headquarters in Norwich. No more was heard until – fortunately as things transpired – John was alone in the house a week later and received a telephone call from a police officer who introduced himself as Inspector Andrew Willets. He was PC Edwards' superior officer and Sir Arthur van Vliet's friend. He reminded John he was the officer who had been able to provide some information in strict confidence about the nature of the charges against Harry Kett, for which he was later convicted at the Quarter Sessions and was serving five years. Then came the body blow. Inspector Willets said there was a small collection of jewellery that had been seized when Kett was arrested but that none of the owners of the burgled houses had claimed as theirs. They matched exactly he said, the items on Mrs Farrow's list.

John Farrow drew up the chair adjacent to the telephone table and sat down. 'Good God!' he said. 'Well, Kett has never to my knowledge been inside this house – but we all know who has – his very good friend and my wretched son-in-law Frank Atmore. Either Frank took the items himself or, my guess is that he tipped off Kett and gave him access when we were all out. How the hell did he think they could get away with it? They must have known we would find out sooner or later and it's only by good fortune that Phyllida – that's my wife – hasn't needed the items for some time.'

The conversation continued for several minutes, John explaining to Inspector Willets about Charlotte's dreadful marriage and that she had not seen Frank for over a year. Because his name was kept out of the reports of Kett's subsequent trial at the Quarter Sessions, she knew nothing of her husband's almost certain involvement in his crimes, and most definitely nothing of Frank having spent the proceeds on prostitutes. 'Do you have a daughter by any chance?' John asked the inspector, who confirmed he did indeed have a fifteen-year-old. 'Well, as a father, I know you will understand this,' said John. 'It would break my poor Charlotte's heart if all this came out, just at a time when she is putting her life back together.'

The telephone line went quiet for a few moments and

the inspector then spoke again. 'I fully understand, Mr Farrow, so this is what I'm going to do – though heaven knows what my superintendent would say if he knew. Kett is serving time, and even if this extra offence was known about, I doubt if he would have been given any longer. Where is your son-in-law now by the way?'

'He's at sea, in the navy,' said John.

'Right then, there's nothing to be gained by making all this too official. If you come here to headquarters, identify the jewellery and sign for it, I shall return it to you and say there was a belated claim so it looks all right in my books. You can say to your wife and daughter that it turned up among some other stolen items but we have no knowledge of how they came to be there – which is of course true. There is no evidence other than the circumstantial.'

John expressed his heart-felt relief and sincerest appreciation to the inspector, drove to Norwich to collect the items and when Phyllida returned home later in the day, he told her what had been agreed. 'Just take this at face value and be pleased you have your jewellery back,' John said to her, 'and don't ask any questions.' Phyllida looked him in the eye. When a wife has been married for over thirty years she can read the runes. Phyllida was an intelligent woman and could all too easily add together two and two. There was little doubt she knew what had happened but she also knew not to pursue it further. 'Will you let Charlotte know what I have told you?' her husband added. 'And let's consider it the end of the matter.'

That was not, however, the end of the matter as far

as John was concerned and he mulled over this further betrayal of the trust, of the faith, of the love his daughter had misplaced with this dreadful man. Until the matter of the jewellery theft came to light and Frank had been implicated, John Farrow had put his son-in-law temporarily out of his mind. But the jewellery theft was but the first of two reminders, the second of significantly greater moment and one that portended far-reaching consequences.

But before then, he took a telephone call from Margaret Fraser, the doctor's wife and nurse. 'Mr Farrow,' she said in her most glorious Aberdonian, 'Callum would be grateful if you will call in at the surgery. Could you manage it tomorrow?' John said he could, and the next morning he was sitting opposite the doctor's desk in his consulting room, gazing idly at the government propaganda posters on the wall while awaiting his arrival. He read most usefully how not to waste water and electricity, how to keep secrets and how to avoid venereal disease.

After a few minutes, Dr Fraser entered clutching a brown folder. 'I've had the results back from Fenton Bishop,' he said, before drawing up his chair, sitting down, and taking out some documents and from what John could see, several X-ray images. 'Now, please don't become unduly alarmed, John, but I do need to be realistic with you. Your blood results are fine. No problem there. But two of the shrapnel pieces have moved slightly since your last X-ray and they are now really uncomfortably close to your heart. The experts aren't really sure how or why this is happening. It may be something to do with you having lost some weight and the tissue shrinking, but they have calculated the rate at which they seem to be moving and it is possible – but only possible – they may actually cause serious damage. And as you know already, they will not operate. It's too risky.'

Ever the blunt farmer and former soldier, John Farrow had no hesitation is asking, 'Right, don't mess around, Callum. How long do I have?'

'It's not that easy, John. They may never move again and you will be good for another fifty years. But if they do move again and at the same rate, then, well, the feeling is that nothing will happen for at least a year but it might some time thereafter.'

'So, a minimum of twelve months?'

'If you put it like that, then yes; but it may well be an unduly pessimistic prognosis.'

Chapter Thirty-two

John Farrow was essentially his own man with an overabundance of pride, and also a man who kept many things, even from his wife – in the way men must do, he told himself. But he sometimes felt the need to share his thoughts and sound out others on what was in his mind. He quickly determined to say nothing to Phyllida about his visit to Dr Fraser, but opted instead to invite himself to The Manor. It had been a long time since he and his old army friend Arthur van Vliet had had a man to man, heart to heart and this seemed as good a time as any. The male bonding evening was arranged for a few days time.

The day before his visit, however, John was sitting at his desk in the room that doubled as study and farm office. It was some while since he had looked at the dates he copied in his notebook on the day in August when he met Meg, the flame-haired prostitute – the dates recording the occasions Frank had visited her. Apart from noting, to his abject horror, that they confirmed he had been doing so repeatedly over the months he was married to Charlotte, John had taken little notice of the actual days and months. There had seemed no need. He knew there was probably nothing he could do with the information without subjecting his dear daughter to untold and pointless distress. So he had mentally put it all to one side. A week after speaking to Inspector Willets, however, and soon after seeing Dr Fraser, he needed to check some ideas relating to the farm he had jotted down in the same notebook a while previously. He was on his own. It was the first time he had had cause to open the book since the visit to Meg and he could not avoid flipping through the three pages on which he had recorded the dates of Frank's liaisons. He later told himself he could not decide whether seeing these pages again was by predestiny or serendipity. Phyllida's giant three-year planning calendar was on the wall in front of him. All significant family events – forthcoming and in retrospect – Phyllida marked assiduously in her own short-hand. The chart was covered in her handwriting but there was no mistaking the meaning of her entry for 7 July 1938. She had marked it in small letters with 'C-mis' followed by 'Dr Fraser'. It was the date of Charlotte's miscarriage.

This was the moment John Farrow discovered the meaning of having one's jaw drop. He glanced back and forth from calendar to notebook. He could see that on the same day, 7 July, Frank had been with Meg. Charlotte's account of the reasons for that appalling event now came flooding back. She had taken it upon herself to climb the ladder and shift the bales because no-one had been available to help. She said afterwards she had not asked him, her father, because she knew it would be too much effort physically. But among the others she asked for assistance was her husband Frank – in his case she had effectively begged for help. Everyone else had sound reasons for being unavailable. But Frank? Frank had claimed to be seeing a new client, one of those new clients who mysteriously never materialised. Small wonder Phyllida had said he behaved strangely when he first heard the news.

Charlotte's father next discovered the meaning of another oft-repeated expression. He now understand all about the final straw, the straw that broke the camel's back. For him it was the camel's back of his forbearance with his son-in-law. He was now perfectly clear in his own mind – to add to all the multitude of other sins, Frank had been responsible for the death of John's unborn granddaughter. In the next few minutes, he decided what had to be done. Dr Fraser had told him there was a possibility he might not live much more than a year. That would be quite long enough for a lasting legacy of retribution to be wrought on the wretched Frank Atmore, a vengeance for all the hurt, all the infidelity, cruelty, lies and deceit he had inflicted on Charlotte – about some of which she herself was, of course, thankfully unaware.

John took out a key, the only key, to a locked cabinet at the back of the office and opened the door. It contained a pair of shot guns. Charlotte had her own gun, a present when she became eighteen and which she kept separately. It was, her father had said at the time, part of becoming a farmer in her own right. John's own guns were quite different and he removed one and laid it on the desk. It was a rare and magnificent example of the English gun-maker's craft. He stroked it fondly, running his fingers over the twin over-and-under twelve-gauge barrels and the beautifully polished stock of figured walnut. He read the engraved inscriptions. On one side was the maker's name: Boss & Co. And on the other, that of his father Montague Farrow with the date 1912. John had inherited it on his father's death in 1928. In his own and his father's hands, it had killed countless pheasants, partridges and grouse in addition to a multitude of rabbits, crows and other vermin. John thought one more vermin should now be added to the list. Or, on reflection, should it? Surely Frank Atmore was unworthy of meeting his fate at the hands of something as distinguished as a Boss shotgun. John had an alternative idea. Replacing the gun in its rack, he used another key to open a small inner compartment at the foot of the cabinet. He was the only person who had ever seen inside it, with good reason.

The compartment contained a small bundle wrapped in khaki cloth. John removed it carefully to reveal a German Luger automatic pistol together with a precious clip of 7.65 mm ammunition. He was fully aware it was a weapon held by him unlawfully because the British Army forbids the taking of trophies of war. John had liberated it in 1916 from the body of the last man he had killed, and spirited it back to England in a manner known only to himself and to the battlefield medical orderly who bandaged his wounds. He turned the weapon over in his hands and checked it was still lubricated, checked again it was not loaded and pulled the trigger to hear a resounding click as the firing mechanism proved itself in perfect order. He then looked at the silver-framed photograph of himself on the desk, dressed in the uniform of a Second Lieutenant of the Eighth Battalion, The

Norfolk Regiment. The uniform was immaculate and the jacket bore no medal ribbons because it was taken shortly before he embarked for France in 1914, a deployment that was to end prematurely following his wounding on the Somme. Two days before his enforced repatriation, his platoon was engaged with the British 53rd Brigade in the action at Thiepval Ridge. A small group of German infantry led by a young Oberleutnant – an officer just one rank higher than his own – broke away and reached within fifty yards of John's trench. With his farm and country upbringing, John had always been an extremely good shot and despite the whirling clouds of artillery smoke, he ensured the young German fell dead with a single Lee-Enfield bullet in his heart. His fellow German troops, even younger than him, then fell back as a British machine gun opened up. Under the covering fire and smoke, with no superior officer seeing what he has doing, and motivated from nothing more than simple foolish bravado born of adrenalin and the wildness of youth, John rushed forward and relieved the dead German officer of his side-arm. Two days later came the end of John Farrow's war when a German mortar shell landed directly in his trench, severely lacerated his left leg and embedded several large pieces of shrapnel in his chest. He and his illegal Luger were soon on their way home.

John's principal hope now was that he would live long enough to be able to add one to the number of his fellow men he had killed. But there was no knowing how long Frank would be away; how long it would be before John could arrange the 'accident' he had now decided would befall him. Perhaps he would be given shore leave before a long deployment. Perhaps he was already deployed in some far-flung place and would be away until the war ended. John kept all such thoughts in his head but determined that if things went according to plan, the unlawful Luger would be fired one more time.

He also determined this was something he could tell no-one, not even Arthur, his dear friend and – John never forgot – magistrate, when the two men settled down for their planned heart to heart the following evening. They were in his study at The Manor – more of a male sanctuary than a study Arthur liked to think. It was in one of the oldest and most evocative parts of the great house, a gloriously oak-panelled room with spaces every few feet along the walls occupied by shelves lined with predominantly leather-bound books inherited from van Vliet ancestors. The furniture was what might be expected in a London gentlemen's club – deeply padded, leather chairs and sofas arranged before a large stone fireplace emblazoned at the top with a beautifully carved representation of the van Vliet coat of arms, outlined in slightly faded colours. Below it in gilt lettering was the ancient family motto: "Van Vliet Unitum Heri, Hodie, et in Aeternum". On the wall facing John was a small glass display case with several photographs of Arthur in uniform and a clasp of medals. John recognised the 1914-1915 Star, the British War Medal, and the Allied Victory Medal, all of which he had himself received. But alongside was also the white and blue ribbon of the Military Cross, awarded for an act of gallantry that Arthur had never disclosed.

In the centre of the room was a large low mahogany

table stacked with well thumbed copies of magazines embracing country matters – farming, fishing, shooting, forestry and estate management. A large silver tray stood on another low table, this time of beautifully figured and polished rosewood, and bearing fine sparkling glasses and three bottles of single malt Scotch whiskies.

'Yours will be the Islay as usual, John?' asked Sir Arthur, lifting a half empty bottle of gloriously golden liquid and pouring a good measure from it into one of the crystal glasses. 'And neat, I hope. I've just managed to obtain a few more bottles from my merchant and I suggest you do the same. Mark my words John, before long, this stuff will be as scarce as hen's teeth.' John nodded positively, took a substantial drink and started by telling his friend about Dr Fraser's prognosis. 'It doesn't surprise me, John,' said his friend, 'but doctors are always a bit gloomy – I suppose they have to be for fear of giving folk unwarranted grounds for optimism. But for what it's worth, John, I would put a different slant on it. You've had these bits of German hardware in your chest for about twenty-five years. I'm no medical fellow but I'd be very surprised if they moved much now. And if Fraser's right and the concern is because you've lost some weight, then feed yourself up, man!'

'Thank you, Arthur. You are always good at putting things into perspective and that does cheer me up no end. But I'm pleased we have this chance for a chat for another reason because I've been turning over and over in my mind the shocking thing that Frank did. How could he, Arthur, almost from the start of his marriage to Charlotte? It's not as if there's something wrong with her – at least as far as I know. She's a beautiful young girl. She was his wife – well, in name I suppose she still is. Why would a man in that position want to have an affair and even worse, pay for sex? I'm a man of the world, Arthur, but it's quite beyond me.'

'As you've raised it, John, I shall have to be blunt. It wasn't a normal marriage, was it? Not like you and Phyllida, or me and Matilda. They were never in love. They married out of necessity. I'll be even more blunt and this will hurt. I don't see Charlotte ever being anything more to Frank than a casual date. They never walked out in the accepted sense. So why should he treat her any differently, knowing the sort of person he is? Marriage didn't mean anything to him. Charlotte just fell into the category of one girl tonight, another one tomorrow and so on. From what I gather Phyllida said to Matilda, you both think the only reason he behaved with anything like a shred of decency in the early days was because he saw a chance to get his hands on Six Oaks. I've had the same thought. So when you scotched that idea, and then when Charlotte lost the baby, all interest went.'

John glanced across at the whisky bottle. Sir Arthur took the hint and topped up both their glasses. 'Oh, God, Arthur. I'm afraid you are right but it makes me utterly sick to think of it. Our dearest little daughter. Not at all what we planned for her.'

'Matilda and I have said just the same about Hannah – but for a very different reason. We could never in our wildest imagination have ever thought she would end up living with another woman. But here we are. Emily is certainly a fine girl and there's no doubt they are in love and I've had to accept it. The world is changing John. I expect one day even marriage will become a sort of random thing – women with women, men with men, trebles even, take your pick, make your own permutation.'

'I'm truly glad I shan't be around to see it. I've said to Phyllida I can't understand how you cope with it. Having a daughter who is – well I'm sorry to say it, Arthur – but who is frankly unnatural, who behaves unnaturally. It can't be right. And in your own house too. You must know what they get up to. I just can't come to terms with it. If ever Charlotte was like that I just don't know what I'd do.'

'You *would* come to terms with it, John, if you really love her. I know all about Christian values and the Bible and all the other things you might want to throw at me. I've been through the gamut of emotions and *I* have now come to terms with it. Matilda and I have talked it through endlessly, as you can imagine, and we are now of one mind. Who are we to define love? Who are we to say what is right and wrong in human relationships? Yes, I grant you it's unnatural in one sense – actually in a lot of senses – but when I see Hannah and Emily together, well I just don't have it in my heart to condemn them. You've been blunt with me, John, and I'll now do the same. I'd far rather Hannah was in a loving relationship with another woman than in a marriage like Charlotte had with Frank.'

John Farrow just shook his head as Arthur continued. 'But I haven't answered your question have I – about Frank paying for sex when he had a beautiful young wife? I really don't know. Perhaps he is basically just a bad person with no care for anyone but himself. There are occasions when I can understand a man using a prostitute – his wife has left him, he doesn't want a relationship but has a man's needs, or perhaps in war – far away from wives and loved ones and under the kind of stress no-one who was not there can ever imagine. In that sense, using a prostitute is almost more understandable than having an affair. Not that I am necessarily condoning any of it, but at least there are obvious explanations. But with Frank, no – inexplicable, unforgivable.'

'Now you've mentioned the war,' said John, 'we've never talked about this and I have never admitted it to anyone – to my shame not even to Phyllida, though she's an intelligent woman, and a former nurse so I am sure she knows – but did you do it? Did you do what I did in France? Did you use some poor anonymous French girl to ease the pain and give you a few moments of relief?'

'I didn't, John, but I came very, very close. I was actually waiting my turn in a queue when we had a call to go back to HQ. But you do not surprise me, my dear friend, because many – perhaps most – of my fellow officers did and it's certainly not for me to condemn you or anyone else for it. The oldest profession and all that.'

John continued. 'I think I can forgive what I did for myself – I just use the old cliché about things happening in war – but I can't forgive it for the poor girl with whom – or rather to whom – I did it. She may even have been under age, God forbid. I have been wondering what happened to her. If she survived would *she* forgive me? War is so terrible. You and I know, better than most, what is happening at this very moment in towns and villages right across Europe. There are occasions I lie awake at nights thinking of it. Phyllida knows I still wake up sometimes in a hot sweat, not knowing where I am and still hearing those terrible sounds and seeing those awful sights. Some things never disappear – even all these years later. In fact I had a bad episode a little while ago. But – can you understand this, yes I am sure you can – among the sounds of the artillery I am now again hearing the voice of that little French girl and what terrifies me is that if the clock was turned back, I am sure I would do it again.'

'Don't beat yourself up about it, John. I can see it's helped to confess, to get it off your chest and it will go no further than this room, but you know I'm always here if ever you want to talk – about anything, anything at all. We haven't done it often enough over the years. Everyone needs a private – secret almost – confidant. Now, more Lagavulin?'

'Yes, thank you. All right, Arthur my friend, now we have come this far with confidences, I must come absolutely clean and tell you what else I know – but please, my dear old friend, you must not, cannot, breath a word to anyone.'

And with that caveat, John told Arthur how he had discovered that Frank was unable to help Charlotte with the straw bales on the day she had her miscarriage because he had arranged to be with his favourite prostitute.

Sir Arthur van Vliet gasped and took an uncommonly large drink from his glass. 'That is bad,' he said. 'That is really, really bad.'

'As far as I'm concerned,' continued John, 'what Frank did was not far off murder. He was responsible for the death of my grandchild. And he deserves anything that comes to him. The fact that I might – just might – not live for much longer has given me a great deal of food for thought.'

'I'm not sure what you mean by that, John. I do hope it's not what I fear it might be. Don't answer this, but promise me you will not do anything that smacks of desperation, retribution or revenge. Promise me.'

John Farrow looked his old friend and comrade-in-arms straight in the eye, said nothing but emptied his glass.

Chapter Thirty-three

Charlotte knew that when certain important items of personal news have to be conveyed, they are announced by telegram delivered personally by a messenger. The messenger's knock at Six Oaks Cottage came at just after ten o'clock on the morning of Monday 30 September 1940. Annie and Gordon had been collected as usual by the school bus, William was preparing to go to his surgery, Phyllida had called round to collect some papers and John Farrow was searching the bookshelves for a volume on pig husbandry he had managed to lose. A motorbike engine sounded in the yard outside. The noise was not of a big black 1000 cc machine like the Vincent that used to call here, but that of a small, red Post Office messenger's Bantam. It was a young man in GPO uniform who had knocked and when Charlotte opened the door he handed her an envelope. For its significance, it was a pathetic little thing, buff in colour and measuring just a few inches. 'Telegram for Mrs Atmore,' he said, 'I'll wait for a reply.'

Charlotte had never personally received a telegram before and she tore it open so rapidly that the hand-written message sheet inside was ripped in half and it took a few seconds of rearranging the two parts before she could read them. She stared at it and her mouth went dry. Completely oblivious to the fact that all eyes in the room were now on her, she swallowed hard and said two words: 'Frank's dead.'

There was a chorus of shock all around but it was noises rather than words that emanated from William and her parents. Charlotte passed the two pieces of the telegram to her father who took his spectacles from his pocket and read: 'The Admiralty deeply regrets to announce that your husband Ordinary Seaman Francis Atmore is reported missing presumed dead. Details to follow.'

'Any reply, then?' asked the messenger, waiting by the door. 'No, no reply,' said John and the young man re-mounted his machine and was gone, leaving behind him the dismay and misery that had already become the stock in trade of GPO messengers.

Charlotte sat down and said, 'Dear God! Well, that's that. What a shock, though I suppose I shouldn't be surprised, but I don't really know how I feel. He was my husband but I hadn't him seen for almost a year. I wonder what happened. I hope he didn't suffer. I don't think I told you but I bumped into Vic and Clarice a few months ago and they said Frank was serving on a corvette – I think that's some kind of small warship – and that he wrote sometimes but never mentioned me. So, yes, I have to be sad but I feel I can now move on with my life. Is that terribly hard and callous?'

No-one else in the room at first said anything, but then words including sorry, darling, dearest, worry, love, surprised, inevitable, conclusion, free, future and solution were mumbled from various lips. And anyone who was listening extremely carefully might just have detected 'bastard' and 'shit' among them.

But no-one was by this time actually looking at John Farrow, whose face would have spoken volumes had there been anyone in the know, which of course there was not. Was it relief, gratitude or abject frustration that some unknown enemy intervention had thwarted his plan and spared him, as he saw it, from avenging the rape of his daughter and complicity in the death of his granddaughter – and indeed spared him, John Farrow, from becoming a murderer?

After an hour or so, during which much tea and coffee – and even at that early hour, a couple of whiskies – had been drunk, Charlotte suddenly said, 'I wonder if Clarice and Vic know. I must telephone them.' Which she did. It was the normally silent Vic Atmore who answered and as soon as he heard Charlotte's voice said, 'Yes, we know. We've had a telegram. Now we'd like to be left to grieve in peace. Goodbye. Don't ring again,' and replaced the receiver.

'Well, I suppose we all react in different ways,' Charlotte said. 'I now need to telephone Hannah and let her know,' and the others replied that they would leave her to make the call in private and return later.

As the telephone rang at The Manor, it was Sir Arthur van Vliet who answered and when Charlotte asked after Hannah, he said she was away with Emily for few days. 'How can I help?' he asked. 'Very sad news, I'm afraid, Arthur,' Charlotte replied. 'Frank, my husband is dead, missing in action somewhere.'

'My dearest child,' was the response. 'I am so very sorry. Do you know what happened?' Charlotte explained they were awaiting details. 'Please accept our most sincere condolences,' said Arthur. 'I shall write of course and I'll let Hannah know as soon as I can contact her. I think they will be back on Saturday. If there's anything, anything at all, that Matilda and I can do in the meantime, you will of course let us know.' Then as Sir Arthur replaced the phone, he turned to his wife who was standing nearby. 'Frank Atmore, Charlotte's husband, has been killed,' he said.

Matilda asked, 'Should I change into black?' Her husband told her not to be quite so ridiculous.

Two days later, a grey military staff car with the letters RN on the side arrived in the yard at Six Oaks and Charlotte went out to investigate just as a tall young man in naval uniform emerged, stood smartly and extremely briefly to attention, and then stepped forward with an outstretched arm. Charlotte saw his sleeve bore two gold rings. 'Mrs Atmore?' he asked, simultaneously shaking her hand firmly and then without waiting for confirmation, announced himself: 'Lt James O'Keefe, madam, Royal Navy.' Charlotte was immediately struck by the fact that he appeared far younger than her and was decidedly handsome. 'Yes, I'm Charlotte Atmore,' she replied. 'You'll be here about my husband. Please come inside.'

Once in the parlour and having removed his cap, seated himself and accepted Charlotte's offer of tea, Lt O'Keefe outlined all he knew – or at least all he was permitted to say. He confirmed that Frank had been serving on His Majesty's corvette *Sunrise* which had been in action on convoy escort duty in an area of the Western Approaches that he was unable to reveal in detail, when the vessel was struck by a torpedo fired from a U-boat. There was an explosion and it sank within minutes. A destroyer nearby rescued four members of the crew of fifty and several bodies but regrettably OS Atmore was not among them, and although the destroyer fired depth charges, it was deemed too dangerous for it to remain in the area because it could also have been torpedoed. The lieutenant continued. 'Please be comforted, Mrs Atmore, by knowing your husband was a very brave man who died serving his country.' Charlotte immediately recalled in her mind how Frank's wish to serve his country had extended to him going to all possible lengths to avoid the call-up while his bravery encompassed hitting a defenceless woman whom he had previously and in all probability raped. But she thanked Lt O'Keefe for his personal expressions of sadness.

Normally, the navy man said, this would all have been posted to her but as he had other Admiralty business nearby, his superior officer had asked him to deliver it personally. He then handed Charlotte the letter which he said contained the same information. He added he was about to visit Frank's parents and asked Charlotte to confirm how he could find their house.

'And that's really all there was,' Charlotte said to William and to her parents when they returned later. 'I've obviously not thought about much else over the past two days but honestly I'm still not sure how I feel. Of course, in wartime, one always knows this can happen and we were still married – in theory. I know one shouldn't speak ill of the dead but it wasn't a happy marriage – or, let's be honest, a marriage in anything but name. We have all known that for a long time. I don't think he really ever loved me, and…' turning to her parents, added 'well, you know all the rest,' realising that was not in fact entirely true. John Farrow had rather similar thoughts from a quite different point of view. Charlotte then faced William. 'I'm sorry, darling,' she said, 'there's a lot you don't know but perhaps one day...'

'Of course,' he said. 'I do realise how frightfully difficult this all is but I do want you to know, Charlotte, I am deeply sorry for you and if I can do anything at any time…' although in his heart William knew he was merely mouthing a platitude.

She responded, 'I hope no-one minds, but I'd really rather be on my own for just a little while please, just to reflect and come to terms with everything now I know what happened. I'd like to do that now if you don't mind.' And with no-one daring to gainsay such a request, she departed for her bedroom.

Once there, she sat on her bed for about half an hour and did as she had said she would, and reflected. The room was full of memories, few of them good. She knew she was sitting on the bed where her husband had used her new and carefully chosen underwear as an aid to masturbation when he was prevented from subjecting her to loveless sex. She saw the vanity case that, had Frank known it, contained the scissors with which he had wanted to cut off her glorious hair. She looked round and everywhere she could still hear his voice, but it was not a kindly loving husbandly voice but a voice saying

'Lottie take off your bra...now your knickers.' Charlotte shuddered and decided she had heard enough. Even in the silence of her own head she had heard enough. She returned to the kitchen and made herself yet another pot of tea.

As soon as Hannah and Emily arrived back in Felsingham on the Saturday morning, they drove over to Six Oaks and were barely inside the cottage when they enveloped Charlotte in a succession of intense hugs and embraces. 'This is going to sound awfully trite, C,' said Hannah, 'but we've talked about nothing else since my father told us and we just don't know what to say. We don't know what to think and we don't how we should be reacting. But before we say any more, what's really important is what about you? How do you feel? Do you know yet how you feel? Has it all sunk in? Has it hit you?'

'Now I've had a few days to think about it and come to terms with it all, things are becoming a bit clearer in my mind,' said Charlotte. 'The first thing of course is that there can be no funeral, no burial, no grave where I can pay my respects – but come to that, no grave to remind me. But beyond that, although initially I felt numb, I'm ashamed to say I don't feel any different from the way I would if anyone I knew had died – let alone a relative or a husband. He's gone. That's simply a fact and I cannot wipe from my mind the terrible things he did and said. To be truthful I find it really hard to think of occasions when we were actually happy together – apart perhaps from the few days at Caister on honeymoon. Everyone knows it was a ridiculous marriage and everyone knows it was all my fault and everyone knows it was doomed to fail. If Frank hadn't been killed, we would have divorced as soon as possible. I realise it's now so very soon, but I want to move on.'

Emily was the first to respond. 'It seems to me that you are being very brave but also very sensible, Charlotte.' And Hannah said, 'You know, C, we shall always be here for you to give support in any way you want, but the rest of your life is now in your own hands.' It was a truth Charlotte simply had to accept.

Chapter Thirty-four

Charlotte now needed to clear her head. She needed to rationalise. She felt that in so many ways she had reached a cross-roads in her life. Frank was dead so that probably meant she and William could marry, if that was what they both desired – and she had become increasingly sure it was what William wanted. That said, he had even skirted around using the word marriage when he raised the subject of adopting Annie and Gordon, let alone come close to anything resembling a proposal. And she hoped he would not propose – certainly not yet – because she really did not know how she would respond. However, despite Torquil's touching recent overture, she now knew he was not right for her. She still adored him but had come to realise he was more of a brother figure than a potential husband and she could not reconcile wanting to share his bed with the fact he had slept with another man. Charlotte was uncomfortable. It just would not feel right.

She was concerned because she knew William needed her, and she had professed her love for him and given him every hope that their relationship would endure. Had she misled both herself and him? Oh, hell! she thought.

Everything goes round and round in circles. It's like one of those dreams where you are somewhere, anywhere, but can't find your way out, can't find your way home.

Annie and Gordon miraculously seemed to have settled down after the appalling tragedy of losing their parents although try as everyone did, no-one could discover or guess what was happening inside their little heads – or the background to the fact that they may have been abused. Moreover, Charlotte had been unable to put out of her mind the adoption idea that William had floated. Could they in fact adopt the children and become their mam and dad? She decided – just for her own peace of mind – to check the legal position and telephoned Simeon Palfreyman, the lawyer of Casterbridge as he had become known.

It was much more complicated than Charlotte had imagined. A new Act had been passed in 1939 and although the war had prevented its full implementation, the adoption of any child under the age of nine must be notified to the local authority. And Mr Palfreyman confirmed that for adoption, the couple certainly had to be married, but then surprised Charlotte by telling her there was insufficient age difference between her and the children. She had to be twenty-five, which was fine, but she also had to be at least twenty-one years older than the children which would just about work with Annie but not with Gordon. At least, that is if they stayed strictly within the law, but as William had pointed out, hundreds of children were still being adopted informally – even being bought and sold. Surely therefore, as Charlotte was over the minimum age, no-one would object to

Annie and Gordon being given a secure and loving family environment. But Charlotte kept asking herself, why was William so keen on adoption and so much less enthusiatic about any talk of wanting to father his own children? Why had William still never brought up the subject? Why had he and Jane never had children? After all, Jane was a fair bit older than him and might have been expected to want to try for a child sooner rather than later. William had said he and Jane hoped for a family. The time was arriving when Charlotte simply must confront him.

But even if William could become a father, it raised other anxieties. Could Charlotte herself face pregnancy again? Was she psychologically prepared for it? And like prospective parents everywhere in 1940, she pondered if in any event it was right to bring children into a world of such an unknown future, a world in which the most unspeakable horrors were revealed in the news day after day. Was there, in fact, any certainty that marriage to William, to anyone, would work for her? She had tried it once – admittedly without any forethought – and it had proved a comprehensive disaster. Was she not meant to marry?

Then there was the secret she still kept from William. There was Julia. Charlotte had had her chance to reveal everything when William asked about the marmalade pot, but she had let it go, and some days she cursed herself for having done so; but then was pleased and relieved she had not. She kept telling herself Julia had been absolutely true to her word and she had never heard from her again after they parted that morning nearly two years ago. But nor had she been able to bring herself to throw out the little pot which still stood on her windowsill and so intrigued William. That very morning, Annie had re-filled it with a small bunch of tiny late season Michaelmas daisies. She looked at it every day and unashamedly drew warmth and affection from the memories it stirred. Try as she might, Julia would not leave her mind. Charlotte had tried to analyse it. Was it in a literal sense, a case of absence making her heart grow fonder? Was the distance from Julia in both time and space causing the memory of their hours together to become magnified and distorted in her brain? Was she now inflating the pleasure she had derived from just one night of Julia's company? And then again she found herself asking if she was being unreasonable, hypocritical. She had found it impossible to imagine sharing a bed with Torquil, knowing his sexual ambiguity, yet surely she was not so different herself. And perhaps that increased the problem of telling William. Now she knew her own feelings about Torquil having slept with another man, would it be even less likely that William could understand and accept the fact of her having been with another woman?

In her mind she had often compared sharing a man's bed with sharing a woman's, something she felt she was unusually in a position to assess. A man's body was stronger, firmer and when a man embraced her, it engendered an inescapable feeling of safety and security. But it could also make her feel a lesser being, a weaker being, in some way beholden. And she was not at all sure that was in Charlotte Farrow's psyche. Was she just too free a spirit? Perhaps she did not want to be that safe and secure. Perhaps she needed more independence. A woman's embrace was the embrace of equals. It was softer, gentler and spoke reassuringly of all the things they had in common, womanly things, physical and emotional, and experiences shared.

There were so many aspects – almost too many aspects – to consider and she needed some time on her own. Going away for a few days was out of the question because even if she could be spared from the farm, petrol rationing and general travelling constraints meant it was unrealistic. But a few hours alone here and there were more feasible and sensible. So it was, on what was to prove the most extraordinary Monday morning of 28 October 1940, exactly two weeks after Charlotte had learned of Frank's death. William was away in Derbyshire visiting a sick cousin. The children were on half-term holiday and John and Phyllida had taken them out in a bus for a long-promised day at the seaside, while it was still permissible.

The weather was fine. Charlotte had used scarcely any of her monthly 'motor spirit' ration – which could not be carried over to November – so she decided to indulge herself, give an airing to the MG which had been languishing for several weeks under its protective cover in the barn, and spend the day in Norwich.

Charlotte wrapped up with scarf and warm coat in readiness for what would inevitably be a decidedly chilly journey in her open top car. She left Six Oaks after breakfast, a few minutes later joined the A146 and drove the remaining fifteen or so miles from Felsingham. She was reminded again of how quickly petrol rationing had cleared the roads of all except important – or in her rare case indulgent – traffic. The signs to the local villages had now disappeared or been painted over to try and confuse any would-be German agents and Charlotte smiled at the thought of any spies who asked for directions trying to understand the accents of rural Norfolk. The imposing large circular yellow and black AA sign that proudly told motorists they had arrived at Felsingham St Margaret had also gone, spirited away by the authorities. Not that Charlotte needed any directions as she passed through countryside she considered her own. This was her home, her county and no amount of war could remove its appeal and beauty.

The streets in Norwich were surprisingly busy because the local Eastern Counties buses were operating regularly and on most days were packed with shoppers and people who were denied the use of their cars to come to work from outlying towns and villages. The market stalls with their striking striped awnings were thronged with customers seeking the best bargains, as people have always done in markets everywhere. The shops were still reasonably well stocked and although there was nothing in particular Charlotte wished or needed to buy, browsing and window shopping on her own offered pleasure and satisfaction enough. She could be anonymous in the crowds and let her thoughts roam free.

She visited the cathedral, not knowing it was there that Hannah and Emily had learned the awful truth about Frank, a truth that had effectively terminated her marriage and in a real sense brought her to where she was today. She sat for almost an hour, again not knowing she had found the same corner where Hannah and Emily sat after hearing Nigel's appalling revelation about Frank and his view of her as the ultimate challenge.

Charlotte knelt on the hassock and joined her hands in silent prayer. As always, at home or church, her first prayer was for her lost Ophelia, followed by a request for forgiveness, a forgiveness to which she no longer believed she was entitled. From the ledge on the pew she picked up a Book of Common Prayer and a Bible. They were well used copies she noticed, the prayer book with its worn red cover and the Bible, emblazoned with the cathedral's insignia, bound in blue. She then absent-mindedly flipped through the prayer book pages, noticing but not lingering on the Service of Marriage. She then turned to the Bible and as she journeyed slowly from the Old Testament to the New, she kept telling herself she must be a hypocrite. She had committed unnatural acts, she had fornicated with a man and with a woman and she was an adulteress. She had slept with a woman who had also fornicated and committed unnatural acts while a man who was a cherished friend, with whom she had once fornicated and whom she had considered a possible partner, was now a practising sodomite. The only person who seemed pure and innocent of all sexual malpractices and misdemeanours was her dear, kindly friend William.

Charlotte stayed for several more minutes trying to rationalise; trying to rationalise her Christian upbringing with the way she had conducted her life. She reached no conclusion other than that she could not bring herself to believe she was innately bad and when she left the cathedral, she felt she could still hold her head high.

Knowing she would be preparing dinner for her parents and the children that evening after their day out, Charlotte decided to miss lunch but spend another half hour alone and take the opportunity for even more quiet contemplation. So she bought a newspaper and headed for her favourite tea shop off Princes Street. It was housed in an elegant half-timbered building that was once an accountant's office, and for many years it had proved a delightful meeting place where Charlotte and her mother had entertained friends over tea or lunch. As she opened the door, it rang a small bell to attract the attention of the staff, but there was no need for it today because the room of around twelve tables, all with neat blue and white gingham table cloths, was busy, already half-full of customers and imbued with a calm hum of conversation. Everyone it seemed was speaking at the same time but so quietly that no individual voices or subjects could be discerned. A small blonde girl wearing a rather becoming traditional black and white waitress's outfit was in attendance behind the counter, taking orders.

Charlotte approached her and apologised that she did not want lunch but ordered a pot of tea for one. She then noticed a tray of appealing looking scones marked "Made on the Premises". They looked almost as good as her own – the scones that had first tempted William in to her home and her life. 'I don't suppose there's any butter for them,' she asked.

'Yes, we do have some, madam, because restaurants don't have such severe rationing as we do at home – at least not yet!'

'Of course, I'd forgotten. That's perfect. And I assume you have jam of some sort.'

'Yes, we have several kinds but may I suggest our delicious home-made damson if that's all right? Things made from wild fruits aren't rationed either, you know.' Living on a farm, Charlotte did know that – it was one of the small blessings of rural life. 'That would be excellent,' she said and the girl lifted a 1lb jam pot from behind the counter and proceeded to transfer an appetising spoonful to a tea plate. It was then that Charlotte froze. Attached to the pot was a label – "Julia's Jams" – and underneath in the most familiar handwriting "Damson, 1940". Her mouth went dry but she just managed to say, 'May I ask please where you got that?'

'Yes, a lady makes it locally and she brought in half a dozen new pots this morning – in fact you can tell her what you think of it – she's sitting over there having lunch by the window.'

Charlotte could not recall feeling anything like it. It was as if electricity suddenly ran though her entire body. For a few seconds she could not move. Her legs felt more than a touch insecure and her face flushed hot and pink. Her heart was thumping. She gripped the edge of the counter. The waitress asked if she was all right.

'Yes, yes, I'm fine. Sorry. I just remembered something I'd almost forgotten.' Her mind was racing. It raced back to a Boxing Day night in a little cottage, several glasses of a gloriously rich red wine – Valpolicella she seemed to recall – some wonderful conversation, laughter and relaxation, a night in an unforgettably warm, inviting bed and some remarkable new experiences; and a pot of marmalade. Then it raced back further, ten years further to a school sports pavilion and a beautiful young girl standing in front of her, exposing her breasts and imploring her to respond.

In the next moments, much of Charlotte's recent life passed through her mind in a series of flashing images. There was handsome, kind, caring William, still in love with his dead wife; her bedroom where so much good and so much bad had happened; her parents, especially her father who had survived the hell of the Somme to bring her up in a loving Christian home as his adored only child; the heartless, unkind, unloving Frank in a sailor's uniform floating face-down in the sea and also Frank the father of the lifeless embryonic Ophelia whom she had failed; Annie and Gordon, two abused little orphans needing a new mam and dad; her treasured confidantes Hannah and Emily; her beloved Six Oaks Farm; Felsingham village; even Holy Humphrey.

Charlotte knew she now had a choice. She could do exactly as she had done at school. She could look away, turn her back and put Julia out of her mind for years, this time probably for ever. She could take her tea tray to the opposite corner of the restaurant, to the vacant table hidden behind that great oak beam and sit there anonymously; or even, and more positively and simply, make her excuses and leave. Or she could walk towards the window, towards that elegant, handsome, assured and confident woman with the black wavy hair and slim, beautifully dressed figure who had told her she could love her and more than anyone had given her the strength and self-belief to renew her life again. In that instant,

Charlotte was fully aware that whatever she decided, it would probably shape her entire future. And after a few seconds more, decide she did.

THE END